THE PRINCE OF THE DEEP

THE PRINCE OF THE DEEP

F. R. BLACK, BOOK 4

F.R. Black

Fairy Godmother Inc. Series

Heir of the Beast
The Elven Crown
The Crystal Commander
The Prince of the Deep
The Palace of Frost
The Siren Prisoner

To all my readers with thirsty hearts and a love for adventure, this is for you...

CHAPTER 1

CAMILA

The moon lies.

I want to be angry, but I do not have the energy.

The moon has this miraculous ability to produce an abnormal amount of excitement in its victims, casting a veil of deceit. This excitement leads to bad judgment, red flags being overlooked, disguised by ecstasy and the thrill of the moment.

Did you know blood sparkles like diamonds in the moonlight?

Deep hues of black and stunning hints of scarlet have me in a trance. Only a full moon could produce such splendor. I reflect as I take a labored breath.

The color could be called ~betrayal.

I think most people would agree that when pinning a color to the damning word, they would approve with my assessment.

I look up, seeing the luminous orb in the night sky, and realize that a full moon is not an invitation, but a dire warning. I think I have heard that bad things happen on a full moon. You should stay inside and lock your doors.

Well, if it has the ability to transform a mere man into a ten-foot wolf, then there is some truth to that saying. Maybe if I had remembered this earlier, I would have had my guard up.

I mentally laugh, tasting metallic blood on my tongue as I cough.

My tickets to Paris are now a soggy mess next to me, the dashed dreams of my life in luxury.

This was the gig of a lifetime, a job we have worked toward for the past three years. Being so careful, honing our skills almost to perfection.

Lucas had promised me this would be our last job, with a payment beyond our imagination. Diamonds. Thousands of them.

Well, he was half right—this would be ~my~ last job, but not his.

Vetrov Yankovich had been my Russian prey tonight. The bisexual billionaire was perfect with his thirst for extravagance. His harem-like tastes and massive orgies made him an easy target, a clear mission.

Vetrov and I shared the same feelings for wealth and the more beautiful things in life. We became fast friends and moved in the same social circles, giving me an easy in.

What can I say, I have always had high tastes.

Since I was a little girl, my father had always spoiled me with lavish gifts. The infamous drug lord had more money than he could spend.

But when he died, I couldn't walk away from the life I knew so well and loved. I needed it, yearned for it. I wanted ~extravagance. ~

And I did what I had to do to keep it.

I steal expensive things from billionaires. But I was ~fucking stupid ~tonight, for lack of better words.

Lucas is probably on a one-way flight out of here, sipping champagne while getting a shoulder massage to ease the guilt and tension he must be feeling. I make a sound of disgust.

It's not easy being a monster. The poor thing.

I can still remember looking up at the glowing moon with a silly smile on my red lips, my glittering gown swaying in the slight breeze. The thrill and adrenaline were still coursing through my veins, powered by this energy that I had felt.

~We did it~, I had thought.

In my bag was over three hundred million dollars worth of precious diamonds.

Lucas and I were flawless, getting by security like seasoned thieves.

This heist was executed with precision and extreme talent that took years to master. Vetrov will probably not notice the fakes in his massive safe, at least not for a while.

But I was not focused on the real threat.

The blaring threat that told me he ~loved ~me and that he would buy me the moon if he could.

How fitting . . . the moon. Such a mysterious thing.

I wonder how many red flags I missed tonight, like when he was on his phone and quickly hung up when I glanced in his direction. Or when he told me that we should take separate flights so as not to draw unwanted attention to us.

In hindsight, he had been distant lately. But I had thought it was just the nerves, the impending obligation that we had to do this job without fault.

I had been so imprudent that I can't even get mad at Lucas. I should have smelled the bullshit a mile away. Now my life in riches is but a vague memory. Poor Camila.

Poor ~Camila~. . .

"Camila," Lucas had said, coming up to me with a broad smile, dashing as always, "do you have the bag?"

I grinned back at him, the alleyway hiding us from curious eyes. "That depends."

His black suit matched the darkness around us. "On what?" He was still grinning. "You going to skip town without me?"

"Never," I said too fast. "But I want the biggest diamond ring to wear on my finger," I purred, my arms snaking around his neck.

"And you shall have it, ~mi reina."~

~My Queen~.

He always called me his Queen, something that I found quite endearing—until now, that is.

My vision blurs for a moment, then rights itself.

Lucas had grabbed my face and passionately kissed me, saying, "I will take the bag, ~cariña."~
I remember frowning. "I thought we decided I would take it?"

"I don't want you to risk it. Let me handle this."

I had smiled at him, thinking that this man must truly love me to protect me like this, and I handed over the bag—which was my death sentence.

The knife in my stomach happened so fast that I was still in shock when he kissed me again, saying how sorry he was before impaling me harder. He slowly lowered me to the ground and kissed my head for the last time. He told me that this hurt him more than it did me, and left without looking back. . .

More tears stream down my face as I feel my heart pounding against my chest, laboring. I let my head fall back and wait for the darkness to consume me.

Maybe I will get to see my father again, and we can laugh together over our dumb life choices. . .

~Footsteps~.

I hear them echoing.
~Hope~.
I open my heavy lids as a flash of adrenaline courses through me.

"E . . . lllllppp," I try to wheeze out. I'm not sure how much blood I've lost, but I know I have but minutes left.

I try to focus my vision as I see a tall, burly figure stop in front of me. I look up at him, wondering why he is not calling for help at the shocking sight of me.

"Mister," I moan. "Help. 9-911!"

He kneels right in front of me, his features coming into focus. He is very handsome, I realize, but not recognizable.

The man tilts his head at me with a bright smile. "Camila, is that you? Almost didn't recognize you with the wig."

I frown at him.

He knows me? And why is he talking to me like I am not dying?!

The man shakes his head and holds up his hand. "You don't have to answer that. I see that you have gotten yourself in a little bit of a pickle."

A pickle?!

Is this guy nuts? I am about to die!

"Help," I wheeze. "I'm s-stabbed."

Why is he happy? Smiling?!

The man frowns suddenly and steps back as if to not dirty his shoes with my pooling blood.

"Sorry, these are my favorite shoes," he says apologetically, making my mouth drop open.

He studies me with his hands in his suit pockets, making me think he might have been at the same party as me. Maybe he knows what we did—a detective, perhaps.

"I know that you are confused, and honestly, this has not been your night. Am I right?"

I can't say anything.

He looks around then back at me. "Well, Camila, your luck is about to change. I have an offer for you, and the fact that you're dying might alter our mission, and we can't have that.

"When Fate picks us a girl, we take it very seriously." He gives me a pointed look. "The universe depends on you . . . maybe. You have like a one in five chance, actually. But, still."

What?
~I must be hallucinating~.

I wait for him to say "AND WELCOME TO HELL!" as fire explodes behind him and he turns into something horrific.

"I'm dying, call 911!" I plead, as my vision spots with black dots.

I really don't want to die. I want revenge.

And this man is a lunatic!

He shakes his head. "No point. You have lost too much blood for that, I'm afraid. By the time you arrive at the hospital, your body will be a cold corpse." He tilts his head.

"So you must listen carefully. I have a job for you, and if you sign this contract," he is now holding a glittering piece of paper, making me think I may have died already, "I will save your life."

"Am I dead?" I whisper.

"Well, not yet," he continues. "I'm trying to prevent that if you have not noticed."

My hands and feet feel numb as I stare at him. "You can save m-me?"

He smiles and studies me. "Of course I can. I just need you to sign your name, my dear. Fairy Godmother Inc. would like to employ you. We are the keepers of balance, sustaining the universe by true love's kiss."

I stare at him.

He is serious.

Did he say Fairy Godmother Inc.?

I am good at reading people—er, until tonight, that is. Maybe he is a doctor? A billionaire with a chopper on one of the skyscrapers nearby? Flight for life?

"I-I'll sign." I know this is ridiculous, but beggars can't be choosers.

This is my only hope.

He holds the glowing letter right in front of me and it looks real. Like, ~real~ real. I know I am dying, but something tells me that I'm really seeing this.

My eyes trace over my full name that is written on the first line. No one knows my real name.

No one.

I look up at the man, my breathing labored, my lungs stinging.

"Who are you?" I whisper in awe.

He grabs a pen from out of his perfect suit and holds it out to me. "This is your lucky day, Camila."

I reach to grab the pen, but my arm will not move. The man leans closer and grabs my limp arm, lifting it. It's strange, but I can smell the spice of his cologne.

"Do I have your permission to help you sign?"

"Yes," I rasp.

He places the pen in my limp fingers and guides it to the glowing letter, helping me sign my name on the dotted line at the bottom. It's messy, blood dripping on the magical contract, but it's done.

I look up at him, waiting for him to call for help. To do anything.

He stands up quickly and touches his ear as if he is wired, confusing me. "Randy, I need an extraction now. This is a code triple X—Medical staff on standby." He looks at me. "Camila. I want to formally welcome you to Fairy Godmother Inc."

I think I am frowning.

Maybe he is a nutbag.

"Welcome, Camila."

I am about to sputter curse words at him when something strange happens to my person. My whole body feels prickly and fuzzy, and before I can panic everything goes utterly BLACK. The last image I see is that strange man winking at me.

CHAPTER 2

CAMILA

"Camila?" The sound echoes beautifully in my mind. I can hear the voice, and it sounds like an angel.

I have died, I realize.

"Earth to Camila!"
~That's odd~.
~Why would God be using that harsh tone~?
~Am I in trouble~?
Panic hits me.

"I do not mean to be insensitive, but we do have a schedule to keep. Can you hear me, child?"
~Child~
~That's . . . not God~.
~More like a bossy female~.
I open my eyes and sparkles of light seep through, resembling the diamonds that I once had in my possession.

Can we still want revenge even after death? Will I be eternally tormented by Lucas's betrayal? Walking the city's alleyways, howling with the wind on the eve of my brutal death?

Naive teenagers will dress up as me for Halloween, draped in the stolen jewels with a knife sticking out of their stomachs. Fake blood everywhere. It would catch on like fire, the new fascination with my death. Hollywood would catch wind of the shocking legend and want to monopolize on the gold mine.

My sad life suddenly becomes a blockbuster hit, gaining me the ultimate fame I always wanted!

What irony.

"Any slower and she'd be dead."

I blink, seeing faces looking down at me.

What. The. Hell.

Am I in Hell? My brain is misfiring.

"Ahh, there she is. You see? She is not brain dead like you thought," came the voice of~that~ ~MAN.~
The man from the alleyway.

That means I am not . . . dead. I think.

I look at a lovely woman with silver hair, who is scowling at me. "You sure? She looks a little slow. I'd run the brain scans again."

"Excuse me," I get out as my voice breaks. "I am not dead, right?"

Where the hell am I?

The man from the alley helps me sit up, and I look around. My head is dizzy. I'm in some sterile hospital, everything almost blindingly white with virtual technology. I hear a beautiful electronic woman's voice talk in the background.

I glance at the man and notice his bright blue eyes as they regard me, studying me.

"Where am I?" I whisper, my heart thudding.

I'm breathing. I am alive, then?

"Great question," he says, and removes something from his shoulder, then glances back at me. "You were just in surgery, and it went very well." He winks at me. "We cut it close."

I immediately feel my stomach where the knife was sticking out.

No pain.

"You are a doctor?"

He laughs and nods to the woman standing next to him. "I think we are ready for briefing. Her scans are clear. I will meet you and the girls in five."

The woman sighs and glances at me with a sly smile, then turns to leave with three men in black following her. "We are a day late, and I hate being late," she says over her shoulder.

"She does hate being late," he says with a wink.

FBI?

Am I being detained?

"Call me Pierce."

"Pierce," I repeat, taking a big breath, calming my pulse. "Why am I not dead? Are
you with the FBI?"

"FGI—not FBI. We have the best medical staff in the universe," he says, and walks up to me. "I am going to be blunt because I think you can handle it. You are not currently on the planet Earth anymore. This place is, in other words, not Kansas anymore.

"You are now in the fifth dimension and employed by Fairy Godmother Inc. For the next three months, that is. Think of this as extreme speed dating."

"Fairy Godmother . . ." I trail off. "I remember you saying that."

"Impressive, seeing how you lost fifty percent of your blood by the time I got to you." He gives me a pointed look. "This is real, Camila. This is an opportunity that will never come again in your lifetime."

I look around. My mind is rejecting this but . . .

But I'm alive, and this man is right—I was minutes from dying. No flight for life could have saved me that fast. A wound like that was a kill shot, and Lucas knew it.
He would not have given me the chance to live if someone found me.

Unless a real-life miracle happened.

"I can see you are working this around in your head, and I can already tell that you will be more open to this than most of my Darlings.

"You are a dreamer, and I like that about you. Always dreaming for bigger and better things beyond your means." He puts a cigar in his mouth and lights it, puffing it as he stares at me.

I swallow, looking around with newfound awe. "Is this real? Are you sure that I have not died?"

He laughs, smoke escaping his mouth. "Quite the opposite, my dear. This is where your life begins."

My eyes widen. "Why am I here? What do you need from me?" I look around the sterile room. "And what did I sign?"

"Do you like games?"

I stare at him warily. "Of course. Life is a game."

A game that I played poorly.

He smiles at me, and that smile, I know, hides a secret meaning.

"Well, this is the ultimate game. You will be competing against five other women in this '~life'~competition. You all will be an FGI agent," he continues at my intrigued expression.

"Think back to your childhood. The Fairy Godmother, as you know from growing up, is about love, one's dreams coming true, correct?"

"Well, yes," I say. "It's make-believe."

"Or is it?"

I stare at him. "Are you saying that she is real?"

"I am." He takes a pull from his cigar. "Not quite in the way you know from
childhood, but she is a miracle worker, yes."

I laugh. "You have got to be kidding me. The bitchy woman that was in here earlier?"

He gives me a dry look. "That bitchy woman has the power to make your dreams come true. I would show a little respect."

I close my eyes. This is crazy.

"The ultimate prize is true love."

I open my eyes to stare at him. "True love?"

Like the one I had with Lucas?

I want to vomit.

He shrugs. "True love's kiss keeps the universe in line, changing the hearts of the powerful. It keeps evil at bay and makes room for compassion—a flooding of empathy like a chain reaction."

"True love's kiss keeps the universe in line? How? There are more worlds out there?" I snort.

"Thousands."

My heart starts to drum again.

I can tell he is being serious, which blows my mind.
I swallow. "So . . . what? We all compete for the same man? A competition? Is this ~The Bachelor~?"

"In a sense, yes."

"I don't want a man," I blurt. "Not sure if you know how I almost died or not," I bite out, "but men are not high on my list right now."

Pierce shrugs. "I thought as much. A lot of women come in here thinking just that, but let me tell you, I have yet to see one that did not change their mind."

"I am not a lot of women."

"But I know your weakness," he says. "I do my homework."

I narrow my eyes.

"Wealth. Fame. You want riches without having to steal or to pretend to be someone you're not," he murmurs, seeing too much of me.

My accent always gets thick when I am annoyed. "Maybe, but how does that involve a man?" I get out, feeling my anger rise.

"Well, you have a chance to make a prince fall in love with you, which would result in you becoming a queen or something like that. I'm sure you can see what I'm getting at."

"A prince . . ." I trail off, my mind wandering. He'd have to be rich, very rich, to be a prince.

The cunning feline in me has just opened her eyes.

"Oh yes, a prince is the main target. A very wealthy prince."

I don't care about the man.
But I do care about diamonds, gold, and a lavish lifestyle. The con artist in me can't resist.

"I'm in."

Pierce winks. "I thought so. Here's the kicker: You must win to get it."
"Then I will win."

Piece of cake.

This time I will not be blinded by love.

***

I sit in a giant room with four other women. Apparently, there was one that left.
The women seem shocked, but we all drank this sparkly pink drink, and we all feel better now. Relaxed. Not on the verge of a mental breakdown.

If they were going to poison me, they would not have wasted their time saving my life.

I can feel my adrenaline coursing through my body as I try to imagine what this game will consist of.

I laugh, covering my mouth. My father is turning over in his grave, like, right now.
Any doubts that lingered in my mind are now gone. I'm shown some of the most advanced technology that is way beyond anything I have ever seen.

I just sit here in silent awe, trying not to freak out and get the boot for still being crazy. A surge of exhilaration courses through me.

The impossible ~is~ ~possible.~

"Ladies," Pierce says as the virtual screen behind him shows a world of blue, with clouds moving around it, "you will all get more details later. This is just a brief overview of the destination and male target."

~Male target~. I almost laugh.
Barf. Let's talk about better things, like gold, perhaps.

I glance at the woman with silver hair that is piled high on top of her head like a bun. She wears a glittering black dress and red pumps, matching her lipstick.
She is stunning.

Elegant in that French way.

She touches her chest and puts on her cat-eye glasses. "Pierce, you have to make this quick."

He nods and looks at us all. "I have spoken with each and every one of you already. As you probably have determined, this is very real." He pauses. "This is exciting!" He points at the world behind him.

"This is the planet of Valturn. Now, this world is very fantastical, so pay attention. Sometimes we have worlds that mirror Earth very closely, others are more alien to you. This is a dangerous planet full of magical energy."

The fairy godmother speaks up.

"We have been here before with a successful mission in the past, and we can do it again. This is a water planet." She looks up at us. "The landmass on this planet is the size of the United States. Everything else is water."

My eyes widen. A water planet?

I am not sure how I feel about this.

She continues. "There are two primary races, amongst other smaller ones. The Valkyries and the Water Nymphs. The Water Nymphs look human, mind you, but they can breathe in the water."

"Mermaids?" asks an Asian woman sitting in the front row. Her long black hair is silky and she has a pretty face. ~Very pretty~, I muse.

They said names earlier, but I was too shocked to remember any of them. I think her name was Sun Hai or something.

"No, Sun, no tails or gills. They can process oxygen through their skin, which changes color."

"Weird," I hear someone say.

Sun is frowning. "So they live in the water then? How do they talk?"

Pierce chuckles. "They do not live in open water. Pay attention. They have a city under the water that is water-free. They prefer to breathe air, and their underground palace is stunning, full of wealth and riches. They have land allies who visit all the time.

"I have seen the main throne room, and the windows are ten stories high, letting you see into the deep blue ocean."

"I need to vacation there," the Fairy Godmother murmurs as she stares at her paper. "Quite stunning."

That actually sounds amazing. I need to pinch myself.
I hear a lot of ~oohs ~and ~ahhs. ~

I'm getting excited, and I can picture all the jewels and silks now. Queen Camila, ~everyone bow before her greatness~. I hide my smile.

"Now, the land Valkyries also have stunning cities. The vast tropical islands are a sight to see, make no mistake." Pierce glances at the Fairy Godmother.

"Let's talk about the mission real quick before we split up and bring out the Bowl of Destiny." Clearing her throat, the Fairy Godmother begins, "Ladies, Poseidon Iphanthei is the king of the water realm who is married to the very powerful Kalypso Syrinx

.

"Now, this is Poseidon's second marriage. His first wife was killed by Valkyries, causing bad blood." She pauses like she is reading, frowning. "Thetis Iphanthei is our man, everyone. He is the son of Poseidon and his first wife. Thetis is turning very dark due to jealousy and rage."

Pierce chimes in. "Ladies, we need you to work your magic on Thetis. He is the heir to the throne, but there is family drama that you will get briefed on later. Mainly caused by Thetis's stepbrother, Raine Syrinx, who is also the king's adviser."

I am on the edge of my seat listening.

Thetis?

"The Bowl of Destiny!" Pierce claps as everyone forms a line.

I frown. The what?

"Pssst. Come on. You missed a lot of information. We went over this yesterday, while we were waiting for you," whispers a petite blonde who looks like Kristen Bell. "Get in line. This is when we find out what our positions will be."

"What? Positions?" I ask, and stand behind her, arms crossed over my white medical robe. I look at every girl and note that I am by far the curviest. I really hope this prince likes that, or I am screwed.

I have a J-lo butt and breasts that sag just a bit due to their size. I smile. But my tan skin looks gorgeous draped in diamonds—no one will argue with that assessment.

My body was meant for rap videos on million-dollar yachts. Not Water Nymphs . . . mermaids . . . whatever they are.

"It's all chance. Whatever position Fate picks for you, that's what you will be for the next three months," she whispers.

"Oh shit," I murmur. "So we can't just pick to be a princess?"

18

She laughs. "No."

Dread washes over me. I don't want to be a low-life.

I can't get a prince being a slave or something.

I bite my lip as the first girl puts her hands in the bowl. Her name is Crystal and she looks very nervous, her skin pale. She has the girl-next-door look, with brown hair and a cute face.

The screen reads: Zebia Empire royal family — Valkyrie~.~
Pierce nods. "They are the clan that killed Poseidon's wife. But don't get discouraged, they are working on peace treaties."

Crystal nods.

That sounds like a shitty position to be in.

Next is a girl named Joniqua Hodge, who sounds Jamaican. A curvier girl like me. She places her hands in the bowl.

We all wait.
The screen reads: Poseidon's Empire — Light Activator.

She looks happy, and Pierce gives her a little clap.

Next is Sun Hai and she seems like the most confident. A tough competitor, I can tell.

The screen reads: Poseidon's Empire — Royal family.

The Fairy Godmother nods her head. "Sun, that is a prize position."

I can tell the rest of the girls are not happy about that. The look on Sun's face says it all, the arrogant bitch.

I don't know how I feel about this Bowl of Destiny yet.

Amanda in front of me turns and gives me a weak smile before leaving to place her hands in the bowl. I feel nervous for her, my stomach twisting.

The screen reads: Gaya Empire — The Light Air Force.

I let out a sigh of relief.

Pierce claps his hands. "A very exciting position. The Gaya Empire is the Nymph's biggest ally. They have each other's backs."

I swallow as I step up to the bowl and see the eerie metallic water. I say a silent prayer, ~Please do not make me a slave. ~

~Please. Please~.
"Camila."

"Right," I say, and place my hands in the substance. It feels cold and weird, making my arms tingle.

My heart is pounding.
~Please~. . .
The screen reads: Gaya Empire — Royal family. Betrothed to Prince Brayja.

I can't believe what I am reading, relief washing over me. I am to marry a prince?! Excitement explodes through me at the thought. I will have to ask if we can stay in the position we are in. Who cares about this Thetis guy.

Pierce looks thoughtful. "Interesting. Brayja is very close to the Nymph family. Like I said earlier, the Gaya Empire is their close ally. I believe Brayja is Raine's most loyal friend, and most hated by Thetis."

So what? I am to be married to a prince!

Bring on the next stage, baby!

CHAPTER 3

CAMILA

We are led to our briefing rooms where we will be paired up with an FGI agent.

I thought we were the agents?

I usually work alone on jobs. I am not sure if I like the idea of working with someone. The last person I worked with tried to kill me. I sniff as I lean back in my chair, eyeing the empty room.

This place is surreal. My mind is still having trouble believing that this is all real. I sit in the metal chair, drumming my fingers on the white marble desk, deep in thought.

I am to be married to a prince on a different planet. This is so extreme. I close my eyes, imagining what it would be like to have royal blood. I have always faked my positions to steal costly things in my life. This will be the first time I will not fake who I am.

I muse on that.

I guess I am still faking, but this is different. Right? Who cares, though. I was invited to Harry and Meghan's wedding, and I watched with silent envy, wishing it was me up there.

Now it will be me that everyone will envy. For once in my life, my cards are aces.

Nothing can beat an ace.

The door suddenly opens and in walks Pierce with a little, weird-looking . . . person. It's like four feet tall with large eyes.

What is that?

"Camila, sorry for the wait." He smiles at me and nods to his left. "This is your FGI personal agent."

"Heya, toots."

My eyes widen as I take him in. He looks like a 1980s gigolo, complete with gold chains and an oversized beige suit for his chubby body. His sandy blond hair is long and pulled back into a pony, and his large purple eyes are heavy-lidded.

He takes a pull of . . . weed?! I can smell it. The smoke trails from his lips, and he coughs a couple of times. "Shiiiit."

"This is Steve," Pierce says, and gives Steve a stern look.

Steve holds up his hand, eyes watering from the hit. "How many times do I have to tell everyone? It's ~Steven~."

Pierce rolls his eyes slightly. "His kind are amazing shapeshifters, and he will be your guide through this new world. Steven, are you briefed for the mission?"

I stand up. "Excuse me. I am not having a pothead as a partner."

Steve looks at me, eyes bloodshot. "The babe has a bite. I like it. ~OUUUCH~." He shakes his hand like I actually bit him, putting his finger in his mouth.
This can't be my partner.

Pierce checks his watch and glances at me with a sigh. "You want him smoking weed, otherwise he is not brilliant in the least. A few years back he won a mission by a long shot, surprising us all."

"Hell yeeeaaah we did!" Steve laughs, and it sounds like Seth Rogan. He fist pumps the air then starts to hip thrust.

I want to slap my forehead.

It's whatever. I am still to be wed to a rich prince. It does not matter who I am paired up with, honestly.

"Fine. What now?"

Pierce grins at me and tilts his head. "Most find this part the fun part. You may change three things about yourself to give you an advantage. I will be back shortly to prepare you for extraction. Think really hard about your wishes because you will be stuck with them."

My eyes widen. "I can change anything?"

Wild.

"Yes, but I would focus on abilities. This world is very alien to you—dangerous." Pierce points at Steve. "Guide her. I will be back."

Pierce leaves, and I glance at Steve.

He stares at me.

Awkward silence.

He looks down with a frown and I grab a piece of lint I see on my sleeve. After a couple painful minutes, I break the ice. "So we are stuck together," I mutter, crossing my arms.

He takes another pull, eyes squinting. "You know, Pierce is right. I am a weed genius, fifth generation."

"What does that even mean? Your family members are potheads?"

"We are mysticals."

"Uh-huh."

"So mystical."

"I think it's just called being a pothead," I deadpan, and walk over to the large book on the table. "So do we all have to go after the main target? This Thetis man?"

Steve frowns. "That's the game, toots."

I expel a breath. "I am to be married to a prince, though. I have already won by default."

Steve's eyes look blank, then he laughs, coughing a bit, almost falling backward in his chair. "So you are playing to be a Sweet Heart?"

"Sweet Heart?"

"As long as the main objective is met, you may choose to stay in your position. I would prefer a Darling win, but a Sweet Heart has a pretty great payout." He sits up and looks around.

"I have to pay some knockers back home, if you know what I mean. I barely escaped them to make it here on time."

I muse on that. "Do you think the other girls can handle the main mission on their own?"

Steve makes a face. "FGI women are significantly hotter than any other women. So the odds are always in our favor. I am down with cheating the system. I could use an easy win."

I might like Stoner Steve.

"Alright then. New objective," I say.

Steve nods. "New objective."

"Will Pierce be onto us?"

Steve laughs. "Dude, Pierce knows shit before you even think about it. That man is a ninja. He is a king. We are all kings."

I bite my lip and rub the bridge of my nose. "Will he be okay with this?"

"Don't know. I guess if you fall in love with the guy." Steve leans back in his seat again, his gold chains catching the light.

"I have to fall in love?"

Shit.

I can fake it. It's what I do.

"That might help. But there are some things you might want to know about your position first." He takes a candy bar out from his large dress coat.

I sit down in front of him. "Well, tell me. Is he ugly? Fat? Mean? This . . . Brayja?"

Steve takes another hit and grabs the book to open it. "Activating mystical talents," he whispers to himself.

I raise a brow.

What a strange little man.

"Okay, this dude Brayja is a prince, but he is engaged to three different women." Steve looks up at me. "You have some competition."

"What?!" I yell. "Are you serious? You're just now telling me this?"

He laughs. "You should see how red your face gets." He laughs harder.

I take a large breath and look the other way. "Are the other women pretty?"

"Have no clue." Steve flips through more pages as I glance back at him. "But he has one month of courting to decide which noble daughter will be worthy."

I close my eyes. "Shit."

"I GOT it!" he yells, making me jump. "I have just tapped into my mystic brains."
Steve's eyes are wide, bulging. He makes sounds with his mouth like he is gaining divine guidance.

I frown as I watch him hold up his finger to silence me when I start to talk. I huff. "Please enlighten me on what your ~brains ~are telling you."

"Your extraction is perfect to get in with Brayja over the other girls."

I stare at him to expound.

"Okay, your man Brayja is captured by the Kingdom of Qokar. They are Orc-type people, scary as hell." He looks back to the book, reading, pausing.

"I was looking over the map late last night when I was in mystic mode. Brayja was with Raine of the Nymph realm and Eluno.

"Eluno is mentally challenged, only knowing battle. He is intellectually slow, but is a crazy warrior—Brayja's loyal bodyguard."

"I am confused. Brayja, Raine, and Eluno are all captives?"

"Yeah. They fell into a trap that I think Thetis set up, though I do not know for sure. This Thetis guy really hates his stepbrother. Like, a lot. If they all just smoked, they might get along." He snorts.

"That does not matter to me."

Steve takes another pull. "Well, Raine is Brayja's best friend, they are like brothers. Raine is the son of Kalypso. The dude is super powerful. Like, he blows Brayja off the scales."

I frown. "I don't care about that. What point are you making?"

That this Raine guy is not to be messed with?

"Just don't get on Raine's bad side. He could sway Brayja into not picking you," Steve says, like I am an idiot, rolling his eyes. "You're a chick, you always know to get on good terms with the bestie."

"True."

Very true.

Maybe Steve is not as dumb as I thought.

"Kalypso knows her son is caught and is coming for them, along with the Gaya Empire." Steve is still turning pages.

"Some more info: Kalypso wears the pants in the relationship with Poseidon. She is one bad bitch to cross. Very powerful — which is why Raine is dangerous not to have on your side."

I shiver, excitement and nerves coursing through me.

A real-life adventure.

"Got it."

"They are all held in dark prisons on the side of a cliff with Orc guards patrolling everywhere. So I was thinking you could sneak in and bring Brayja cookies and shit to get a head start on him picking you."

"Cookies? He's not a pothead, ~Steven~."

"Or just your company, but I bet he'd love cookies. They are tortured there, already been in captivity for a week." Steve exhales. "These Orc people are vicious."

"So why am I there?"

"You were on the Gaya ship that followed them. Your ship was sunk and you are a brilliant woman and put on a disguise as a slave to help Brayja escape."

He looks at me like he is some wise monk, raising his chubby chin, eyes half shut.

I frown. "Right . . . that would make me look worthy in his eyes."

Steve starts laughing, face turning red. "You'd have it in the bag, man."

I smile. "Money in the bag. How do I break in?"

He gives me another heavy-lidded expression. "This will be very tricky. You have to break into Eluno's cell first and wait an hour until the guard leaves to make it to Brayja's."

My mouth falls open. "I have to stay with Eluno for an hour? The slow guy?"

"It's the only way you don't get caught and use a lifeline. You only get three lifelines before you are ejected from the game, by the way." Steve looks like he is ready for a nap, eyes barely open.

"Stay awake. Is Eluno dangerous?"

"Very." He pauses. "Like an animal. But he is tied up with a mouthpiece on. You will be safe, just don't get close to him. From my calculations, you would have a week's worth of time before they are busted out. Us agents get top-secret information when we are briefed."

"That's like seven hours with Eluno."

"Maybe bring him cookies." Steve looks at his large gold watch. ~Dammmmnn~. We have to pick your three traits—hurry, before the king comes back. We will go into more detail once we are there."

A flash of nerves washes over me. "So, any pointers on what to change?"

28

Steve is sitting in the metal chair still and leans back on it, two feet leaving the ground. I raise a brow. He looks like Zach Galifianakis and Seth Rogan had a baby.

"You're super fly."

"I'm fly?"

His eyes widen slightly. "Big ol' booty." Steve winks at me. "Nice rack too. Your face is golden."

"Should I be offended?"

"Yes—er, no." He looks a little confused. "But you're packin' a lot of curves, so you might need to be in superb shape."

I almost laugh. This Steve is something else. "I am in shape. Just because I have curves does not mean I can't run."

I just need a legit sports bra.

He takes a pull of his joint. "Doubt it."

I can feel my cheeks heat. "Fine, ~Steven. ~What else?"

"I would be an exceptional swimmer." He laughs. "A lot of water there, kinda a no brainer, toots"

"Don't call me that, it's weird." I think for a second. "Right, because I don't swim that well," I say, more to myself. I am more of a doggie paddle kind of girl, and I think that will not fly in this world.

"Does that mean I can hold my breath for a long time?"

Like James Bond.

"No, but being in shape will make your lungs perfect," he says, nodding like he is the Godfather, the all-knowing.

"Okay, what else? What does this man Brayja like in a woman?" I ask, looking down at myself.

I have long black hair that I always keep plaited or braided, and my heart-shaped face is delicate and exotic. My eyes are slanted, and my lips are full. I have a face to entrance people, while my hands are quick to steal from them.

Cold truth.

Steve leans up. "You need a talent. You are super fly. I don't think he will complain after FGI airbrushing. Airbrushing is a freebie, makes the dames super sexy."

"It's weird hearing you say sexy while looking half asleep," I say, hiding my grin. "What talent, then?"

"I am not half-asleep, I am in mystic mode. Being a Valkyrie, you may not possess Nymph abilities," he says, and frowns in thought. "Let me look through the book. I thought I saw something when I was eating a pizza pie."

"I want my talent to be special, rare," I say, leaning closer. "What are Nymphs weak to? Since they are our enemies."

Steve points at me. "I like the way you think. They fight with electric currents. Especially Kalypso and Raine. Poseidon and Thetis's blood-line is more physical strength, brute force.

"There are so many different bloodlines it's hard to pick one to oppose." He looks at me. "What are you naturally good at?

Very deep for a pothead.

"I am good at stealing," I say, and shrug. "Pretending."

I look down, feeling a bit uncomfortable.

His eyes widen. "I got it."

"A manipulator," Pierce says from behind us.

We both jump and turn to see him leaning up against the door with an amused expression.

"Right on, my ninja," Steve says in awe, like Pierce was his mystical weed God.

"You two have hit it off just like I thought you would." Pierce has his hands inside his pockets like he's on the cover of ~Men's Warehouse: Most Interesting Man Edition~.

"A manipulator is a talent of an ancient Warlock bloodline. Rare. It allows you to temporarily steal abilities off the people around you for a short time, like five minutes. If you get good, you could be very dangerous."

"Yes," I breathe. "That actually sounds like me."

Perfect.

"Into the pod you go," he says as he studies me in that weird way. Pierce is a very strange man. "You are the last to be extracted, so we must hurry."

I'm so excited and terrified. I nod and walk towards the alien-looking pod, stepping inside. I feel a burst of cold air. It closes around me and I gasp, seeing pink writing on the screen.

~"Alright, Camila. The first trait?~" Pierce says over the intercom.
"In shape."

~"An FGI favorite.~"

"Then the ability to swim."

I hear him laugh. ~"That would be wise.~"

"And then the manipulator."

~"Alright, this might . . . tickle.~"

I roll my eyes then instantly hiss and suck in a breath as I see a white flash

31

all around me. I think I scream. My body feels hot and foreign.

"Holy shit!" I place my hands on my head. "Let me out!"

After a few minutes, the door opens with a pressurized sound. I stumble out and Pierce grabs me, steadying me.

"Sorry about that, but you look amazing," Pierce says. "The dizziness will pass."

"Duuuuuuude," Steve says, covering his mouth.

My gaze finds the large mirrored wall and I scream. "~La concha de tu madre~! I look like I am a Latin Barbie Doll." I touch my hot body. "Look at my skin."

Pierce nods. "We mean business here at FGI. We play big, if you have not noticed."

"My eyes!"

They are violet and slightly swirling with colors.

"Yes, that is part of the manipulator trait. Very rare—and stunning," Pierce agrees, and looks me over. "I need to prepare you for extraction. Spin, please."

Spin?

"Toots, like Cinderella."

Pierce rolls up his sleeves. "Now."

I spin and my whole body tingles, making me scream again. "What the hell?!"

Pierce laughs. "Extraction in 5." He touches his earpiece.

"What?"

"Steve will brief you once you have landed on Orc mountain."

"It's ~Steven~."

"Steve," he looks at him, not really paying attention to what he said, "you will be her adviser, as you already know."

"You got it, my ninja."

I look in the mirror and see that I am in a brown dirty cloak, hiding my body. How the hell did he do that?

What kind of shit is this?!

"And 5 . . . "

"Pierce," I plead.

"3 . . . "

I close my eyes and grit my teeth, trying to control my erratic pulse. "Ahhh! Ahhhhhhhh! Ahhhhh!"

Pierce is frowning at me. "2, 1!"

Blast off.

Camila out.

CHAPTER 4

CAMILA

I suck in a breath as my vision rights itself, my skin prickling in awareness. My gaze widens as my brain desperately tries to make sense of what I'm seeing.

~Impossible~.

This can't be real.

Sea mist hits my face as I try to take in the menacing scenery around me.

"Oh, ~Camila~," I breathe. I can hear the deep rumble of the ocean waves and the cracks of lightning as it hits the mountain peak, making me tense.

I slowly lower to my knees, scared my legs might give out. I barely restrain my scream as I cover my mouth to ensure I do not do anything stupid. My heart beats against my chest so hard it hurts as my eyes frantically take in this new world.

This is real.

I'm on the edge of a landing that looks out over a black sea. The sky is angry and flickers with flashing lights. I'm on a jagged black mountain about two hundred feet into the twisting sky.

An entire dark city is embedded in this spiky landmass.

I look behind me, seeing glowing orange lights illuminating the perimeter with distant people walking on faraway ledges. The mountain looks like a crystal shard that has been broken and is now puncturing the angry night sky.

I look to my left and see metal doors leading inside the menacing rock. It looks like a gateway to Hell.

I am not going in there.

"Duuuuude," I hear Steve say beside me, where he's covered in a brown cloak. I feel like we are Frodo and Sam here about to toss the ring into the fire. "Get down! You see that Orc up there?!"

I look up to another rough landing and see a creature you would only see on ~The Lord Of The Rings~. It's tall and looks like a troll or reptilian creature. Ugly as sin.

"Steve," I breathe, and run over to the rock wall, flattening myself against it. "What the hell are we doing here?!"

"It's Steven, and I already told you," he whispers. "You will be hanging out with your man until help arrives. Here, put this on and act like an Orc. Walk with a limp and be hunched over. Just keep your head down."

We put mesh face covers on, only our eyes showing.

"I need to smoke," I hear Steve say.

"Me too," I agree, feeling the biting cold of the wind.

A lot.

We both stand in silence, listening to the thunder crash. "We need to make it to the lower level where the prisoners are held," he says finally.

"How are we going to stay here for a week?!"

"Pierce has a room for us in the Orc city," Steve says.

"Are you serious? We have to go inside this hell hole?" How generous of FGI to get us a room.

He laughs like a stoner.

I curse.

The things I do for wealth.

"Let's go," he says, and starts moving his hand like he is typing on an invisible computer.

"What . . . are you doing?" I ask, then flinch as another lightning bolt hits this nightmare of a mountain. I flatten myself against the jagged wall even further.

"This place is terrifying. I wonder if the other girls are relaxing in luxury, seeing the wondrous sights that this world has to offer," I hiss. I feel like a cat with her ears back who has just been dunked in freezing water.

"Can't I just meet Brayja back at the Gaya Empire? Is this necessary? I'm starting to think it's not. Why did we have to spawn here?!"

"I'm getting directions."

"Are you listening to me?!"

"Trying not to."

I expel a breath, and Steve does his dumb laugh.

"Messing with you, relax and ~chilllll, ~man. I can't do anything until I smoke and tap into my mystic powers. So follow me," he says, and starts to hobble away like his whole body is broken.

He looks ridiculous.
"You're overselling it, ~Steven~," I whisper, and follow him, lowering my hood over my face. I can't believe I am doing this.

This Brayja guy better pick me after this, or I might slip him some poison. Make him die a slow and painful death, after threatening him until he puts me in his will.

We hide behind this and that, dodging one ugly Orc after another. My heart is
pounding as we wait for the guards to move to their next post. They are terrifying creatures, reptilian-like with long sharp teeth and slimy skin with gills on the sides of their faces. My gag reflex kicking in.

I can't imagine spending a week here in the dungeon.

A nightmare.

I feel for Brayja and I haven't even met him. I am also very curious to find out what this man looks like. Is he handsome? Not that it matters, but it would be a plus.

We finally make it to the dungeon entrance and we sit against the rock wall, out of breath. "When are the guards back?"

Steve is lighting a joint. "Ten minutes."

"Shit," I breathe.

"You need to go in with this universal FGI jail pick. Do you know how to pick a lock? Pierce thought you knew very well. The locks here are pretty basic. It only works on the doors," Steve says and blows out smoke, eyes squinty.

This is the first time I actually look at Steve in the face without his mesh on. He looks just like a human version of his natural self. So, in other words, he looks more like Seth Rogan but with long dreadlock hair in a pony.
Not a great look.

I glance at him and give him a ~duh ~look. "Of course I do." I could pick locks when I turned six, learning from my dad's shady friends.

"Sooooo you need to hide out in Eluno's jail cell, which is the first metal door you will see. I will let you know when it is clear, and you can make your way to your future lover's cell. "You will only get fifteen minutes with Brayjo before the guards' return. It's not long, but better than nothing." He takes another hit and hands it to me.

I stare at it. "It's Brayja, not Brayjo, and an hour with the braindead guy?" I moan in misery, not really seeing a point to all of this.

"That's why I'm giving you a hit. Pierce is not fond of agents smoking, but it will wear off by the time you leave." He pauses with his hand up.

"Eluno is super mean and dangerous. I need to tell you this before I get too high and forget. Already killed a couple of female Orc slaves, Pierce said."

"Perfect," I mutter, and take the hit. I immediately start coughing, eyes watering.

"Steven, this is strong!" I cough more into my hand and feel fire in my lungs.
"Don't cough too much." He is laughing, eyes almost shut. "You'll be flying too high."

I curse and laugh too. "Can't believe I'm getting high on Orc mountain, in a different parallel world. I can cross that off my bucket list." I pause in thought.

"Can you get me a music player and headphones? Please? An hour in a jail cell is brutal with nothing to do."

He is looking at me like he is a drug lord—must be in his mystic mode now. "I'll talk to some people and get back to you. I have a few favors owed to me."

I laugh, feeling a little spacy. Hopefully I don't fall off the side of the cliff to my death. "You can do that?"

I was only half kidding.

"We are not supposed to, but I can just say I got too high and forgot. Steven's got you," he says, and shrugs. "Go now, and don't get caught." He waves his hand like he is a king.

A heavy-lidded, high-as-F, king.

I take a deep breath. "Great. Thanks, Steven."

I sigh and get up, making my way into the dungeon. This is what I am good at—sneaking around and being in places that are ~restricted~.

My eyes quickly adjust to the darkness and I slow my breathing. It's dark and scary, fire torches lighting up the caves. If an Orc pops out, I'm going to piss myself. I swallow and find the jail cell that faces the crashing waves with jagged rocks below.

This has to be it.

I take another breath and quickly work the lock, sticking the FGI pick into the rusted hole.
~"Hurry! The guards are coming back sooner!~
"You just talked in my head!" I yell, and curse, lowering my voice. "Shit." I drop the pick and say a stream of swear words. The pot is making my fingers clumsy. I feel sweat dot my forehead as I try again and finally hear the gears shift and open.

I hear the ugly sounds of the Orcs right as I open the heavy metal door and slip inside, locking it back up, hoping they did not just hear that.

Note to self: Don't get high and try to pick locks again. I'm breathing hard as I wait by the door, praying they do not come in here. I place my ear on the cold metal to listen, hearing their heavy footfalls walk by the door.

I exhale in relief.
"~Dude. That was close. You're safe!" ~I hear his sloppy laughter. ~"Dude. I'm a bug right now and I'm flying super high. It's kinda tripping me out. I'm flying high, and I'm high.~"
I roll my eyes. "Don't kill yourself," I mutter, turning around. I yelp, not expecting a pair of fire-colored eyes regarding me.

"Holy Mother of pearl, you scared me," I whisper, my heart thudding, placing a hand on my chest.

He is big. Frightening.

The only thing I can see on this man are his eyes, for he is draped in a huge, ratty cloak. I swallow seeing that half of his face is restrained in some kind of spiky leather contraption.

It's slightly unsettling.

Maybe he bites people like a vampire?

I shiver.

My face is covered except for my eyes in this mesh mask, so I'm not sure if he is alarmed by my presence. Hopefully he does not think I am here to torture him or he might try and kill me. He can't be all bad if he is Brayja's bodyguard. Right? He is mentally challenged, so I'm not sure if he can feel fear.

Strange.

His abnormal gaze follows me. Such is a shocking shade of orange. It glows slightly.

I wave my hand. "I'm just going to sit over here for like an hour. Just ignore my presence, I will be here all week. Sorry about that," I say awkwardly, and lower down to sit against the wall.

I can hear the crashing waves through the cracks in the rock. "A little drafty in here, huh?"

He says nothing and closes his eyes.

I expel a breath. "Sleep away, don't mind me."

Shit.

What am I going to do for an hour? Talk to a guy who is meanly unable to have a conversation? I sigh and look at him, feeling sad that he has been here for a week already.

"Your name is Eluno? Am I saying that right?"

Crazy how FGI automatically makes us speak their native tongue.

His eyes are still closed.

"I don't like silence," I admit, talking to myself, resting my head against the freezing stone. "Since I was a little girl, I could never handle it, not sure why. I asked ~Steven ~to get me a MP3 player." I laugh, feeling very high.

"Do you guys have music here? In this world? I'm sure you must," I muse.

His eyes are still closed.

No matter.

"Do you like to fight? You must, being a bodyguard and all," I say, not expecting an answer. "I took some karate classes when I was younger. I liked it. My dad was always big on self-defense."

I laugh, thinking back on it, missing my dad very much. "Eluno, I'm sooooo high right now." I laugh more, wondering how Steven can do this all day and function.

"And you have no idea what I am talking about."

Apparently, I talk a lot when I'm high.

No movement from him.

"So is Brayja rich? I mean, he's a prince, so he must be. As you can probably tell, I'm not an Orc." I laugh and close my eyes, then immediately open them. "Do not close your eyes. Do — not. Verrrrry trippy."

I sigh and sit in silence for a while. I can hear dripping, and it seems to echo in my head. I think I might be sweating.

"Do they feed you?" I finally ask. "I'm a very good cook. I can make some mean-ass tacos, and I bet you would like fish tacos. Seeing how this whole planet is water." I realize that I'm ravenous. "Oh shit, I have the munchies."

So hungry. Steven better have food on him.

"Steven! How much lonnnnggger. Speak in my head and tell me, oh great mystic!"

It's probably only been ten minutes.

If Eluno were of sound mind, he would definitely think I'm crazy. His eyes are still closed. Most likely he does not even hear me, poor guy. If I were stuck in this place as a prisoner, I'd probably kill someone too.

No judging here.

"This place is super scary, by the way. I can't imagine being here for a week. I'd have so many nightmares.

"And get this—I have a room here. I can't imagine what it looks like, something out of ~Hotel Nightmare Magazine: Hell Edition~." I snort. "I'm not touching the bed, trust me. I'd rather sleep on the ground. So gross."

I pause, trying to get my thoughts together through the weed haze. "I bet the place you are from is beautiful. Not like here. I can't wait to see it, actually. This will be one looooong week."

One long-ass week.

"You know I'm not from this planet?" I laugh and exhale, feeling so loopy. "I'm from over the rainbow." That really makes me laugh. "Over the rainbow where bluebirddddds fllllly," I sing.

I am an idiot.

Why can't I stop laughing? Why is everything so damn funny? I laugh more, my voice echoing off the rock walls.

Someone kill me.

My stomach hurts from laughing—I'm literally crying. I'm now laying on the ground, staring up into the dark rock of the ceiling. Maybe Steven does enter mystic levels. Not going to lie, I am feeling a bit mystical.

"We are cellmates. You know what, Eluno? We could become best friends after this."

That makes me laugh harder.

I roll to my side and lift my legs up, my feet now on the wall. I pull up my cloak, exposing my fabulous legs. Huh, Pierce put me in a ratty brown gown. No matter, my body still looks hawt.

My legs were sexy before, but now they are ~fire~! My skin is a perfect golden brown, and my legs are toned but also very curvy.

I bet Brayja will definitely like them.

I pull up the cloak even higher to see my prized possession: My arse.

Yes, ladies and gentlemen, my rear is big and perfect with a tiny waist. My eyes widen. "Holy shit, Pierce, what have we here?" My underwear is super hawt! I didn't even realize I was wearing a skimpy golden thong, being so distracted and all.

How sweet of him.

Pierce is very naughty, but also thoughtful. Maybe he knew I'd be going after Brayja and wanted me to~, ahem~, accidentally show him.

The golden string sparkles against my tan skin, almost entrancing me in my ~mystic ~brain. I laugh, feeling slightly delirious.

I look over to Eluno and gasp.

His fiery gaze is roaming over my legs and half exposed rear and hip. I sit up quickly, pulling down my cloak. Wow, this man is probably so confused.

"Sorry, Eluno. I thought you were sleeping."

His gaze sears me, making me shiver.

Strange.

Eluno's gaze does not look . . . slow. In fact, if I did not know this man was slow, I'd think he was very intelligent. The way he is looking at me makes me nervous, almost alarming me.

Maybe I upset his delicate sensibilities?

Maybe he has never seen a woman's naked legs and butt before?

"I am sorry," I say slowly. "If my," I look down, "indecent exposure offended you. You see, my friend gave me some weed." I wave my hand. "I'm sure you don't know what that is, but trust me, I should not have done that and taken such a large hit. Stupid, I know." I sigh and shrug. He has no idea what I'm talking about.

"I'm usually not this careless on missions. Maybe I'm losing my touch."

Oh, Camila.

I look back at him, and he regards me very intently now.

His eyes, though. Maybe this hardened warrior is hot?

"You have amazing eyes, if you don't mind me saying. Where I'm from people do not possess that brilliant eye color." I bite my lip as he stares at me, and I slowly crawl towards him.

"Don't be scared. I just want to see your eyes closer." I have never seen such entrancing eyes before.

Maybe Brayja's will be similar?

I hope so.

I'm closer, and I swallow, my pulse hammering. I can hear the rain pelt the side of the mountain wall, breaking up this deep and peculiar moment. His gaze is so fierce that I dare not go closer. Eluno's eyes burn into me. I can see him trace over my hidden face then over my body as if he were intelligent.

Well, he is not brain dead.

Definitely not.

But I can feel him—his extreme power. It's my gift. I'm able to spy on people's abilities and steal them for a little while.

I feel so much power from him, which confuses me.

No wonder he is a bodyguard. I'm surprised that these Orcs were able to restrain him. I wonder how they did it. I look at what he is sitting on and it appears to be a rubber platform.
Odd.

I look back at him and see so many swirling colors in his irises—orange and bits of fiery yellow.

"I'm not sure if you realize, but you really do have stunning eyes."

His eyes narrow.

"That's a compliment, Eluno." I wonder if he has ever been complimented before. With eyes like that, I would think that he would have been. But maybe his harsh demeanor scares everyone off.

~"Sweet tits! It's time to go!~"

Holy shit, has it been an hour? How long was I lying on the ground exposing my legs to Eluno?!

I close my eyes—so embarrassing.

No more weed for me.

At least Eluno does not understand. I need to be more careful or I will make a lot of trouble for myself.

Day one: Camila gets super high and exposes her ass to a man who has been tortured for a week on Orc Mountain.

Winning.

CHAPTER 5

CAMILA

"This could be worse," Steve says, and sits on the stone bed huddled in the corner.

Maybe.

Our room is a cubby hole carved out of the black rock with a thick curtain covering the entrance; one low hanging light glowing like red embers. Surprisingly, the city is slightly more civilized than I had initially imagined. But this is still bad.

"At least we are safe in here," I mutter. In our tiny rock sanctuary.

Orc City consists of deep tunneling that extends way underground. Like an iceberg, under the water is a massive structure. Luckily, if you walk hunched over and keep your head down, no one really notices you. I feel a sense of panic walking through the towering tunnels.

I feel so closed off, almost like I can't breathe or escape.

I can't wait for this week to end.

I met Brayja, and surprisingly, he was able to talk to me. I told him I was hiding out, and he needed to keep this between us, but I was going to help him escape.

He seemed very enthused.

"So Brayja already likes you, eh?" Steve takes a hit.

"I only got to talk with him for a short while, but I think so," I say. "Maybe this is not such a bad idea. He told me how brave I am and that he will make it up to me." I grin, not being able to help it.

Steve laughs. "You can't already be in love with this guy."

"With his money, I am," I say, and roll my eyes.

I know that sounds bad, but I can't help what I want.

"So you're a high-class FGI gold digger. I dig it." He laughs more. "Get it? Diiiigg it?"

"Clever," I say, and huddle against the opposite corner. "I can't help it. I just know what I want and what I want is not to have to worry about being poor. I was homeless for five years, living on the streets after my father died." I shrug, not wanting to think about how I was so skinny that I would pass out in public.

It would land me in the hospital, and at least I would get hydrated from an IV for a little while. But that was only temporarily, then I was kicked out to fend for myself again. The staff knew me, and I remember not being able to stand the looks of pity. ~Poor Camila~. They would feed me and give me clothes, but then ultimately it was up to me. I grew up fast.

I swore never to experience anything like that again.

It traumatized me.

It jaded me.

"I can relate," Steven says, looking very thoughtful. "I do have a craving for gold watches and chains. It compliments my skin tone."

I smile, realizing he is serious.

He glances at me. "So, do you not want love and all that happily-ever-after stuff?" he asks, and takes another hit. "Don't all females want that crap?" He blows out smoke.

I chuckle. "I'm not against having a mutual fondness for a man, but love? I'd rather not. It's what got me killed. Or, ~almost~ killed. Love is blind, and it makes you vulnerable."

He thinks for a second. "I'm hearin' what you're barkin'." He takes a breath and rests his head back. "To get a Sweet Heart Necklace, though, you will have to fake it. It has to be a real love match. or you will not get any benefits from FGI after the mission. And trust me, you want FGI benefits.

"You get tons of shit; it's like a retirement package. One thing I will say, FGI takes care of their own. But they won't cover gambling debts, FYI."

I bite my lip. "You think I can fool Pierce?"

"That man is a ninja. If you do, I will be very impressed." He laughs.

"Your lips are sealed then?"

He winks at me. "I don't know what you have experienced, but I'm a loyal partner." He continues with a slow smile, "Just don't fall in love with me toots, I don't need the extra drama. I already have three baby mamas back home." He gives me a half-smile that I'm assuming is his ~pick-up ~grin and raises his eyebrows over and over.
Wow.

Stoner Steven just got creepy.

I fight a grin and lean my head back on the cold stone. "I will try my best, Steven."
We both chuckle and close our eyes in exhaustion.

Brayja, ~my future husband~. I think about that and realize he didn't have a mouth cover like poor Eluno, and I could see his face.

Shockingly, he was handsome even after being a prisoner, to my slight relief. I look at my nails, expelling a breath. Hairy, but good bone structure. It will make my case more believable when I confess my love for him.

I almost laugh. I think Brayja will clean up nice enough to not make sleeping with him horrible.

Because I do enjoy a mutual attraction. I'm not into pretending to love an eighty-year-old man for his money. I love money, but not ~that ~much. I draw the line somewhere.

It's good to know I have some boundaries.

Though I will say, his bodyguard owns the eye department. Brayja's nondescript eye color cannot compete with Eluno's shocking orange-hued orbs. Maybe I can tease Brayja about that?

If only he had Eluno's eyes, then I would surely fall in love with him.

"What did Eluno do to receive a mouth cover on half his face?"

Steve shrugs, eyes still closed. "Not sure, probably just violence. Though Raine got the worst of it, I think. Orcs hate Nymphs more than Valkyries." He opens his eyes and looks distant, must be in mystic mode.

"Raine's kind are bigger threats to Orcs, generations of passed down hatred. Raine, from what I read, does this weird thing with electricity like his mother, so they jam this bendy rod down his throat to ground him."

My eyes widen, thinking how painful that would be. "Morbid."

"Yeah. If he talks, he could choke and die."

"~Mierda~," I whisper, shivering. "Do you think they did the same thing to Eluno?"

Steven shakes his head. "I wouldn't put it past them. Orcs are evil sons of bitches to other races but their own. They might do it just for fun."

One week and they are out.

"Two weeks is a long time to endure this torture," I say.

Steven nods. "Dude. These fantasy worlds are brutal. Too much power and shit here, way too many power trips. These creatures have zero empathy." He shrugs. "But if you smoke, it's not that bad."

I don't say anything, biting my lip.

"Okay, toots, day two. Let's get you to your fake, rich lover."

Back to the dungeons we go.

***

We are breathing hard as we flatten ourselves against the wall. This mountain sure takes a beating from the elements.

Dodging guards and security teams are my specialties, but this is ~slightly ~different. It's hard to see in the darkness, and everything looks the same.

An air of malevolence surrounds these dark passageways. Sounds carry, so a water droplet can sound so close when it's not. But we manage to make it, the crashing waves gently misting us. Strong wind currents carrying the droplets far and wide.

It's good to have fresh air, away from the muggy and suffocating atmosphere inside the hellish mountain.

"Did you get me an MP3 player? I could use something positive instead of all this darkness."

A small luxury in this hellhole.

Steve lifts his chin. "Who's the best partner?" he says, like I'm a dog.

"You are?"

He chuckles. "That's right, sweet tits! I did get you one, and I also personally put some music on there for you. Consider it a partner's gift. Oh, and the music is translated into this language so you can understand it. So it will sound the same to you — it's undetectable. "

Strange.

"First, don't call me sweet tits, it's weird, Steven. And secondly, thank you," I say, and take the small music player with tiny headphones. "You're awesome."

He beams.

I pat him on the head. "Okay, see you soon. Wish me luck," I whisper, and try to calm my pulse as I leave with my head down.

Finally, I get to Eluno's jail cell, and this time I'm not high, so the lock picking goes
a lot smoother. I look around as I hear the gears shift, making a small echo.

I expel a breath, hoping no one heard that. I swallow and open the large door quickly and slide inside.

Safe.

I'm not going to lie. I did have a slight night terror about those eerie orange eyes. I take a breath, and slowly turn to see Eluno open his eyes to look at me from under the hood of his cloak.

He is much larger than Brayja, but I guess he'd have to be.

I shiver.

"Hello," I whisper.

I suck in a breath when I see that one of his eyes is black and blue. I bite my lip as his gaze follows me, his fire stare pinning me and very alert.

"I'm going to get you out of here," I whisper, hoping he understands. I wonder what pain they were putting him through.

Eluno's barely visible eyes widen slightly. Like he understood what I said.

I need to ask Steven what level of understanding he has—maybe I'm not giving him enough credit. I slowly sit against the wall, thankful I'm not high. That was probably bizarre for him to witness last time.

"I know the Gaya Empire is on their way. It's just a little bit longer," I say, trying to ease some of his pain.

His stare burns into me.

I shiver. Was Eluno this intense last time? I don't remember much from the weed high, unfortunately.

I look around, feeling oddly exposed, not sure what to say with his full attention on me. I clear my throat and pull out my MP3 player. His gaze lowers to it, then back up to me, eyes narrowed.

I smile. He's curious about it.

"Eluno, this is a music player to pass the time," I say, and shrug. "Not dangerous."

He looks down at it as I turn it on, the little screen lighting up. I plug in my headphones and put them in my ears. "Alright, Steven," I say to myself. "What did you put on here for me?"

I cringe.

"Ricky Martin? Seriously?" I whisper to myself. What am I? Ten? There are like four songs on here—didn't Steven know that this could hold a lot more? A lot more ~current~ songs?
Sigh.

Beggars can't be choosers.

I grin.
~Livin La Vida Loca~, ~here I come on Orc Mountain, ~oh no~, someone stop me. I push play, and instantly the song blares in my ears, making me laugh slightly.~
The familiar tune of the Latin song immediately boosts my spirits.

Eluno tilts his head slightly, regarding me from under the hood of the cloak.

I start moving my head and my shoulders to the beat. "Eluno, if I were not scared of you, I'd let you hear." I start moving my legs.

"~Her lips are Devil red, and her skin's the color mocha~," I sing along with the song then quiet my voice. "~She will wear you outtttt" ~And bob my head.

He sits up slightly, making me stop singing.

"Sorry," I breathe. "Blink twice if I'm irritating you."

He just stares at me then glances back down to the player.

I'm curious if he knows what I just said or if he is just bewildered. "Blink once if you want to see me dance."

I'm not going to, just curious if he understands me.

Eluno blinks.

My eyes widen.

"You want to see me dance? You understand what I said?" I ask, my mouth hanging open in shock.

His eyes lock with mine, and he blinks.

I shiver slightly, feeling weird. His gaze is making me feel . . . how should I describe it? Uncomfortable?

He looks too intelligent—which I know is not the case, but I'm starting to wonder.
Maybe he is interested in me?

I clamp my mouth shut. I wonder if Eluno has ever had an experience with a female before. It would be very natural for him to be curious. I mean, I did show my thong stupidly.

He has almost seen me half-naked thanks to Steven's weed.

My cheeks stain red, remembering his eyes tracing over my legs and round butt.

"I'm not going to dance for you, Eluno. Trust me, it would shock your sensibilities. You would never be the same again. Traumatized. Where I'm from, our dancing is very," I pause, searching for the word, "inappropriate."

Naughty.

I'll save that for Brayja.
~Mierda~.
His gaze narrows, making me curious.

"Eluno," I say, "do you have any experience with a woman? Blink once for yes."

Just curious.

He does not blink, confirming my suspicions. He just watches me in that intense way. I bite my lip as I ponder him. It seems he is able to have basic conversations, making this a little less boring.

He still observes me, and he keeps glancing down at my MP3 player.

I shimmy a little bit. "Latin music, Eluno." I smile through my mesh covering. "The beat is very fun." I tilt my head. "Do you want to hear?" I ask. "Blink once—"

He blinks.

I expel a breath. "Steven warned me not to get too close to you. You could kill me."

His eyes narrow again.

I bite my lip, thinking about how much this man has been tortured. It would not hurt for him to take his mind off this dark place with a little fun, and it would be entertaining to see his reaction to Ricky.

I do have lifelines, right?

Yes.

"Eluno, will you hurt me?"

He shakes his head ~no~,and I can hear the chains around his neck echo off the hard rock.

My mouth drops open. He is responding more. His eyes burn into me, and I can't recall anyone with that amount of expression in a gaze. Fascinating, actually.

His eyes are liquid fire.
~Mierda~.

I will have to ask Steven more about Eluno because he is not looking at me like he is ~slow. ~Actually, I feel a blush rise to my neck and face from his intensity. I shake my head and clear my throat.

"If you try anything, I will not help you escape. I'm excellent friends with Brayja, so there will be repercussions."

He nods.

I think I'm a special kind of stupid. Play stupid games, win stupid prizes.

I sit up and crawl very slowly towards him. The way he watches me is quite unnerving, like a predator luring in the small, naive prey.

"No funny business," I murmur, swallowing.

He is a very large man, I realize, as I'm now right in front of him. I wonder if he can smell me. Pierce lathered me in this magical vanilla-coconut scent that is luxurious and potent.

I thought Brayja would like it.

I can feel my pulse hammering as he watches me.

His eyes look even more exotic up close, and I have to repress a shiver. Why did I offer this? I can tell Eluno is extremely muscular by the sheer size of him in his dark cloak. He is a bodyguard, for crying out loud. He could snap me in half.

He nods his head as if to urge me on.

I swallow again. "Okay," I breathe.

I can feel the power in him, and it scares me. Maybe fate wants me dead because I cheated it—~Final Destination~ coming after me.

Eluno could snap my neck.

Game over.

On shaky knees, I kneel right next to him.

"I'm going to put these in your ears, do not be alarmed."

I lean in really close to him, our faces mere breaths away. Eluno can probably hear the rapid beat of my pulse. He can only see my eyes, just like I can only see his, and they are mesmerizing.

"Eluno, has anyone ever told you," I pause, swallowing, "you have very vibrant eyes?"

Never mind the black eye he acquired.

He just stares at me, not blinking.

"Well, you have a very stunning eye color. That is a compliment," I say, making sure he understands. I look down and frown. The cord to the headphones is too short, making me curse. Not long enough for this distance.

He nods to his lap.

"You want me to sit in your lap?" I whisper in awe.

This is such a strange scenario.

He nods.

My eyes trace over his leather mask then to his spiky dog collar with large chains hooked to it. I swallow, trying to see more of his face. If I didn't know any better, I'd say this bodyguard is not bad on the eyes. I'm thinking he could be . . . hot.

Like, ~really ~hot.

I close my eyes. No. I'm not getting turned on by Eluno. I'm not.
~Nope~.
Only if I was into Doms and Subs.

~He is just curious~. I take a breath and dive in. I lean over him and straddle his lap, which brings us to a very awkward position.

Bad idea.
~Mierda, Camila~.

I'm breathing fast as I feel his hard body beneath mine. He feels like titanium— so much restrained energy. My senses are on overdrive, my thoughts malfunctioning.

Eluno is extremely powerful.

Dangerous.

I wonder if I could tap into his power and free him. I will have to ask Steven about that.

I clear my throat, my cheeks staining red as I feel him shift under me, chains clanking. I'm not going to think or dwell on what I am feeling under me. My girl parts are right on top of his man parts.

Stop.

It.

I need help.

I will not sexualize a man who has been tortured, and who most likely does not understand what he feels. I give myself a mental shake, not meeting his gaze.

"Okay, listen, and I will get off." I slightly glance at him and he is looking down at my bare calf, my brown gown riding up from the position.

He raises his gaze to mine, and I feel lightheaded.

What is happening?

Why is he looking at me like that?

I feel like I'm experiencing hot flashes. He looks down at me and nods to my player, jolting his hips a bit to get me moving. I take a slow breath.

"You understand more than I thought, Eluno," I whisper, feeling like I ran a mile. I rise to my knees bringing myself almost eye level with him. ~What am I doing?~

My fingers feel clumsy as I pull back his hood slightly and reveal glossy black hair. I bite my lip as my gaze locks with his. I swallow, finding his slightly pointed ear. No, I will not think about how my earlier assessment of this bodyguard's attractiveness is spot on.

I think Eluno is quite a stunning creature.
~Focus, Camila~.

"Okay, this song was really popular for a long time where I'm from. Now, it's an oldie but a goodie," I say, trying to defend it.

He probably has no idea what I'm saying. I'll have to remember to pop Steven on the head to get me more current songs.

He nods.

I put the buds in his ears, and I push play, a smile forming on my lips as I watch him. His eyes are narrowed on me, then suddenly his gaze widens.

I laugh, able to hear the song.

I'm crossing so many things off my bucket list right now.

I mouth the lyrics that I hear, '~*I feel a premonition, that girl gonna make me fall . . .'* ~

I smile as he looks down, listening to the foreign music. This must be so weird for him.

I start to slightly dance, making him look up at me and I mouth, '~*She'll make you take your clothes off and go dancing in the rain...'*~

~'Once you've had a taste of her you'll never be the same...'Upside, inside out she's livin' la vida loca!~'

The air between us shifts.

I stop moving as I realize his chained hands are now gripping my thighs, hard, slightly squeezing. I suck in a breath—I hadn't thought about how he might react.

It's a sexual, playful song.

I thought he might not understand the lyrics and just think it's bizarre, fun even.

I look down and see his hands loosen and let go of my upper thighs. Glancing back at him I can still hear the song, and I slowly take out the buds.

"Eluno, I am going to get off now, okay?" I am tense and alarmed.

He nods and closes his eyes.

I want to groan — he must be frustrated, confused . . .

I glance at his exposed hand and frown. Is everything about him pretty? His hands and fingers look long and graceful, strong. Not at all what I expected.

I think I have done enough here today.

I get off of him feeling odd, shaken, and confused. I guess I have more in common with Eluno than I thought.

We both are not very smart.

Or maybe that's just me . . .

CHAPTER 6
CAMILA

We have been on lockdown since yesterday. Since I came back from my . . . ~Ricky Martin ~experience.

~#headdesk~

"Update from Pierce: It seems like you might only have two more days here. Raine's mother Kalypso is closing in fast. She is bringing hellfire with her." Steve makes a sound.

"Or, actually, a literal hurricane. The Orcs might have made a grave mistake by capturing Raine." Steven looks back at me, one hand on the curtain of our small rock room. "I think the Orcs are detecting Kalypso's arrival and are preparing for war." He laughs.

"Dude, they're so scared right now, looks like they are preparing for Armageddon. But so would I if some pissed ocean queen was after my ass.

"Not sure if they thought this through when they jammed a rod down Raine's throat. Someone's going to pay dearly for this."

I shiver at the thought, hoping we won't get caught in the crossfire. The Orcs are grisly creatures. I hope this Kalypso woman drowns this place.

"What about Eluno?" I ask, and I quickly add, "And Brayja?"

~Stop with Eluno, Camila~.

Steven glances at me. "Well, Raine will not let his best friend stay in captivity. Not sure about Eluno. I'm sure he will come too."

I bite my lip, not being able to help myself. "You said that Eluno is mentally challenged, right?"

Steve turns, eating some brown bread loaf, bits of crumbs sprinkling to the cold ground.

"Yeah. What? You spending an hour with him is making you crazy?" He swallows and coughs a bit. "Shit. I'm gonna need something to drink with this."

"Yes," I say—that's one way to put it. "Well, how dumb is he? Because honestly, I'm starting to think he is not dumb at all."

Steven laughs, dry crumbs flying out of his mouth. "You serious? Eluno is a killing machine, and has not uttered more than three words his whole life. There was not a ton of information in his bio, just that he is mentally stunted. A loyal son of a bitch, though." He pauses. "Not that his mom's a bitch. An expression."

I take a breath, thinking of the intense look he gave me when I was on his lap. I feel a wave of guilt. I know he was interested sexually, but I'm not sure if he is smart enough to recognize it.

"That has to be wrong."

Has to be.

Steven raises his brows. "Pierce sent me the information, by the way. This man does not make mistakes—trust me. Pierce is a genius. He's a king." Steven smiles and shrugs.

That does not make sense. "Fuck."

"Whoooa, language."

I give him a hard look. "Steven. Are you sure I have been breaking into Eluno's cell?" My heart is beating now, the more I think about it. "Oh shit, what if it's not Eluno's cell, Steven?! This guy's eyes look pretty intelligent!" I shriek, my face heating.

I place a hand over my mouth as I look around in silent horror. I wonder if I sang Ricky Fucking Martin to a sane person, who ~now ~knows I'm definitely not from this planet.

Complete embarrassment.

Mission botched over weed and an MP3 player, and a pothead for an agent.

"Calm down, toots," Steven says, and holds up his hand. "Pierce ~himself ~told me that this was Eluno's cell that you must wait in." He makes a face at me.

"He sort of guessed that you're after Brayja, so Pierce said he wanted to help you out. The whole dungeon-hopping thing was actually Pierce's idea."

"I thought that was your mystic-mode idea?" I ask, eyes narrowing.

Lies.

His cheeks heat. "Well…" He frowns. "Well, we were sharing wavelengths, connected to the mystic and spirit realm."

"Wavelengths? Right."

I think about that, trying to calm my hysteria. Would Pierce deliberately lie or set me up? I doubt it. Given my trust issues, what would be the point of that?

Or would he?

I swallow, trying to calm my pulse. "Pierce never makes mistakes? You're sure?"

"Never. "

I take a deep breath, giving myself a mental shake. "Okay." I bite my lip. "It's just that Eluno seems intelligent."

~Beautiful.~

I bite my lip harder.

Stop.

Steve takes another bite and offers some to me.

I decline.

"Toots, I'm not saying he's brain dead."

"What color of eyes does Eluno have?"

Steve raises a brow at me. "I don't know, why would I know that?" He gives me an expression like I'm way out of line.

I groan. "You're an agent!" I continue and lower my voice, "You must know all the details, being an agent. Right? This is a mission, not a game." I point at him "You're going to make me look like an idiot."

He raises a brow. "But are you an idiot?"

"No," I deadpan.

"Well, then there you go." He takes a large bong from out of his cloak.

"How did you fit that in your cloak?" I ask, slightly impressed.

"I fit a whole bag of weed up my ass once." Steve looks down, a frown showing on his pudgy face. "It broke, and I was high for like a month."

"Steven," I say with a concerned frown, "maybe you should not smoke so much."
His eyes widen. "How ~dare ~you."
We stare at each other.

He raises his chin as he lights his bong.

"Can you find out the color of his eyes?"

"Probably."

"And," I say, "why are there only four songs on the MP3 Player? And Ricky Martin?!"

"You're Latina—Latinas looove Ricky," he says, and raises his eyebrows. His eyes go round and he speaks in a high voice.

"~Ooooh Ricky Martin! I love you! Ahhhh~," he takes a breath, "~Ricky you are so hot~!" He gives me a pointed look. "I have seen videos, Camila."

I slap my forehead and fight a smile. "Yeah, maybe in the 1990s."

Steven nods to the large pale of soapy water that took my heist skills to steal. "And why do you need this water again?"

"I thought Brayja would like to clean up a bit. It's very dirty in the dungeon. He expressed to me that he'd kill for a bath."

I don't know. The amenities here are nonexistent.

Steven is laughing, puffs of smoke leaking out of his mouth. "You really are trying to butter this guy up, aren't you?"

"Duh, Steven." I tilt my head at him.

He is laughing more. "Soapy water, though?!" He wipes his eyes. "Just show him your sweet tits!"

"Steven."

"Sorry."

I get up and take a breath. "Two days."

"Two days."

"I'm ready." I lean down and pick up the heavy pale of water. "The things I do for wealth."

***

My heart beats as I squeeze my eyes shut. That was too close.

For a second, I thought I would not make it to Eluno's cell. The Orc guards are off of their regular schedule due to the hysteria. I had to wait in the shadows for far too long.

I set my bucket of soapy water down quietly, my heart beating hard. Brayja better enjoy this, I swear.

I go to work on the lock, praying no beastly Orc comes running by.

~Click.~

I can feel a trickle of sweat run down my neck as I pick up the pail and slip inside. I could probably get caught at any time.

I hold my breath as I shut the door.

I'm in, and I'm instantly aware of Eluno, though I do not turn around. I take a breath and try to act normal. I slightly turn to see him with his head back against the stone wall, eyes closed.

I expel a breath.

"Eluno," I whisper.
He does not open his eyes.

I bite my lip.

I take the pail of water and sit down by the wall across from Eluno. Can he hear me, or is he deliberately ignoring me? Wouldn't one have to be smart to ignore someone? I curse, feeling so confused.

Time ticks by as I sit, staring at him. I wonder if they shoved a rod down his throat too.

"Eluno?" I ask. "Can you hear me?"

Finally, he tilts his head up and those vivid eyes of fire pin me. I feel a slow shiver wash over me and my skin prickles. Damn, this boy has a penetrating stare. It's such a crime of nature that he does not know how stunning his eyes are.

Damn shame.

"Miss me?" I ask playfully, then regret it.

Doubt he's in a playful mood.

I glance at the bucket next to me, and a pang of sadness washes over me. How inconsiderate of me to bring this only for Brayja. I look back at him and see him also regarding the pail. I tilt my head, a grin pulling at my mouth.

"Eluno, would you like to wash your hands?"

It seems so meaningless, but it's all I could find.

His gaze slowly raises to mine, and I can almost see the blaring question there. I swallow and shift uncomfortably.

"I brought it for Brayja," I say carefully, "but there is plenty for the both of you." I meet his gaze and I wish I knew what he was thinking, if anything. My pulse jumps as he regards me, his orange gaze traveling over me.

He then closes his eyes and does not open them again, leaning his head back. I sit up, confused. Shit. Did I somehow offend him? But, to be hurt, one must possess an IQ.
"Eluno?" I whisper.

His eyes remain closed.

I narrow my gaze on him. He thinks to ignore me?

I raise my brown skirts to reveal my shapely golden leg. A part of me wants to prove that this man is not dumb. Pierce needs to go back through the paperwork because a moron can see the intelligence in his stare.

"Fine, I guess I will just use the water myself," I whisper, knowing he hears me.

I bet he could hear a pin drop.

I take off my slipper and dip my toe in the cold water making a light splash noise. I sigh in fake pleasure, watching Eluno's gaze slowly open to zone in on me. His fiery gaze flickers over my exposed leg then pins me, tilting his head just a bit.

I feel my skin prickle.

I move my foot around in the water, my dress pulling dangerously high and he watches me. I can hear the chains as he moves, sitting up straighter.

I'm sorry—in hindsight, I'll probably call myself an idiot for tempting Brayja's bodyguard, but I'm just too curious.

I'm helpless.

It's the way he looks at me that makes me not think clearly. After this Brayja needs a ~new ~bodyguard, or there may be some issues.

It's like staring at the hot pool boy as I lower my shades and watch him, licking my lips. I'm not even sure if he is as hot as I'm thinking, but if he is, I can see a lot of women taking advantage of him.

I shiver, not wanting to imagine what he is capable of when he is at his finest, not in a dark dungeon. I close my eyes and put my slipper back on, feeling like a cat in heat.

Shame on you, Camila.

I need to get laid for Pete's sake.

69

I hear knocking, startling me, and I glance at Eluno. His exposed hand is taping on the stone with his knuckle, and he nods to the water.

I clear my throat, lowering my course gown with shaky hands. "You want the water now? You changed your mind?"

He makes a slight nod accompanied by the sounds of chains.

I take a breath and force a laugh.

"Okay, a little jealousy and you want the water. Go figure." I force a grin, trying to ignore how his eyes follow me like a tiger ready to pounce. Or to strain against his confines.

Play it cool, Camila.

Down, girl.

I stand and pick up the water, carrying the heavy bucket to him as gracefully as I can. I suck in a breath, my power picking up on his once again when I'm this close to him.

A low hiss escapes my lips, my body craving to feel his energy.
~Mierda~.
So much power.
~It's delicious~ . . .

I lower to my knees, knowing something is wrong. How can a mere bodyguard be this dangerous? I am like an addict, seeing my poison for the first time.

One of my FGI wishes was to have a talent that steals other abilities for a short time. It feels like an addiction, almost. I want, ~need~,his power.

If I could just lock my lips with his, I could suck in his power. I almost moan at the thought, giving myself a mental shake.

~Stop~.

I open my eyes, and he is studying me intently.

I clear my throat. "Eluno, let me see your hands."

I go to grab his hand, and he pulls out of my grasp, dunking his chained hand into the water himself.

I gasp, feeling a slight pulse come off him.

"What was that?" I ask, scared to move.

I felt it like a slight shock.

He tilts his head at me and lifts his clean hand out of the water, the suds sliding down his hand into his chains. I swallow, feeling the tension.

Maybe it's only me, but whatever it is, it's driving me wild.

I don't meet his eyes. "Eluno, nod if you have a rod down your throat." I glance up at him, wanting to help him.

He watches me, then puts his hand back in the water and closes his eyes, not responding. I glance at his hand as he moves his fingers through the water.

"Eluno, can I try and take off your mask?" I ask. "Maybe I can try and break you out."

Eluno opens his eyes and shakes his head, ~No~.
"No?" I ask, confused. "Why?"

I close my eyes, knowing he can't respond.

"Can I please try?" I whisper.

He just watches me but does not respond, his fiery gaze moving over my face. I still have my mesh covering on, and it looks like he is trying to picture me without it. Just like I was doing to him, wondering about the man under the mask.

I bite my lip and slowly raise my hands to his face, and he does not flinch away.

~"Hey, Steven here! I think the Nymphs are coming faster than I thought! There is a massive storm brewing and I don't think it's natural!~"

I pull my hands back and turn to peek out of the cracks in the rocks and notice the sounds of the howling wind is much louder. I expel a breath and glance back to Eluno.

"The Nymphs are coming," I breathe. "Don't worry, Raine is Brayja's good friend, they will not leave you here. They will come for you, I will make sure of it." I try to reassure him.

I see the lines around his eyes crinkle slightly.

That makes me curious. Is he smiling? Grimacing? Snarling? Taking a breath, I raise my hand to his mask and my fingers lightly touch the metal lock at his ear. I could potentially pick it, but I would need more tools. Steven said the FGI pick only works on the door. I want to roll my eyes—why only the door?

It's hard to think clearly when he is staring at me like he is.

I need a closer look, but I don't want to straddle him again and make him sexually confused. I rise up on my knees and lean in closer, now grabbing the lock.

We are so close, but I try to ignore it.

The lock is old and rusted.

I could break it, but I would need something heavy. And the lock being on his face would compromise that unless I wanted to knock him out.

I could steal his power.

I bite my lip again. "Eluno," I whisper, "I'm going to attempt something." I look at him and we are just breaths away from one another. Eluno's eyes narrow as he slightly tilts his head. I swallow.

"I may have to sit in your lap again, if that's okay?"

I feel like the air is charged around us. But I know it's just me, poor Eluno is most likely just in a constant confused state. I bet that would be horrible, never understanding what everyone else does.

His hand moves out of the water and he touches my thigh, pushing me on top of him. I straddle him with a frown on my face. He understood me then?

It would appear that way.

I can feel his body under mine and I notice again that this man feels like solid muscle. I look at his hand and see that his fingers are gently caressing my leg through my course gown.

What the hell?

I look back at him and he raises his gaze to mine, his hand becoming firmer.

"Eluno," I ask, "what are you doing?"

His hand strains against his chains as his finger finds the bottom of my gown and lifts it up, his hand disappearing under my dress.

I am breathing hard, completely confused by what he is doing. He must be curious, wanting to experience something sexual.

"Eluno, you're not supposed to put your hand up a woman's dress without permission," I reprimand a little breathlessly, feeling his large hand now gripping my naked thigh.

Oh boy.

What should I do?

Stop him?

But I don't, curiosity getting the best of me. A little part of me wants to see what he will do. A man with no experience will not know what to even look for. Right?

Eluno just watches me as his hand squeezes and massages my thigh, making a slight moan escape my lips. I curse myself.

~Please don't be such a hussy. Get a hold of yourself. ~

He sits up a little straighter, bringing me chest to chest with him. I don't know what to do, my heart is pounding against my chest.

This is so wrong, but I can't stop it.

"Eluno, you have to stop what you are doing. I'm having a hard time focusing," I breathe as his hand now grips my bare ass, pushing me against his very ~hard ~erection.

His erection! He's hard. He's hard. OMG. What do I do?!

"Eluno," I moan, feeling the long length of him.
~Mierda~, this man is huge.
I feel dizzy. I need to stop him.

Does he understand what he is doing?

"Eluno," I pant, as I feel his hips move against my girl parts. Hot flashes exploded over my body, knowing this is escalating too fast.

I cannot believe he is hard, and I'm not helping with my slight moans.

Eluno looks down and I feel his hand making his way to my lady parts.

Will he touch me?

There is no way he will know what to do if Pierce is right about him. If he knows what to do, then someone made a grave mistake. Either Eluno is smart, or this is NOT Eluno.

Eluno looks up at me and I want to climax from just his intense gaze. He's a lady killer—those eyes are panty-dropping eyes. I can't believe I'm feeling this way when I have not even seen him fully yet.

His fingers find my thin underwear and pull them away from my lady bits. I hold my breath as our eyes lock. Time freezes for an instant.

Will he?

Then I feel his fingers slide through my slick folds and I gasp, my body sizzling, igniting on contact. He closes his eyes for a few moments then opens them, his fingers sliding back and forth.

I can see his broad chest rise and fall fast, his hand expertly moving over me. A part of my brain that still works wonders if that is why he washed his hand in the water.

Did he know he was going to touch me?

That is smart.

Not dumb.

Not dumb.

SMART.

I gasp when two fingers dip inside me and immediately he finds the spot that makes me scream a moan.

"Eluno!" I pant, my brain firing off red alerts.

I feel a shock. A pulse.

Like he shocked my vagina and now I'm tensing around his fingers, a powerful orgasm racking my body from head to toe.

I'm grabbing into him for dear life, my body shaking with a forceful sensation I can't even begin to describe.

I see stars and colors.

What the hell was that?!

This is not right.

I hear a loud explosion outside, shaking the walls, bringing me back to reality. I jerk away from him right as his hand tries to stop me.

I'm breathing hard, crawling to the opposite wall, hearing another explosion, rocks falling from the ceiling. Eluno flexes his muscles and thrusts his arm forward, the chains breaking free, the rock wall splitting.

I scream, scooting more against the rock wall.

He is trying to break out.

To get me.

~"Steven here! Sorry, I got the munchies and passed out. Kalypso is here! Get out of there! Meet me at the west landing where we arrived.~"

"Steven," I whisper breathlessly, as I watch Eluno try and break free from his confines, the rock wall cracking more. His hand is working on his face mask. "What was Eluno's eye color?"

~"Oh, uh, like brown.~"

I feel the blood leave my face. My heart pounds.

"What is Raine's eye color?" I barely say.

~"Raine? Why?! Get out of there!~"

"Fucking tell me," I hiss.

~"I think I read like bright orange or something.~"

I close my eyes, my world spinning. "Camila, you fool." You were the moron all along.

I see Raine rip off his mask and pull a long cord from out of his mouth, coughing into the ground.

Oh ~shit. ~

He is breathing hard as he looks up at me and I feel faint. Good lord, he is beyond hot. Well, he is the son of a mythological sea goddess. Of course he is fucking beautiful.

My mind cannot even process him right now, shock overwhelming me. I slowly stand, my whole body on alert, shaking.

"You are not Eluno," I whisper.

"Don't go," he whispers, his voice rough.

I'm to be married to his best friend. He could tell Brayja my secrets. Mission compromised.

I turn and run, and I can hear him yell in fury. The sound sends a chill down my spine.

I have to lie.

Raine cannot know who I am.

I have to lie.

CHAPTER 7

CAMILA

The rain hits me in all directions.

I run. Away from him.

Raine.

My mind is in denial as I sprint, my emotions flaring out of control.

~"I see you. Over here! I'm waving my hand! Holy shit, Kalypso is raining hellfire on this mountain.~

~"I also received updates that ships from the Gaya Empire are closing in, but they can't come too close due to the hurricane. These Orcs are screwed, man!~"

I can still hear his yell of rage echo in my head, making me sprint faster.

I'm running blindly, trying not to get hit by falling rocks as explosions wrack this horrid mountain. My mind is in fight or flight mode.

I scream as a large boulder smashes right beside me, making me almost fall off the mountainside. I wave my arms to regain my balance, breathing hard.

I curse and do a Hail Mary, my eyes seeing out into the black, angry ocean. The waves crash against the mountain side violently. This is probably a level ten on the danger scales.

~"Keep your lifelines handy! I'm permitted to use one on your behalf. Don't get smashed~——~run faster, woman! Poseidon's army is here!"~

I look behind me, knowing Raine will be hot on my tail if I don't move fast. I heard him yell when I left, this man is not just going to let me get away.

Raine is the eye of this storm and I'm caught in the middle.

I see Steven and I run up to him, breathing hard, my eyes flinching from another bright lightning strike.

"Shit!" I look around. "We need to get out of here," I say, and catch my breath. "Like right now, Steven!"

"Company," Steven says as he squints through the rain to the cliff's edge and points.

I gasp, seeing vampire-looking people climbing up and over the edge with sleek weapons. "Oh shit," I murmur. "Who are they?"

"Nymphs," Steven says. "Poseidon and Kalypso's army."

They look like vampires. I can see the sharp canines even in the darkness.

"Pull your hood down, show that you're not an Orc!" Steven orders, and lowers his hood.

I follow Steven and see them make their way to us, weapons raised.

We both hold our hands up.

"Madness," I whisper, my heart pounding.

I just sexually frustrated a dangerous Nymph with razor sharp canines. ~Fan-fuckin-tastic~. I shiver, glancing in the direction I came, praying I don't see Raine.

I need time to collect my thoughts, to get my fake storyline in order. I need to prepare, I'm not ready yet.

I know Raine will want to report me to Brayja, so I need to be ready. I curse, wondering if the other players are having as hard a time as I am.

I seriously doubt it.

Steven clears his throat. "Gaya Empire!"

I see a Nymph soldier walk up to us and I notice that half the skin on his neck is bluish green, but it's slowly fading to skin color. They look human, but you can tell they are not.

They seem to be leaner and almost elegant, like an elven race. Not like brute warriors, but like magical creatures. I think that when I reflect on this experience, when I'm not scared shitless, I will appreciate this in awe.

I glance at Steven, just realizing I have no idea what my alias is. "My name?" I hiss through my teeth as rain pelts me in the face, soaking my hair.

"Oh, right." He smiles nervously at the Nymph, who is eying us suspiciously, some sort of gun aimed at us with a spear on its end. Steven clears his throat and speaks to them.

"Daphine Laromedia, fiancée to Brayja of Gaya."
~My name is Daphine~?

Crazy how FGI can just create a life like this, like I have always been this Daphine Valkyrie.

The Nymph's eyes widen.

I can feel my body shake with impatience, begging this man to take me away before Raine breaks free. Please . . .

The man turns to yell at his men, lightning reflecting off his wet skin.

I expel a breath, shivering.

Steven and I glance at each other as sounds of explosions get more frequent. I can hear echoes of Orcs yelling their battle cries, making me tense.

The Nymph looks back to us.

"Come with us quickly, we have recused Brayja already. You will accompany us until the weather passes. You will be our guests." He bows slightly to me, holding out his hand.

"Brayja has already informed us that you were to be saved and located."

I almost forgot that I'm from royal blood and engaged to the up-and-coming king of the Gaya Empire.

A real smile spreads across my face for the first time since being here as I think of all the riches waiting for me. Finally, time to get off this horrid mountain and to start my fantasy.

The future queen has arrived.

~Mierda.~
~Raine~.
I'll deal with that later.

***

Pinch me. Is this really happening?

I'm living my wildest dream.

I take a steady breath as I gaze around my room with ten servants running around me, assisting me with every single need as if I were already a queen. My skin is perfectly scented, my body is luscious and smooth, and my makeup is sultry. I bathed in hot water perfumed with the smell of tropical fruits.

I had not had the pleasure of a mirror on hellish Orc mountain, so it's a shock to see my new eye color. Swirling red with blue and purple outer tones. I take another calming breath as I feel hands on my gown, making slight adjustments. I look mouthwatering, goddess level. Brayja is going to lose his mind when he sees me.

I have seen the other two contenders for Brayja's hand, and to my benefit, they can't compete with an FGI agent.

We are just too damn hot.

~Ouch~.

But my eye color is a bad shock.

The color is very rare, because my talent is rare. Which means Raine will most likely recognize them if he was observant in the dungeon. If, in fact, he is still searching for me. There could be a chance that he's not and I will get off the hook.

I'm horrible about running worst-case scenarios through my head obsessively.

I bet that boy has women at his feet night and day. I mean, I know he had his hand up my skirts, but that's hardly anything to fuss over, right?

Right.

I'm not married yet.

I sniff.

Closing my eyes, I bite my lip, praying this Raine guy does not make my life a living hell. When I'm ready, I must go to Brayja, who is in the main hall. He requested to see me at once.

I'm curious to see him when he is not dungeon-dirty. He could be a real catch, and I could pretend to be head over heels for him.

I tilt my head as I gaze into the golden-rimmed mirror. They pierced my nose; the glittering nose ring is a sign of royalty. I'm draped in golden jewels and I'm wearing a stunning headpiece that compliments my jet-black hair.

Even my fingers have glittering jewels adored on them making me feel like a goddess of wealth and beauty.

This is unreal.

I was transported to this stunning underwater city in their Atlantean submarine. The palace is made mostly out of glass or some transparent material.

I met up with other Valkyries from the Gaya Empire, taking me back into their protection while the Orc war is happening.

The enormous hall is a great dome, probably a hundred stories high. I feel like I'm in some enchanted aquarium, seeing foreign sea life swimming through the massive glass panes.

It's straight out of a magical ocean fantasy.

Each room has a ramp that disappears into the ocean, like a water doorway. They also have normal doors with halls just like any other palace—for use if you're not a Nymph, I guess.

Air pressure, I'm assuming, keeps the water from flooding in and drowning this magical place. I did dip my feet into the cool water, seeing the aqua sea splashing up on the marble incline. I didn't go any further because Steven said there are tons of sea creatures out there that have very sharp teeth.

So I will postpone my ocean swim and not get eaten on my first day here.

I shiver.

I raise my chin to all my servants. "Leave me, please," I say in a commanding tone, and almost laugh.

This is so wild.

I hear Steven's stoner-laugh behind me, gaining looks from the other servants. What? They've never seen a chubby pothead garbed in golden chains, looking like a love guru, before?

It's a first for me too.

Once they all leave, I turn to him. "Look at me! We have to talk."

He sits up, chains clanking together. "Thank god they left. I need a smoke. I'm losing my mystic talents."

I glare at him. "I think your mystic talents just landed me in some deep shit, Steven!"

He lights his blunt, frowning. "What do you mean?"

I can barely contain my rage. "Pierce—the wise ol' Pierce—was wrong. I'm so screwed!" I close my eyes, starting to panic. My house of cards is starting to come down.

"Pierce is never wrong."

"It was Raine's cell all along, you moron!"

Well, I was technically the moron. But still. He should have known.

He laughs, smoke coming out of his mouth. "Ooohh, that's why Pierce told me to tell you, ~sorry~. His little mistake."

"What?!" I yell then look around, lowering my voice. "What? A little mistake?"

Steven shrugs and frowns at me. "So what? It's not like you made out with the dude."

I stare at him, face heating. Deafening silence.

He starts coughing, eyes wide. "No. W-way."

I bite my lip and feel a crash of embarrassment. "This is so bad," I whisper. "I sang Ricky Martin to him, Steven! I didn't think it mattered because he was supposed to be mentally challenged."

"No. Way."

I hold up my hand. "I also told him that I'm from another F-ing planet when I was high off your strong-ass weed. And," I take a breath, "all sorts of other dumb shit like being an agent."

"Nooo. Waaayy."

I groan at this part. "He also made it to third base with me."

Steven's mouth drops. "NOOO. WAY." He takes another hit. "Duuuude. You took advantage of a guy with little mental capabilities?"

"He was not slow, obviously! It was Raine! Not Eluno!" I shriek in self defense.

He is laughing now, smoke coming out of his mouth in fast puffs. "But you didn't know that at the time!" He laughs more. "How embarrassing."

I cross my arms. "He seemed smart, because he ~was~," I mutter.

A woman enters with half her face covered with lovely silks and bows in front of me. Steven thankfully shuts up, but I can still hear him snorting.

"Prince Brayja asks your whereabouts, Daphine of Gaya."

I'm in a mess. My nerves take flight.

"Of course," I say, and give Steven a pleading look.

My golden gown sparkles as I walk towards the guards, Pierce having adjusted it to fit my curves deliciously. The material is waterproof, apparently, but it feels like the purest of satin.

My fantasy is short-lived, though. I now wish my breasts didn't look mouthwatering in the dipping neckline, and I wish the glittering jewels didn't make my brown skin look luscious.

I should stay in the shadows till Raine moves on, not draw his attention. I'm not playing this game smartly—I'm almost on strike three.

***

This underwater palace is Gothically stunning. The Nymphs are like underwater vampires, dressed in their dark beauty. Everything is silver and the color of gunmetal while the Valkyries are the opposite—golden riches galore.

I am in awe.

My eyes are wide, I think I have blinked maybe once. The great hall has hundreds of people in it, mostly Nymphs. You can tell them from the Valkyries by their pale skin and Gothic appeal.

In the center of the hall is a massive ramp leading down into the deep blue ocean.

So bizarre, but remarkable. Fish and whales can be seen through the towering glass dome.

Nymph guards dive into the water and some emerge with full clothing on, dripping wet. But their clothing seems to dry within seconds. Small submarine vehicles emerge also, carrying Valkyries.

It's incredible to see all of this in real life. It's like a massive doorway into the palace.

Steven nudges me. "Go sit next to the other two fiancées. Up on the platform, do you see? Brayja is to your left, ogling you with his mouth open. "

I notice a lot of stares directed my way. I feel a flash of intense nerves.

I nod, seeing the platform for royalty, dark metal chairs with red rubies embedded into them. The craftsmanship is astonishing here.

I look to my left and see Brayja walking up to me, holding out his hands. I instantly recognize him.

My future husband.

I raise my chin.

He looks handsome with his finely manicured goatee and brown, slicked-back hair. He is giving off definite Jude Law vibes. Brayja wears white breeches and a golden overcoat fit for Buddha. Rings on every finger, and in his slightly pointed ears.

"Daphine, my holiness, you are a vision, and here I was not looking forward to having my marriage arranged," he says, and brings my sparkling hand to his lips. His voice is slightly higher than I remember, but still nice.

I can do this.

"I'm so glad you're not in the horrors of captivity," I say carefully, easily playing the part of the seductress, beckoning him with my eyes. "You were so brave."

He makes a sound, his gaze traveling over my face. "I could stare into your eyes all day, stunning creature you are. It's a surprise we have never actually met before this, our families being relatively close.

"My mother has informed me that you lived up north, which is why our paths never crossed until now," he murmurs, kissing my wrist. I'm so glad you did not slip past me, and, my dear, I will correct you if I may. You were brave, not I."

He keeps kissing my wrist, smelling it even. Brayja continues as his gaze moves over my body. "You have shown me your true colors, breaking into a dangerous place just to see about my health," he says, beaming at me, his hazel gaze intent.
He likes what he sees, pausing at my breasts, ~a lot~.
"Later on, my mother would love to speak with you. She will be arriving tomorrow."

I totally have this in the bag. I smile and nod.

Brayja leads me up to the other women like I'm already queen, and they openly glare at me as I sit down.

Sorry girls, but the game is over. He's mine.

~"Hey, your boy Raine is coming. Still can't believe you got dirty with him!" Steven says. "Just keep your head down, you hussy." He laughs.~
~"By the way, I'm super high right now. This chick in front of me has like three heads and five eyes . . . creeping me out.~"
"No, no, no," I breathe, having forgotten about Raine.

The hairs on the back of my neck rise and I feel a wave of nerves.

"Aye, Raine finally shows!" I hear Brayja say to the men around him. He leaves, off to wherever he sees Raine.

Shit. Shit. Shit. Shit. My pulse pounds and I feel faint.

Camila, do not overreact.

My gaze slowly raises, and I see a group of men emerge from the massive ramp, and every bone in my body knows. I swallow and feel my pulse beat against my neck like an axe.

~Raine Syrinx, son of Kalypso~, I hear someone announce.
People cheer like he is some celebrity, rushing over to him.

I don't clap, my mouth just hangs open for heartbeats. It's like watching the rockstar finally emerge onto the stage. Raine rises fully out of the water, soaking . . . wet.

The droplets run down each hard ripple of his wet shirt, tantalizing every female who sees. He is big, muscular, and darkly sexy.

I sensed that in the dungeon, which ultimately made me make dumb choices. That animalistic, fiery gaze will haunt me—the way he looked at me while I let him touch me.

Stop.

This obsession cannot escalate.

I look away for a second and see other women eyeing him like candy, giggling.

"Raine!" I hear Brayja yell and walk up to him. "Someone told me you had a better cell than I had."

~"Yea, because Raine made it to third base in his," Steven chimes in with a snort. "Dang, homeboy is huuuge—I really hope you did not piss this dude off.~"
~Mierda~.
"Shut it," I hiss. "Get out of my head."
They start talking like long-lost buddies.

I take a steadying breath. I can get through this.

He's easily double the size of Brayja, his body dressed in all black clothing. His thigh alone is the size of Brayja's two legs put together. But he is not bulky — strangely elegant, like an Olympic swimmer.

He looks dangerous.

Powerful.

This is not going to be easy.

Brayja's best friend just happens to be some sex god who just happened to get me off in a dark dungeon, after being tortured for a week.

Ahem.

Without even trying.

I hear a commotion and I look up to see Raine inspecting Brayja's servants very intently. Looking at each face like he was looking for a hidden criminal. I suck in a breath.

"Steven. He's looking for me," I whisper in fear.

~"Yeah, no shit. The dude must have liked third base. Nice job, you just made this complicated.~"

I'm holding my breath, watching Raine grab each female's face to inspect them. Brayja laughs and points in my direction.

Oh no . . .

Raine's gaze snaps in my direction and I can't breathe.

I look down. Heart pounding.

I hear, "Raine, we have already located the maiden stranded on the mountain. She is my future wife, astonishingly enough . . . " Brayja says right in front of me, and his voice trails off in the fog of my mind.

He is talking me up to Raine, and all I can hear is the rushing of my ears.

Soon-to-be wife.

I force myself to look up and our gazes collide, hard.

I can't speak.

Raine's fire eyes look shocked and they sear my face. His chest is moving up and down as his gaze lowers to my body, not hiding his absolute shock.

Did he think I was just a slave girl?

Brayja laughs and slaps him on the back. "I finally have something the mighty Raine wants! I shall celebrate tonight. Stunning creature, right? Can you believe that this is the first time I'm meeting her?

"I tell you, Raine, it's love at first sight," he murmurs as his gaze lands on mine, and I think he actually means it.

I want to groan.

Love at first sight.

Raine coolly regards me, jaw clenching. "She is stunning, Brayja. Congratulations," he finally says in a dangerous voice, with an accent that has me squeezing my legs together. His gaze slides over my body again and a small smile flickers over his lips as his gaze meets mine. The smile is something you'd see on a hunter, a predator.

"Yes, we shall celebrate. I look forward to hearing more about your chosen wife, Brayja. I must see for myself if she is worthy." He winks at Brayja, causing him to laugh.

I shiver. I'm in trouble.

Raine looks back at me before he leaves. "Until we meet again," he all but hisses.

I feel a flush wash over my face.

I hear Brayja whisper, "Don't worry, he's always like that. He will warm up to you."

That's what I'm scared of.
~Mierda~.

CHAPTER 8

CAMILA

I'm hyper-aware of him. I don't feel like myself, and it's as if I can't catch my breath.

Raine has not once glanced my way since our meeting in the main hall. Nymph soldiers rush in and out, taking orders from Raine. He looks furious, yelling orders to his men.

I would too if I spent almost two weeks being tortured by morbid Orcs. Hopefully, though, he had one positive experience in the dungeon.

Ahem.

I close my eyes, knowing I have a problem now.

I have a Raine obsession. It happened fast.

Swift.

It's best if I acknowledge it—the first step is identifying that I have a problem. I can't fix something I don't accept. Right? This is going to be emotional hell for a short while, watching him while being engaged to Brayja. Don't misunderstand me. I still very much want to be engaged to Brayja.

I will be a queen with untold power and riches beyond my imagination. I mean, I already have it in the bag—Brayja can barely keep his eyes off me. He already informed his adviser, Amete, that he made the decision to choose me.

I bite my lip. I might be wrong, but I'm sensing some severe possessiveness from Brayja, almost excessively controlling.

He tells me what to do—no, ~commands ~me—like it's the most natural thing for him.

I have not known him long, and it's already grating at me.

~My Daphine, stand next to the ladies in waiting~.

~Do not get in the way or talk. We need no distraction from pretty things~. I roll my eyes.

He called me a ~thing~. ~What a turn on—not~. ~Hardly groundbreaking, I have been called worse. The thing is, I really don't care.~

Brayja has no idea I'm just using him for my own advantage, not pining after him like he thinks. Call me what you will. I will not lose sleep over it, trust me.

But it does not mean it's not irritating as hell, eye-twitch worthy.

~Are you forgetting to lower your head around other men~? ~He laughs to lighten the blow~. You're not my queen yet, my beautiful flower~.

~Let me take you to the throne room, so your beauty does not distract the other men~.

Well, to be fair, he is to be king, so maybe it's in his blood to be commanding of everyone. Steven said that the Valkyries in the Gaya Empire are incredibly wealthy.

They use extremely vibrant colors, so opposite of this underwater haven. I also observed that Valkyrie women dress very scandalously, with tons of sparkles and jewels galore.

They like to flaunt their wealth, which is fine by me.

I love it, actually. I would rule over millions. I'm happy. But I'm ~slightly ~bothered by Raine.

The palace is beautiful. This room possesses giant statues of Poseidon and a clear dome that sits behind the central throne. This is not where Poseidon and Kalypso reside, Steven tells me, but it's still breathtaking.

Stunning.

I tilt my head as I watch Thetis. Yes, that's him. The main objective.

I also saw Sun Hai earlier. I wonder how it feels to breathe underwater? She is very pale with blood-red lips and long black hair that's plaited. Stunning, really. I wonder if she has made any headway with Thetis.

I have not seen any of the other girls yet, but I'm sure I will.

My eyes narrow on Thetis, lounging on his throne, listening to his council talk about the spreading Orc war, and what steps to take.

I'm permitted to sit on the sidelines and watch with a few other top-ranking Valkyries. I nod to them, but apparently there is no talking.

I take a breath.

Brayja led me here and then left somewhere, saying he'd be back for me. I sigh and glance back at Thetis. He's handsome. There is no doubt about that with the timeless elegance they all seem to possess. His blonde hair and piercings make him look like a gothic elven king. I can definitely see his appeal.

To be honest, he gives off an air of being spoiled rotten, almost rolling his eyes when his military men talk to him. He looks extremely put out as if he does not have time for this.

I have not seen Poseidon or Raine's mother yet, but I can see why his father prefers Raine. I can see and understand the deep jealousy that has taken place. It seems that no matter what dimension or planet you're on, scenarios repeat and reflect each other.

Seeing how Raine is more respected, in my opinion, makes him sexier. Raine has that mysteriousness about him that drives women wild—including me. I want to know what he thinks when he looks at me, and I can't tell which drives me more mad.

I take another bored breath and gaze out into the ocean, seeing the exotic sea life. I could not help but watch Raine in the main hall when Brayja was not watching me like a hawk.

I was helpless not to salivate over him, and trying to hide it from Brayja was hard.

I wonder if Raine knows he was set up by Thetis. The jealous and bitter brother.

That might just be FGI knowledge.

~"So, Sun Hai is the top runner with Thetis thus far. A couple of the girls have not even met him yet due to the Orc war. Are you certain you do not want to try for Thetis? He's is in line for the throne.~"

"Steven, I already have the queen thing in the bag," I whisper. I look to my left and see the man sitting next to me is still staring straight ahead.

~"True, but Thetis is the main objective.~"

I sigh. "Look at him, way too much drama. Too much work. Where are you?" I whisper under my breath, and see the man slightly glance my way.

Great.
~"I'm the beetle on the chair next to you. Please don't squash me. Dude, I have like eight eyes. Shapeshifting when high is kinda fun.~"

"Cant. Talk." I mutter and raise my chin.

~"Dude, but what about Raine? I think a tsunami is headed your way if you stick with your position. Thetis might actually be a safer bet, he's not

Raine's best friend~.

~"Haven't kingdoms fallen over a single woman? I just want to win. I need the money for my kids back home.~"

"Bullshit. You just want to buy more watches," I get out as quietly as possible.

~"You a mean bitch,~" he laughs like he is a broken record, "~but that's true.~"

I take another breath and glance over to see Thetis rolling his eyes and stifling a yawn.

"I can deal with Raine," I whisper. I don't mesh well with entitled brats.

I hear a disapproving grunt from the man next to me. Don't glare.

I don't need him telling Brayja I'm out of control. I need that ring on my finger before I start doing what I want.

~"Another thing~ — ~I think Riane knows that Thetis is a piece of shit."~ I almost laugh.

Even Eluno could see that. Oh, funny, I saw Eluno. A large brute of a man, like a massive Viking.

Yeah.
The FGI girls have it cut out for them because I'm sticking with the safe option. I will be rooting for them on the sidelines though. ~Go team! Whoo-hoo! Shake that fine FGI ass! ~

I suddenly hear a loud commotion coming from the entrance. I sit up straighter, frowning. My eyes widen when I see Brayja sprinting in with a couple of Nymphs, making his way to me.

"Get back!"

Get back?

"Get back!"

Thetis slowly stands, and for once, he does not look tired. I stand and move back right as I see Raine enter in all of his glory and rage. He bares his sharpened canines as he pins Thetis with his gaze.

Raine might know.

"Raine! So glad you're back and unharmed, brother." Thetis's smile is cold and sinister.

Oh, I don't think sarcasm is helping this ~not ~to escalate.
The next thing I feel is my body being catapulted backward. My vision swims, and I realize I'm on the ground with broken wood around me.

I hear lots of sounds. Yelling. Screaming.

I feel my nose as I try to right my vision, and realize it's bleeding.

~"Dude, get out! Get up! The brothers are in it deep. Raine is giving Thetis a massive beat down!~"

I stand as I feel another shockwave that almost makes me lose the contents of my stomach. I glance at the men and see that Raine has Thetis up against the glass dome, hand on his throat, arm radiating electricity.

The color drains from my face.

It's breaking, cracking.

Raw fear washes over me.

I look over to see Brayja yelling at me, waving his arms for me to run. I turn to run, but it's too late. The sound of the dense sea waters smashing through the glass is earsplitting.

Dark water pours in at an alarming rate and I scream.

"Steven!"

~"You'll have to swim out once it fills up with water or use a lifeline! They're shutting off this wing to prevent the water from flooding everywhere. Get ready to hold your breath!~"

"Daphine!" Brayja tries to make his way to me, but gets swept up with the raging currents. Within minutes I'm underwater, being thrashed around.

I can feel my lungs. I can tell I have about ten minutes of lung capacity.

Bubbles everywhere.

Survival instinct.

I'm thrown off balance, not sure which way I'm facing, my hair floating around me.

Must get out.

Adrenaline pumps through my body as I kick, starting my powerful swim, thankful it was one of my talents. I can see now as I squint, the water having surprisingly good visibility. I also realize I'm the only one left in the room, the backlash pulling all of them out but me.

I kick more, the pressure from the electric pulse making it feel like I'm swimming in mud, oddly enough, confusing me. A wave of panic hits me.

~"Camila! Pierce says use your lifeline. Don't be stupid! FGI is watching your vital signs. I'm permitted to use a lifeline on your behalf!" Steven yells in my head.~
~"By the way, I'm the little fish to your right. I'm kinda cute.~"
No lifelines yet.

I see a tiny little fish to my left with large, bulging eyes like someone squeezed it.
In a weird way . . . it looks like Steven.

I kick more, the dress I'm wearing hindering my legs. I stop and reach down to grab the end of the dress and pull hard, trying to rip the material.

I curse.

The effort is wasting my oxygen. But it finally rips.

I'm now able to move my legs in a better motion. ~I can do this~. I don't need to waste a lifeline this early in the game, which would put me at a major disadvantage.

Swiping my hair out of my face, I notice a current. I'm wasting a lot of effort making my way to the giant glass hole. Something is pulling me, and I notice I'm going around in a circle like there is a mini hurricane in here.

~"Camila, you might have to throw in the towel. Raine has created a tunnel current! Hold up five fingers if you want to activate the lifeline!~"

I fight even harder and it does nothing, my body is pulled around. Desperation floods my emotions as I kick harder. I can feel my pulse beating in my neck as I ready myself for a lifeline activate.

I have just a little air left as I kick one last time, and I see a large figure swim through the massive glass hole.

My eyes widen.
"~Oh shit. It's Raine! I'm out."~
Raine.

It only takes him a few leg kicks to make his way to me, like the strong currents are nothing. My heart is beating hard as he grabs me around the waist, pulling me to his large body aggressively.

I give him a panicked look.
~Air~!
His gaze glows orange under the water, and his hand grabs my chin, lowering his mouth to mine. I suck in the air he forcefully blows into my mouth like a lifeline, and something happens.

99

Something major.

I didn't just suck in his air. A shock courses through my body, and I know immediately what happened.

I took some of his power. Or stole it.

Beautiful air fills my blood cells as I look at my hands, which are now metallic maroon and orange-yellow.

I look up into Raine's handsome face as he also regards my skin, which I can see matches his. His neck and what disappears into his black shirt is the same color.

He touches my arm, then looks back up at me.

We both float together as I wrap my arms around his neck, my body molding to his. I will argue later why I did this—mostly reasons to do with him having to carry me out of here.

But right now, I just want to feel him.

I can't help it.

His black floating hair and piercing gaze underwater is a heady combination. The grip around my waist tightens, and I wrap my legs around his hips, thanks to my ripped dress.

Not sure what's happening, but something is.

My dark hair floats all around us as he holds me, his hands now grabbing my thighs. Finally, he turns his head and looks behind him, carrying me with him while he swims with one arm.

I can feel his muscles working.

I dig my head into his neck as he swims with powerful strokes. He exits the hole like it was a walk in the park, not the hurricane from hell. He does not go to the surface like I thought he would, but keeps swimming. I hold on tight, not sure how long Raine's abilities will be present in me.

I open my eyes and see that we are swimming under the rooms at the palace. Lots of ramps leading up into apartments are visible with glowing blue lights.

I stare in awe.

Where is he taking me?

Then I realize where, as he swims up into ~my ~room.
Nice to know he knows where my room is.

We break the surface and I take a large breath, looking around, confirming that this is my room. Still hooked to his shoulders, I also realize that we are alone.

Raine sets me on the ledge's entrance and stands between my thighs, water sloshing around us. He is wet, water droplets running down his neck and face.

"Daphine," he breathes, his fire gaze roaming over my face. "I think we should talk."

I swallow, trying to ignore how hot he is. His powerful arms on either side of me, pinning me.

"First, thank you for saving me."

I can feel his body heat, his slight breathing. Raine glances down then back up to me.

"How long did you know you were engaged to Brayja?"

I shift, realizing my golden gown is hiked up around my waist. "Well, just for a little bit, but only just today he chose to marry me."

"Did he now?" Raine whispers.

I look away and nod.

His gaze is so intense it's hard to keep his stare without blushing. Raine tilts his head to gain my attention again.

"Daphine, I'm still trying to piece together who you are. What's your real name? Because we both know it's not Daphine."

Shit.

I make a sound. "I'm sorry. What I told you in the dungeon was all fantasy—a friend of mine gave me this drug that I regret."

Raine laughs, and his gaze lowers to my breasts then back up. "I remember."

I shiver.
Raine is banned from laughing.

I repress a moan.

"Steven? Was that your friend's name?"

I blush. He was paying attention.

"Yes," I say.

"Thank him for me, will you?"

I don't say anything.

Raine's eyes lower again as if just realizing my dress has hiked up, revealing my ass. Now I'm thanking my lucky stars it has. Thin underwear is all that stands in the way.

I feel heat pool inside my body as I watch him expel a breath, jaw flexing.

"Thank Steven for letting me see the real you." He glances up at me. "Are you going to play coy with me, Daphine? I didn't get to be who I am today without being able to read people."

I raise my chin. "Sorry, Raine, ~baby~. But you can't prove anything." He makes a sound. Maybe he likes the pet name.

"I can," he says, pulling me slightly to him like he could not help it. "I might not be able to locate your music player or make Brayja believe that I got you off in two minutes in the pits of the dungeon. Or tell him that you're an agent from another planet.

"But I can prove what you just did in the water."

I swallow, eyes narrowing.

"You should know that your people obsess over bloodlines. Brayja may under no circumstances marry a woman with tainted blood, nor would he want to." Raine tilts his head at me, his hands moving higher to cup my ass. Raine takes a breath as he rubs me into him. "Royal families are all alike, you should know this."

I stifle a moan when I ~feel ~him. "I'm n-not tainted."

I feel like I can't think.

What would it be like to have Raine make love to me? Raine's lips graze my neck as he slightly grinds into me, rolling his hips masterfully. "I can. That talent you have is from Nymphs."

"It's not," I hiss, feeling hot all over my body.

Lies.

Did I just pick a talent that will screw me? But didn't Pierce pick that for me?!

"I think I know better than you, seeing how I'm from this planet," he whispers against my skin. "Valkyries do not have such powers. But, if you don't believe me, feel free to ask Brayja."

Fear washes over me through the desire.

"He will never believe you," I get out quickly, and try to kick Raine away from me.

He catches my leg. "Go away."

"I want you to back out of the engagement due to tainted blood," Raine says, eyeing me. "Not that I care about tainted blood, but I do care about the Gaya Empire alliance. I don't know who you are and I can't have the next queen ruin everything. We are strong because of Gaya. Otherwise, my kind would be outnumbered."

"I'm no threat," I hiss back. Maybe to the Gaya bank account, but other than that, no. "I will not back down."

"I will break you then," he threatens.

I swallow. "I'm not scared."

Lies.

He smiles, and my pulse flutters. "I hope Brayja can tame the desire you have for me." His gaze lowers to my breasts and I feel hot all over. "I can sense how much you yearn for me—hear your rapid heartbeats, your rushed breaths. Honestly, it was hard to concentrate earlier." He tilts his head at me, licking his sensuous lips.

I can't breathe. "Not true."

He makes a sound. "Don't you want to feel what it's like for me to devour you, every inch of you, not in a dirty dungeon? I promise it's worth it—or so I'm told."

I swallow and take a shaky breath. "You're arrogant," I say breathlessly. I need to get out of here. I'm so in trouble.

Raine laughs. "Hardly, and you know that." He leans into me, his knuckle grazing over my hard nipple, making me suck in a breath. "Do you want to see what I can do with my tongue?"

YES!

"No," I pant.

I hate this game.

"I will give you a short time to end it with Brayja, or I will do it for you," he threatens. "Until then, think of me when you get yourself off, and I'm sure that will be quite frequent."

Steven was right. Thetis would have been a safer bet.

He leans more into me, his hands gripping my thighs hard again. "I'm going to call you ~Aora~." I feel his breath on my neck.

A moan escapes my lips as his hands squeeze harder. "What does that mean? Should I be offended?"

"I don't think so, you might be used to it." He laughs into my neck and turns to leave. "It means 'little liar.'"

Chapter 9

Camila

It's madness here, and all I can think about is the feel of Raine. It's like he's bitten me with this dark venom and it's now taking over my soul, slowly and painfully.

"Now, m'lady! Brayja is waiting!" my chief servant, Lorahi, reprimands, looking pale even though half her face is covered. "It's not safe." Her voice is very high pitched, almost like a chipmunk. "Thetis has quite the temper. It's the clash of two powers I always knew would happen."

Steven raises an eyebrow at her, decked out in gold chains. "We hear you, lady," he says like he is annoyed.

Her eyes narrow on him, and she mutters something under her breath. I know they all look at Steven, wondering where he came from and why I would choose him to follow me around. It is what it is. I like chubby little potheads as my advisers.

Nothing weird about that.

We're leaving this underwater haven because Raine could not keep his temper in check, not that I blame him.

I have learned there are many underwater cities, but they all are under the rule of Poseidon. Each dwelling has its own ruler, though, and Thetis prefers to reside here. This means Raine has no power here unless he wants to fight all of Thetis's guards.

So we have to leave ASAP to avoid more conflict.

It seems like Raine is the source of a lot of people's pain, good and bad. Mostly mine, and I'll fight Thetis for that title because I can think of nothing else but him. I'm in mental torment, seeing his burning eyes and his seductive mouth. I need to get rid of him or I will go insane with this secret obsession.

But mainly, I need to get rid of him because he knows what I'm capable of — my ~tainted ~blood.

Brayja just needs a new damn

best friend. Maybe after we are married, I will find him one. One uglier than Brayja so there are no issues.

One that is not the object of my sexual fantasies.

At the moment.

I have to fix this. Raine just caught me off guard, that's all. ~That's all. ~I laugh and shake my head, expelling a breath. This is something I can handle.
I just need a moment to take in this experience. Being in a new world like this is overwhelming my brain, too many mental shocks.

And I need a margarita.

We quickly follow a long line of servant women and guards through transparent tunnels. I gaze through the tubes, seeing sea life swimming by, knowing that this is spectacular, despite everything. I sigh and look down at my glittering gown of yellow sunlight. It's transparent except for the main parts. It was an apology from Pierce for picking me a talent that threatens my goal of being queen.

I need fifty more dresses, or a potion to make Raine forget what he saw.

Apparently, that's against code B12-00.

I roll my eyes. I swear Pierce is setting me up on this mission, so I can't lay back and relax. Aggravated is an understatement. It's almost like he wants me to fight for this when I already had it in the bag. I'm confused. Does he want me to fail?

I'm wearing a golden, mesh face cover that is in high fashion at Brayja's request. I guess it shows that I'm taken by a man, and not just any man, but a prince. It's adorned with diamonds and gems of all colors and makes my eyes pop. It draws attention to the part that I do not want to draw attention to, at least until after I'm married.

Or if Raine leaves and I don't see him again for the rest of this mission, and my libido can have a break.

I grit my teeth.

My eyes practically glow now. It's like they have a life of their own, swirling scarlet surrounded by brilliant purple. Steven said that they are brighter than they were at Qokar. He said that maybe it's because I used the power with Raine, thus awakening it.

I will not panic yet. Crazy tears will be on standby, though.

I have one hand hovering over the big red button.
I'm just going to have to keep my eyes down, a lot. "Thanks a lot, Pierce," I mutter and glance at Steven who walks beside me. "Where are we going? Away from here, I hope."

"I think to Brayja's submarine that just arrived. I'm not sure where after, but I'd bet your sweet tits we are leaving here." He gives me a look after I glare at his comment. "Dude. I need a smoke. You might have to cover for me in a sec. You have to help me, my mystic mode is wavering," he says with a pained expression.

I expel a breath and look around. "Yeah. Is Raine coming?"
~"Please no~. ~Please, Fate, don't be so cruel," ~I whisper. and look up, right as my stomach drops. There is a fork in the tunnel and I see Brayja and ~Raine ~with lots of their men.

I look away and want to punch the wall.

"Daphine," Brayja walks up to me, and I keep my head down, "we are ready to leave. Thetis is backing down. He does not want to anger me too much, given our alliance. We will let the World Council handle it from here."

Freaking Pierce.

He tilts my chin up, and his eyes widen, tracing over my face with fascination. "It shocks me every time I see you, my dear. You're stunning." He turns towards Raine, who is talking to his men, seemingly ignoring us.

"Does she not have the most beautiful eyes you have ever seen?" Brayja chuckles, and I hate that he makes me feel like an object.

Raine almost looks pained to look at me.

When his fiery gaze lands on me, I see no emotion or expression. He looks like some dark vampire king—uncaring, cold, incapable of ~passion~.
Well, I'm not going to think about that. I suppress the shiver that slithers down my spine.

He is so arresting, and I hate that.

Despise. That.
I wonder if the men secretly loathe him—having their woman fantasizing about him all the time must be hard.

Raine's pale skin contrasts with his stark black hair and vibrant eyes in that deeply erotic way. Yup. I hate him, I realize.

I mean, you can't hate him because he's beautiful . . .

Or can you?

"What do you think, Raine?" Brayja looks back at me. "I place a bet you will not find a prettier set of eyes than hers." Brayja watches me intensely.

I swallow, taking a breath. "Beauty is in the eye of the beholder," I say lightly, wanting the attention off of me. I can feel eyes on me from everyone, and I shift nervously.

"Well," I hear Raine finally say in his low voice, "at least your kids will have a fighting chance, Brayja." He pats Brayja's back hard and walks away, just like that, not even looking at me.

Brayja laughs hard. "I believe I was just insulted!"

I hear a few chuckles.

I'm surprised he didn't just out me in front of everyone.

Raine glances back at Brayja with a slight smile that makes my pulse quicken. "And yet we are still friends," he says, and leads us into a massive arena-type room.

"Not after Raine bangs his wife," Steven whispers beside me. I shoot him a look, my face blushing. "Shut up," I hiss.

"I need weeeeeed," he hisses back.

I curse.

My eyes widen when I see an Olympic-size pool with a massive submarine contraption floating in it. I gasp. This must be where the big ships come in.
"Aw, there she is!" Brayja claps. I see guards walking around on the top of the giant sub. It's like a mini cruise ship that's been converted into a sub. It's gold and purple, glistening under the lights.

This arena is gigantic. I feel like we are in a football stadium. The deep blue waters of the ocean make ripple effects on the roof and walls of the dome. I look to my left and see a group of women who are walking up to Raine and his men.

Raine hugs a short woman, clearly a Nymph, and smiles down at her. She covers her mouth and shakes her head, wiping her eyes.

"Steven," I hiss, "who's that?"

She's pretty, with her long blonde hair woven with green and blue ribbons. My eyes scan her skinny body and decent sized breasts in her dark bodysuit.

I'm immediately on alert even though I try to tamp it down.

Steven, next to me, is blinking and using his hand to type.

Great.

If Steven could appear any weirder to everyone, I'd be shocked.

"Dude," he whispers.

"What," I say as I watch her hug Brayja, Raine watching her with his hands on his hips.

"That's his sister."

I expel a breath. I hate that I'm relieved.

"But she is in love with Raine. The file I'm reading says that they have gotten intimate on multiple occasions." Steven almost laughs. "Weeeeird, dude."

"What?!" I hiss, gaining looks from my servants. "No, impossible. That can't be right, Steven. You need to smoke."

NO. WAY.

I can't.

"Wait," Steven says as he blinks rapidly. "Oh, I see."

My eyes nearly fall out of their sockets as I wait for him to expound.

"It's Thetis's sister, Raine's stepsister. Nomilia Iphanthei, it says. No blood relation." He holds his finger up. "My bad."

Raine.

Unbelievable.

Stepsister?!

"That is still horrible, Steven," I hiss.

"Well, it says she has been in love with him since before his mother married Poseidon. So . . ." Steven looks up at me. "Tell me again why you care?"

I curse.

No wonder Raine acts like he is over me. It's because he is. Dear lord . . . this is a one-sided obsession.

I shall die a thousand deaths tonight.

"I don't . . . care."

"Dude, you have not stopped staring at him," Steven says. "I sure hope you don't cause a world war with your obsession."

Shit.

I look away and make my way to the sub, cheeks on fire. "Not obsessed," I whisper as I see Brayja making his way to me.

"Yeah, and my ass is not hairy," he says behind me.

I cringe.

"Daphine!" He smiles, his gold and silver overcoat catching the light. His goatee is perfect and his eyes hold intensity. Except not the kind that has me panting on the ground.

Not the ~dangerous ~kind.

I smile at him, seeing him staring at my breasts in my yellow dip-neck bustline. My skin looks luscious and radiant, like warm honey.

"This is beautiful," I say, and look at the sub. It is breathtaking.

He nods. "This is the first time I'm riding in it. It took us two years of work building this before I was satisfied." He pauses and glances at me. "It takes a lot to satisfy me." He beams at the hidden meaning, licking his lips.

I smile. He's handsome. I can do this.

Pep talk time.

He suddenly walks up to me and grabs me around the waist, pressing me to him. I feel his hands skim the top of my ass. "When we are inside, you may take off your mesh. I want to see those luscious lips," he whispers. "I want to get to know you."

I swallow.

"Of course," I whisper. "I would also like to know the man I'm marrying." But do I?

Not really. Unless he gives me a diamond necklace.
"Your voice is lower than I would have expected it to be. I was telling Raine that earlier. Throaty, even. Sensual, " he says. and leans into my ear. "I find it extremely ~arousing~."
Yes, I'm aware of my sex-hotline voice. Now I'm cursing it.

"Brayja." I hear a woman's voice.

Brayja pulls away from me and turns. "Forgive me. This is Daphine Laromedia, not sure if you know of her mother from the North?"

Raine's stepsister.

I raise my chin. "I don't think we ever met," I say, trying to keep a neutral voice.

"No, I don't think we have. Who is your mother?" she asks, and looks me up and down. I hope she is jealous.

Just . . . because.

Wait. Mother?! I look over to Steven, who is gone, probably smoking behind the far wall.

Brayja beams at me. "Nomira and Nyson. You remember them from years back, don't you?"

"Ah, yes. " She holds out her hand and I take it, hoping I'm doing the right thing. I'm going to kill my pothead agent. "You may call me Nomi," she says, her blue gaze assessing me. "Congratulations, what an honor it is."

"Thank you," I say.

She smiles. "She's beautiful, Brayja," Nomi says, and I can't tell if it's a compliment or something soaking in frigid water.

"Yes, she is."

I hate how they talk like I'm not standing here.

"And so are you. I love the colors in your hair," I say — and actually mean it, it's quite pretty. She looks surprised and touches her hair. "Oh. Well, thank you."

I tense, seeing Raine walking up to us. It does not escape me that he only looks at Nomi and Brayja. I feel anger rise in me, feeling slightly invisible, meaningless to him.

I hate that I care, but that's how obsessions work, right?

I look at Nomi and see her eyes light up when she stares at Raine. "Are you riding with us, Raine?" she asks, voice significantly softer and breathier.

I want to roll my eyes.

He takes a breath and looks at Brayja. "I'll join you later. I'm going to see if my mother needs help before we hit the coast."

Nomi grabs his hand. "I'll come with you."

I cross my arms over my chest and I see Raine's eyes slightly, ever so slightly, look. It happened so fast that I think it's all in my obsessed brain.

I cringe.

I'm now obsessing that Raine slightly looked at my breasts, though it has not really been confirmed by reality yet.

I will die a thousand deaths tonight.

"No. I'm taking my men, Nomi. Your father would have my head," he reprimands lightly, and she blushes.

Brayja points to his men. "Let's go!" He looks at Raine. "Stop being so noble all the time. You deserve to be bad sometimes."

Nomi smiles, eyes traveling over him. "I agree."

Raine coughs in his hand and smiles, turning to leave, motioning to his men. I turn to leave too, my mood going to dark places where little girls crawl out of wells. They have lowered a long ramp to board the sub, and I start the journey up.

"Sorry, I'm back," Steven says beside me, out of breath from running.

I'll lay into him later. Get me away from here.

I look to my left just in time to see Raine take off his shirt and my heart skips a beat. Time slows as my eyes travel over his ripped torso, never before seeing such glorious pec muscles.

His waist is so narrow, but his shoulders and arms are built like a god's. Swimmers have the best bodies, and Riane's is off the charts. I clench my thighs together and try to keep walking.

Walk!

He is strapping weapons to his body, and I can't help but watch. Raine's tight black pants show off the part of him that I really shouldn't want to see, but desperately do. An impressive bulge, especially when he clips things to his thighs. I feel my heart beating out of my chest, an intense desire washing over me.

"Walk," I hear Steven hiss.

My eyes widen, seeing his skin down by his happy trail turn colors like a mermaid. It spreads up his rippled abs to his pecs. Maroons, yellows and oranges. Like fire, matching his eyes.

I notice all nymphs change different colors, but this is . . . this is . . .

I don't realize what happened until I feel my body hit the water. My brain screams in denial.

~Dear God~, I walked right off the ramp into the deep ocean.

Shock courses through me, and I suddenly feel a strong arm wrap around my waist.

I break the surface, sputtering, yanking off my mesh mask.

"I got her!" I hear Raine yell.
~Raine~.
The object of my pain.

My eyes focus on his burning gaze staring down at me. We are shielded by a large engine propeller, his arm pressing me to his hard body as he holds me up.
"Are you okay, ~Aora~?"
I stare at him, breathing hard, feeling his heat, his energy. "D-don't call me that."
~Red alert, red alert~.
I just fell off the ramp. This is not happening.

A thousand deaths.

He tilts his head at me, making a sound.

"I forgot to tell you that your eyes are going to give you away without any help from me. I'll just let you crash and burn all on your own. I'm glad you gave me a chance to tell you."

I feel my anger rise, my heart pounding in my ears. "I'm getting the impression that Brayja might not mind. He seems quite taken with me, not sure if you're paying attention."

I see amusement in his eerie gaze. Or maybe I hit my head on the way down.

I try to ignore Raine's black hair that curls around his ears, droplets running down his porcelain skin. "I haven't noticed," he says, and raises a brow. "Was I supposed to?"

My eyes go to his sharp canines as I swallow, ignoring the desperate desire to feel his lips on mine.

Focus.

I glare up at him, hoping he sees how much I hate him. Raine slowly smiles and presses me tighter to him as if my anger turns him on. Is he a sadist?! He leans his head down to my ear,

"~Mmmm, ~you're so easy to anger. I can read you like an open book. It's also shocking how much you want me—you'd better tame that down in front of Brayja."
My cheeks flush. Embarrassment.

I turn away from him. What an arrogant pig!

"Leave me the ~fuck ~alone," I hiss, not caring that women here probably don't talk like that. "I can swim back myself," I try to say as meanly as possible, my pride taking a big hit. I kick him as I try to push away.

"Raine! Is she alright?!" I hear men yelling. Raine's jaw clenches. "Yes!" he yells back, and glances back at me, pulling me back to him, his eyes intense.

"This will just get harder, ~Aora. ~I have not even started to break you down yet. Back off from Brayja. Tell him the truth."

"Kiss my ass, Raine," I say, not needing to hide who I am anymore.

He already knows I am not from here, so fuck it.

Raine expels a breath, eyes clearly shocked. "Is that an invitation?"

I almost laugh. "In your dreams." I see other men swimming up to us.

Then I think I hear: "~You have no idea."~

CHAPTER 10

CAMILA

I breathe in and out, the sound echoing in my head.

You got this.

I sit in a beautiful room full of golden luxury, wrapped in a warm blanket—not that I'm cold. I'm numb, actually. My brain is too busy frantically trying to talk me off the ledge to appreciate the beauty of the massive submarine.

Something is happening to me. I can feel it. I close my eyes and curse, knowing this is not usually how I operate. How could I let my desire for a man ruin what I want?

A ~want~ that I would generally do anything for, and would let nothing get in my way. I'm never that rash and, to put it bluntly, that damn stupid.

I saw the way Brayja looked at me when I exited out of the water.

I rub my temples, cursing Raine.

Someone needs to take the fall for this, and it's not me. Did Brayja see the intense desire in my gaze—and my embarrassing plunge into the water? My right leg shakes from my nerves.

Of course he saw me fall into the water like a moron, that's a given. It's the ~why~ that matters.

~Here's the next queen to the throne of the Gaya Empire, wading in the water with a man set on destroying her ~. . . ~Boo! Booo! Boooooo!~

Raine said that he would just sit back and let me ruin myself. He was so arrogant, insinuating that I'm so out of my element that I would just crash and burn myself.

Is he right?

My leg taps harder on the glistening marble floor. Raine has done nothing to me, if I am honest, which disturbs me more. I hate to admit that he is right. I'm destroying this with the help of me, myself, and I.

And Steven.

I grit my teeth. This obsession stops here.

I glance at the clock, wondering where the hell Steven is. I just keep seeing my body fall off the ramp, eyes alive with want, passion, and shameless desire. It's like I'm in a trance, not able to help it.

"Can you . . . stay away from Raine? Please?" Steven says, suddenly next to me, eating something crunchy. "I mean, unless you want to change your results. If you remember correctly, I need a win. Either Sweet Heart or Darling. Not picky."

"I'm messing this up," I whisper, fear seeping into my bones.
My mind keeps flashing to Raine. Want . . . desire . . . ~need . . . ~uhhh~! ~
"Um . . . Well, from my vantage point, Brayja didn't see you up close. So all he could do is speculate why you fell.

"I was doing some damage control, saying you were experiencing dizziness and plunged into the sea. Which I think went over nicely, considering all of the drama."

I sigh and rub the bridge of my nose. "You told Brayja?"

"No, he was with Raine, but I'm sure he will come here and ask you himself." Steven shrugs, "You have got to stay away from Raine, dude. You mess up that friendship and that could create so many problems."

He holds up his gold card. "I don't want to lose my gold membership. I'll starve."

I jerk my head up, only hearing one word. "Raine . . . He was supposed to go and see his mother . . . or something. He's not supposed to be here." My pulse is pounding again, feeling so much arousal when I think of him. He can't be here. He can't! I have not figured out what is going on here!

What is going on?! I almost laugh.

I place my hands on my forehead, my body feeling overheated.

"You alright?"

"No, Steven," I say, gritting my teeth.

He raises a brow.

I look up at him. "Are Valkyries, like, super horny? Like, more than usual Earthly humans?"
Steven almost spits out his food. "What?" He raises his brows at me. "Am I turning you on? Be honest." He swallows his food, mouth hanging open.

I groan in annoyance. "NO, Steven. I'm just asking for basic information. You know, the stuff you're supposed to be telling me instead of getting high." A sensation washes over me, and I hiss. I need Raine so profoundly it's driving me half mad, making me stomp my foot on the floor.

"I need a therapist."

Steven holds up his hand. "Alright, alright, let's not get testy. I was only kiddin'." He plops down on a plush sofa and looks around. "Dude, this place is so crazy though. Brayja must have so much money. I was gettin' high on like a solid gold chair like I was a king or some shit. The king of vaginasssss. It was awesome."

He laughs in his irritating way, eyes heavy-lidded, humming to himself.

I can't even think about the lushness of this place.

That's how messed up I feel.

It's like feeling nauseous and trying to appreciate chef-cooked food. I know I could just go and ~relieve ~myself, but my pride will not let me.
Because that's what Raine said I would do.

So I can't.

He will not have that on me.
"Logging on," Steven says, and shakes his head. "Almost fell asleep."

I lay back in my animal print chair and try to mentally draw devil horns on Riane's imagine in my head. Bad, Raine. Bad, bad, bad, bad, bad, bad—

"I think it's all pretty standard from what I'm reading," Steven says with one eye open.

I open one eye as well. "You're missing something."

"Or," he holds up a finger, "you just need to get laid. Damn. My mystic powers say that you just need to stop being so horny and lock in this mission." He gives me a pointed look.

"Please don't say that to me again," I say, nose scrunched up.

"It sounded more encouraging in my head," he admits, and closes his eyes again.

The door suddenly opens and in walks Brayja, making me sit up and tense.

"Leave us," he says to Steven.

I've never seen Steven move so fast. It's impressive. I look back at Brayja in his black and purple dress coat. He seems relaxed and happy, but it's hard to tell.

I swallow, not knowing what to say.
"Daphine," he murmurs, his gaze tracing over my wet appearance.

122

~Mierda~, I should have had Pierce fix me up. I pull the blanket up tighter.

"My heart nearly stopped when you fell. How are you feeling? Are you sick?" He slowly sits down beside me and smiles, showing me his perfect teeth. He does look like Jude Law, I muse.

I can't read him. He's a hard one. "I just remember feeling very dizzy, but I'm much better now." I smile at him, trying to connect.

To force Raine out of my thoughts.

"Thank goodness for Raine. He moved so fast one would think he knew you were going to fall." Brayja laughs. "That's Raine, though. Sometimes I wonder what I would do without him."

His hand rests on my leg, and he squeezes it.

"Yes, I must remember to thank him," I say, feeling his hand move higher.

"Well, I'm having a little thing tonight—drinks, food, great company. We all need a night to relax and forget about all the drama. I, for one, am sick of it. Thetis will pay for what he did to me, but that can wait," he says, grabbing my blanket and yanking it off.

I look at him in confusion.

"I know you are frightened and confused, not realizing you are soaking wet and sitting on my fine fabrics." He smiles and tilts his head at me. "I like the way you break the rules, Daphine."

My cheeks redden, and I sit up to stand. "This is where they led me, Brayja."

"Well, I think your adviser needs a better briefing." Brayja stands with me, his gaze traveling over my body.

I feel so out of place.

His arms circle my waist, making me drop my blanket. "I have embarrassed

123

you?"

I force a smile, my pulse beating with uncertainty. "No, I just need to be better informed," I say, and feel his head lower to my neck as he inhales.

"I'm beginning to like your bizarre ways, Daphine, my queen. If I may say, it's quite refreshing, and I cannot stop imagining you on our wedding night," he whispers, his breathing escalating. "I was telling Raine that I have never felt this way so fast, even having barely talked to you, in fact. I can see the intelligence and defiance in your gaze, and it makes me crazy," he whispers.

His lips kiss my shoulder, his hands pulling me into his body. I can hear his shaky breaths like he is trying to keep himself in line.

This will be my husband.
~You need to connect with him, Camila~.
I have to try.

I feel his tongue swirl on my neck, his hands lowering to my ass with a deep, drawn-out moan. "I'm very observant, my Daphine, and I can see such passion and desire in your eyes that it entrances me. I want to taste that wild energy so badly it hurts."

Warning lights flash in my head. I can't read him.

Did he see me look at Raine with desire or not? I need to change his mind about me if he did.

I force my arms around his neck and that produces another deep moan, his lips almost hurting me as he kisses. Slightly alarmed, I try to respond in a way he might like.

I moan—I'm great at faking it.

"Daphine . . . " His lips move up my neck and it hurts, his sucking past erotic. "Am I hurting you?" His lips are on mine and I barely whisper a ~no~, which is a big lie.
Why did I lie? Maybe I just don't want to upset him.

"Mmmmm, my kitten likes it rough, then?"

124

My eyes widen. What's happening?

I try to respond ~no, ~but he licks my lips then aggressively takes my bottom lip in his mouth, biting and sucking. I make a sound, the pain shocking me.

The crush of his mouth on mine is that of punishment, not pleasure. His tongue thrusts into my mouth, hurting my lips, and I squirm, making a sound of pain. I am pushed back on the couch. He groans loudly as if this turns him on, and his hips start to rock forcefully. I look around the room for anything to distract him from me.

I have no idea what this man is doing. It's like he is having this seizure on top of me — zero finesse. Brayja's head leaves my mouth and rapidly descends to my breast, messily kissing his way down, aggressive.

"Yes!" he yells, and groans, taking my nipples in his mouth through my yellow gown. "So sweet! Like honey. Moan for me, my love." He tugs painfully with his teeth and I have had enough.

I sit up instantly, completely weirded out by Brayja.

I feel him push me back down and his lips are at my ear instantly. "My bride is bashful?" he whispers, his lips brushing my neck. "That's even more of a turn on, Daphine. All the things I can't wait to show you."

I'm tense and watch as he raises his head to peer down at me. "I have picked out your dress this evening. It will please me if you wear it just for me, no one else. I want to see your body, all of those delicious curves." He makes a sound and glances down at my breasts. "Do not be scared of me, Daphine." He raises his hand to touch my chin. "You already have my heart, do not worry."

I nod and force a smile.

"Good girl." He gets up and fixes his coat, as he watches me sit up, and I can almost sense his strange nature like a dark cloak. "I have to go see to some meetings. Raine wants me to put pressure on the council." He laughs. "It will be fun to watch Thetis sweat. I wish I could see Poseidon's face when Raine tells him of his piece of shit son."

He tilts his head. "Raine will have a target on his back after this." Brayja chuckles. "It's a good thing he has me for an ally, right?"

I swallow.

He is not threatening me, is he? Or am I in my head?

Brayja smiles. "I can see you have a big heart, and don't worry. Raine will be fine. You can rest knowing that."

The hairs on my neck raise and I shift. "I don't care about Raine. Forgive me, I know the alliance is important and it needs to stay intact."

He winks at me. "If something happens to the mighty Raine, there will be war, my dear. Have you met his mother yet?" He tilts his head. "One woman you do not want on your bad side. My father can't stand the woman personally." He leans down towards me and does the ~shhh~ movement with his finger.
"So, we make peace with Poseidon because of her and Raine. I also have a hunch that my good friend Raine is more powerful than he lets on. That's why I like him—he's smart. Thetis would be wise to stand down. The fucking little pig-dick is going to get burned, one way or another. Excuse my harsh language."

He pats his sleeve for anything dirty. I take a steady breath and ask, "So your friendship with Raine is merely political?"

Brayja raises his eyebrows. "What a perceptive creature you are, I'm impressed. But, no, I do enjoy his friendship very much. It's hard not to like Raine. He's so irresistible, right? But that does not mean it's not political." He chuckles and heads to the door.

I blink at him. This man is so strange.

I am getting little hints that it's slightly more political than warm fuzzies.

"Rest up, my love. I will see you for dinner." He blows me a kiss and leaves, then says before the door closes, "I will have my servants show you to your room where you may shower and clean up for me."

This man.

"Thank you," I say.

I can do this, right?

Right?

***

I must have passed out. I'm lying on silks and plush pillows. My room is extravagant with deep purples and animal prints, accented with glittering golds. I feel my forehead. The brilliance of the room is going unnoticed.

"Camila, you're in trouble, girl," I whisper, and roll over on my stomach, squeezing my eyes shut, digging into the silks.

I scream.

Something happened.

I can't.

I take another labored breath and roll onto my back, visions of Raine flashing through my mind. I had a very vivid dream and it's messing me up. It was scorching HOT . . . like, the sexiest sex I have ever experienced, or even dreamed.

This obsession is now unhealthy to my mental state. I'm having erotic dreams now, for fuck's sake!

Yeah, I had a damn sex dream about Raine.

Not a shocker though. I feel even more on fire for him, confusing my brain. I close my eyes and see him walking up to me in the dark on the beach, with the seduction of the moonlight . . .

I should have stopped once I saw the moon.

The moon lies.

I shiver, seeing his shirtless torso dripping with cool water droplets. They ran down each hard ripple of his muscles, showcasing his contained power. But what had me arrested was the look in his eyes—the glowing orange embers had me breathless as I watched him come closer. His wet hair was wild, blowing dry with the slight breeze.

I groan into the pillow as my mind replays the scene. I have flashes of myself moving my hips for him, lying in the sand, seeing his body come over mine in heated passion.

I sit up in bed and shiver, recalling him picking me up and throwing me over his shoulder as I screamed with excitement.

"My goodness Camila," I whisper harshly, and rub my forehead.

This is a first for me. Embarrassing.

Raine had kissed me so hard that it nearly had me undone, holding my face and not letting me go. I laugh and pinch the bridge of my nose, forcing myself to take a calming breath.

It was not like Brayja's awkward cruelty, but done so skillfully, so erotically. The pain was welcome this time. He knew how to tease the senses like I have never experienced before.

It sounds crazy, but it was almost like he was showing me how to be kissed like Brayja had tried to do but failed. His lips even trailed down my neck as Brayja's had done, but this time I felt Raine's teeth. The suction of his lips had me panting, straining against him for more . . . He made me wild.

OMG.

I'm talking like this is real. My subconscious is playing tricks on me.

"Steven!" I hiss, hating myself, feeling an angry tear. Another image flashes through my mind as he rips the wet, sparkling clothing from my body . . . his head between my legs as I scream his name . . . his tongue . . . grabbing his hair . . . his lips devouring me . . .

My cheeks heat. This is unhealthy.

Soooo wrong.

"Hey, you're up," Steven says. "I was about to come and wake your ass up. We don't want Brayja displeased," he mutters with an eye roll, then laughs.

I stare at him, my mind in fragments.

"You okay?"

NO. Not even close.

"Uh, yeah," I mutter, not wanting to share my shame.

I will take this to my grave.

"Well, you need to hurry, cuz everyone is, like, in this lounge area. It's really cool actually — low blue lighting and legit drinks." He winks at me and nudges me. "Dude. Perk up, man. This is what you want! The luxury and the parties! This is livin', man." He claps his hands. "Finally, right? Let's go have some fun, shiiiieeeet." He starts hip thrusting and bobbing his head. "Want some weed?"

"No," I say too fast.

Maybe.

No.

Yes.

Absolutely NOT.
~Be happy, Camila. Smile~.

When Steven says it like that, I want to cringe. Really though, I wish I could stay under the covers and try to piece my emotions together.

"You want Brayja to come and get you?"

My eyes widen. "No."

"Get. Yo. Ass. Up."

I get up and pretend I am okay. Because I am . . .

"Logged on, by the way. Pierce is asking how you're doing." Steven frowns at me and shrugs.

I grit my teeth. "Tell him I'm peachy."

"Okay. Pierce says the dress Brayja left you . . . he will alter it just a bit." Steven nods to his left and rings the bell for my servants. This would have thrilled me before.

After the servants leave me, I stare into the gold framed mirror.

"Damn, Brayja tryin' to give all the men boners or what?" Steven pauses. "Well, the other girls are wearing similar outfits, but they don't have your curves. High five, girl!" Steven raises his hand.

I stare into the mirror at what looks to be some belly dancer-inspired gown. It's stunning, the color of sparkling pink champagne, making my skin glow.

"Dude, you left me hanging. Spin. Pierce says this will not do," Steven says.
I look at Steven. "Really?"

"He's making it a bit more elegant, not so slutty," Steven says with a frown.

"Spinning," I say, and twist.

My skin tingles as I swirl and a white light flashes, making me gasp. I stand there out of breath and look in the mirror. "Pierce," I breathe.

The dress fits better, and it is stunning. My breasts are mouth watering in the V neckline. The two-piece dress connects at the bustline and is fitted to my body perfectly. Not too tight like before, but elegant. "Thank you, Pierce."

My hair hangs down my back like black silk, and jewelry adorns me everywhere. My nose ring glitters with diamonds, and my fingers are dressed with gold and bright gems.

I look like a queen with my sparkling headpiece.

Will Raine look? I clench my jaw.

"Let's go, horn dog," Steven says as I shove him in front of me.

"Wanna get slapped?"

"Yes."

I ignore him as my eyes take in the brilliance of this underwater hotel. Sweet diamonds, this place is outrageous. Just like Brayja, I'm coming to find out. It's like I'm in some grand hotel made of bright fabrics and golden craftsmanship.

I follow my servants as they lead me to double doors, music emitting from them. I take a breath as they open the doors for me, and I'm immediately greeted with bowing heads and low lighting.

The place looks like some underground lounge for the elite.

Brayja immediately sees me and his eyes widen slightly, excusing himself from the group he stands in.
~You can do this. Wipe your brain free of him~.
"Daphine, my love." He walks up to me and kisses my hand, his tongue swirling on my wrist. Then he puts my finger in his mouth and sucks, surprising me. I can tell he's had a few drinks.

I force a smile and slightly, ever so slightly, remove my finger from his mouth.

"This is beautiful, you should be proud," I say, looking around, feeling out of my element. The music almost has a futuristic sound to it. It's instrumental, but with a slight beat. A club beat.

I . . . like it.

"Come, dinner will be served soon. Have a drink. I would like you to meet some of my cousins." Brayja pulls me with him, his arm wrapping around my waist.

I meet many of his family and his high advisors. I nod and try to ignore their lustful gazes as they drink heavily. It does not bother me as it should, but what does is the fact that Brayja will not give me space.

I'm handed a drink by a server, and it's okay. It tastes like a glass of strong wine. As I stand next to Brayja, I resist the urge to down the whole glass. I feel Brayja's hand rubbing my waist as he talks with animation, sloshing his drink as he makes his point. I sigh and scan the room, seeing no Nymphs, only Valkyries.

I wonder when dinner will be served, praying it's not something weird. I might have to use Steven's gold pass later.

My gaze widens as a door to my left opens and I see Nymphs emerge. My heart starts a fast drumbeat, trying not to focus on the people emerging. They were obviously in a meeting—plotting Thetis's demise no doubt.

But I'm not sure if I am mentally prepared to see Riane.

Maybe he is not here?

"About time!" Brayja yells, sloshing more of his drink. "Raine! Nomi!"

~Double fuck bitch shit~.

Pardon my French.

~"Hey, dude! Just giving you a friendly reminder that Raine is headed your way. Don't blow it. Like, don't stare at him and knock over a table or some dumb shit like that.~"

I roll my eyes.

I have tunnel vision. Raine has no idea what naughty things I dreampt up earlier. If he knew, I would die a million deaths. I can already feel my face heating, and I take a shaky breath. I can feel Brayja's eyes on me.

Don't look at Raine for more than a moment. The hairs on the back of my neck stand up when I hear his hypnotic voice.

"Brayja," I hear him say. The tension that only I feel is choking me.

I don't look, but sip my drink, taking generous gulps.

"Daphine," I hear Nomi say to me. I look at her and notice she is in a dark blue gown. It's pretty enough. "You look beautiful. Nice to see you again."

"I should say the same to you, dear." I can hear a hint of hostility.

Brayja laughs and grabs me around the waist, jerking me to him. "Nomi, she has me around her finger." His lips are on my neck, making me tense. I feel the tension escalate — in my own head, that is.

I still do not look at Raine. I can't.

I hear Nomi laugh. "I have never seen you like this."

Brayja kisses my neck and lifts his head to look at Nomi. "That's because you have never tasted her." He laughs at her shocked expression.

My eyes widen, my face heating.

Against my better judgment, I look at Raine. He leans against the pillar, looking like I thought he would.

Sexy.

Dark.

I feel a heat wave wash over me as I stare at him from over my glass. Brayja is busy laughing with Nomi. I'm good to ogle him just for a second.

Damn . . .

His silver coat is a dark metallic, almost like metal, such gothic beauty. So opposite of the bright Valkyrie style that I see everywhere. His black shirt is unbuttoned at the neck, showing his gunmetal necklaces and red rubies.

Nymphs really do look like vampires.

My eyes roam over his hair that is combed back save for a few wild, tantalizing pieces. I look away, making sure no one is watching me, playing this smart.

I glance back and see his fiery gaze zoned in on Brayja with a look of indifference. But there is something dangerous in his eyes that I can sense.

I could be imagining it.

Maybe, maybe not.

Brayja looks at Raine and hands him a drink from a waiter. "Raine, you look tired." He continues, "Drink, relax!"

Not tired. I'm betting he's irritated.

Nomi walks up to Raine and bites her lip, looking like I must. Honestly, I don't blame her. I can't because I do the same thing. I curse and look away, wanting this night of torment to end.

I feel Brayja grab me again and pull me in for a kiss on the lips, his tongue forcing its way in my mouth. I nearly gasp.

What is Brayja doing?!

I try to turn my face away and catch Raine's intense gaze before he downs his drink in one gulp before leaving.

Is Brayja taunting Raine?

Impossible.
Raine would have to give a shit.
~"Dude. I just saw that. What's going on? I thought Raine was going to slit Brayja's throat. If looks could kill! Good thing Brayja didn't see cuz he's shit-faced.~"
I'm frowning as Brayja kisses my jaw.

"You're wrong," I whisper.

~"Um . . . I hope you're right. I have a bad feeling about this. Too much testosterone in that Raine guy. Those Nymphs look like they could slit your throat with their teeth if you piss them off~.

~"You could be starting a war on your behalf. Not sure if Pierce will like that, and I really don't want to lose my gold card.~"

"You're wrong," I whisper again.

I squeeze my eyes shut, lost in confusion. I need another drink if this is an indicator of the rest of the night.

Raine wants to destroy me.

Simple.

Nothing else is happening here.

CHAPTER 11
CAMILA

Dinner is served in an extravagant room, decked out in riches and bold colors—much like everything else in this glittering submarine.

It almost feels like a sparkly prison.

The air is thick, and I see so many faces staring at me when they think I'm not watching. It's almost in slow motion as I see each face, each look, each whisper. I know they are sizing me up, picturing me as their next queen. Or the queen that will keep the allies secure, preserving the peace.

I can't tell if they approve or not.
But I raise my chin anyway, keeping my breathing easy.

I curse. I'm seated directly across from Raine, and it's like watching a giant tiger sitting in front of me. Don't show him fear—the man can probably smell it.

Brayja is to my right and his cousin to my left, thankfully giving me something to look at instead of the man in front of me. I take a large breath of air as I sit, trying not to let Raine consume me.

I bite my lip hard, trying to reset my thoughts with pain. I hate that he is always the subject of my thoughts.

I laugh and shake my head, noticing Nomi sitting next to Raine with a strained expression. This is going to be an awkward dinner, I can already tell. I'd rather fake a headache and leave, go anywhere but here.

The tension is suffocating to put it gently, even with all the liquor flowing like water. Raine's expression is indifferent but . . . not.

I can see the rigid set of his shoulders and how he looks everywhere ~but ~at me.

I sniff. I can almost feel the hatred. He knows I'm an imposter to his best friend.

Ahh, because of Ricky Martin, amongst other things.

I grab the wine that has already been poured in front of me and take the sparkling glass in hand, swirling it around. I might be the only one to feel the strained vibrations droning around me, depleting me of energy.

I hear muffled chatter surrounding me and these couple of minutes feel like freaking hours. I pause with a frown, clearing my throat . . . feeling weird again, more intense.

It's like a wave of energy just washed over me, making my skin tingle.

I'm curious if my talent makes me . . . stimulated? Being around all this talent and power. Because I'm still in a constant state of ~arousal~, confusing me—exhausting me, even.

Steven has got to be wrong about Valkyries because they must be hypersexual creatures. Either that or it's my talent.

I mean, I would say that Brayja is overly sexual, but I'm not sure if it's an act or if he is just genuinely creepy.

But this constant feeling is getting me into trouble.

I let out a calming breath, crossing my legs. What I'm feeling is not normal. It goes beyond the man in front of me. Raine is insanely sexy, but what I'm sensing is more than that.

"Daphine," Brayja's cousin whispers next to me, "do you travel to the underseas often? You being from the North, I wonder about that."

I look at him. I bite my lip, forgetting his name.

"Argon," he says, as if reading my thoughts. "You must be feeling overwhelmed. It's written all over your face."

What am I feeling? That makes me want to laugh.

I look down, then back at him with a smile. Argon is handsome enough, though not quite as much as Brayja. Still, I can see the family resemblance in his hazel eyes.

"Yes, nearly drowning will do that to you," I say, and take a sip of my wine with a forced smile.

He laughs and nods his head, his gaze flickering over my face. "Yes, that would put a damper on anyone's day." He turns more towards me, eyeing me. "That's what happens when," he looks at Raine, "you have bad blood in powerful places."

I don't look at Raine. "Yes, it would seem the family drama is turning dangerous," I say under my breath, hating how Raine is sitting right in front of me. Nomi leans on his arm, whispering something into his neck.

Sweet little somethings. Ignoring that she is his stepsister now.

Something tells me that he is aware of me, even though he has yet to acknowledge me.

"Dangerous? Thetis is the man that could shift the peace treaties set in place, destroying everything. Look, he put the prince of the Gaya Empire into the hands of the Orcs."

He pauses with a strained expression, and slightly looks in Raine's direction, lowering his voice. "If something happens to him, this will be a world war we would barely recover from."

I swallow, now understanding why Thetis was on the FGI radar. I look at Argon, taking a breath.

Argon shrugs and murmurs, looking down. "Brayja would be wise to stay away from Raine in my expert opinion because the man will be hunted and silenced."

I whisper back, trying to block out Brayja's loud laughter, "Could that happen?"

"Thetis is cunning, much like a snake. Look what just happened—they were imprisoned for almost two weeks on Qokar mountain. I was shocked they were not dead when we found them." Argon glances at me. "You also need to be careful, my dear. Brayja is a survivor, and witnesses are often dealt with."

"You think Thetis has allies? Possibly someone close to Raine or Brayja?"

Argon chuckles. "You're intelligent, Daphine, which is refreshing. When I first saw you, I knew something was different. You do not act like most Valrykie women." He studies me and takes a sip of his amber colored drink. "But, yes, I would not put it past Thetis to have spies. They always do."

Brayja grabs my arm and places a kiss on my shoulder. "Argon, stop filling my future queen's mind with conspiracy!"

I laugh and the two banter back and forth in good spirits.

I look up and see Raine sitting quietly, studying something on the table, jaw clenched. I doubt he hears Nomi's constant chatter, or at least it doesn't appear that he does.

Brayja looks at me and I tense, realizing I was looking at Raine intently. Brayja smiles at me and tilts his head. "I hope you are enjoying yourself."

I sit up straighter and smile at him. "Of course."

Brayja side glances at Raine. "Raine! Be careful. You might set the table on fire with that brooding look." He laughs and glances at Nomi. "Nomi, stop boring Raine to death."

Nomi frowns at Brayja, making him laugh loudly, clapping his hands.

Brayja is strange.

Raine finally looks up at Brayja and smiles.

It's not a genuine smile. Raine's fiery gaze shows the opposite emotion, something dark and aggressive. I think anyone who is not drunk could see it.

Raine glances sideways at Nomi and gives her a reassuring grin that has me looking away with shocking jealousy.

Am I that easily riled up?

Why is Raine in such a dark mood? Because I'm sitting here as the future queen, and Raine is seething, wanting to expose me?

Maybe.

Probably.

Though I'm curious why Raine is waiting. Oh, wait, I remember — because I will crash and burn on my own.

I look back to Argon and smile at him, wanting a distraction. Argon smiles back then suddenly I curse, tensing, grabbing the table in front of me. I 'm breathing hard, feeling a wave of sexual desire that renders me speechless.

I want to moan but clamp my mouth shut.
~Mercy~ . . .
~What in the actual F?~
"Are you alright?" Argon is frowning at me, concern written on his features.

"Fine," I get out. "I'm fine." My voice breaks a bit, and I try to act normal. My knuckles are turning white. I might just need to run to the bathroom and relieve myself, like immediately. I can feel myself perspiring slightly.

I look up at Raine and see him talking to Nomi, completely distracted. I take another shaky breath and try to calm the sensations that consume my body.

I need to talk to Steven.

This can't be normal.

"Are you sure?"

I look at Argon and smile, holding back pants, gritting my teeth. "I a-am just feeling a bit . . . hot." I almost curse, then desperately fan myself with my small glass plate.

I see Brayja glance at me, then look at Argon. "What's wrong?"

Everyone looks at me except Raine, thank ~goodness. ~One look at me and I feel like Raine would see what I'm feeling in my eyes.

The sensations intensify.
Oh my . . . hold it together . . . ~please. ~

I ever so slightly grip the table in front of me, and I force a strained smile. "Oh, just a bit overheated."

~WTF~.
I'm sweating.

Brayja snaps at the waiter for some water.

"Thank y-you," I barely whisper as a delicious sensation splashes over me, never feeling anything like it. I'm going to scream in front of everyone.

This is torture.

"Maybe it's something she ate?" I hear Argon say through my sexual haze.

Dear goodness. If I orgasm in front of everyone, I will never live this down. I'm not confident I can conceal a climax in front of these people.

Panic hits me as I feel it build, faster and faster.

My knuckles are white as I grip the table. I see Raine nod at something the man to his left says and take a sip of his drink, poised and relaxed.

Completely unaware of my internal crisis.

I grit my teeth when I see Raine look at my hand, clutching the table as if I would fly away if I let go. He slowly sips his drink again but does not make eye contact with me, looking up at Brayja, grinning at something he said.

That grin.

I find it odd that he does not care enough about my bizarre behavior to even look at me. I'd think anything weird concerning me would gain his undivided attention—any opportunity to call me out in front of everyone.

~Mierda~.

I jump up from the table, mumble something about being sick, and leave like I have the plague. I have tunnel vision. I don't know where I'm going, but I turn a couple of corners as the intense sensation racks my person.

I fall to my knees and muffle the sound in my arm, panting, moaning.

The most erotic sensation consumes me, leaving me confused and gasping on the ground. I'm breathing hard as I look around, making sure no one saw that shameless display.

"Steven," I hiss, closing my eyes and gritting my teeth.

I want answers. If this continues, I will no doubt ruin everything.

"I got it! I will see to her. No—really, I've got it, she's fine!" I hear Steven yell, then he kneels beside me. "Duuude. You okay? Should I get a hold of Pierce?"

I look up at him, seething. "Get me out of here."

His eyes widen. "You got it toots."

142

***

"Dude, you should smoke, though."

I turn on my bed, finding the darkness comforting.

"Be horny and high?" I laugh into my pillow. "Oh hell no. I might actually try to make out with the real Eluno," I mumble into the silk, pausing. "I saw him again. He grunted at me."

I hear Steven blowing out smoke. "You think Brayja will come check on you? He looked concerned."

"I hope not. He was pretty drunk, so that makes me nervous," I say. "Anything from Pierce yet?"

"Not yet. So explain to me what happened again?"

I groan. "I already told you. I constantly feel in a state of desire . . . and I . . . well, you know . . . had to leave . . . before I embarrassed myself."

He is laughing so hard I think he might choke.

I feel my cheeks heating. "Steven, I was like thirty seconds from orgasming in front of the entire dinner table! That would have put a big CRAZY stamp on my forehead! Ruining everything."

"Dude." I hear him take a breath. "Not going to lie. I'm not sure if that is disturbing or hot." He continues, "Everyone got up to search for you though, they all looked super concerned."

"Everyone?" I say, sitting up. "Even Raine?"

He laughs. "Oh, I forgot, you're obsessed with him. Just kidding. I didn't forget, because you remind me every second." He says, playing with the chains around his neck. "But, no. He is the only one who stayed seated, sipping his drink because he's a gangsta. He's a king."

My brain is misfiring as the realization hits me like a ton of bricks.

143

Confusion clouds me, swarming my senses with fury.

"Steven . . . Could Raine be messing with me? All this time? Ask Pierce."

Could he?!

I feel hot with anger.

I think hard, biting my lip. Raine did say he was going to take me down by letting me destroy myself. My heart pounds, and I think of all the sexual feelings that almost felt like caresses, my body humming to a silent, erotic tune.

Was he . . .

Has he been . . .

"Liiiike . . . What do you mean by messing with you?

"I don't know, mentally . . . making me feel, you know, turned on?" I ask, and feel awkward, saying that to Steven.

He is laughing again, making a whistling sound like I am out of my mind

.

"Leave the brotha alone, man. I think you just need time away from Riane. He's making you ~cray-cray~." He says the ~cray-cray ~super high.

I grit my teeth, my gaze searing him. "Ask Pierce if Nymphs have that ability, Steven. To like . . . make you feel things without touching."

His eyes are wide. "Okay, okay, maaaaan, chill." He blinks his eyes. "This is some weird shit I just smoked, by the way. Good thing you didn't take a hit. It literally looks like my hands are super tiny . . . like baby hands." He is typing with his hands, looking weirded out, then curses. "Shiiieeet . . . forgot my login information."

"What?"

"Hold on. Sometimes this weed makes me scatty-scat," Steven says, and laughs, shaking his head, hitting it with his hand. He needs to find the breaker switch.

Off and on.

And I need Advil.

"Steven, are you kidding me?! Have you not told me important information?" I ask desperately, wanting to strangle him. I wonder if anyone in history has killed their FGI agent before. "How did you win a mission being so damn high all the time?!"

I can barely see him smiling in the darkness, and he waves his hand as if he is actually seeing the baby hand.

"Can't really remember, but calm down, toots. I just logged in, forgot that all my passwords are the same. ~Mystic_KING. ~Last word in all caps, because we are all kings and queens."

I stare at him and expel a breath. "Ask. Pierce. Steven." I feel like it's forever before Steven responds.

"Oh," he makes a weird face, "I guess there was this folder uploaded to my file."

"Folder?! What does it say?"

"Pierce told me to look it over, and he is looking into Raine's bloodline ASAP," he says as he types. "He's also telling me to stop using the ninja emoji so much. A little testy, sheesh."

I shake my head. "Why? Why look into Ranie's bloodline?" I might . . . strangle him, slowly, loving every minute.

I am right. It makes sense now.

"Well." He holds up his finger, making a smacking sound with his mouth as he reads. "Yes . . . Well, Nymphs can make Valkyries feel things, even sexual things."

I expel a breath, my mind flatlining. "Shit." I place my hand on my

145

forehead.

All this time.

Steven makes a whistling sound. "Pierce says to hold on, though. It's also revealed that it's rarely used because it takes a ton of energy. Like, a ton. If used for too long, it can be excruciating." Steven looks at me. "Pierce wants to know when and how long you experience this?"

"Almost every second," I whisper.

Steven frowns as he types. "Right now?"

"No, but before this."

My dream . . .

No . . .
My heart is pounding harder as I look at Steven. "Can they enter dreams?"

"Asking," he says, then nods. "Yes."

My cheeks heat to dangerous heights, remembering all of the things we did. His lips scorching a trail down my naked body under the moonlight. The hot sounds I remember him making, the carnal look in his fiery gaze when he pinned my arms over my head.

But the moonlight lies.

It's an illusion.

He was not physically touching me. My mind was confused by his manipulation . . . I have no idea what's happening here, but my mind is trying to piece everything together. The brain is easily tricked, of that I am sure. What is Raine capable of?!

No wonder Brayja thinks he is hiding things.

Again, I should have known.

But it was so ~hot, hot, hot ~ . . .

Did he pick and set the scene on the beach?

How much was . . . real?

I tap my chin, wondering if he saw me naked. Raine is trying to bring me down by mentally seducing me. That's alarming. "Can he see me naked if he tries to seduce me in my sleep?"

That's a violation.

"Whoa! That's a loaded question." He types. "Hold on." Steven cracks his neck, and after a few moments, he says. "Pierce does not think so. Raine just puts the images in your mind. Like, he tells you what he wants to do to you and you are the one that projects it into your suuub." He points to his brain.

My eyes widen and I feel . . .

Why do I feel like I'm turned on by hearing that?
He tells me what he wants to do to me? Well . . . I bite my lip, remembering all the things he did to me in my dream. I feel like I'm overheating. I take a shaky breath.

"You okay?"

No!

Are you kidding?!

"Yeah, but how do I stop it? I can't have another episode like tonight," I say, my mind blown. How do I look Raine in the eyes again without being embarrassed? Raine knows I dreamed of him—and liked it.

A lot, a loooottt.

"Well, I guess I will take the blame for this. Valkyries at an early age have a jewel embedded into their skin, it says. It stops Nymphs from brain hacking." He looks up at me.

147

"Really? That's pretty important," I say, feeling so much irritation. "You need to be a better mystic, Steven! Raine could have ruined everything for me, and for you."

"You can wear a bracelet or a necklace as well," he continues quickly. "I can get one for you tomorrow."

"Okay. Will Raine know . . . that I know about him? If I put it on?"

"More than likely. He seems pretty smart, and when you put it on, if he is linked to you, it will cause tremendous pain."

Cause him pain.

I smile.

"Like . . . how much pain? Enough that people will notice?"

"Oh yeah." He smiles at me, clearly thinking the same thing.

Payback is a BITCH.

"I think I will wait for the perfect time to put on the bracelet, like when there are a lot of people around him."

The same thing he did to me.

"You, Mistress Daphine, are sooooo bad." He starts laughing like some evil villain.

I can't help but laugh too. Now I must get through this night without the bracelet.

Ahem.

Not excited.

Nope.

CHAPTER 12

CAMILA

I wake up, breathing hard. Placing a hand on my forehead, I take a steady breath.

I glance around my room and see that it is still dark, but that doesn't mean it's not morning. The deep sea is always somewhat void of light.

I roll over and realize that it's four in the morning, thankful for that bit of certainty from the glowing gold clock. Steven was supposed to be scouting, but I'm sure that he is passed out high somewhere.

Or eating cookies.

I take a shaky breath, needing to process what Raine did to me without Steven here. This time it was not steamy beach action but something darker, sexier.

I shiver . . .

This time I was tied up and blindfolded by a red silk scarf, the deep scarlet obscuring my vision.

I close my eyes, trying to remember all the erotic images that Raine fed me. I hadn't realized how kinky he was—or is. I sit up in my bed, frantically wondering how much information I gave away.

I was helpless, and he knew it. I rub my forehead.

The man will pay.

My hand goes to my neck as I remember. I felt his lips on my stomach as he kissed his way up my rib cage until he got to my neck, whispering questions, urging me to respond with his roaming, caressing hands.

He used ice on my flushed skin followed by something hot, creating so many conflicting sensations.

I glance around my room, the darkness reminding me that it was all imaginary.
It's weird, but I felt the pain of his teeth, then his soothing tongue.

It must have taken Raine an insane amount of energy to produce this naughty scene. He is putting a lot of effort into me, not knowing that I ~know.
~
Was he by himself while he envisioned doing those things to me? Did he enjoy it as much as I did?

My cheeks flush. I can't help but wonder if he relieved himself while picturing doing those things to me.

I remember that he was on top of me, holding me down, and I can barely recall that it felt like he was wearing leather or something similar. I remember moaning and saying something to him as he pulled my hair back, his lips on my neck.

What did I say?

Panic hits me.

"What did I say?" I whisper to myself. "Camila, you fool . . . I've lost my touch." It seems I'm being taken down by my weakness yet again.

~Desire for a man~.
~And not just any man~.

But I can't remember anything that I told him. Did he plan it that way as he brought me to a climax? Knowing my brain would be mush?

He is extremely smart. I'd place my money on the fact that he made sure I would forget.

"Steven!" I hiss.

I wait.

Minutes pass.

". . . Steeevennn." I grit my teeth, but before I can yell his name again, Steven lands on the bed next to me in a messy heap.

"Toots," he says as he sits up, eyes wide. "Dude, I think something is about to go down."

"What do you mean?" I ask, frowning at him. Is there ever a dull moment in this place?

"Well, Raine is on high alert. We broke the surface an hour ago. Brayjo—"

"Brayja."

He rolls his eyes. "Brayjaaa is all scared and shit."

"Well? You're not telling me why."

"I don't think Raine knows, but he is sensing vibrations or something like that. I heard him saying that it has something to do with Thetis."

I look at him with a frown. "Are we under attack?"

"Well, Raine and his men went into the sea a while ago to see what the disturbance is. Nymphs are weird—able to sense things that Valkyries can't," Steven says, and stares at me. "And they can get laid in their sleep." He raises his eyebrows at me.

My cheeks flush.

"Raine still attached to you?" He is typing, looking at me like he is a medical doctor.

I shift. "Well, yes. What do you mean attached?"

"So I was talking to Pierce after I smoked earlier. Apparently, Nymphs can, like, attach to Valkyries and other Nymphs. Well, Valkyries without the lunar gem, which I'm working on getting you. "It's actually quite alarming that the soon-to-be queen is un-gemmed. Brayja would have a fit. So I have to get the gem on the hush, hush because you are already supposed to have one," Steven says.

"Anyway, it's like Raine has a tracking device on you. He will know where you are and can sense your emotions. This dude has a mental GPS on you."

My eyes widen, my pulse thudding. "Can he hear what I'm saying?"

"No, just hints of your emotion and your location," Steven says. "Annnnnd," he drawls out, "it takes a lot of energy to do this. Breaking it off could take a day or two. Which is why when you put on the gem bracelet, it will hurt like hell."

I take a steady breath. "I don't know how I feel about this," I whisper. "Is he sensing me now, do you think?"

Steven shrugs and looks at me like I have three heads. "How should I know? If he reaches out, then yeah. I doubt it though, seeing how we could be under attack right now."

"By Thetis?"

"Again, I have no clue, but I doubt Thetis is that stupid."

"I'm confused. Why is Brayja scared if it's not Thetis?"

Steven laughs. "Well, he is scared for this submarine. He does not want it ruined by something Thetis does. I guess it took a lot of money to build."

Of course.

I can't blame him—I'm worse than he is.

"So it is or isn't Thetis?"

"I don't know."

My brain hurts.

Steven laughs. "I mean, like, Raine thinks his evil stepbrother planned something. But it could not be him. Another cover, a lie, a trap."

"Revenge."

"Yeah."

I gasp as the submarine violently tilts to the left. I look at Steven, pulse jumping.

"What was that?"

"Shit."

"What?!"

"Red alert. Quick, we need to get up to the top. I forgot that Brayja's men asked me to bring you up. I would loathe using a lifeline if water starts to come in and we get trapped again. "Between you and me, I'm not that great at shape-shifting into fish, as it turns out. I can't get the eyes right."

I stand. "Try shape-shifting when you're not high."

"Never," he hisses.

I roll my eyes. "What do I wear?"

"Pierce uploaded a couple of packages to pick from. I already told your servants to get lost earlier. They were bringing in more slutty clothing picked by Brayja. So maybe something you can swim in." He pauses and nods, blinking.

"Yeah, there is this silver bodysuit thing that Valkyries wear. Like a wetsuit—helps with body temperature and shit."

"Perfect."

"With diamond earrings."

I raise a brow. "I think Pierce is after my heart."

Steven laughs. "No, he just wants to win."

I give him a dry look. "I was kidding, Steven."
"Spin."

I spin, and my body tingles and feels electric, making me suck in a breath. The flash of light makes me flinch as I gaze down at myself in awe.

The power FGI has.

The material is stretchy and sucks to me like a second skin. I feel over my stomach, loving the smooth and slick feeling of the suit. "This is awesome."

"Yeah, it makes your honkers look niiiiice," Steven says, and winks at me.

"Steven."

"Sorry, I know, creepy." He stands and walks to the door as I realize Steven is in a wet suit of his own. I make a face, seeing every fat roll in his super-tight black wetsuit. "Let's go—"

We both side-step as there's another violent jolt. We look at each other and quickly make our way past everyone rushing about like the rig is under attack.
My servants and bodyguards immediately locate me, saying that we need to talk about ~Steven~. But, for now, we need to go up top.
"What's going on?" I ask a guard.

He looks at me, and I notice everyone is also in wetsuit gear, black and gold, with weapons strapped to them.

154

"Your grace, we are still trying to understand the threat, but do not worry. I believe Raine and his men are due back anytime," he says as he opens a door for me. He is a handsome man, but a little hairy with his long hair and sideburns. "I tried to come and retrieve you earlier, but your trusted adviser," he looks back at heavy-lidded Steven, "gave us orders to stand down. May I kindly suggest that perhaps your adviser is putting you at risk?"

I take a breath as we take some narrow stairs.

"I will have a talk with him."

He steps in front of me and opens a large latch that leads to the upper deck of the submarine. "Well," he grunts and pushes the door open fully, "you need to be guarded every second. You are of noble blood and our future queen, and if I know Brayja, I would suspect that he would not approve of the liberties you give your advisor."

I curse.

"I understand," I murmur as I climb up a ladder, and instantly suck in a breath. I emerge to an angry, wicked sea. The sky swirls and flickers with the three moons glowing in the clouded sky. The wind hits me as I stand, holding onto the rail with dear life.

"Climb down the ladder with caution. The lower deck is safer," he says from my right.

I think I nod as my heart pounds against my neck painfully. The ocean scares me, especially at night. It's so big and mysterious, not to mention infinitely more so seeing as it's on a foreign planet.

I don't know what the hell is in that water.

I shiver, feeling the pull and rocking from the high waves. I hear Steven behind me saying something about needing a vacation with lines of coke.

I don't even have the presence of mind to smack him on the head.

The lower deck is massive and adorned with golden luxury, much like everything else. But I can't appreciate that right now.

I make a sound as my eyes take in the open sea, feeling like I'm on the show ~Deadliest Catch~. I feel like I'm going to throw up.

A giant red rail is all that separates us from the violent sea. How comforting.

"Daphine!" I hear Brayja run up to me. I see tons of people on the deck and focus on Brayja, who is also in a wetsuit but still wears his golden overcoat. "My love, I almost came down to get you myself."

"What's happening?" I ask, ignoring his concern.
Brayja takes a moment. "I hope nothing." He looks out towards the sea, and I can see his jaw clench. "Raine should be back by now. This is just precaution, being up here." He glances back at me. "Think of this like a drill, nothing to worry about, my pet." His hand grabs my chin, this thumb moving over my bottom lip.

The sub jolts to the right as a large wave hits us hard.

"Son of a bitch!" Brayja yells, eyes wild. "When can we go back underwater? This is ruining the damn paintwork!" He storms past me, yelling at someone like it's their fault. "And where the fuck is RAINE!"

"Dude, he's pissssssed," Steven says beside me.

"Yeah, that's an understatement," I whisper, and back up to the wall, trying to get as far away from the rail as possible. I have my lifeline ready, yes I do.

"Please stay here until something changes," the guard says to me, and runs to help Brayja and his men.

I look around and see the female servants huddled together, fear in their gazes. I hear gasps and look to see the Nymphs climbing up the red rail.

"Bout' fucking time!" I hear Brayja yell as he runs up to them.

All of the Nymphs are shirtless with varying colors of skin. If I were not terrified, I would say they are beautiful creatures and marvel at them. But right now all I want to do is scream, watching the dark waves beat against this submarine, desperately trying to tip this golden rig over.

My eyes widen when I finally see Raine climb up, his fire-colored body reflecting the streaks of lighting, his muscles flexing as he sits on the rail.

Brayja holds up his hands. "Alright, my brother. Tell me some good news!"

Raine acts like he doesn't hear him at first, his eerie orange gaze peering out over the sea. He reminds me of a cat, with that intense and watchful look. Nymphs have very inhuman eyes, and Raine's are borderline unsettling.

He looks back to Brayja and says, "I'm sorry, my friend, but I believe Thetis wants us dead."
Brayja laughs loudly and holds his stomach, putting me on edge. "Raine, this better not involve my submarine! You know that would upset me."

Raine's gaze flickers as he watches Brayja. "Please tell me you equipped this golden tube with weapons."

He stops laughing and looks around. "Of course I did! You think I'm an idiot?" he yells, then holds up his hand. "Don't answer that." He points at Raine.

Raine takes a deep breath. "Brayja, I sense that Thetis might have released a Pirahnopus," Raine says, the thrashing wind blowing his wet hair.

I hear murmurs and gasps.

Brayja stares at Raine for a few painful moments, fists clenching. "How the fuck did he get access?! Those are on lockdown!"

Raine gets a better hold on the rail, his skin turning back to its pale luminosity, seeming to glow in the moonlight. "As I said earlier, he has someone working for him, covering up for him."

Raine's gaze slightly flickers towards me for the briefest of moments, then back to Brayja.

"You need to turn off everything in this sub. It will attract the Opus like blood in water. No noise, no vibrations."

Brayja's face is flushed, and he grits his teeth. "Son of a bitch. I'm going to kill Thetis with my bare fucking hands!" he yells so loudly that spit flies from his mouth. "You tell his daddy that if any damage is done to this submarine, I will rip that peace treaty up and eat it—then shit it out and feed it to him!"

My eyes widen.

Raine's face doesn't change, but I can see the intensity, the undercurrents of something dangerous. "Brayja, if you do not do as I ask, you will lose a lot more than this submarine," he says in a chilling voice.

Thankfully Brayja is not a complete lunatic and can see the warning in Raine's gaze. He turns and points at his men. "Go now and turn off everything!"
Then he looks at everyone on the deck. "Do not make one sound or I will toss you over the edge," he threatens.

"I want you to run your evacuation," Raine says to Brayja.

"Evacuation?! Are you telling me the mighty Raine can't take out an Opus?" Brayja hisses. "Forgive me, Raine, but I know what you're capable of."

Raine laughs coldly as he turns to give Brayja a dangerous smile. "Unfortunately, Brayja, so does Thetis." He says something to the Nymph next to him, and he nods, running off. "Run it."

I think Brayja's face could not get any redder. "Run it!" He points to his men.

I see men tossing life rafts over the side of the sub, lots of them. I swallow and see Brayja with his head down, shaking it.

"Raine! Tell me, what is worse than one Opus? Enlighten me."

"Three of them," Raine responds with a wink, and takes a silver crown from the returning Nymph, with five high points on it.

Brayja's eyes widen. "You need the crown for this?" He runs his hands through his hair like he is losing his mind. "Thetis is a dead man!"

I see Raine put on the crown and instantly the lights glow, causing Raine to hiss in pain.

I look at Steven, who has wide, horrified eyes. "What's happening?"

"Uhhh, well, Raine has most of his power locked onto you. That's the elephant in the room."

My eyes widen. "Are you serious?"

"Yeah." He looks up at me.

"I told you it takes a lot of energy to be linked to you. That is his birthright crown that is connected to his mother. He needs the extra power, and Brayja does not know that half of it is sucked into you."

Raine grips a tall pole with his eyes closed. "Does it hurt him? The crown?"

"No, but being connected to you does," Steven says, and swallows. "Dude, I need a smoke. Getting red alerts like crazy."

I take a shaky breath as I watch Raine. He looks like some ocean god — powerful, mythical. In the back of my mind, I can't believe something like him is even giving me the time of day.

I close my eyes — well, I keep forgetting that it's because of my deception and marriage to his friend and ally. Still, though, he seems overly sexual with me when he probably doesn't have to be. I bite my lip. Maybe he can sense a weakness in me? His dark plan is backfiring on him — he didn't anticipate this.

"He is in pain because he is linked to me, but he can't unlink himself?"

"No. It takes meditation and requires precious time to do that. Raine screwed himself," Steven whispers.

"Can you get the bracelet?"

Steven makes a face. "Yeah, if you want to die. That would seriously hurt him—not a good time for that if you have not noticed."

Raine opens his eyes and takes a scary-looking spear from one of his men, about four yards long. The silver spear shimmers in the dark, and immediately I feel a pulse of pure energy.

Raine stands up on the top rail along with his men, who are also holding spears. He twirls the spear as it flickers with electric power, Raine's muscles flexing with each pulse of energy.

"Don't miss, Raine! So help me!" I hear Brayja's crazed voice.

All of the Nymphs lower their heads and close their eyes, along with Raine. I shiver as we wait in silence, feeling droplets of rain.

The strained silence has my heart palpitating in anticipation.

The sub jerks left then to the right as waves hit us hard, intensifying the emotional friction. I take a steady breath, my eyes fastened on Raine, whose eyes are still closed.

His crown and spear make him look deadly, like some god of war. He wears black wetsuit-type pants that showcase his muscular thighs as they grip the rail.

I wonder if he regrets trying to manipulate me.

I bet he does now.

Raine's head jerks up with the rest of the Nymphs. It happens so fast that my eyes barely register it as Raine throws the spear into the water with lethal speed, the sound like a woman screaming.

I see the ocean flicker with light like a bomb is going off under the water.

Then I hear a loud sound, almost like if you amplified a whale's call underwater but more monstrous. Tentacles shoot out of the black waters making me scream, flattening against the wall.

"RAINE!" I hear Brayja scream. "Oh my—GET THE FUCK BACK!" Brayja turns to run in my direction.

The long tentacles tower into the night sky as Raine fires off more spears with deadly precision and speed. Raine turns and yells at Brayja's men to shoot their golden spear guns.

I see another set of tentacles to our right rise out of the water after being hit by Raine's electric spear.

"Steven!" I gasp.

"Dude." Steven says. "Lifeline, r-remember . . . Oh, mama! Those are big as hell!"

This is insanity.

I might rather be back on Orc mountain.

My heart hammers against my chest as the rain pours down on us. Brayja, I notice, is freaking out as the tentacles get closer to the submarine.

"What is it, Steven?!"

"Like a monster octopus, dude!" He says as we both stare at the towering tentacles in the night sky, lightning flickering around them. "It could squeeze this rig in half like an anaconda. And there are three of them!"

Oh shit.

I swallow, trying to calm my breathing.

Raine turns to see what Brayja is screaming his head off about, and out of nowhere, a massive tentacle comes out of the water, seemingly right next to the submarine. Raine tries to jump out of the way, but being distracted by Brayja, he is struck hard.

He is gone.

Overboard.

I scream, covering my mouth.

"Steven!" I gasp. I see full-blown panic from everyone as the tentacle lands on the side of the sub, making the rig tilt violently, almost going vertical.

I'm sliding down the deck, hearing the eerie calls of this sea monster echo in the night. I'm ready to call my lifeline as my body slams into the red rail, right next to the monstrous tentacle. My body enters fight or flight mode, adrenaline pounding. I think it's time to jump ship and try to find a life raft.

Or drown.

I scream as I feel someone grab me around the waist and haul me up. I turn to see Raine right next to me, pulling me over the red rail like I'm a rag doll.

I have no time to react.

My first sensation is the pain of hitting the monstrous waters, being submerged in blackness.

Raine still has me around the waist as I kick with all my might, bubbles rushing by my head as I violently thrash.
We break the surface as I cough and grab Raine around the neck. We swim up to the half-tilted rig and Raine grabs onto a golden ladder embedded into the side.

A wave slams into us, making me sputter in his arms.

"RAINE!"

He is looking at me, holding me tightly to him. "I need you to look at me!"

I blink through the sting in my eyes and try to calm my breathing.

"I need you to help me!" he yells, and shields me from another wave.

"I need you to steal my power, and we both can produce a shock wave! It will buy us time to save this submarine and make an escape."

My brain can barely function.

We are in the water with these monsters.

"I need you to do it now!" Raine squeezes me harder as if to bring me back to reality.

"I don't know how to create a shock wave!"

Raine pauses for a second and looks at the second tentacle claiming the rig. "Don't worry—I will guide you!"

How?
~Oooh, I know how~.
He's linked to me.

"Now!"

I try to think, my body almost forgetting how to steal power through all the fear and adrenaline. ". . . I n-need to kiss you!"

That's how I did it last time.

I don't have time to figure out another way.

Raine stares at me, and for a second I think he'll refuse. Then he leans his head to my lips, and the contact shocks me. My mind is vaguely aware that I'm finally being touched by him, and it is not a figment in my imagination this time. I can feel his warm lips as he deepens the kiss, his mouth claiming mine.

Time seems to stand still, oddly enough. I feel him shift as if to get a better hold on me, and that's when he starts to devour me.

163

We are kissing in the middle of a crisis.

Insanity.

His tongue is in my mouth, almost making my brain flatline, defeating the purpose of kissing him in the first place.

The way his lips move with his tongue in such a fluid motion, like he's been perfecting the art of kissing his whole life . . .

Raine lifts his head back as more water crashes into us. "Again?"

If it were possible to blush, I'd be a cherry. "Again, sorry!"

I see something in his fiery gaze, and I can't tell what it is. Almost as if he knows why this didn't work, and quite possibly, he finds it amusing.

His lips are on mine again, but he does not use his tongue this time, gently kissing me.
Dear goodness, he knows I was too ~mushy ~to concentrate.
I will die a thousand deaths . . . later.

But right now, I can feel his power, and I suck it in through his mouth. His essence.

Everything slows to a slower time frame and it's shockingly bright. My body is on a high. My skin is hot and cold at the same time.

It's so bright, like someone raised the exposure.
I feel Raine come behind me and wrap his arm around me, his hands grabbing mine. I can see that I'm the same color as him — the color of ~fire~.

I think I remember feeling his lips on my neck as a surge of energy blinds me.

I try to stay conscious, but my eyes flutter, utterly oblivious to everything.

Whatever I did, I hope it worked.

CHAPTER 13

CAMILA

"CAN YOU HEAR ME?"

I flinch, blinking as Steven's face hovers over mine.

"Steven," I whisper, my brain quickly gathering information. My heart jumps to life as I sit up, looking around the golden room. "We are back in the submarine?"

Steven shakes his head. "Uh, yeah. Dude, you were out for hours, though. We are almost to landfall—the Gaya Empire."

I swallow and try to slow down my bubbling hysteria. "Tell me what happened."

Steven covers his mouth and laughs, his chubby body shaking. "Dude. Like, I don't know how to explain everything."

"Try," I hiss.

"Okay, well, this is the first time I'm actually alone with you. You're being heavily watched. Brayja is in here like every five minutes, I swear."

I stare at Steven. "Okay . . ."

"Yeah, so, like . . . " Steven frowns at me. "You missed Raine saving everyone while Brayja screamed his head off. The shockwave you and Raine created bought us enough time to power on the sub and make a quick escape. Though a lot of damage has been done, which has Brayja in an even worse mood."

I don't say anything.
"And . . . "

"And?"

Strained silence.

"Do you remember kissing Raine? Like, I don't know, in plain view?" Steven shrugs.
"Not sure if you remember that juicy little tidbit. And your skin was the same color as Raine's."

The color drains from my face. "Fuck."

"Yeah." He takes a breath. "So Brayja saw you two with lips locked like hot and heavy lovers. I was like, 'Oh shiiiiit, duuuuude.'"

I close my eyes and grit my teeth. "So where is Raine now?"

"With Brayja."

I feel sick. "So is Brayja beyond pissed? The engagement's off? He clearly knows I have Nymph blood. I'm not pure, there is no way he will want me as his queen," I whisper to myself. "I suck at life."

"Well—"

"I had this in the bag, Steven! It was literally foolproof!" I feel my eyes well up with angry tears. "Self-sabotage at its finest."

"Well, I was going to say that Raine is pretty smooth. He got Brayja to calm down, but I don't know what was said between the two. I have not heard

Brayja yelling for at least an hour." Steven says, and takes out a snack-size bag of ~Lay's ~potato chips. "This Brayja guy is pretty weird, you have to admit. Are you sure you're even sad about this?"

"I was to be a queen! Of course, I'm pissed!" I yell, then lower my voice. "I don't care about Brayja."

"But he would be your husband. He seems a little off. Like an I-will-kill-you-if-you-make-me-angry ~and ~cover-it-up-as-if-it-were-an-accident type of dude."

I snort. "He will tire of me eventually, maybe even take other lovers, and I will be free to do what I want."

"Well, I don't think that will happen now." Steven looks in the chip bag with a frown. "You know, they barely put any chips in here."

I close my eyes again and whisper, "What a mess."

All over a man.

Again.

Raine just needs to leave. I can't function with him being here. It's like my lady bits don't agree with my brain.

"I need that bracelet."

I can't have another hot night with him and mentally survive.

"Yeah. When we get to the palace, you will have one," Steven says, and offers me some chips as he chews.

I decline, feeling like I might vomit.

"Why don't you switch dudes?"

I look at Steven and frown. "Raine?"

"Yeah. The one you were sucking face with, remember?"

I bite my lip. "He hates me."

Steven laughs loudly. "Yeah, suurrrreee. I kiss all of my enemies too, and make them have sexy dreams with me." He snorts.

I shiver, my face heating.

I would not be opposed to that, actually. He is the son of a sea goddess—life with him might be all that I'm looking for. And, let's face it, Raine can make me hot with one damn look.

"You're thinking about it, I can tell." Steven laughs.

I take a large breath. "But I'm a Valkyrie."

"True. There are half-breeds all over the place, but normally they like the royal family pure. It's kinda the same with royalty everywhere," Steven says, and shakes the crumbs into his mouth, chips landing all over his face.

The possibility of being with Raine excites me more than it should. "Shit. Well, is it against the rules? Could Raine pick me if he wanted?"

Steven shrugs. "Not sure, I will have to ask Pierce. But I know it's, like, never done. There are no Valkyries in the royal family currently."

"Perfect," I whisper. "I'm screwed."

"Well, we still don't know how Brayja will react, so let's wait and go with the flow," Steven offers. "You could still be queen."

"Unlikely," I mutter.

I will end up alone. Back to planet Earth with shame consuming me.

I hear the door open, and I stand up as my pulse hammers.

Steven is gone, save for his empty chip bag floating to the ground.

"Daphine?" I hear Braya's voice, and I almost die with nerves. He walks in with Raine, and I forget to breathe.

Deep breaths, Camila.

"You're awake, thank goodness," Brayja says, making me frown. He walks up to me and grabs my face, lowering his lips to mine. My whole body is tense, not sure what is happening. Brayja's lips are hard, and I barely refrain from gasping in pain. "My brave Daphine, you must have been so terrified."

I glance past Brayja and see Raine leaning up against the wall with his arms crossed over his chest. He's dressed in all black save for his dark jewels, the rubies on his fingers catching the light.

I repress a shiver. "Yes," I whisper.

Brayja laughs and turns to look behind him. "Raine knows I was distraught at seeing my queen kissing my best friend."

Raine's expression is carved from stone. Zero emotion crosses his features as he looks at me with eyes of fire.

The object of my obsession and my downfall.

I swallow, still having no idea what to say.

"But then Raine exposed a little secret you were hiding, my love," Brayja murmurs as he glances back at me. "He assured me that the kiss was necessary for saving my submarine and the people on it."

I can still remember the feeling of Raine's tongue in my mouth. If Brayja saw the way Raine kissed me, I don't know how he'd let this slide.

It was not innocent. A moron could tell that.

Guilt washes over me.

"Yes," I say, feeling Raine's gaze searing me.

Brayja looks down and back up to me. "I thought there was something different about your eyes," he murmurs. "Extraordinary."

We stare at each other, the tension thick. "Forgive me, Brayja. I know you want a queen that is pure of blood—"

"I do, and you are correct. My parents will be appalled to learn that I chose you with Nymph blood." Brayja eyes me, his gaze lowering to my breasts in this silver wetsuit.

I feel exposed when he looks at me like that, and it's giving me unsettling vibes.

"That is why they will not find out."

My eyes widen as I look past Brayja to Raine.

Raine looks down, and I can see the tension in him. Anger radiates off of him.

"Raine has promised to keep this a secret. No one will know of this little setback but us." He grabs my face, forcing me to look back at him. "Daphine, my love. Nothing will tear us apart, which I'm sure you were scared of that happening if you were exposed. Please do not fret."

I'm not sure how I feel about this.

I was getting excited at the possibility of being with Raine. Well, the idea of it—not that ~he ~would be excited about it.

If I bet on Raine, I could end up alone.

What a mess.

Brayja studies me in that odd way, like he has a secret. A smile always plays on his lips, as if he could reveal something horrid at any moment. "I find your power and ability to be very curious, desirable even. Your skin was the color of Raine's, which baffled me!" He laughs and glances at Raine, shaking his head.

"As long as Raine keeps his tongue in his mouth, no one should know of this particular dilemma." He laughs at Raine's glower. "I'm giving you a hard time, brother. Relax! If I actually thought you were in love with my future wife, we would not be standing here laughing. You know me better than that." He smiles, looking too happy and pleased with himself.

I can feel a dangerous tension floating about. The house of cards is teetering with too much unstable weight on top.

"Daphine, we will be arriving at your new home within the hour. Please make yourself presentable. My mother and father will be thrilled to meet my intended wife," he says with a wink. "I must leave, Raine, and I have to figure out a way to prove Thetis's guilt. He will pay for the damage done to this submarine. He will pay with his fucking life."

And with that, he leaves.

Raine pushes off the wall to follow him without a second glance in my direction, like I mean nothing to him. I must be acting like a lover continually scorned when he has made no promises to me.

In fact, it's been the opposite. He wanted to ruin me, not love me. I laugh, feeling like my sanity is also teetering.

I feel pain sting my eyes, so I blink it away.

I don't ~want ~to want him, and that's producing this rage inside of me. I hate him for making me desire him as I do—it's cruel.

It's his fault that I have this need for him. I mean, he sexually torments me in my sleep. The way he kissed me in the water is not easily forgotten. I do understand the concept of fatal attraction. It's like wearing a rare diamond necklace only to have it snatched away and given a string candy necklace in its place.

I need to talk to him.

Alone.

But I can't forget that I will still be the queen.

It's enough. It's all that matters.

***

The palace left me with my mouth open half the time on my brief tour before Brayja had to leave. Golden splendor with vibrant colors fit for the highest of tastes, like a massive version of his precious submarine. It's tropical and lush here—incredibly extravagant.

The gigantic white columns should be a world wonder.

Maybe I can do this with Brayja.

It's enough.

I don't want the feelings for Raine to ruin this for me, because I feel like I'm teetering on the edge of a cliff and the slightest wind current could push me either way. I'm no stranger to temporary obsessions. It just takes time to clear my head. I need to talk to Raine. I need to get closure, in a sense.

I curse.
Or do I want to talk to him because I want to see if he feels what I'm struggling with? Maybe that will be my end to this mental fascination.

I walk down the long golden hallway, seeing Brayja's men and Raine's men filing into the massive banquet room. Brayja is already there, and he told me that I may watch from the high seating.

I have yet to meet the king and queen, and I'm mildly dreading it.

"I think we go into the large double doors on your right," Steven says.

"Is Raine already in there?"

"Not sure—"

I suck in a breath when I see Raine walking with a couple of his men from around a corner, seemingly deep in conversation.

Steven nudges me. "Unless he has a twin, then no."

"I need to talk to him," I whisper, and look down at my golden gown glittering in the evening light. It flows like golden dust embedded with diamonds and emeralds. My breasts are displayed in a dipping V-neck that Pierce altered to fit me perfectly.

"I think that might be what got you into this mess in the first place," Steven whispers.

I snort, feeling nervous. My high ponytail is plaited with braids and shiny twists, and my long black hair hangs down my back beautifully. I look like a queen, so I'm not sure where this nervousness is coming from.

I almost feel sick.

"I have to get answers. Cover for me," I murmur.

"Roger that."

I shiver, my eyes tracing over Raine. He is larger than almost everyone else, and his shoulder span is impressive, pulling against the black and scarlet dress coat. Nymph's style is very gothic Victorian, with a hint of something magical.
All of their clothing adapts to the water, almost like it shape-shifts at their command.

Raine's orange gaze raises to mine, as if sensing my stare.

I stop breathing, and I can feel my heartbeat in my neck, begging me to take a breath of air. Suffocating right now would be a shame. I would go down in FGI history for being the biggest moron ever to play the game.

I finally take a large breath as his gaze moves over my body, slowly and deliberately.

So different from his usual indifference.

"Make it quick, dude. We don't need any more drama," Steven says, and leaves.

Raine says something to his men and they nod, leaving to go into the large double doors. He glances back at me and takes a breath, hands on his hips.

"You look like you have something to say," he murmurs as he eyes me suspiciously.

I do?

Yes, I do.

Focus.

"I think you know we need to talk," I say under my breath, and look around, smiling at random people.

He looks around as well, then back to me. "I have five minutes. Follow me."

I follow him, praying that Brayja does not jump out of the shadows. Raine turns to glance back at me with a half-smile.

"Relax, I can feel your tension." His voice is deep but also beautiful with his accent, and I hate that I notice it.
Relax? ~Yeah, right~, I want to say.
He leads me to an area that no one seems to be in, though my brain isn't taking in the scenery at this point. I'm too sick with these butterflies and nerves. Surely he must feel this also—he has to.

I will be mortified if this is one-sided.

What am I doing?

I close my eyes.

~Get your shit together, Camila.~

"Are you okay?" he asks softly, leaning up against the wall opposite from me, studying my silent battle.

"No," I say, and hug myself. "I want to know what is going on between us."

There.

He takes a long breath, his fiery gaze moving over my face. "Nothing. I have misjudged Brayja's fascination with you, unfortunately. It seems he does not care what you really are, strangely enough. So I don't think it matters anymore if I expose you as an imposter.

"Congratulations, you will be the next queen," he says in a soft tone, but I can sense that he is holding back something dangerous.

Or is he?

I blink. "Congratulations?"

He does not say anything.

"What about the way you kissed me in the water?"

Raine closes his eyes, and takes another breath, pinning me with his gaze once again. "What about it?"

Down girl, I can feel my anger rise and start the slow boil. "You want more from me, admit it."
He still does not know I know about him being linked to me, and the naughty dreams. You don't do that to someone, put so much energy into it, and not feel something.

He laughs, and it makes me shiver. Raine looks away and takes a moment like he is searching for words.

"Brayja is very unstable. Like I said before, I was unaware of his desire for you. We are in a very dangerous position." He pauses. "I can't want more from you because it could start a fucking war," he says in a low voice, putting me on edge. "I have known Brayja for most of my life, and I can see that he already does not trust me with you, testing me. I need his alliance if I want a chance at taking Thetis down."

I feel a flood of emotion. That sounded like a hidden rejection.

As I stare at him, all I want to do is to have him kiss me again — or hold me in real life, not in a dream world.

I take a breath and try to ignore the lock of black hair that hangs in his face, or how sexy he looks with his dark jewelry. My brain is just not making this easy for me. It's mental anguish to want something you can't have.

Thetis is the FGI main target, so I doubt he will be taken down. The mission is to change his heart, not kill him. Raine will lose on that account.

"I don't know what to say," I whisper, and look down, feeling my eyes tear up and my jaw cramp. I have too much raw emotion to deal with this. "So you don't want me . . . or try to fight for me?"

He makes a sound, and he shifts. "I can't answer that, and please don't make me," he pleads, making me raise my gaze to his.

Raine searches my face, probably seeing the hurt and pain written there. I take a shaky breath. "Answer it."

I hear him curse as he closes his eyes, wiping a hand down his face. "I'm sorry, but I will not give you the answer you want."

I feel a tear stream down my face as I try to keep it together. "You kiss other women like you did me? So I'm just a silly girl who imagined something more?"

Raine's eyes widen when he sees the tear on my cheek. "Don't do this," he whispers. "Stop."

"You want me to stop?"

He glances around then takes a step toward me, his chest rising and falling. "You have to," he gets out, coming closer, making me back up.

I raise my chin. "You're the one that's a liar, not me," I get out through gritted teeth.

I hear him say something under his breath, his hand coming to my chin to tilt it up higher. "If you are to be queen, you have to be stronger than this."

My eyes widen.

"You're such an asshole," I whisper, feeling another tear fall.

He expels a breath. "Do not talk this way to Brayja. You will get punished severely, and he will know you're not from here. You must be submissive to him."

I'm not sure if I'm cut out for this. This is heavy. It hurts.
"Thank you, ~kindly~," I get out sarcastically.
His jaw clenches. "Brayja will destroy you if you can't learn to shut your emotions off. You're falling apart."

"I wonder why," I hiss, and glare at him—a glare that would make anyone doubt my sanity. I move closer to him, our faces but breaths away. I bet he can hear my erratic heartbeat, see the crazy in my gaze. "You want me to shut off my emotions, then? The pain?"

His eerie gaze lowers to my lips, then back up. "I will get hurt worse than you, trust me," he whispers.

I laugh and shake my head, not buying it.

"You must like pain then, Raine, because if you do nothing, you're about to hurt a lot more." I shove him in the chest and it's like pushing a brick wall.

"Move," I hiss, and he steps back.
He grabs my hand to jerk me toward him, but I hear my name being called, and I pull my hand out of his. I wave at the female servants walking towards

me. I smile even though I want to scream and knee Raine between the legs.

"Camila, it has to be this way," I hear him say as I turn to walk towards my servants.

I pause.

He just called me ~Camila~.

I grit my teeth and take a breath, remembering him touching me, kissing me as I must have told him my real name. Raine played me, and now he just told me ever so gently that I'm not worth fighting for.

His revenge is worth more.
~It has to be this way~ . . .
Blind rage.

So be it.

I don't remember finding my way into the massive banquet room or being led up to the second floor that overlooks the room. I have tunnel vision, the beat of my heart echoing through my chest. I guess I didn't realize how much I wanted Raine to tell me that he also wanted me.

I'm a silly girl. I guess I always have been.

"Dude," Steven whispers, "take a breath. Breaaaathhhe. You're turning purple."

I look at him as he sits beside me. "Do you have the bracelet?" I ask indifferently, reminding myself to breathe.

He looks around then back to me. "I take it the talk with Raine didn't go well?"

"No. He's just been using me," I whisper, and feel my eyes water.

"Shit." Steven is quiet. "Sorry, toots, but you're going to be queen. His loss, screw his ass," he murmurs, and pats me on the shoulder, giving it a squeeze. "Well. Okay, so do this with ease." Steven holds out the gold bracelet with a beautiful diamond-looking stone embedded into it.

I look back over the ledge and see Raine walk in with a few other guys. Brayja walks up to him and pats him on the back. The king, Brayja's father, walks up to Raine also, showing him glory and respect.

I roll my eyes.

"Dude, Brayja's mother looks like a toad," Steven says with a look. "Don't understand how Brayja was born. Like, that woman had sex . . . ?"

I look at Steven with a frown then glance to where the queen sits on her throne. She is definitely toad-ish, with zero neck and an expression like she is two seconds from shitting her sparkling gown. She is adorned in so much golden material that I'm surprised that she can breathe correctly, let alone walk. I shiver—she looks like a delightful character.

Her severe bun pulls at her eyes, making them tiny little slits, and I half expect her tongue to dart out and catch a rogue fly.
~Mierda~.
I'm beginning to see why Brayja is . . . strange.

"Oh no . . . "

"What?" I whisper, glancing at him.

"I'm picturing it . . . Them having sex, the king and queen," he whispers, and scrunches up his face. "The weed is giving me a lot of detail, dude." He sucks in a breath. "MAKE IT STOP!"

Everyone around us looks in our direction, frowning. "Sorry," I whisper to them, and pinch Steven. "Shut up," I hiss.

He whines, closing his eyes.

"Give me the bracelet," I whisper, still nodding at the curious stares.

Steven looks at me, a little pale. "Look, if you hold the bracket close to your skin, Raine should be able to feel it and know it's coming. That's how powerful this is.

"Homeboy about to be pissed," Steven says, and hands me the bracelet, careful not to let the gem touch my skin.

I stare at it, realizing that I will lose my connection with Raine for good. I look down at him, and immediately he looks up and he finds me like he already knew where I was.

Our gazes clash, and I raise my chin.

I see him curse, and he closes his eyes, tilting his head back. Raine looks back at me and slightly shakes his head, ~NO~. I narrow my gaze on him, saying, ~Too bad. ~

"Oh man, he looks scared. Or pissed, I can't tell with him," Steven says, and looks at me.

Raine looks back at Brayja and everyone else, responding to something someone said. Why does he not want me to break this connection with him?

I feel anger over that.

He still wants to control me. Keep tabs on me.

I move the gem closer to my skin.

Raine turns and walks towards a pillar, leaning against it, bracing himself for the pain. Our gazes meet again and his stare is still pleading, but I'm not giving him this hold over me.

I slowly stand and he all but glares at me.

There is an electric current about to be broken forever.

Do it.

I put it on and instantly, Raine hisses in pain, falling to the ground, sliding down the pillar. Men run over to Raine, trying to help him up. A crowd has gathered around him.

I immediately feel the disconnect like someone dumping ice water over me. I didn't realize how different I would feel. My eyes sting as I watch Raine in intense pain on the floor.

I can't watch this.

Anger, pain, and vengefulness all course through me. I don't know where I'm going, walking past people like I'm delirious.

~"Dude, Raine is leaving, claiming to need fresh air," Steven says. "Watch out~ — ~I think he saw your mad dash."~

I tense, realizing I'm by the back entrance to the banquet hall.

The door opens and the Raine I see is livid, seething, breathing hard.

"Shit," I whisper.

He stumbles to the left a bit, but walks towards me, eyes of burning fire searing my insides.

"Take off the bracelet," he whispers harshly.

I back up, breathing hard. "It can't be removed," I breathe. "It's over."

He closes his eyes, gritting teeth. "No, it's just begun."

I turn and run, hearing him laugh behind me.

What in the hell have I done?

CHAPTER 14

CAMILA

I don't get far.

I gasp when he grabs me from behind, and somehow I twirl into him, my heart pounding. All of my senses are on high alert, my intuition sounding the warning sirens.

I might have screamed from how quickly I collided into his broad chest. Raine looks different as I stare up at him, and I wildly wonder how badly I hurt him with the bracelet.

He's dangerously pale, and there are deep circles under his eyes. His black hair is wild and hangs in his face like some wicked vampire king here to take my soul.

"Raine," I breathe.

"So now you want Brayja?" he whispers. "Now that I broke your golden heart?"

I swallow and look around to see if anyone sees this, which could be devastating. I can't let this man be my downfall. I need to see the red flags instead of ignoring them because he's beautiful, lust altering my decisions.

I guess I'm just a sucker for pretty things . . .

"Searching for him?" he whispers, and it sends a warning thrill down my neck.

"What do you care?" I say, challenging him. "You're upset that you cannot control me?"

He tilts his head then pulls me with him, tossing me against a wall, barely hidden from Brayja's guards. My heart is beating as I watch him walk up to me, taking off his black overcoat, tossing it to the side.

"Control you?" He laughs. "Poor Camila. How does it feel to know that I'm aware of your secrets? I know your desires," he murmurs as he looks at me, rolling up his sleeves.

I swallow, noticing how dangerous he looks, muscles flexing with each careful movement. From a young age, I have learned to notice dangerous men for survival.

Men with dark intentions always surrounded my father, and right now, Raine is giving off those vibes.

Did I miss this about Raine? Lust hazing over the fact that this man could be more dangerous than Brayja? I thought Brayja was more on the lines of crazy, but Raine is making the hairs on my neck stand up.

"Seeing that I can't sense what you're feeling, will you tell me?" he asks lightly, his eerie gaze studying me.

I can hear people in the distance, making me nervous.

"I'm confused, that's what I'm thinking. Help me understand. What do you want with me?" I get out, trying to ignore the way he is watching me.

He sidesteps and glances around the wall, nodding to someone, then comes back to me.

"What do I want with you?"

I stare at him, seeing the smile pulling at his mouth. He makes a sound as he watches me, eyes roaming over my breasts deliberately, then back up to meet my gaze.

"It would ruin everything if I told you, sweet Camila. But I will say that I loved seeing and sensing how much I turn you on," he whispers, smiling now. "And how much Brayja repulses you, which is why he's still alive."

My cheeks are fire, confusion clouding my brain.

I swallow. "You still make no sense, Raine."

What the hell is going on? Does he want me or not?

"Good," he murmurs. "All you need to know is that you will never become queen. Never. I'm sorry because I think you were looking forward to it. I got to sense how much you desire it, and for that, I'm sorry. " He gives me a pitying look. "Truly."

I suck in a breath. "You cannot dictate that," I say, my heart pounding. "Brayja does not care that I'm not pure."

"I can, actually."

He's going to ruin me after all.

Raine walks up to me, and I flatten myself against the wall, trying to control my hysteria. His gaze sweeps over me.

"I hate that I do not know what you're feeling." He pauses with a dark grin. "But I did learn that when you're sexually turned on, your eyes turn a stunning shade of purple."

I look down and hear him laugh.

He watches me for what seems like an eternity.
"Are you turned on now? Look at me, and let me see," he orders in that voice that makes me want to do stupid things.

"No," I hiss, and make a move to run past him, but my attempt is shut down. Now I'm pinned between his arms, his face but breaths away, and I avert my head.

"Let me go, Raine," I whisper.

"Raine," I hear a woman's voice.

Nomi.

Raine pushes away from me and takes a deadly looking sword from her with a holster. Her eyes go to mine, and the glare I get makes me on edge.

Will Nomi tell Brayja? What the hell is going on?

Raine says something to Nomi as he puts on the buckle, her eyes round as she whispers something back to him. He clasps the straps to his muscled thighs, and I have to try not to look at him ~there~.

It's very pronounced, making my cheeks redden, and I mentally slap myself in the face.

Again and again.

I look between them, trying to calm my bubbling panic. Nomi looks back at me, and I can see the jealousy in her eyes as she walks, or storms, away.

~"Dude, sorry to interrupt, but, like, Brayja is looking for you. Your ass is going to get caught, man! Get away from Raine. Braja is with his parents – the King and QUEEN!~"
I mentally curse, p

anic coursing through me. "Brayja will see us, let me go," I hiss, hearing voices in the distance.

"I'll let you go, but look at me first," he orders in that voice that has my stomach fluttering.

"Promise you'll let me go?"

What am I, five? I know I can't trust him.

I hear Raine laugh as he walks back to me, and his head lowers to my shoulder, lips feathering over my skin. "Promise," he whispers against my neck.

I shiver, feeling his tongue on my neck. I finally look at him and try to keep my emotions in order, focusing on the anger instead of him.

His gaze is swirling fire, making my stomach twist. Something is different about the way he looks at me, as if something shifted. Whoever he was pretending to be vanished the moment I put on that bracelet.

"Camila, I find you intoxicating. I could feel your doubts about my desire for you, which I found humorous for a while and played along with. Someone that looks like you, surprisingly, has low self-esteem. Pity. You make yourself easy prey for someone like me."

"I don't understand," I whisper as I watch him.

"It's complicated," he whispers, his lips on my neck again. I tense, holding back a moan. I feel him start to suck, his hands grabbing me firmly around the waist.

"We will get caught," I get out, pleading.

Alarms ring in my head.

I can't scream, that will only bring more drama.

"Then be quiet," he whispers, and grabs the back of my head, his lips taking mine, surprising me. My brain is flickering on and off, hating that I love the taste of him.

"Kiss me," he whispers as his lips take mine hard, his body forcing me into the wall.

I try to fight it, but the taste of his lips makes my stomach melt into lava, my body
flushing against my will.

"Don't fight me," he breathes into my mouth, and I can feel him smile against me, kissing me harder. "I know you want it. Open," he whispers between his heated kisses. "It was addicting sensing your desire for me, almost making me break my poise a few times."

"Raine—you have to stop," I pant, hearing voices coming closer now, trying to move my head.

I will get caught.

Pure panic.

He grabs my chin, making me look at his lustful expression, my heart pounding.
"If you don't kiss me back," he threatens against my lips as his hand applies more pressure on my hip, "I will make you scream so loudly they will run in here to help the poor maiden in need of saving."

He kisses the side of my lips, the heat of his body engulfing me.

"You're threatening me?" I pant, losing control.

He laughs against my mouth, and in the next instant, he picks me up, making me gasp. My legs wrap around his waist, my arms circling his neck. I'm breathing hard as he gets a better grip on me, hiking up my golden skirts.

"Raine," I moan, instead of reprimanding him.

"Are you going to kiss me like you mean it?" he whispers into my neck, his hands squeezing my ass.

I'm breathing so hard I might pass out, and I'm actually hearing Brayja's voice mere feet from us, on the other side of this wall.

"Raine," I plead.

"Hmmmm." He nips at my neck, his sharp canines scraping my shoulder. "She's not convinced. Calling my bluff?"

I feel his right hand let go of my thigh, and I suck in a breath when I feel his fingers brush over my heated center. His hand plays with my panties, one finger hooking into the fabric, pulling it away from me.

I gasp, my eyes widening.

"Raine," I whisper in a moan.

He watches me as his finger rubs over me, his thumb pressing into my sensitive spot.
"I remember this, don't you?" he rasps, his hand becoming more aggressive. "You're so wet." Raine closes his eyes with a slight moan. "Fuck."

That did it.

He wins.

Raine's mouth on mine is wild, to an almost alarming degree. I give it back, drinking him in, feeling his tongue sweeping against mine. We are both starving for each other, as I feel his fingers deep inside of me.

An electric pulse wracks my person, making me barely able to keep in a scream. I hear him laugh against me as his fingers plunge into me deeper.

"Raine," I pant.

"Shhhh," he coos, watching me, fingers swirling. "You'll get us caught," he whispers with a playful flick of his tongue against my lips.

I hear Brayja yelling orders to determine my whereabouts, but Raine's fingers are magic. I try to hold back an orgasm, perspiration dotting my forehead.

I can't . . .

He is kissing me once again as his hand thrusts for the last time, making me lose control, fireworks exploding behind my eyes. I bite my lip, stifling the shockwaves in Raines's shoulder, almost weeping.

That was the hardest thing I have ever done.

I'm breathing hard, feeling dizzy, my body tingling still.

"Impressive," Raine whispers. "I went easy on you, but next time I won't." He lowers me to the floor.

~Next time~.

Raine sucks his fingers and grins at me. "You'd better go to your prince," he whispers, looking insanely hot with his wild look, "before I throw you over my shoulder."

I think I nod, not fully realizing what we just did.

Fear creeps into every bone in my body as I hear Brayja yelling his head off, thinking I have been kidnapped.

Which is very accurate.

Raine leans against the wall, adjusting himself, and my cheeks flush again, heart pounding. I have to leave before I do something foolish.

Tunnel vision sets in as I leave, seeing Brayja talking to his guards, yelling. Funny how we were so close and they didn't think to look around the wall. I'm sure they wouldn't believe that someone would be that stupid, take that big of a risk.

Brayja stops mid yell as his eyes locate me walking towards them. "Daphine!"

I slightly smile, feeling lightheaded still.

Confused.

"Where were you?" He grabs me by the shoulders. "I thought you were taken by
Thetis!"

"No," I say. "I'm fine," I say in a weak tone. "Just took a walk."

"A walk?!"

"I was feeling overheated," I think I say.

He studies me. "You look flushed. Are you sick?"

"I might be," I say.

In the head.

Brayja looks up and his eyes widen. "Raine! Where did you go? You collapsed."

I freeze, not looking in that direction.

What a mess.

"Brayja," Raine says. "Touching that you care."

Brayja laughs. "Of course, brother. You also look sick."

He glances at me, then back to Raine, a frown on his face, and I can see the connection being made. I close my eyes, wanting the ground to swallow me up. I look around and see a lot of Nymphs, more than usual. I frown as I look to my left, noticing that they are holding weapons.

I look back to Brayja and I realize he is seeing the same thing.

The king walks up to me, his wrinkled expression eying me from head to toe. "So is this the woman, Brayja? Particular eye color she has, eh?"

Brayja does not seem to hear him. "Raine," he whispers, "tell me. Where did you go after you left the banquet room?"

I hear Raine laugh, and now he stands next to us.

~"Steven here. Something is definitely wrong, man!~"

I glance at Raine, and he is staring at Brayja. It's not a nice look.

Brayja is now frowning, stepping closer to him. "Tell me."

Raine glances at me with a wink. "I was making your queen ~feel ~better. I hope you don't mind." He whispers the deadly words.

Brayja's eyes widen in furry.

Everything happens so fast I don't have time to scream.

I feel Raine grab my arm and jerk me backward, landing in the arms of one of his men. I stare in horror as Raine pulls the sword from out of the king's chest, then he moves so fast I don't even see him slit the queen's throat.

I can feel my heartbeat in my head, hearing only muffled screams as Raine's men close in, holding the Valkyries hostage.

"~Dude! What the fuck, man?"~

I look at the rage on Raine's face as he pushes Brayja to the ground. "You're mad!" Brayja screams, holding up his hands.

"Possibly," Raine says, and puts his foot on Brayja's chest.

"You're a dead man. You have just made your grave!" Brayja screams, and hisses in pain as Raine applies pressure on his foot. "Y-you have just made your g-grave," Brayja gets out again.

"Consider yourself lucky I let you live this long, old friend. I was going to have you killed on Orc mountain, but plans changed."

Brayja's eyes widen. "Thetis set us up! I don't believe you."

Raine expels a breath. "No, actually, I did. You think I would be dumb enough to fall for a trap Thetis set up?" He laughs.

Brayja's eyes bulge. "You were also imprisoned!"

"Correct. I was willing to be tortured for weeks if that meant you would be killed and it blamed on Thetis, but alas . . . " Raine sighs.

I'm in shock. I can't even breathe.

I see Raine draw his sword and hold it up to his chest.

"Why are you doing this?" Brayja pleads. "You don't have to do this! They will have your head. This is suicide!"

"I think you know," Raine hisses, looking down at him.

His face pales, and I see him visibly swallow, hands shaking. "It's not true, Raine. I swear it," he whispers.

A thought occurs to me. If Raine kills Brayja, I will have nothing. I cannot become queen if Brayja is dead.

I will have nothing, game over.

Whatever Brayja has done to Raine does not affect me, but killing him will be game over, and from the looks of it, Raine will be an outlaw after this.

My lavish lists of wants are now burning in Raine's fiery gaze of revenge. I can't let this happen. I feel my eyes sting with anger.

It seems that Fate is over me, wanting me gone.

"Don't!" I plead, my heart pounding, trying a last-ditch effort.

Raine slowly looks at me, and I realize what this might look like.

Like I care about Brayja emotionally.

Not good.

A tear streams down my face and Raine's gaze widens, obviously not realizing it's because I suck at life. Nothing to do with Brayja, but just how I can't do anything right.

Raine looks back at Brayja in complete furry, and raises his sword, swinging downward.

"Nooo!" I scream. Then I do the only other thing I can think of. "Lifeline activate!"

Everything slows right before Raine's sword hits Brayja's chest, and my vision turns fuzzy until I see nothing at all.

***

~Phones ring~.
"Camila?"

"She should be able to hear us . . . "

"Pierce is on his way."

My head hurts, and the blinding white light is not helping. I see faces in front of me, and I realize I'm at FGI headquarters. My eyes water as I blink, seeing men and women running around everywhere in their business attire like this is the CIA.

"Camila, you have defaulted on the lifeline," a woman tells me as her face comes into focus. She looks at the man next to her. "Violation of code-345?"
The man in thick black glasses frowns. "B-345, I think . . . "

She nods. "That sounds right."

A man's voice from behind them speaks. "Actually, it's more of a program glitch. It's been acting up all week."

The woman moves out of the way. "Of course. I will consult with I.T."

I look at the man in a pristine navy blue suit paired with a lavender dress shirt. It's Pierce, and he is smiling at me. "Camila, I didn't expect to see you so soon." He looks down with a frown, "No, I thought you'd be here sooner, I mean."

I try to keep my anger in check. "You sabotaged me countless times—

why?"

Pierce looks thoughtful. "Have I?" He pauses with his hands in his pockets. "Well, I guess you can take advantage of the software glitch and I'll answer some questions. You see, the system thought ~you ~were going to die, not Brayja." He makes an apologetic face. "Happens sometimes, and it's the damnedest thing."

I stare at him, ignoring what he just said. "You want me to fail?"

He sits down in front of me. "Never. Actually, you are taking this rather well. In the past, I have had plant vases thrown at my head."

I do not understand this Pierce guy.

"So you mess with people . . . a lot?"

"Only when they are being lazy," he says with a wink, and studies me.

My mouth drops open. "You think I am being lazy?"

"That, or you don't know what you are capable of." He shrugs. "That's why I am here." He smiles at me. "Any other questions?"

"I want to be Brayja's wife! What's wrong with that?" I yell, gaining some looks.

"I always tell all of my girls to trust me," he says, still looking at me like he's trying to find something. "This is not easy, and it's designed that way."
"Why?" I sniff. "Why can't it be easy? It hurts." I feel my jaw cramp as I try to keep it together.

"Great question, Camila," he says, and looks down, then back up. "Because I want to see who you really are, that's why. I want to know why you crave a lavish life—is it something you self-medicate with? You're willing to be with a man who may be very wrong for you all because you feel stable in wealth."

My eyes widen.

"You see, I think you don't give yourself enough credit to be able to make a difference in anyone's life because you were hurt. This game is designed to strip away every wall you have up, and expose the true you." He shrugs. "That's why our success rate is untouchable here at FGI. We don't put bandaids on issues. We expose them, aggravate them, then make people thrive once again."

I swallow. "So you're saying I'm in for some hell."

He takes a breath. "I'm not saying that, but you have put yourself in a bit of a pickle because some of your walls are falling, and now you don't know what to do." He tilts his head.

"Brayja is going to be killed by Raine! And Raine, I'm just now realizing, is a monster! I don't see a way out of this." I feel more tears stream down my cheeks.

"Well," Pierce dusts something off his sleeve, "no matter how flat a pancake is, there are always two sides."

Who is this guy? A life guru?

"Thanks," I say. "I'll remember that."

"Perfect," Pierce says with a bright smile. "That's all we hope for."

"Guys! Dudes! Sorry I'm late, got stuck in the third dimension and almost had a panic attack," Steven says as he appears next to me, out of breath.

Pierce looks at Steven. "That's not possible."

"Trust me, it is," Steven says with an eyeroll. "That's what happens when you enter mystic mode with some heavy weed," he says, looking proud of himself.

Pierce looks thoughtful. "Interesting. I heard some people in the design department say that you landed in the air vents blocking the main suction valve, almost causing a meltdown in sector five."

He snorts, and his face reddens. "No."

Pierce nods and stands. "Camila, you must return. But let me tell you that you are stronger than you think you are and you deserve to have it all—and I want that for you."

I close my eyes and sniff.

This FGI fantasy is turning into an FGI nightmare.

"Fine," I say, and stand. "Do your worst."

Pierce winks. "That's the spirit."

I feel my body tingle as I prepare myself for some good ol' fashion pain and suffering, FGI style.

CHAPTER 15

CAMILA

Loud sounds.

I'm back in my body, though everything is slower, and maybe ten seconds earlier. I see Raine look at me before he raises his sword over Brayja. Instead of screaming this time, my eyes lock with Raine's, and I don't let him go.

I grit my teeth as I hold his stare hostage. I see the fire in his eyes, the rage, the anger, and possibly . . . the ~pain~.

I hold up my hands like I'm trying to calm a wild animal.

~Shhhhh . . . don't do this~

The sword stops just over Brayja's chest, a frown on Raine's face as he stares at me, chest rising and falling. He finally closes his eyes and tells the man next to him to take Brayja away.

I expel a breath in relief. But the scene before me is still bloody and horrific.

Confusion clouds my thoughts.

Why would Raine murder the king and queen of the Gaya Empire?

As soon as this news gets out, there will be war, intense backlash. All of Brayja's allies will come on his behalf.

This is bad for Raine.

What of his mother? What will she think? That her son has lost his damn mind?

So many questions run through my head as I feel the man behind me grab me tighter.

Is Nomi on Raine's side then? She sure looked like it earlier.

I look around and see even more of Raine's men, like he has a secret army no one knew about. But I guess I don't know Raine at all, really.

The Nymphs look rouge and mean, not like the finely dressed ones with Thetis. I watch as men tell Raine that they have the entire palace on lockdown, the Gaya army is no match for Raine's.

No match?

That means he must have a pretty substantial army.

A surprise attack.

My eyes widen. How long has Raine been planning this, then?

Raine turns to face me, looking like the dark villain, the wicked lord. My pulse jumps as I try to tamp down my hysteria, hoping they do not kill Brayja.

I still have a slight chance that my destiny is not just a killshot.

Raine looks dangerously pale and deadly. The circles under his eyes almost make his fiery eyes glow.

He looks at the dead bodies being hauled away and wipes his long sword on a cloth, an indifferent expression on his face. I swallow as he walks up to me, glancing at the man behind me with a nod.

The guard hands me to Raine, and he grabs my arm, pulling me with him. I have to tell myself to be calm and think with a level head. Pierce thinks I'm lazy? That I do not have what it takes to become something great? I raise my chin as Raine leads me away.

Well, I will prove him wrong. My pride will not allow me to give up.

I will not lie. I want to . . . but I can't.

I look at him and try to pull my arm out of his hard grasp. "Are you going to tell me what's happening?" I whisper, my heart pounding.

He does not look at me as we keep walking, nor does he say anything. I bite my lip as I'm led through a series of golden hallways. Raine's men are everywhere, holding deadly looking weapons as they patrol.

Two large double doors are open, and we walk through them. It's lavish and bright with a massive purple bed in the middle, fit for the queen. My stomach dips, praying it wasn't hers.

"Is this my prison?"

Raine slams the doors shut, making me flinch, still not say anything. He closes his eyes with his hands on his hips, deep in thought. I wonder if he knows that he has lost his mind, or that he has waged war.

Is reality hitting him now? Is he regretting it?

"What happens now?" I whisper, taking a steady breath.

He opens his eyes to stare at me, but instead of answering me, he walks to the balcony that overlooks the massive waterfall. Raine takes off his shirt in one swift movement, making me suck in a breath, then makes an attempt to wipe off the remaining blood with his shirt.

"Raine," I say.
He turns to look at me. "You will stay here until I can get you out

unharmed. It's going to get ugly for a bit, but I will keep you informed. I'd imagine you will be transported to the North where your family is from."

He winks at me. "Or, your ~pretend~ family."

I swallow. "Why did you kill Brayja's parents?" I pause. "Tell me."

He takes a breath. "Because I'm an evil man," he whispers, and walks out onto the balcony, stepping up on the rail like he is ready to jump to his death.

"Raine!" I run out onto the deck to stop him, heart pounding.

He looks back at me, and the slight smile that tugs at his lips has me confused. "Please tell me that, after what you saw earlier, you're not still worried about me?"

I feel my cheeks redden. "I'm not."

He steps down and walks up to me, lifting my chin. "Don't be."

"I'm not," I whisper.

"Liar."

I look the other way, hating myself for still craving this man after what I just saw him do. "Go then," I hiss, clenching my jaw. "Go about the destruction of your life."

"I will see you later tonight," he whispers.

I stare at him, and I can feel panic consume me. "How long have you been planning this, or was this just a spur of the moment thing?"

He leans up against the rail and crosses his arms, making his biceps bulge.

"Definitely spur of the moment," he says, and tilts his head. "Any more questions? Happy to answer."

I can't read his mood, making me on edge. "Will you kill Brayja?"

Raine's eyes flicker slightly, and he looks up towards the sky like he is thinking about it. "Of course."

I close my eyes, the little hope I had dwindling. " Why are you doing this? What's the end goal here?"

"I told you, I'm doing this because my soul is black." He suddenly reaches for me and pulls me to him, even though I resist. He spins me around to where I'm pinned against the rail, his arms on either side of me.

Raine's bare chest is so close it's hard to think correctly, his massive pecs at eye level.

I'm waiting for him to say, ~My eyes are up here, lady . . . ~

"What is my end game?" he repeats. "Tricky question. An answer I don't think you'll like."

I stare up at him. "World domination?" I almost deadpan.

He laughs, his fiery gaze traveling over my face. "Witty little thing. But no. I'm after just one man, and after I kill him, my life's work will be done. I will be complete once again, and I can die a happy man."

I shift my leg's weight. "Revenge?"

"Too noble," he says, and sighs. "More of good old-fashioned hatred littered with jealousy." He tilts his head like he is thinking hard. "Possibly some bitterness in the mix."

I frown. "Who would you possibly be jealous of?"

He frowns. "Good point." He smiles at me, and I feel my stomach dip. "Let's just stick with the hatred then."

I notice he is closer to me, and I lift my chin. "Who's the lucky man? This hated man that is responsible for the death of a king and queen?"

He makes a sound. "Sweet Camila, it's slightly more complicated than that. It's a list, actually, but this particular man is really in for a treat, right at the top."

"A treat? Just like the king and queen got?"

Raine leans down and nips at my neck. "I love your wit. I would think something similar, yes, though I'm open to ideas."

I make a sound when I feel him suction his mouth to my skin. "Tell me who he is?" I ask as my voice breaks, feeling his tongue now.

"My beloved brother," he murmurs as his hands smooth down my hips, gripping me hard.

"Thetis?" I breathe.

"I believe that's his name, having trouble thinking right now." Raine lifts his head to stare at me. "You're surprised?"

I take a steady breath. "No, but why kill him?"

"Because I want to." Raine looks down at my breasts as his hands become more aggressive on my hips. "You never just wanted to kill someone?" He is grinning now, his gaze rising to mine. "Just randomly end someone's life?"

"Yes, but for a good reason," I say carefully.

Because he tried to kill me first. Justified.

Raine nods. "You see, I just merely want him dead. I don't like his face. It irritates me."

I'm so confused by Raine. I've never seen this side of him.

"You're messing with me, Raine," I say. "I don't believe you." I have a sense he is testing me or pushing me to see my reaction.

These can't be his real thoughts.

"I don't believe you," I say again.

"You also do not know me well enough to make that judgment," he reprimands. "I have a question for you, sorry to stray from this intense interrogation."

I bite my lip, trying to figure him out. "Should I be scared?"

"No," he says.

"Ask," I say.

"Where is that music player you had with your songs on it? I tried to," his eyes lower, "coax it out of you, but you told me you didn't know as you screamed my name." He licks his lips. "I think you were slightly distracted."

I swallow. "That was a violation."

"You're joking."

"You did things to me that I do not remember," I say, now feeling his hard body against mine. "You manipulated me."

His hand brushes over the tops of my breasts, making me shiver. "Manipulation is what I do best, if you have not noticed. But a violation—that is not true. For me to enter your dreams, you have to want it just as bad as I do. I knock and you open the door. Simple."

I frown at him. "How can I trust you?"

"You can't." He shrugs. "And, if I were you, I wouldn't."

I gasp.

I look down as his hand cups the full weight of my breast through the golden fabric.

"Why are you touching me?" I ask, my pulse hammering against my neck, my hand grabbing his wrist.

I forbid myself to get turned on right now.

Forbid. It.

I should slap him.

"That's an easy question." He rubs my nipple between his fingers, causing me to grit my teeth, his fiery gaze scorching me. "Because I want to."

"Stop," I say, holding back a moan.

"Stop?" He tilts his head at me. "But I'm ~not ~done," he barely whispers in his sexy accent. "I can already sense your arousal, and it's making me want to drive you crazy."

I grab his wrist harder, halting his movements. "This is wrong on so many levels," I whisper. He laughs and slowly lowers to his knees, making me tense, his mouth kissing my stomach. "What are you doing?!"

Raine lifts my golden skirts as he looks up at me, his hands traveling up my smooth legs, ~thanks to Pierce.~

"Relax," he whispers. His hands cup my ass and he makes a primal sound, his eyes closing for a second. "Your ass is so luscious that when I saw it back in the dungeon, I thought I was hallucinating."

I take a shaky breath. "I was high, now let me go," I plead, but I make no move to push him away. My heart is pounding, feeling his large hands caress me. I can't think straight, not when he is now kissing his way down my stomach to my girl bits through my dress.

I expel a harsh breath and hear him groan into me, vibrating me ~there.~ ~Oh~ . . .

~I'm in trouble~ . . .

I feel Raine pull my legs apart and his mouth kisses me through my gown, groaning as I feel him settle between my thighs.

"Raine," I breathe, not even sure what I mean.

Raine is breathing hard as he leans back, yanking my skirts up and over his head, making gasp.

"Spread."

I hear the command and feel him tug at my thighs.

I'm panting now, hyperventilating.

This is happening.

The first contact with his hot mouth is shocking bliss. My body is tense until I feel his tongue and the heat of his lips covering me, followed by a low, sexy moan as he tastes me. My legs nearly give out and I feel him steady me as his tongue swirls and dips into my hot core over and over again, relentlessly.

I vaguely remember what he said about his tongue and that he knew how to use it.

My head falls back, my neck unable to support it any longer. ~I believe him . . . I believe him~.

He has a rhythm, a technique, that has me seeing stars. My body's at a dangerous temperature as I feel him devour me. I'm now grabbing onto his head and I feel his hands grip me harder as he raises the tempo, as if that was even possible. I yell, or scream, or cry . . . not sure at this point.

Not sure of anything at this point.

But I come hard.

My body is vibrating, tingling, humming with the electric energy that Raine loves to yield.

I don't even notice him move until he kisses me hard, his lips taking my mouth in almost desperation, my legs wrapping around his waist as he picks me up.

"Do you want it?" he rasps in my ear. "I want to hear you say it."

I'm a lunatic, I realize.

Any Earthly woman would have zero defenses against someone like Raine. The sexual energy overrides the brain.

I will kick my ass later.

But now . . .

"Yes," I pant, and feel his tongue sweep into my mouth.

"Mmmmm," I hear him groan as his right hand works his pants.

We are kissing again, but I pull back, wanting to see him, taste him as he did me. I bite his lip and whisper against his mouth.
"Do you want my mouth?"

Raine's eyes widen, his chest rising and falling fast, the air around us practically crackling with raw energy.

My hand moves and it does not take me long to feel his hard erection through his tight pants. Raine closes his eyes and whispers something as I rub up and down the thick length of him.

I feel my face flush. Yeeeeeah, he's a big boy.

I feel dizzy with blind desire.

But yelling from outside draws Raine from out of this lust haze we both are trapped in. He makes eye contact with me as I caress him through his pants.

"Fuck," he hisses, jaw tense, and glances outside again. He grabs my wrist and holds it still, squeezing his eyes shut.

"What is it?" I whisper, my pulse still hammering.

"The rest of my men. I have to leave," he says in a low voice, and looks at me. His expression is dark and carnal. "I will see you tonight." He puts me down and leans into my neck. "Don't wear underwear tonight," he whispers, and leaves.

Raine leaves with that wicked order, jumping off the balcony into the far waters below like he is Aquaman.

I'm still reeling, breathing hard.

That just happened.

I cover my mouth, feeling my stomach dip and dip again.

What in the hell am I doing?

I close my eyes and want to bash my head into the wall.

I'm sooooo in trouble.

I'm falling for a man who will most likely get killed or imprisoned at the end of this, not giving me the life of riches I hoped for, and this man also wants Thetis dead, which will ruin the FGI mission.

If Thetis dies, the purpose is incomplete, and we all have to go home.

I couldn't stay with Raine if he kills Thetis, even if I wanted to. If I don't stop Raine, we will all lose.

"Steven!"

After a few minutes, he appears, looking pale.

"We need to talk," I say, eyes intense.

He laughs and takes out a joint. "Uh, yeah. We do. And I need to be in mystic mode for this crazy-ass shit."

I nod and rub the bridge of my nose. "I need a plan, Steven. Like, I need to escape, free Brayja, save Thetis from Raine, annnnnd have a happily-fucking-ever-after. "

Steven expels a breath. "The things I do for my gold membership."

I need a brilliant plan.

I need one now.
And, if at all possible, one that does not involve ~Ricky Martin. ~

CHAPTER 16

CAMILA

I look in the mirror and take a deep breath, trying to make sense of my thoughts. "Steven, I'm ready."

Am I though?

This is what I do best. The only thing I can do.

"Talkin' to Pierce right now," Steven says as he sits on my bed. "This is going to be almost impossible to pull off, dude. Just saying." He shakes his head.

"Fate chose me for a reason. Maybe that reason is to save this damn mission from Raine. I'm the only one that can keep Raine from killing Thetis at this point," I say, and look down.

There has to be a reason I'm here, because I know it's not for a happily-ever-after.

That ship sailed as soon as Raine showed his true colors. I have come to terms with the fact that I will be going home after all of this is over. But for now, at least I can help save the mission.

Raine is on a suicide mission that does not include me. I don't feel like falling in love with someone who will be imprisoned. I bite my lip, pushing down those deep emotions that want to roar to life and make me weak once again and call me a liar.

He can't control me the way he thinks he can, and I can't forget that.

He is out of his mind — and just because he is incredibly sexy, that does not make it okay. You can't fall in love with someone who is crazy because that's ~crazy~.

Back on Earth when I would prepare for a mission, I would do deep breathing to clear my mind of thoughts. All drama was forgotten — life's letdowns not remembered.

I was an impersonator, a manipulator.

Someone told me that I had the quickest hands in the west — I mean, upper Manhattan.

"Ouch, Camila," I whisper, and almost laugh. I guess Raine and I have something in common. Maybe that's why Pierce thought we would be good together. We're both good at being someone we are not.

Bless Pierce's heart, but he could have ruined the mission on that hunch.

Can't win them all.

But the big difference between Raine and me? I pretend, and Raine does not.

Right?

Right.

I never failed at a job because I had the ability to become an actress, to blend in and become whatever part I was portraying, stealing whatever jewels I was after. But I can feel my nerves scratching at the walls because of Raine.

He makes me nervous, which is messing with my game.

I have never tried to manipulate a manipulator.

"Okay, dude, you have to be quick . . . Like, really quick. We need that keycard that Raine keeps on him. The file that I'm reading says he keeps it under his shirt in a strap case with two latches. Must have taken it from Brayja before dragging him to the lower levels. I'm seeing that it looks kinda like a gun holster." Steven looks at me in the mirror.

"I really don't know how you are going to do that without him knowing. Raine seems weirdly perceptive. The dude's a mind-ninja."

I tamp down the panic. "I can do it," I murmur. I know the man's weakness. All men are the same—I have deceived many. I'm not gloating, but it's something I noticed with each job I took.

I need to steal the golden master key. It's the key that I always saw Brayja holding; he had it on him at all times. There is only one. He is the only one that had access to everywhere, and now Raine does.

Why do I need it?

Well, the word about what happened here has leaked, according to Pierce, and Poseidon has ordered Thetis to take Raine in.

The fall of the golden boy. Raine, the one that could do no wrong in Poseidon's eyes. Sun Hai's agent logged it in, informing all of us to work together. No hiding information.

Sun Hai and Joniqua are neck and neck for Thetis's time, and I'm not sure if I trust them just yet. But only some information qualifies to be shared. I'm not sure about what makes the cut for this twisted game, for I didn't want to read the thousand-page activity log guidelines. So I decide that logging that Thetis is walking into a fatal trap does not make the cut.

I have to get the key from Raine, then break into the central hub room where they communicate with other empires and kingdoms. It's like Skype, but with much more fantastical elements.

This world is still so alien to me. They harbor some crazy Atlantis power that is very advanced. Steven said it has a lot to do with conscious transfers, whatever that means.

I can imagine the smile on Thetis's face when he heard of what Raine did. This is a dream come true for Thetis, except for the fact that he is walking into a deadly trap that will kill him by electrocution.

Their Nymph crafts underwater cannot block the deadly currents Raine has in store for them. Raine is extremely dangerous, for the amount of power he possesses is paired with his insanity.

"So, did you ever figure out why Raine went apeshit?" Steven asks me, chewing gum. "Asking for a friend."

I turn and bite my lip. "I asked, and honestly, I think he is just out of his mind. Some people just snap, you know?"

I can't even imagine what goes on in his brain.

Steven gets up and stretches in his tight wetsuit, making me want to laugh. He looks like an egg with legs. "You want a joint? It will make you feel invisible. I use it all the time at FGI headquarters when I don't want to be noticed, works like a charm."

I give him a look. "Steven, no. Do you realize that even if you feel like you're invisible that it does not mean you are? We learn this at a young age when we play peek-a-boo. Just because you cover your face does not mean you disappear."

He stares at me with a frown.

I frown back.

"Well, you're entitled to your opinion."
"It's not my personal opinion, it's a fact, Steven," I say, mouth hanging open.

"I think you should go."

I snort and roll my eyes. "Oh, right."

"Not to change the subject, but Pierce really made you look like a black widow." He raises his eyebrows. "You look like trouble."

How come all weird men say that?
~Here comes trouble~ . . .

I told Pierce I needed to distract Raine, and boy did Pierce not hold back. The glittering black dress is scandalous indeed. The lace is suctioned to the curves of my body, but the top of the gown leaves little to the imagination. It's a large V, making my girls the center of attention, and the off-the-shoulder feather sleeves add to the seductive magic. I'm fit for the red carpet, wowing the media in my sexy choice.

Pierce said to take all jewelry off and do a seductive natural look, without all of the glam — which is weird for me, but looking at myself now, I agree.

My skin and ashy lashes are killer paired with my nude lip. My black hair is in a bun at the nape of my neck, adding to the elegance, the mysteriousness.

I take a breath.

Get your mind right.

"How much time do I have?"

Steven expels a breath. "Like ASAP. Thetis is nearing Raine's trap as we speak, and two FGI agents are on board. Raine is out for blood and needs to be stopped, maaaan." He continues, "Go out the door and down the long hallway. I think he is out on the main balcony. Go before he moves, and don't forget what we talked about. The exit plan."

Raine, like the true villain. Who happens to be the sexiest man I have ever seen. What irony.
I open the door by jamming the lock with a sleek butter knife I stole earlier. I slightly peek out, holding my breath. My heart pounds as I see the guards talking to one another, laughing in a lively exchange. I can do this. Their backs are to me, giving my first stroke of luck.

~1 . . . 2 . . . 3 . . . ~

I take a slow breath and exit, light and swift on my feet. Like a shadow, I pass them without detection. My heart pounds as I'm now out of sight, staying in the shadows. If I were to get caught, everything would be ruined—mission over for everyone.

Minutes seem like hours as I continue to walk, dodging this guard and then that. I flatten against the wall as I peek around the corner.

Raine is in the distance.

Finally.

If I could just calm my nerves. He's alone—my second stroke of luck—but for how long? I just pray he doesn't send me away immediately without me getting to manipulate him.

That's what the dress is for: Distraction. My natural look will make him look twice, forgetting that I should not be here.

Or, that's the hope.

I grab the corner of the wall and frown.

Raine sits on the marble bench with his head in his hands, seemingly in deep thought or mental torment. I bite my lip as I watch him, the first time I have been able to evaluate him without him putting on an act.

It's like I'm watching an exotic animal in the wild.

He is rubbing his hands through his black hair, and now I know why his hair always looks wild. Something strikes me as I watch him—it's not what I expected to see, not even close.

I can almost feel his anguish, which is silly.

My heart twists.

Raine lifts his head back and his eyes are closed, and there is no denying that he is not doing well. I have seen that look before, and it resembles something I thought Raine was immune to feeling.

Living on the streets when I was thrown out of the place I grew up in, you see that expression a lot.

Pain.

That's as bluntly as I can describe it. It's such a simple word, but the meaning runs deep, leaving destruction in its path. Raine is in pain, and I'd put money on the fact that if he knew I was watching him, he'd be furious.

I close my eyes, feeling a sense of guilt wash over me. I don't have the time to figure out what torments him so much. And more importantly, I don't have a choice, even if I did.

Rule number ONE.

Do not get emotionally involved—that's when mistakes happen. I look back to Raine, and his head is back in his hands. He is a threat to FGI, and I have no choice.

Game face.
~"Dude, you have it yet?~"
I curse. "Shut up, not yet," I whisper, feeling sick. I swallow and start my walk towards him, feeling out of sorts. I don't mind being deceitful to insane, evil Raine.

But this is broken Raine . . .

His head looks up at the sound of my heels, and my pulse jumps. I will never get over how he can render me breathless with one blazing look.

I try to slip into my detached, mission mode, but it's hard.

The way he's gazing at me right now has me wanting to stop, turn around, and run the other way. But I can't.

I see something in his gaze that I'd rather not think on.

It's not anger.

It's like when you are told your whole life that unicorns don't exist, and one just appears before you.

That look.

I stop in front of him and I see his eyes trace over my natural face, devoid of the Valkyrie's heavy makeup. I must look foreign to him, but Pierce did me a solid.

"Need some company?" I ask, trying to ignore how hot he looks in his disheveled appearance.

He makes a sound. "Well, well, the kitty-cat has come out to play," he barely says with a slight grin, but makes no move to stand.

They have cats here?

Noted.

Cats are everywhere.

I can see that the circles under his eyes are deeper, making him look very dangerous. I take a deep breath, feeling the hairs on my neck rise. "You should try sleeping, Raine. You look tired." My plan is to steal his power with a kiss, so I need to cut the small talk.

That makes him laugh and he licks his lower lip.

I shift as he just watches me, feeling my confidence crack. "Are you just going to stare at me? Or are you going to kiss me?"

Damn. Shit. Bastard.

I sound nervous.

Raine laughs again and tilts his head, his gaze still roaming over my face. "You look different. I like it."

I shiver, cursing the heat flashing through my body at his praise.

"Relax," he says with a sexy grin.

I quit.

I feel like he can see right through me, turning me into putty on command. "Maybe I should leave then," I say, and turn, but I'm jerked back. Raine is standing right in front of me now.

"You want me to kiss you?"

I take a calming breath and look up at him. "Yes."

"Why?"

"Do I need a reason?"

His hand grabs the feathers at my bare shoulder. "Where did you get this gown? This is not Valkyrie fashion, Camila," he chides, his hand falling to my cleavage. My skin tingles as his fingers brush over my breasts. "You're trying hard," he murmurs with a heavy breath. His expression probably mirrors mine.

"Is it working?" I ask breathlessly, feeling a tad light-headed as his hand rubs over me. I just want him to take me to his room and lock me there, never letting me leave.

Focus.

Raine groans and lowers his mouth to mine, and the shock of his lips is delicious, luscious. My arms circle around his neck as I feel him kiss me harder.

I moan, loving his tongue, the erotic taste of him. He's not sloppy, but precise, having this rhythm that is easily matched.

He syncs with me instead of trying to be aggressive and overpowering. I'd imagine that's how he makes love—perfectly matching his partner's rhythm, taking them to the next level with him.

Raine's hand holds my head to his mouth as he tastes me and devours me expertly.

"Let's leave here, us together," I whisper, wanting desperately not to betray him. I kiss at his lips, my teeth grazing his lower lip.

If I could just get him to come with me and to drop this Thetis thing, then I would not have to steal his power. I would like to avoid drama at all costs, for once.

"Please."

He raises his head to look at me, his body pressing into me harder, his arm wrapping around my waist. "Mmmm. You're adorable," he murmurs with a smile.

I frown, feeling his hands on my ass. "Why not?"

Raine leans down and kisses my neck. "Because I'm selfish," he says as his hands squeeze me hard. "You have no idea who I am to make that rash decision, which is very naive on your part. But I can tell you that you are mine," he almost hisses in my ear. "I will kill Thetis and still fuck you every night. Do you understand?" he asks, and sucks my neck. "Tonight, I have something quite special planned for you, though you might not be able to walk tomorrow."

My pulse is pounding.

Damn it.

I can't talk.

Should I be upset or turned on?

"You think to save me?" he asks, and looks at me, lifting my chin. "Or have you something else swarming around in that pretty head of yours? It's driving me insane, not knowing what you're feeling."

I swallow, trying to focus on anything but Raine making love to me. ~Oh boy~.

Think of starving baby animals. Get pissed. Focus.

"I . . . "

He looks over my shoulder then back to me. "I have to go, but go down to the lounge and have a drink. I want you relaxed for me. I'll come take you shortly."

I shiver.

Mercy.

Yes, please, take me.
~"Dude!!! Hurrrrrrry!~"
My brain snaps back to reality.

Shiiieeeeet.

"One more kiss," I moan, and bite my lip, giving him my come-get-me eyes, rubbing myself on him.

He groans as he watches me, his thumb rubbing over my bottom lip as my tongue darts out to suck on him. Raine closes his eyes and takes a large breath, lowering his mouth to mine.

Do it, Camila.

You have too.

I sucked in his essence so fast I bet he didn't even know what hit him, but I'm sure he felt it. Raine jerks his head up in complete horror, almost in slow motion.

I feel his power coursing through me and I react with the first thing that comes to my mind. I see the rage in his gaze as I blast him against the wall so hard he lies still, sliding to the ground.

My ears are ringing.

What . . . just happened . . .

"Dude!! Come on!" Steven says beside me. "Holy shit, did you kill him?!"

No . . .

I crawl over to Raine on my hands and knees, my vision still blurry.

"Raine!"
Steven opens Raine's black shirt to retrieve the key card. "I'll do it if you can't. Come on, focus!"

I look at Steven then back to Raine and immediately feel his neck, in a full-blown panic. I wait as I try to calm my breathing.

"Dude, your eyes are orange! Trippy."

I expel a breath when I feel a steady beat. "He's alive."

I close my eyes, thanking the heavens. My eyes widen as I see Steven handcuff Raine to the stone balcony. "Where did you find those? Pierce?"

"No. Brayja's room. Tons of bondage stuff in the massive wardrobe next to the bed." Steven shrugs. "When homeboy wakes up to find his woman gone, he's going to be livid, dude. Let's get the hell out of here."

I hate this feeling I'm having, like I'm torn.

"You coming?!"

I grit my teeth. "Yes," I say and curse, I have no damn choice.

I hate this.

Raine will be so ticked to find out that I will be on Thetis's ship. Nope, that will not go over well at all. He can't blow up Thetis if I'm standing next to him.

Can he?

Guess we will find out.

CHAPTER 17

CAMILA

I'm running on pure adrenaline.

~Stay focused, Camila~.

Raine will be beyond pissed when he wakes. I don't really know what he is capable of because, as he so calmly pointed out, I really do not know him at all.

Could he kill me? Rage drives people to do horrific acts.

I might not be enough to stop Raine from destroying Thetis.

"Where next?" I say under my breath, staying in the shadows as Steven follows me. "We have to hurry."

Raine could wake up at any time.

I feel sick with nerves.

"This is the last left. Then you are going to have to take out some guards. I'm getting alerts beeping in my ear," he says like it's no big deal. "The control room is heavily guarded."

I turn to look at Steven. "What?! How?" I hiss under my breath. "Throw my heel at them?"

He laughs, eyes heavy-lidded. "Hold on. I have to see what I can get you. It has to be approved by tech support—players are allowed weapons depending on their character's role."

I look down at my glittering gown and frown. "Can you ask Pierce to make me blend in more? I can't do this wearing this skimpy dress." If I run in this dress, everything will fall out, guaranteed.

Steven is typing.

"Hurry." My pulse is hammering as I wait, closing my eyes. I can't stop imagining Raine's rage when he finds out I betrayed him.

I snort—it's not like he has my best interest at heart. I owe him nothing. He ruined my chances at being queen, living a life of luxury.

So I'm confused about why I feel so guilty.

"Pierce says hi," Steven murmurs, blinking. "Yes, he already has an outfit ready to be downloaded." He pauses.
"Oh siiiick, we can get guns that shoot electric currents. Nymphs are sensitive to that, as you well know. Am I right? Or am I right?" He laughs. "I'm so right."

I tense when I hear voices. "Today, Steven, today."

Steven coughs into his hand. "Spin."

I spin as my heart thuds in my chest, praying I don't hear Raine. I suck in a breath when my skin feels hot and tingly, and the flash of light leaves me temporarily blind.

That kinda hurt. I put my hand on the wall to steady myself.

"Duuuuude, nice ass," Steven says.

"You want to get slapped?" I whisper, and blink, looking down at myself as my vision rights itself.

"Maybe. I'm no stranger to a little pain with pleasure. I have a lot of layers to me, like an onion."

I don't comment. ~Gross~.

I'm in the dark wetsuit pants that all of the Nymphs wear with tall grey boots. My midriff tank top is the shade of army green and suctions to my girls perfectly.

Pierce could make a dumpster and a toilet look hot.

I have a gun belt on, along with a small black pack on my back. I look like one of Raine's people, a rebel Nymph.

"Dude, your shoes morph into flippers in the water. It's super practical."

I look down. "Wow."

I feel like Lara Croft.

My hair is in a sleek ponytail, and the only thing I'm missing is face paint. I pull out the gun from my holster and notice Steven has one too. "Pierce gave you a gun?"

"Dude, I could save your life."

"Don't shoot me," I say, and flatten against the wall harder.

He's pointing the gun at his head, inspecting it.

"So we just shoot them? Will it kill them?" I whisper, hearing the voices near.

"I don't know," Steven says as he narrows his eyes. "But it's about to go downnnn." He powers on the gun, and it glows blue. "Let's go, babe."

I glare at him.

"Sorry, always wanted to say that while in combat."

"Fair enough," I mutter, and power on my gun while taking a calming breath. ~You can do this, easy-peasy.~

After counting to three, we charge the men around the corner, who were stunned, shocked to see us running at them.

Screams.

Yells.

Electric currents flow from our guns like invisible flame-throwers from Hell. I'm breathing hard as I watch the men convulse on the ground, clutching themselves.

"Shit," I breathe.

"They will be fine!" Steven yells, and runs past me in his tight suit, his fat rolls jiggling. "Come on! Getting alerts! We have, but minutes before Thetis crosses the trap Raine set up, then they will be toast. Like, burnt toast!"

I tense when I hear loud commotions coming from down the hallway. We both look at each other and expel a breath.

Raine.

"Double shit," I get out, and use the key to open up the room, blasting everyone inside like Rambo. They don't even have a chance as they all fall to the floor in pain.
"Lock the door!" I yell, and run over to a large screen, seeing a map of some sort. "How does this work?!"

Steven locks the door right as I hear Raine on the other side.

"CAMILA! DON'T YOU FUCKING DO IT!"

Steven looks pale as we hear the door being hit with something substantial. Steven turns and runs over to me, eyes wide.

"Here, put these on your temples. Tech support is finding me the number to Thetis's rig."

I flinch when I hear more yelling and pounding. We have but seconds before Raine breaks the door down. I place the metal pieces on my temples, and immediately I'm dizzy. A picture forms in my mind's eye, but it's fuzzy.

"Oh my gosh," I breathe. "I might throw up."

"Hold on, typing in the number."

I hear Raine yelling, making my heart jump. "Hurry!"

~"Who is this?!~" a man yells in my head.
Weird.
"Hi, can you hear me?"

Steven rolls his eyes. "You must think it, not say it, genius."

~"Who is this?~" he asks again, and I can see an image of a man, but it's hard to make out.

~"Hi, can you hear me?~" I think, trying to project it.

"~I can hear you. I will tell you that we are coming and there is nothing you can do to stop this. Who am I speaking to? Please confirm whether Prince Brayja is still living, immediately,~" he says in a forceful tone.

~"I'm here to warn you that you are about to drive into Raine's trap that will kill you by shock. I'm not certain what it is, but I do know that if you do not stop right now, everyone will perish.~

~"My name is Daphine, Prince Brayja's fiancee . . . well, former fiancee.~
"
~"Raine did what?! You will not have me gone that easily.~"

~"It's not a bluff! I broke into the control room to warn you. You have to stop!~"
"Dude, he is right on it," Steven says. "Shit, get him to stop."

~"I need proof of your identity — ~"
I hear yelling and screams.

I look at Steven. "I think they hit it!"

No . . .

"Hold on," Steven wipes the sweat from his forehead, "agents are logging in and saying that FGI agents got the green light as soon as you called. They engaged their shields at the last minute, only wounding some. It lessened the blow of Raine's attack, or they would be dead." Steven looks at me. "Dude, that was like seconds."

"They are safe?"

"Yeah, kinda. They are not dead, so that's a good thing."

~"Where the fuck is Raine's position?!~" the man yells in my head.

~"Oh . . . uh, currently trying to break down the door.~"

~"Get out of there! If you can escape you may find refuge here, we are pulling back from injury.~"

~"Thank—~" I scream as the door smashes in, sparks with sounds of electricity.

"Run!" Steven yells, and we both take off, using the key to unlock the nearest door. I turn to look behind me to see Raine jumping over a long table. I scream as I close the door just in time, locking it.

"Fuck!" I hear Raine yell as he pounds the door. "Camila, don't run from me!"

My heart pounds as we take off, running down long hallways and into random rooms using the key. "Where are we going?"

Steven tries to keep up and holds his side. "Side ache!"

I stop, breathing hard. "Where are we going?!"

"We are a-almost there. We need to make it to the s-subs. Once we are in

227

one, Raine can't stop us. We can meet up with Thetis." He wheezes. "You go ahead. I need to shape-shift, or I might die."

"Raine," I breathe. "Where is he?"

Steven shakes his head and looks around. "Who knows, that man is a ninja. I really don't think you are going to make it far."

I shake my head. "Thanks."

I take off down hallway after hallway for what seems like forever. I tense at every corner expecting to see Raine.

"I can smell the water."

~"Dude, you have to sneak over and get in any small vehicle. There are men out there, so be careful.~

~"Take your next left and you will see Brayja's fleet. It's in an underground cave. It's where they keep their main subs and shit.~"

I curse as I make my way into the massive underground cave. I can hear men's voices yelling back and forth, echoing off the towering walls. I can smell the fresh saltwater and feel a slight breeze. I'm on high alert, tiptoeing ever so gently.

My eyes widen, taking in the sheer size of this place—glistening rock with marble archways, and a massive teal pool that disappears into the dark sea.

~"Stay low. Do you see that small golden rig suspended up on your right? It's a five-person sub, perfect for sneaking into.~"

"I don't know how to operate it, Steven," I whisper, peeking over a massive metal thing with glowing buttons, seeing distant Nymphs with weapons. They are not close to me, on a remote landing off in the distance.

"No one is around here," I say with relief.

A slight stroke of luck.

"~I can drive it. It's a part of our training as FGI agents. I just need to smoke a little more, it helps with my memory loss~."

Memory loss? I grit my teeth. I close my eyes, not feeling confident in Steven's abilities. "Alright, I am getting in," I whisper. "Does it just drop into the water? How do we get it down?"

~"Yea, there is like some release button. Then once it drops, we are home free.~"

Home free?

Yeah right. I'm taking one for the team, sacrificing any possibility with Raine. I want to laugh. He will hate me—like, ~really~ hate me.

Don't think about that.

I quietly make my way up a ladder then onto another landing right next to the small, suspended rig. This is it.

"Okay, Steven—"

I feel a strong arm grab me around the waist and jerk me backward. It happens so fast that my brain doesn't have time to comprehend it before I'm flat on my back with Raine's powerful thighs pinning me to the ground.

His hand covers my mouth, and he leans down to say, "Shhhh."

He looks livid.

"I want a word alone with you without my men here, so don't scream." I can see the threat in his blazing gaze.

I nod.

~"Dude! Shit! You caught by Raine!~"

No shit, Sherlock.

"Camila," Raine says quietly, like he is barely keeping his temper in check. "Pray tell, where were you off to?"

I don't say anything.

229

He makes a sound. "If you think you were the hero back there, alerting Thetis, then you are wrong." Raine's voice makes me shiver, my fear probably showing on my face. "But I'll hand it to you, you surprised me, which is hard to do these days. I thought you just wanted me to make you scream all night," he tilts his head, "not betray me in the worst way."

I almost flinch.

"I'm not yours, Raine. I am not loyal to you. I'm your prisoner," I get out, then instantly regret it.

Did I see hurt in his eerie gaze?

I see his jaw flex, then he leans back on his knees and closes his eyes. It's tough to think when his large package is practically in my face, the tight black pants hiding little.

Different thoughts . . .

"Tell me you were not seeking out Thetis," he hisses, his muscles flexing like he can't control it, blinded by rage.

I want to disappear.

I don't say anything.

He expels a breath and looks down at me. "I'm shocked for the second time today, and it seems I don't know you like I thought I did." His hand feathers across my bare ribs, my shirt hiked up. His thumb apply pressure. "I'm also perplexed by how you were able to change so fast. You look completely different." His gaze moves over my breasts then back up to me.

I swallow.

. . . There is this guy named Pierce Charming . . . he causes a lot of pain for a lot of men.

Raine lifts his hand, and the back of his knuckles graze over my nipple through my shirt, making me clench. He expels a breath as his hand cups me like he can't help it.

"You have help, and a lot of it," Raine breathes, watching his hand intently, practically salivating. "I want to know who," he looks back at me, "or I can cut off your wrist, removing the bracelet."

My eyes widen. I can't tell if he's serious. It's hard to think at the moment.

"Raine, I will stay with you if you promise to not kill Thetis," I say, then realize how that sounds.

His gaze turns deadly. "Why the fuck do you care about Thetis?" he whispers, his hand leaving my breast. "And you're not leaving me, just so we are clear."

Shit . . .

"Um, because I care for you, and if you hurt Thetis, you could . . . " I try to think, "get yourself killed."

He laughs, actually laughs. "Liar."

It's actually not a lie, but why would he trust me?

"I will ask once more: Who the fuck is helping you? Where is that little fat servant you have with you all the time? Steven, right?" Raine asks, his gaze searing me.

"Right here BIIIITCH!"

My eyes widen when Steven swings a metal rod at Raine with all of his might, hitting Raine's broad shoulder.

I suck in a breath as the metal rod seems to fly off of Raine, catapulting twenty feet away with a loud ~clank~. Raine frowns at Steven like he was just hit with a feather and is offended.

Steven swallows and holds up his hands. "Kidding, totally kidding." Steven backs up with his hands still raised, sweaty.

"What the fuck?" Raine says, and looks back at me.

I grit my teeth. "Steven, you idiot. Use your gun!"

MORON!

Steven's eyes widen. "Oh shit, yeah." He pulls out his gun and points it at Raine, his hand shaking. "Get off her, homeboy."

Raine's eyes widen as he studies the weapon. "Where did you get that?" he hisses.

Steven snorts. "From your mom."

Raine looks perplexed. "My mother?"

I groan. "Don't listen to him," I mutter. "I'd get off because he ~will~ shoot you. He's very flighty."

Raine's confusion turns to fury as he gets up with his hands raised. "You leave, Camila, and you are fucking dead to me."

I expel a breath, my heart pounding. "Then tell me you will not kill Thetis." My voice breaks.

Raine's wild hair and stunning features make my chest tighten as I watch him watch me. I want to know his story, but I don't have the time.

The mission comes first, and I'm taking the fall for it.

He glares at me. "You will regret this."

I feel my eyes well up. "Tell me why you want him dead. Help me understand," I whisper.

"Get out of my fucking sight," he hisses. "And now that I think about it, you did me a favor. I wanted to kill him with my bare hands instead, to see the life leave his soulless eyes."

I shiver.

This is heavy. Thetis is in major danger.

I feel a tear stream down my face.

"Leave before I change my mind and shove that gun down his throat," Raine threatens, looking at Steven.

Steven's eyes widen.

He's letting me leave, and it feels like my heart is ripping. "I'm sorry," I whisper, and hug myself. I hate the hurt I see in his expression, and all I want to do is run into his arms.

"Mmmm, not as much as I am," he whispers.

"Are you going to follow me, or blow me up?" I ask, not trusting him.

I can see his jaw ticking. "Goodbye, Camila."

And we leave.
Just like that.

And something tells me that this fuckery is just starting. The look in Raine's gaze was not that of the hungry lion, but the cunning fox.

He let me go for a reason.

CHAPTER 18

CAMILA

We are intercepted.

My mind is in a fog. That unsettling fog that floats around a graveyard, hiding things that don't want to be seen.

Like, maybe, my feelings towards Raine.

I feel like I betrayed him, running off to his arch-enemy to protect him. It's nuts. I don't blame Raine for despising me now, and that thought makes me sick. I close my eyes, thinking about what Raine had planned for me before this.

Raine had said, -"You won't be able to walk the next day . . . I want you relaxed . . . ~"

I shiver just thinking about it.

Something that is now just a fantasy, running scenarios, pretending that I, Camila, won a happily-ever-after with the sexiest man alive.

Swoon.

Not—because RAINE IS CRAZY.

"Dude, pay attention. Thetis is coming." Steven elbows me in the ribs. We are standing in a massive sub close to the size of Brayja's, except their styles are completely opposite.

I look around the large room with windows almost two stories high, the dark ocean visible all around me. I see a crack in one of the window panes that some Nymphs are trying to repair. This rig took some damage from Raine. It was too close — the mission could have been over.

I still have so much to learn about the Nymphs and this underwater Atlantis. I feel so out of place here without Brayja and Raine.

The Nymphs are staring at me like I have two heads. Maybe they are not used to seeing Valkyrie women in rogue-Nymph attire? Especially one that is of royalty, and almost married to the crown prince of the Gaya Empire.

I get it. They don't know that I'm an agent from another planet. It's fine.

A double agent taking one for the team. I still have my gold nose ring in and five sparkling diamonds in each ear, thanks to Pierce. So I should not look too far-fetched. I'm still pierced.

I think about that — maybe I should change my clothes. Maybe it's my tits in this crop top attracting all the attention. Sometimes I don't know if Pierce works for me or against me.

I clear my throat as I look around and ignore the men's stares.

The dark metal gleams like black diamonds, and it's accented with a gothic beauty that reminds me of Raine. I grit my teeth — ~stop it~.

A large man enters, holding a bandage or an ice pack to his head.

Thetis. I remember him.

He is muscular and handsome, but bulkier than Raine. Both very arresting men — I will give credit where it's deserved. But I will say this: Thetis, with my quick assessment, does not possess that raw sexiness that Raine yields without trying. But maybe that's just me. I could be biased.

When you see Thetis, you think, '~Wow, he is very handsome, dashing, and strong~.' Raine, on the other hand, might be more of a reaction like, '~I want you, I need you, I can't fucking breathe~.'

235

I take a breath and try for two seconds to not think about ~him~.
Maybe crazy is sexy.

Steven elbows me again.

Shit, Thetis asked me a question.

"Thetis," I say, and blush.

He lowers the bandage and tilts his head at me, his blue gaze eyeing me up and down. I swallow, my cheeks reddening even more. "Daphine?" he asks with a frown. "Daughter of King Nyson and Nomira of the North?"

I look at Steven. "Yes."

"Unbelievable," Thetis says as his gaze searches mine, hands on his hips. "I saw you after my men saved you from the Orcs, and I could not believe it. Did your parents hide you away all your life, then? I have never seen the likes of you before. It baffles me."

I swallow. "Uh, yes. My parents were very protective of me."
~"I can still talk in your head even though I'm right next to you. Cool, huh? Uh, your parents were very abusive and kept you hidden. The North is very brutal from what I read, it's not a secret. I meant to tell you that but I forgot . . . ~"
Thetis frowns. "Hmm, I can see why, I suppose. Selling you to the highest bidder, a diamond in the rough." Thetis tilts his head as he studies me.

I'm FGI beautiful. I understand his fascination.
"Yes," I say, and shift when his eyes fasten to my breasts again, then my bare stomach. This man is not hiding what he is looking at like most of the men here.
~Just stay cool, don't act like it's bothering you.~
He smiles at me finally, showing his sharp canines. "What an unusual situation. I'm so happy you are unharmed. And please let me say that I'm so grateful for your warning. We all could have been dead, and for that, I owe you a debt. I hope you realize that Raine has lost his damn mind," he mutters, and nods to the men around us. "Leave us."

Thetis looks at Steven. "Leave."

Steven nods, nearly tripping over a dip in the floor. I cringe and look back at Thetis, who is still looking over my body like I'm on display at a museum.

"You should take a picture, it lasts longer," I get out, then cringe again.

Batting two for zero.

His expression does not change, and I want to slap my forehead at the lame retort. He then laughs and sits down in front of me on a ledge, still studying me.

This is awkward.

Thetis has very long blond hair that is tied back tightly in twists, and his black and silver attire speaks of great wealth.

Something I once had with Brayja.

But alas.

Thetis's features are more ruggedly manly, in a sense, rather than Raine's dark beauty. I hate to compare the two, but I can't help it. It's like comparing a lion to a deadly viper. You can't, it doesn't make sense.

"So, let's start from the moment you left with Brayja. What happened to make Raine and my traitor sister betray the crown of Selestia?"

I lean back against the wall, cross my arms over my chest, and exhale. "Raine is a puzzle to me. What happened is confusing to me as well as everyone else. I do not even know if Brayja is still alive."

"Is that so," he murmurs with a smile. "I'm not changing the subject, but you're probably one of the most beautiful Valkyries I have ever seen. It's a major compliment and also a mystery."

I don't say anything to that.

237

He laughs and looks down, then back up to me. "You know what I'm getting at."

I falter. Should I?

"I don't," I say, frowning.

He rubs a hand down his face and exhales. "How sheltered were you?"

"Very," I get out. "Enlighten me."

"Enlighten you?" Thetis frowns at me. "I will try and get this out as lightly as I can," he murmurs with amusement now in his gaze, and his eyes bore into me. "You're intimate with Raine. I know this."

My eyes widen. Thetis should not know that.

He eyes my body again. "You have to be. I have known Raine for most of my life, unfortunately. I would bet my life on it, in fact."

I bite my lip, trying to see what he has to go on besides my looks. "What? Just because you think I'm attractive and that Raine wants me, we must have been intimate? That seems like a stretch, especially since he travels with your sister. I was to marry Brayja, if you can remember. Should I be offended? I think you should watch what you say to me."

Right?!
The fact that he is ~right ~does not matter.

"You are sheltered, perplexing me. No, you should not be offended, but realize who you are messing with," he warns, making me shiver. "Raine is not the man you want obsessing over you."

I glare.

I'm not sheltered. I just have a really bad agent that tells me nothing because he's eating chips.

Thetis exhales. "Daphine, Daphine. Raine is obsessed with Valkyrie

238

women, always has been—claims they taste better—but I think he rejects our own race. Or he's just as insane as he appears," he says, and I can sense the deep vibrations of fury radiating off of him.

"If Raine heard of a Valkyrie with untold beauty, trust me, Raine would have her. He would find her, bed her, and be done with her. Everyone knows of his obsession with beautiful Valkyrie women because it's really the only weakness we know of. It's not a secret, so naturally, it makes me wonder."

I swallow, not sure how to take this.

Raine has a Valkyrie fetish? Did Pierce know that?

"Which is why I think Brayja was so pleased to have something over that crazy bastard." He eyes me. "I bet Raine forgot how to breathe when he first saw you," he laughs, and leans forward. "I have been looking for a weakness in him for years, and I'm wondering about his reaction to you."

When he first saw me? Not sure if he was breathless or utterly confused. I'm not sure how to take this information.

"I'm not sure what you're getting at."

Yes, I am, but still.

"I need to know what Raine is thinking. To get into the mind of the insane, you must understand that this is very important information to me." He leans up. "Did you escape then? Against his will?"

"Yes," I whisper.
Thetis smiles. "I'd imagine so. How intimate were you? Sex? Do you have nipple rings?"

I gasp. "Excuse me?"

"Forgive the personal questions. I just want to know if he will come charging in here to take back his Valkyrie prize. If so, I will be ready. He is not the only one that can set up a trap," he says. "So please, do not leave out any details."

I shift, not sure if I like this man. "If I tell you what you want to know, then you must tell me what I want to know."

"Which is?"

"Your feud with Raine," I say, and raise my chin.

"There is no feud."

I laugh. "That's a lie."

Really? No feud?

"How can you be sure? Raine has lost his mind. He has always been unpredictable." He continues, "Now tell me the level of your relationship? Do you mean something to him? To what level? Or has he lost interest in you?" he asks as his blue stare watches my every movement.

My mouth hangs open. "So your sister is in love with a mentally insane man?"

Thetis closes his eyes and leans back, taking a moment. "My sister is reckless and foolish."

"Tell me how she could fall in love with a mad man," I pry. There has to be some draw to Raine besides his looks. Nomi has to have seen something in Raine to be so loyal to him that she would go against her family and the crown.

He laughs and stares at me. "You will not understand, being from the North. Raine and his mother are from Cerionis Sose, not many know that. Something my father's family tries to cover up."

"Cerionis ~Sose~?" I hope I say that right.

Thetis frowns at me. "You do not know what a Sose is?"

I bite my lip, waiting for Steven to chime in.

~Come on~! I think.

~"Dude, sorry. Uhhh, Soses are not highly looked upon colonies in the deep sea, to the west. They are still under the rule of Poseidon but are considered rebels of the sea. They are growing in numbers and causing major problems. They want independence and all that stuff . . . ~"

"Yes," I say.

That explains Raine's army. He was born a rebel? And his mother?

"Hmm, you look like you don't know much about what I'm talking about. Oddly enough, since you're dressed like one." Thetis smiles and tilts his head. "Now tell me what I want to know. We don't have the time for small talk."

I grit my teeth. "Yes, we were intimate." I swallow. "We have not slept together, but have done enough to be considered intimate."

"I thought so," he whispers, hand on his chin, and he crosses his arms. "Anything else?"

I wave my hand, showing my bracelet. "Before I put this on, he was attached to me without me knowing."

Thetis's eyes widen, sitting up. "He was what?"

"He was attached to me for a few days . . . "

Thetis stands up, breathing hard. "You're sure?"

"Very," I say, and feel my face heat.

Thetis turns and runs up a couple of stairs and presses a button, body ridged. "Opis, I need you to ground here and set up the shifter! Raine is coming, and we need him to engage. Have my men ready. This is what we have been waiting for. Inform my father." He turns to look back at me. "Tell me more."

I save Thetis only to have him kill Raine?!

I can't win.

I feel sick.

"Raine acted normal until I put on the bracelet. He went crazy after that."

"You broke it off with him being attached? Brutal. Tell me, it takes a lot of power to hold onto someone like that, which surprises me. I didn't think Raine had it in him to do that. How did he fend off—"

"A crown."

Thetis looks like he won the lottery, rubbing a hand down his face. "He wore his crown?" he whispers, almost like he cannot contain his excitement.

"Yes," I say, and feel my heart pounding. "Tell me about Raine. Now," I hiss, feeling my eyes cramp. I'm setting up Raine to be killed. "Why the feud?"

Thetis smiles at me, but it's cold. "There is no feud, my dear. He is delusional. It's not as complicated as you think, it's quite the opposite."

"There is!" I scream, and Thetis tilts his head at me, studying me. "I'm not dumb. I can see the hatred in Raine's eyes when he speaks of you. Something happened!"

Thetis exhales and his jaw clenches. "Fuck . . . you too?!" he says, and looks at me. "You're in love with him too? What the fuck is it with him? The man needs to be put out of his misery! He murdered the king and queen of the Gaya Empire and your betrothed. And you fucking still love him? Why?!"

"I didn't say that," I whisper as I see men rushing in.

Thetis almost glares at me. "You didn't have to. I have seen that look in Nomi's eyes, and it disgusts me."

I close my eyes.

There is no feud? That can't be right. I saw so much hurt and pain in Raine's gaze, an amount that you can't fake.

Or can he?

I hug myself, feeling so confused. I need to talk to Pierce and find out what is lies and what is truth. I feel my heart being pulled in two different directions.

"Steven," I whisper as I feel tears stream down my face. "What are they doing?"

~"They have enough explosives to blow Raine to the next orbit.~"

"Fuck," I whisper. "What do I do?"

I can't have Raine killed.

I can't.

I can't breathe.

~"Talking to Pierce. He's saying you need to find Sun Hai. She's on board and may have more information.~"

Sun Hai. I completely forgot about her.

I wipe a tear and nod, trying to pull myself together. I watch Thetis talking to his men and ordering them around frantically.

"You think he will come for her? This is a risk, Thetis," a dark-haired man about the same size to Thetis says with his hands on his hips.

Thetis turns to look at me. "I do. Raine, as far as I know, has never shown this level of attachment." He looks at the man and gives him a pointed look. "Not even for Nomi." He nods and glances at me, eyeing me from head to toe. "She's definitely his type, but will he come for her?"

Thetis's exhales. "She escaped."

"He will want her back," the man agrees, and looks back at me. "It's the best chance we have."

"It's our only chance," Thetis says.

~"Dude. Somehow, I think that Raine is not dumb enough to come for you. I'm smoking right now, and tapping into some deep shit.~"

I frown. "You can't be sure, though," I whisper.

I need to stop Thetis, but I don't know how.

~"Well, Pierce didn't seem panicked to me.~"

"Pierce is weird, and you're high."

~"He's a king.~"

I roll my eyes and pinch the bridge of my nose, feeling like I might throw up. "I need to stop Thetis."

But how?!
~"Dude, think about it. Raine is smarter than that shit. He doesn't seem like the dude to get killed like this. He's a ninja.~"

"Thetis, I'm not getting any readings anywhere near us," a man yells to Thetis. "We have been here for almost an hour and nothing." Thetis turns to look at me, "He has to come," he grits, looking nervous, flexing his muscles. "Daphine," he yells, "anything else you can tell us?"

I swallow as everyone looks at me. "Not that I can think of," I say, feeling my nerves take flight.

Maybe Steven is right. Relief flashes over me.

"What did he say when you escaped? Anything of importance?" the other man says, and walks up to me, his dark eyes intense.

I frown, remembering the look in Raine's eyes when I left.

"What is it?" the man hisses, and holds up his hand to silence whoever started talking to his left.

" . . . Technically, I didn't actually escape."

Thetis's head jerks towards mine. "What?!"

I quickly continue. "Well, I was escaping," I say, and look at everyone, "but at the last minute, Raine let me go."

The man looks back at Thetis, and the color drains from his face, making him even paler. "He let her go, Thetis," he hisses. "That changes everything!"

"Daphine, that would be information I needed to know! I thought you escaped!" Thetis yells, and runs over to the large screen. "Get me a larger view, scan everywhere! Fuck!"

"But I still escaped, and he was not happy about it," I say meekly, but secretly I am relieved.

Steven is right—Raine is a ninja.

I try to hide my smile.

"Thetis, you're not going to believe this."

"Fucking try me," he gets out, breathing hard.

"The Selestia watch has just informed me that Raine is approaching the palace," he says, eyes wide.

Thetis rubs a hand down his face. "Why the fuck would he turn himself in?! That's suicide!" He turns towards his men. "Head to the palace!"

"Only if he is turning himself in," the dark-haired man says.

Thetis is breathing hard. "You mean he is attacking?" He turns toward the man on the radar. "Is he attacking?! Ask!"

The pale Nymph wipes his forehead, "Uh, they are saying he is coming in peace, and he has Brayja, unharmed and . . . happy?"

There is silence around the room.

A pin could drop.

Raine is turning the tables.

"And he is claiming innocence."

Thetis yells and throws something at the wall. "Running to Mommy? I am going to kill him with my bare hands!"

My heart is pounding.

I think the feeling is mutual.

Raine has just become the puppet master.

CHAPTER 19

CAMILA

I shiver as I see the entrance into Selestia, the ancient kingdom of many sea myths.

"Steven, pinch me . . . "

Poseidon's realm. This does not seem real.

We all stand in the central control room, ready to make a hasty exit. My eyes are wide as they take in the scene outside of the sub's windows. I feel like some epic choir music needs to be playing in the background to set the mood.

It looks like a massive mountain that is actually a wall as far as the eye can see. The entrance is a large archway the height of a skyscraper. Giant statues of Nymph warriors line the city's wall, giving it an ancient and mythological feel.

It's terrifying.

The water is crystal clear, allowing me to see tons of sea life and traffic everywhere. Millions of people inhabit this underwater city, and I can see Nymphs swimming everywhere.

I turn towards Steven. "What's happening? Any updates? Thetis's men have been running around like chickens with their heads cut off for the last hour," I whisper.

Steven gives me a look. "That's because Raine is dicking them around, always one step ahead it seems. Can't mess with a ninja."

"What does that mean?"

"Daphine." Thetis walks up to me, seemingly out of breath. He has been yelling at everyone, walking around like he just did lines of coke. "Raine is being held by Selestia authorities. His trial is immediate. He claims innocence!" he yells, then laughs, jaw flexing.

"I don't see how he has the proof for that absurd claim. He is clearly delusional, and everyone will see it. We have received word — proof — that Raine slaine the King and Queen in cold blood, and we have many witnesses. I need you to testify. Can you do that? You might be the one to turn the tables on him — the only one."

His blue gaze sears mine, daring me to say no.

TESTIFY?

Hell. No.

I glance at Steven then back to Thetis. "I . . . "

He tilts his head at me. "I'm not letting Raine get away with this, Daphine. So help me, if you choose to lie, I will have no choice but to act."

I swallow and look around at all the faces staring at me. "Are you threatening me?"

"Yes." He inches closer. "I will send you back to the North so fucking fast your head will spin. I will shame your family's name so that the only husband they can sell you off to will be no better than a butcher's son. Do you understand?"

I can feel the desperation, the panic in him.

I swallow. "You never told me why you hate Raine," I whisper. "If you want me to be honest, then so can you."

Thetis closes his eyes and wipes a hand down his face. "You're ridiculous." He looks like he might slap me, making me tense. "You ask me that again, and I will send you back anyway. You have refuge here because I grant it, understand? Your family and the neighboring empires are on their way here to see Raine's fate. I don't care if you're royalty, I have the ability to make your life miserable."

I take a breath to tamp down my rage. "I saved your life, remember?"

He glares at me, his sharpened teeth showing. "And I will save you from Raine, but you must speak the truth, Daphine." Then he turns to leave, muttering to himself.

I expel a breath as a flash of nerves washes over me.

"Steven, what do I do?" I whisper, looking around at everyone watching me with wariness. "I don't know if I can be the one to convict him. I can't. Why is everything falling on me?"

This is so unfair.

Steven shakes his head. "Pierce is writing, hold on." Steven blinks and moves his left hand. "I don't know what Raine has planned. Pierce is unable to give that information. But Pierce advised you not to lie, it could backfire. He says his team is looking into the situation."

I curse. "I might vomit."

I can't.

With my testimony, Raine will be convicted, then who knows what will happen to him. Even if Brayja is blackmailed into lying, will it be enough if I have to disagree? Will they just take Brayja's word over mine?

I don't know.

"Daphine," a woman says to my left.

I tense, then look, seeing Sun Hai standing next to me, looking beautiful in her Nymph body. Her pale skin and stark black hair look stunning.

I see Thetis notice her and he gives her a slight nod, then resumes his ordering around.

So Sun Hai has caught his interest. I don't understand how she could be attracted to that, but then again, the same could be said for Raine and I.

I look at her. "And your name?"

She looks around then whispers. "Akaria."

"What is going on?" I whisper back.

"Trying to keep this Raine guy from killing Thetis. Pierce tells me you two have a connection? I had to ask to believe it for myself." I can sense her looking at me.

"Have you seen him? Talked to him?"

She makes a sound. "I don't have to in order to know that he needs to be taken out. He almost destroyed our mission and any hope to save this world. How could you fall for the villain? FGI is supposed to rid the world of darkness, and here you are adding to it," she gets out through her teeth.
I tap down the anger I feel. "There are always two sides to the story, ~Akaria~."
"Are you serious?"

I look at her. "Thetis is no angel. That's why he is the main objective. He's not our target for being a saint," I hiss under my breath.

She clamps her mouth shut.

"We have to find a place to talk," I whisper, and look back in front of me like there is nothing to see here.

"I will try and find you when I have the opportunity," she says, and leaves my side to go and stand with a group of Nymphs.

The drama never stops, and something tells me that I have not even made a dent in it.

We enter the city, and my eyes take in this foreign place. If I was not so sick with nerves, I could sit here in awe. Seeing the stunning lights and massive structures, Nymphs riding on dolphin-like creatures, and the glowing plants makes me realize how fortunate I am.

I see enormous jellyfish light up the city like street lights, pink and blue hues that have my mouth hanging open.

"Duuuude, this is so cool. Looks like we just dropped some acid. I had a trip like this once except for the fact that everyone was naked."

"Yeah," I breathe. "That's great, Steven."

I could see myself living in this underwater fantasy. It's so tranquil and mysterious. I wish I could at least take some pictures, seeing how I won't be staying.

I take a shaky breath, trying to stay strong.

After driving through the city, we approach a mountain of a palace underwater. A wave of panic washes over me. Raine's life could ride on me and me alone.

"This is it, dude. Keep your shit together," Steven whispers. "FGI code is to always honor the main objective first. Pierce told me to remind you of that. You could still try and win over Thetis. I mean, I could tell he thought you were super fly."

"No," I whisper, and look over at him talking to Sun Hai, getting all close to her. I tamp down on the curse words I want to yell.

Thetis looks back at me, and I can see in his eyes he is saying, ~Don't fuck this up ~. . .

I feel the sub shift and pull as we enter the docking arena. I hear a rush of what seems like a waterfall as we break the surface into the Selestia Palace. If

I could just stop my rapid heartbeat, I could try to muster what little courage I have left.

We are led into an underwater palace that is so massive that I feel like I'm a tiny speck of dust.

Insignificant.

But that is not true, is it?

I have to testify against Raine, son of Queen Kalypso Syrinx of Selestia. I want to laugh seeing his mother and family.

A thought just occurred to me: Does Raine have any siblings I should be aware of? I know nothing of Raine, it would seem.

On a personal level, that is.

We walk down a series of tunnel hallways with guards swarming around us. I have no idea where Thetis ran off too, but apparently I must get changed out of my offending attire.

I'm royalty and I must look like it, not some low-class rebel. Sose Nymphs are a disgrace here, I'm gathering.

I feel like I have tunnel vision as I'm ordered around by the guards and female Nymphs that follow me. I'm in a place of legends, of myths, and all the focus is on me.

I'm told that after I change my insulting clothes, my presence is needed in the throne room to testify against Raine Syrinx of Selestia.

Don't vomit, ~please~.

I'm now alone. My brian is having odd blackouts, flashes of Nymphs telling me to do this and that. I just want them to stop—to stop ordering me around like I'm their puppet.

I close my eyes, rubbing my temples, willing away the pressure.

"Dude, you look pale. You want a smoke? You're making me nervous," Steven offers next to me in my glass room full of gothic beauty.

How the hell did I even get here? I notice a massive whale-like creature as it swims by my room's windows, making me shiver. I am way in over my head here, and there is nothing I can do about it.

"Duuude, do you hear my VOICE?"

I look at him. "What?"

"You look like you are two seconds from having like one of those bitch fits," he says, and pats me on the back. "We can't have a bitch fit just yet."

"I'M NOT HAVING A BITCH FIT!" I shriek, then redden and lower my voice as I take a breath, my hands shaking as I hold them out. "I'm not having a bitch fit, okay?"

Just a panic attack.

"Okaaaay," he says, eyes wide. "Well, Pierce wants to fix your gown."

I'm dressed like the queen I was supposed to be. I should be thrilled that I'm still considered royalty and that I do not need Bryaja for pretty things. I mean, why wouldn't I still be someone of value? I don't know . . . Maybe now it just seems fake.

I'm fake.

My gown is fit for a queen. The sparkling golden fabric is a Valkyrie favorite, letting everyone see my worth and rank. The glimmering material hugs my body, showing off my luscious curves and heightening my golden skin.

"It's already tight."

Steven looks at me.

"Well, he wants to add a slit and make it only one sleeve and make the bustline a sweetheart. He also said your hair would look better hanging down your back in soft waves, accented with a golden headpiece."

I raise a brow. "Dang, he said all of that?"

"No, I did." He rolls his eyes. "Of course he did, he's a king."

I roll my eyes back and start to spin, not really excited to look like a queen when I have no king. It didn't bother me before, and I'm not sure why it does now.

I want to laugh. I do know why.

Because of Raine.

He is a hurricane, uprooting everything.

I spin, and the gown that could not be any more stunning suddenly is. I look in the mirror and try to find my strength. I am brave. I am beautiful. I am not scared. I can do this.

Raine's a big boy, and he has to lay in the bed he's made.

I'm taken by a fleet of guards, with Steven trailing behind me.
~"Dude, just keep taking deep breaths. When I get too high and I forget how to breathe, I have to remind myself to breeeeeathe.~"
"Thanks, Steven," I whisper with amusement.

Everyone is staring at me.

I feel the guards' eyes on me as I walk, but I just keep my chin raised. Do they know I hold Raine's future in my hands? I'm sure news of what Raine did hit hard, because Raine was Posiendon's right-hand man, even over his spoiled son.
~Just don't think about it~.
I glitter and sparkle as I walk through transparent hallways and rooms like some Egyptian queen.

Why do I feel like I am the one on trial?

I suck in a breath as we round a corner only to see gigantic double doors—

the entrance to the throne room. I suck in a breath, seeing Brayja talking to Thetis, and it's heated.

Brayja is alive.

He is wearing his bright-colored golden overcoat, seemingly unharmed. So Raine let him go? Just like that?

I can feel my heart pounding as I watch them talk. Does Raine want to be charged? Found guilty? Is this his plan? To die in the dungeons, rotting away until his execution?

~"Dude, Brayja is here.~"

"I know," I whisper.

"Your grace," a guard mutters, urging me to keep walking. I swallow, my legs frozen.

Brayja looks in my direction, and of course, spots me. I might be sick. I could potentially projectile vomit if the stress gets any worse—wouldn't that be fun. I can't read his expression as his eyes travel over me, then back up to my face. His mouth slightly opens as he stares at me like he's seen a ghost.

Thetis looks at me next, and his eyes widen, probably expecting me to be in Sose clothing, not dressed like a golden goddess.

They both make their way to me, and I tense. I nod at them both, and Thetis shoos away everyone around me.

"Daphine, a word, please," Thetis says, his gaze still eyeing me from head to toe.

Raine and Thetis make Brayja seem so small. Nymphs seem to be more prominent with twice the muscle than Valkyrie men, and Brayja is not a small man.

I take a breath and glance at Brayja.

"Daphine, this mess will be over soon, and we can get back to where we left off. My people need us—a queen and king—after what happened." Brayja glares at Thetis. "And then we can decide what to do with this broken treaty."

My eyes widen.

We are still to be married? I don't know how I feel about that.

"You look surprised," Brayja says, and I can see the intensity in his gaze. It's practically radiating off of him.

It's anger.

"Not here, Brayja." Thetis glares at him. "Follow me."

Thetis leads us to a smaller room off of the throne room with a large desk and seating. I look at both men, feeling claustrophobic.

"You both should be able to put Raine away," Thetis says as he looks from me to Brayja. "He's a dead man. There is no way out with your testimony. Kalypso is out-of-her-mind upset and is swaying my father to give Raine a royal pass. It won't work with both of your words, your alliance is too important."

Brayja makes a sound, almost a snarl. "I don't know if we will keep the alliance by how you creatures treated me. You will repair all the damages."

Thetis curses, jaw flexing, looking up as if he is seeking divine help. "That conversation is for a different time. We need to take one step at a time. Our focus is on this first."

And here I thought Raine blackmailed Brayja. I close my eyes, trying to figure out Raine's motives in giving himself up like this.

"Why would Raine give himself up? It makes no sense."
Thetis eyes me, and I can tell he's thought the same thing. "I think he was counting on ~Mommy ~to save him."
Brayja frowns. "I have wondered this myself."

I look at Brayja, biting my lip. "What did Raine tell you? Did he try to blackmail you into saying he didn't do it?"

He looks down. "No, he didn't. He just let me go. Laughed, even."

There is silence.

"We need to be prepared for anything," Thetis whispers, and looks at me. "We are prepared for an ambush if that's Raine's irrational plan. The royal army is here. We have Raine heavily restrained."

My chest tightens. "Is he hurt?"

Brayja glances at me with a snarl, his chest rising and falling. The slap across my cheek causes searing, white-hot pain, with pins and needles dotting my face.

For a second, I almost forget where I am, my vision coming in and out.

Thetis slams Brayja against the wall, hand around his neck. "You fucking do that again in my presence and I will break your neck," he threatens in a dark tone, surprising me.

Brayja is breathing hard and nods as best he can with Thetis's hand around his neck. I place a hand on my burning cheek, completely in shock.

Thetis lets him go, and I just stare at him, knowing now that I will never marry him.

"Daphine needs to understand that fucking Raine behind my back has repercussions. If she is to be my queen, I don't want her pining over him or fucking anyone else."
Thetis looks back at me, hands on his hips, livid. "Are you okay?"

"Yes," I get out, and tamp down my rage in this tension-filled room. I'm so angry I am nearly shaking with it. "I can tell you this, Brayja: Find another woman. You didn't give me a chance to tell you earlier that I have changed my mind. I'd rather die than be married to you."

Both men stare at me, shock in their expressions.

Brayja suddenly laughs, bending over. "That's not how this works. I have a binding contract, Daphine. You do not have a choice in the matter. It was signed in blood by your parents."

My eyes widen.

Like hell.

"Daphine," Thetis says. "You may discuss this later. We must go," he says gently, pity in his blue gaze. Thetis does have a decent side to him, so maybe Sun Hai will get lucky. Because there is no luck coming my way. I seem to repel it.

Brayja tries to grab my arm and I jerk it out of his grasp, walking ahead of the men.

"Daphine," I hear him hiss behind me.

When I enter the throne room, it nearly steals the breath clean out of my lungs—it's the size of some mega arena. There are so many people here from many different empires and kingdoms.

My eyes go to the two towering thrones which seat Raine's mother and Poseidon himself on an elevated platform. I swallow as I try to take this in without turning and running away like a coward. The gothic beauty is astonishing, glittering dark accents with blues and silvers.

"Daphine, you are my witness. You will sit next to Brayja and me. Follow me, and I will guide you on what to do," Thetis murmurs beside me. "Are you ready?"

I swallow and feel lightheaded. "No."

"You will be fine. It has to be this way," he whispers, and pulls me with him, his hand gripping me tightly as if he senses I might bolt.
Eyes are immediately on me as we walk, and I can hear whispers and murmurs as we pass. I take a steady breath and glance in the direction of Raine's mother, then look away, heart pounding.

I can't just yet.

We are seated to their right, and I can see a large podium-type structure that looks like it's made of ice or glass, which makes me guess that's where I will be standing. It has a faint blue glow to it and a slight flicker.

I suck in a breath when Kalypso stands as I near them, following Thetis. I make eye contact and my heart constricts.

Mercy, she is frightening and stunning at the same time, and I immediately see that Raine looks just like her.

I feel lightheaded.

Her hair is black as the night, hanging well past her hips in twists and braids, with dark jewels littered in the mix. She wears a glittering deep blue gown with a metal collar that points up towards the ceiling in sharp points. Her crown is intimidating, reminding me of the crown Raine wore.

Kalypso looks powerful.

She is an older woman, you can tell, but that does not take away from the raw beauty this woman possesses. The shape of her eyes and high cheekbones remind me of Raine. The woman is goddess-level beautiful, but it's the expression in her golden gaze that renders me speechless.

Intensity.

Desperation.

She knows what power I have. I feel Thetis nod at her and Kalyspo bares her teeth at him. The look is one of hatred—that is one woman I would not want on my bad side.

I glance at Thetis and he smiles at her smugly, then motions for me to sit.

Poseidon stands, and I shiver, feeling so much power.
He is enormous with a white beard and hair, handsome like Thetis. The blue of his gaze pierces Thetis, and he nods at him.

"Thetis, we are ready to begin."

Thetis responds and my mind goes into a tunnel, then underwater. I look around as I hear them order in Raine.

"~Bring him in~," they said.

I hear the murmurs from everyone quiet to silence as the royal guards walk into the throne room. I feel my pulse, making sure my heart is still beating.

~"Dude, here comes Raine. They have him chained up and shit.~"

I suddenly see Raine, surrounded by guards like he is too dangerous without them. Chains are around Raine's neck, hands, and ankles, and the guards all hold menacing-looking spears.

Raine is twice their size, which is ridiculous.

The place is quiet.

I shiver.

I can see the anger on Raine's handsome face, but also cold defiance. His muscles bulge and flex as he walks, seemingly uncaring about what's going to happen.

Kalypso stands, fear in her gaze as she tries to read her son's face. But like everyone else, she is wondering what the hell Raine is doing.

Poseidon stands and starts talking, his voice booming out over everyone. I can tell he looks just as disturbed as his mother. The shock of Raine snapping must be hard for his family.

I immediately hear hushed voices as Brayja walks up to the flickering podium and tells the audience what happened in excruciating detail. Raine eyes him with cool disdain, eyes narrowed.

I suddenly blanch as Brayja says that Raine wanted ME and was jealous, and that was the reason for him snapping.

If I could kill Brayja right now, I would.

Why would he say that?

All. Eyes. On. Me.

~Dear World, how are you? Could you swallow me up?~

There is a hushed silence as his mother stares at me. Everyone stares at me. The Valkyrie Raine went crazy over. Allegedly.
~"Duuude, like, Brayjo just made it really awkward.~"
Brayja has words with Poseidon's men, then comes to sit next to me.

"Are you serious?" I hiss under my breath.

"It's the truth," he says back with a stern look.

"It's not," I shoot back.

I look back at Raine and he is staring down, then slightly raises his head, and his fiery gaze lands on me like he knew where I was the whole time.

I can't breathe.

A slight smile pulls at his lips, and he winks at me.

He WINKS at me.

Does he find this funny?! Maybe he has lost his mind after all, because what Brayja said was damning. Raine will be prosecuted.

"Daphine, please take the stand," Thetis whispers to me, helping me up.

No.

No.

I can't.
Silence everywhere. The way Raine is watching me now makes me doubt my sanity. All eyes are on me as I stand alone.

Raine tilts his head at me like he is having fun and can't wait to see what I'm going to say. I hate that the smile he is giving me makes my stomach dip

261

and my brain flatline. My eyes lock with his, and I see him eyeing my body like he doesn't care if anyone sees.

I close my eyes.

I feel Thetis stand next to me and whisper in my neck, "Daphine, if you choose, you can just agree with Brayja's accounts. "I can tell Raine is trying to unsettle you. It's what he does best, and you need to just ignore it."

I look at Thetis, breathing hard. "I might pass out," I whisper. "I can't."

He smiles and glances in Raine's direction, then back to me, body tense. "You won't. Just give Poseidon the nod, and I will take care of the rest."

"Will they kill him?"

Thetis looks at someone over my shoulder. "No."

I nod and look back to Raine, and the smile is gone. He looks dangerous now, his pale skin with his black-as-night hair making me shiver.

I'm conversing with the enemy, and I'm a traitor.

Thetis nods to someone. "She will stand by Brayja's accounts."

Whispering and talking everywhere.

It's done.

I hear Raine's mother shriek.
I feel a tear stream down my cheek as I look back to Raine and our gazes collide. I try to say, "~I'm sorry"~, but Raine is being taken away.
"Wait!"

Everyone stops.

"Wait!"

I frown at the female voice.

Nomi.

She comes walking in, wearing her tight black suit, and I hear Thetis curse. She nods in Raine's direction, then looks at her father and Kalypso. "Father, if I may. Raine is justified. I have proof for Raine's immediate release and the capture of Brayja and Daphine of the Gaya Empire!"

I frown.

What?

Me?
~"Dude, why did she say your name? What is going on?!~"
Raine nods in her direction as if to give her confidence. "The Gaya Empire has violated the peace treaty by secret trafficking and imprisonment of female Nymphs. Raine acted on what he thought best and is justified by the many deaths we have uncovered. "We have intercepted a shipment of Nymph children, and the rig is being held for further proof."

Gasps.

I pale.

"Ridiculous!" Brayja yells, looking sick. "It's a setup! I swear it!" He backs up, breathing hard.

Nomi looks at Brayja. "We have your signature on multiple shipments, including King Redul and Queen Hilna's royal stamp, and also have witnesses to confirm these accusations and the horrors that took place."

My mouth is hanging open.
I look at Raine and he is already staring at me. ~Raine ~. . .
"I want proof!" Thetis yells, and walks up to Nomi, who hands him documents and other items. After a while Thetis turns, and the look of horror on his face says it all.

Raine did have a plan after all, and it didn't matter what Brayja or I said.

He had a smoking gun.

"Release my son!" Kalypso shrieks, and turns towards Brayja and me. "Seize them!"

"Wait," I breathe. "I have nothing to do with this!" I yell as men grab me. I look over at Raine as I see him being released, his gaze finding mine.

Dear . . . goodness.

Arrogance.

When I left, it would seem that I was put on his hit list, and he will not stop until everyone pays. Raine is taking everyone out, including me.

Oh, how the tables have turned.

And now, I'm at Raine's mercy . . .

CHAPTER 20

CAMILA

"Dude, I need to enter the ~mystic ~mode. We gotta get out of here."

The guards just left, and Steven is now right next to me in his tight black wetsuit. He puts his hands on his hips and gazes around with his squinty eyes.

I'm in my glittering gown still, sitting on a clean pad on the stone floor. I'm in some sort of small cave with a pool doorway, the air pressure keeping the water from pouring in. The blue of the sea makes aqua designs on the cave walls, illuminating the cave with a faint teal glow.

"Can't we just swim out?" I look around, realizing they did not chain me up. "Maybe they think I can't swim?" I'm on edge, my pulse hammering. The shock of what happened still numbs my senses, confusing me.

What a mess.

We both stare at each other as I take a shaky breath. I slowly crawl to the edge of the pool and peer into the ocean. I put my hand into the water and see that there is a light source down there, illuminating the water.

"Is there something in the water?"

Steven laughs and snorts. "Dude, it's the ocean."

I look at him and give him a hard look. "I'm saying, like, something to keep me in here?"

Steven kneels next to me and squints into the water, his chubby body hunched over. "I don't see anything." He leans closer. "Is that a fish down there? Like, a big one?"

"Steven, scoot back—" Steven's body hits the water so fast I can't grab him. "Steven!"

He breaks the surface, sputtering and splashing like a lunatic. "Ahhhhhh!" he yells, and thrashes around. "Heeeeeelp me!" he yells, and lifts his hand out of the water in utter horror. "No! I lost my watch!"

"Who cares, Steven!" My heart pounds as I see something in the water under him. "Steven, there is something in the water!" I shriek. "Swim! Grab my hand! Or shapeshift!"

Steven lunges to grab my hand and I pull with all my might. His round body lands on the side of the pool, and he rolls to a safe distance. Steven lays there, breathing hard. "Shiiiiittt dude."

I look back into the water and see a shark-like creature swimming a few feet down. "I think I know why we are not chained up." I close my eyes. "You need to talk to Pierce."

"Fuck, man, I lost my watch," he says, staring up at the ceiling, water dripping off of him.

"You were almost lunch." I look at him as he lays there with his hands over his eyes. "I'll get you a new one," I say, breathing hard and looking back toward the water. I frown, peering closer, seeing another large figure. "I see something else in the water," I say, and squint.

Steven looks at me and suddenly sits up, touching his ear. "Oh shit! Red alert!"

He is gone.

I look back into the pool, and I scream, seeing Raine break the surface. My mind flatlines as the water rushes over him like some erotic scene or some sexy Armani poolside photoshoot.

He is shirtless save for weapons and some sort of vest that clings to his orange and maroon torso. It always takes me aback when I see his mermaid-like skin. I swallow as our gazes collide, and I have to remind myself to breathe.

He places his muscled arms on the edge of the pool, half his body still in the water, standing on some lower platform. The blue water reflects off his porcelain skin, rendering me breathless.
"Raine," I get out. "I-I would get out of the water if I were you." I glance at the water that sloshes around his narrow hips, breathing hard~. Ignore his large pecs and chiseled abs that look like titanium~
"Trust me." I look back at him.

Raine tilts his head at me, and a smile pulls at his mouth. I shiver, hating how hot he is when he smirks. He leans back and looks into the water then back at me. "I'll be careful."

"Suit yourself. You won't be so hot if you only have one leg," I say, and take a shaky breath.

He laughs slightly. "Your lack of knowledge of this world is adorable," he murmurs as he stares at me with his orange gaze.

I swallow, feeling the tension crackling.

I gasp. "RAINE!"

Raine effortlessly grabs the head of the shark-like creature and thrusts it to the right, sending it back into the water like it's nothing.
My mouth is hanging open as I stare at him, heart pounding.

He peers back at me. "Here's what's going to happen. I want you to tell me where you're from and your weird little friend. Who is helping you, and why are you here?"

Steven told me a while ago that I cannot say anything about FGI until the end. Even with as much as Raine already knows about me, it's still against the rules. It's a common problem on a mission, but Pierce believes it creates intrigue. FGI agents are always under the suspicion of not being who they say they are.

I swallow. "And if I don't?"

Raine looks around the cell, then back to me. "Get comfortable then."

"You can't keep me here. I have done nothing wrong." I glare at him now, knowing he's not going to let me out.

"I can do whatever I want," Raine says in a low voice. "Why did you run to Thetis? What does he have that you want?" He leans closer. "You will answer me this."

I can see the rage in his expression.

I close my eyes, knowing how this looks. "I want nothing from him."

"Liar," he says. "Tell me."

"Tell me why you want him dead."

"Tell me why you want him ~alive~," he retorts.

We both stare at each other. A battle of wills.

I look away from him. "So you're a hero now? Saving the lives of women and children?" I look back at him. "Why didn't you say anything about that?"

Raine expels a breath and looks up towards the ceiling. "I am not a hero," he murmurs. "It just worked out that way. I could care less about what happens to them. But it seemed to work out for both parties, so I'm not complaining."

I frown at him. "Bullshit."

"I forgot that you know me so well," he taunts, smiling harshly. "You have no idea what my intentions are, Camila."

"I know that you want everyone to think you are a monster, and I don't understand why," I say, my eyes searching over his handsome features. "It's a gut feeling, really. A woman's intuition."

Raine expels a breath. "A woman's intuition?" He stares at me in awe. "You are foolish then," he scolds, his eerie gaze flickering over my dress, my leg exposed through the slit. "You would be wise to heed my warning."

"Why?"

He lifts himself out of the water and walks to the wall to lean against it, water rushing down his muscular thighs. He crosses his arms over his chest and studies me. "Because I will break your heart when you finally realize that I am telling you the truth. You are delusional about my honorable intentions."

My eyes widen, not sure what to say to that.

"You are very arrogant." I feel my cheeks redden. Raine is not smiling, just seemingly looking into my soul with that intense stare.

"It's just a warning."

I slowly stand, wanting to slap him, to inflict bodily harm. "Don't worry. I will heed your warning, but you should also heed mine," I get out, and walk up to him. "Because I will break yours too."

His mouth opens, then he shuts it. "And how would you do that?" he asks, uncrossing his arms and taking a step closer to me.

I make a sound and smile at him, wanting to taunt him. Maybe because I hate him.

I hate how he makes me feel. I hate the fact that every time I look at him, butterflies take flight in my stomach.

"I'm sure you have an imagination." I have no idea what I'm getting at, but it seems to be affecting him.

"Clarify," he hisses.

I bet he can hear the beat of my heart as it pounds against my neck. "I will be leaving soon, and you will never see me again. There will be nothing you can do about it. Trust me."

I hope I didn't cross the line by admitting that.

I did not mention why, or FGI.

Raine looks like he's at a loss for words as his chest rises and falls, his gaze searching mine for any hint of a lie. He steps closer to me, and I retreat, feeling defiant.

"Dry your eyes, Raine. You have Nomi, after all," I sneer.

"Careful," he whispers, jaw flexing.

"Feel free to leave me in here. I will be gone before you know it," I say, and back into the wall behind me.

He studies me, and suddenly he smiles. "Hmmm." Both arms are on either side of me now, making me shiver. "I better make sure you don't disappear then." He leans in closer. "I came here to take you, anyway. You are coming with me."

I swallow, hating how I notice that he smells clean and fresh. I try to tamp down the excitement of his words. "Lucky me. Where are we going?"

I tense as I feel his lips brush my neck. The heat of his breath has me suppressing a shiver or a ~moan~.

"You're my prisoner, actually. Until you have a trial to prove your innocence, your life is in my hands."

My lashes flutter when I feel his hands lower to my waist, trying not to get lost in him. "That sounds like an abuse of power, Raine," I say breathlessly. "When is my trial, then?"

His hands grip my ass, bringing me up against him, making me gasp.

"Not for a long time, actually. You see, we are going to war. Poseidon just made my wish come true, ordering Thetis and me to join forces to fight off the Orcs and the Zebia Empire.

"Queen Luna did not like that I slayed her sister, Hilna. So, naturally, they want to avenge her," he continues at my shocked expression. "We will all be traveling together, giving me ample time to slit Thetis's throat."

I expel a breath.

Not good.

All of us on the same sub?

"Look on the bright side." Raine eyes me, his hands still caressing me, and I can feel how hard he is as he presses me to him. I take a steady breath to calm my breathing before I hyperventilate,

"I'll chain you to my bed every night."

He tilts his head, a smile pulling at his mouth. I feel lightheaded, my thoughts scattered.

"I-I don't want it."

"Liar." He leans down to kiss my bare shoulder. His hand feels the pulse at my neck and he makes a sound. "I can sense your desire even now."

"If you try to kill Thetis, you will have to take it by force," I say, and put my hands on his hard chest to push him back. "And I hope you will not sink to that level."

He laughs, and his eyes lower, eyeing my glittering gown. "I think I can change your mind pretty easily."

"You will not," I say, and push harder.

That's a lie.

"I love a challenge," Raine says, not budging.

I squeeze my eyes shut. "Please, don't kill him. Isn't there another way?" I say, and feel myself panic. "What did he do to you? Maybe I can help."

"He is an honorable man, and I find that irritating," Raine says, and grabs my hands on his chest, squeezing them. "Does that make sense? Didn't I mention that I hate his face? I'm not understanding your confusion."

I shake my head at him. "You're lying, Raine," I say, frustrated.

He opens his mouth like he's offended. "A liar can spot a liar, then?"

I take a moment. "Yes."

"Hmmm." He looks down then back up to me. "We can exit out of here in two ways. I kiss you, and you steal some of my power. Or I have an oxygen mask for you."

"You would trust me with your power?"

He pinches my nose. "No, of course not, but I wanted to see how bad you wanted to kiss me." He smiles with a wink and pulls out a face mask. "Put this on."

"But I want the kiss," I whine, seeing an escape there. "You can trust me."

Raine's gaze lowers to my breasts. "Not until your hands are tied above your head and you're naked save for your jewelry," Raine murmurs, giving me a dark and sexy look like he is picturing it. He makes a sound.
"~Mmmm."~
I shiver, trying not to think about that. "Thetis said you have a thing for Valkyries."

"Did he now?" He hands me the mask with a mouthpiece on it.

"He did," I say, watching him peer into the ocean, hands on his hips. "Let's go, they're most likely waiting for us."

272

"Do you?"

Raine looks at me and takes a deep breath. "I'll let you be the judge of that," he murmurs, and walks up to me and slaps my ass hard, grinning at my shocked expression.

"Let's go before I bend you over my knee for not listening."

I almost don't put on the mask, but I do.

Not sorry.

I'm going on a war submarine with Thetis's men and Raine's men. And I'm Raine's prisoner for who knows how long.

What could go wrong?

CHAPTER 21

CAMILA

"So Raine's justification for taking me on board is that I'm valuable?" I say as I stare in awe at the massive submarine being loaded. "Because I can steal power?"

Steven nods to my restrained hands. "Well, he has a point," he laughs, "but we both know it's because of yo' booty."

I frown at Steven.

"Sorry." He gives me a heavy-lidded smile. "You lookin' fly, though."

I shift my weight as I look down at the black wetsuit they made me change into. I have not seen Raine since he handed me off to his men, and now I'm just waiting to board.

Tensions are high, Sose Nymphs mingling with the royal army. It makes me wonder why Posiendon ordered them to travel together. A parent trying to get the family to get alone with tough love?

I expel a breath — more of like an excellent way to get your son murdered.

"Dude, like, the talk on our message board is that this war will be bloody. The Zebia Empire wants to nuke Selestia, so we have to stop them before they get too close, I guess."

"Will Raine give a shit," I whisper, "or will he still try and sabotage this?"

Steven leans in. "Well, Pierce says that his mother will be in danger, and he loves his mother, from what he's gathered. So I would assume he will take this seriously." Steven shrugs. He might not have a choice. Poseidon is not letting Kalypso leave, almost like he knows Raine's intentions. It's his insurance that Raine will play nicely."

"And if he kills Thetis, that will be one warrior they can't afford to lose. I think Poseidon threw Raine a curveball he was not expecting by keeping his mother in Selestia," I muse. "He might have to wait until this battle is over to take out Thetis."

"Homeboy will be so pissed about that, and we will all be traveling together." His eyes go wide. "I'm going to be high the entire time."

"You better not be," I hiss. "I need you present, not comatose."

"I'm never comatose," he hisses back. "M-y-s-t-i-c M-o-d-e."

I snort. "Most of the time you look like you're the walking dead with your tongue hanging out and eyes almost shut." I look up then back to him. "I have seen you run into a few walls when you thought no one was looking."

I tense when I see Thetis walking with Sun Hai and a portion of their military. I still need to talk to her to pick her brain about the brothers' hatred for one another.

"You sound like a hater," Steven says.

I feel someone grab my arm and pull me towards the sub. He's an attractive Nymph, part of the royal army. His dark hair is tied back, and his dark eyes assess me. "Daphine, you are still in our custody, but you will be helping the army as a part of your imprisonment until your final sentencing."

I look at him. "Will I be chained up?"

He takes a moment as we walk. "That is up to Raine or Thetis, given your cooperation, but you will be treated with care." He gives me a look, and I blush.

Will Raine like deciding that?

This guard is not thinking anything dirty. I need to get a hold of my emotions.

"Where," I say carefully, "is Raine?"

He sighs. "Well, being restrained in a sense. Thetis and Raine got into it, wanting to know how your face became black and blue." The guard glances at my cheek. "Raine had a knife to Thetis's neck, and Thetis said it was Brayja."

My eyes widen.

I frown. Did he care?

I lift my hand to my cheek—I'd completely forgotten about that. So Pierce did not cover it up with FGI makeup then? I thought for sure it was not visible.

"So, naturally, Raine broke Brayja's nose and a few ribs. Possibly some internal bleeding, but we pulled him off before he killed him." The guard stops and glances at me. "I have never seen Raine act like that for someone. So, if I may say this, you seem to hold some power over him. Please, this will be a nightmare of a voyage if Raine is not under control."

I close my eyes. "I don't hold the power that you think I do," I say, and notice Thetis walking over to me.

"Just," he says, "try."

I don't have power over him, right? He was still going to kill Thetis even when I begged him not to, so what power do I hold?

"Daphine," Thetis says, and stops in front of me, "you will be shown to your quarters. As long as you get approval, you may roam freely unless we are under attack."

I nod at him, noting that he looks stressed, his expression wary. "How long is this trip?"

He looks at the sub that resembles a ship hybrid. "That depends on a lot of factors, but I hope not too long. And another thing—if Raine tells you anything I should know, don't hesitate to tell me, understand?"

"I will," I say, and see Sun Hai walk up to us in a gray wetsuit and vest. Her black hair is piled high on her head, complimenting the angles of her face.

Thetis glances at her. "Show her to her quarters." Then he walks off, his men following him.
"Come, we need to talk," she whispers, and I follow her to board.

"Is that your agent?" She glances at Steven's heavy-lidded expression as he follows.

"Yes," I say.

She nods. "Mine is scouting, checking on Raine's whereabouts. He's already on the vessel, cooling off. I'm sure you heard about what happened."

I shiver. He defended me. I can't stop the warm fuzzies that dot my body. We board the massive sub that's the size of a cruise ship. Smaller vessels have already left to scout, I overheard. We climb down a series of ladders and emerge into a massive hall.

It's the central hub for this rig, many stories high, glass all around, controls everywhere, blinking lights and sounds, and lots of men.

"Follow me," Sun Hai says, gaining my attention.

I notice stares directed my way, but I follow her down a series of dark hallways and finally stop in front of a narrow silver door. She opens it, and we both step into the small room.

The room is clean and inviting, but on the small side.

We both gasp.

There, leaning against the small vanity, is Pierce himself, arms crossed over his black suit, looking very ~007~.

"Pierce!" we both exclaim.

"Ladies, looking wonderful and fresh," he says with a smile, and motions for us to sit on the bunk. "A couple of things. I wanted to talk to you both in person instead of through your agents." He shoots me a look. "Seeing how all information I send doesn't always get to you."

Ugh. ~Steven~.

I sit down next to Sun Hai and stare at him.

"Small update. The other players are doing great—we even have another Valkyrie on board. Her agent worked it out so that she could come as a peacemaker for her empire. "Crystal, aka, Iris, has great potential to talk some sense into Queen Luna," Pierce says, and looks from face to face.

A Valkyrie?

A flash of nerves washes over me. I should not be feeling the impact of panic from hearing this.

Will Raine see her and get struck by her beauty? Apparently he's obsessed with Valkyrie women and will notice her. He's not blind. This agent is also not blind, and she will see him and be entranced with his fiery gaze.

I can't blame Raine. I'm a traitor, running to Thetis for protection. Mission first and all that.

"Camila?"

I shake my head. "Sorry, zoned out a bit," I murmur, and blush, looking back at him, my hands digging into the bed.

Pierce's blue gaze seems to see too much, but he doesn't comment on it. "You three, but mostly you two, have to work together."

Sun Hai glances quickly at me. "What do you mean?"

He takes a breath. "We need both men alive. My team has run scenarios back and forth, and if Thetis dies, our mission fails." He pauses. "If Raine dies, his mother will cause more problems than Raine ever could. The apple does not fall far from the tree. if you get my meaning."

"How?" I say, frowning

"Fix them." Pierce shrugs.

Sun Hai laughs. "Are you serious? Raine has tried to slit Thetis's throat already today, and if that man gets another moment alone with Thetis, it'll be a fight to the death."

That might be true.

"Right, he definitely has a chip on his shoulder," Pierce agrees, and squints his eyes in thought. "I think you two would benefit from trying to peel back some layers. I want you two to dig deep and expose what's hidden, and that's an order," Pierce says with a grin, hands in pockets, studying us.

He then stands up straight and checks his watch, taking a breath. "No matter how flat a pancake is, there are always two sides." He glances at us both. "Right?"

I glance at Sun Hai, and she is biting her red lip. I clear my throat and nod.

"I guess it doesn't hurt to try."

I can almost feel her eyes roll. She thinks Raine is a lost cause, and I can't argue against it.

"Well, meet up with Crystal and form a game plan. I'm not losing this mission because we didn't play this smart. If you can't beat them, join them," Pierce says, and touches his ear. Extraction, Matt, and tell Karen I'll have my gray suit pressed for later from my new line, not the black one. Oh—uh . . . please limit her to two drinks."

He looks at us and whispers, "Good luck, ladies."

And he is gone.

We sit in silence for a second. I glance at Sun Hai and expel a breath. "So, do you have any information as to why Raine wants Thetis dead?"

Sun Hai falls back onto the mattress. Minutes tick by, and she finally responds. "Thetis hates to talk about him, but I did get a small chance to talk to Nomi. That girl has stars in her eyes at the mere mention of Raine." She laughs. "You have some competition there. I will admit that the man is easy on the eyes, too bad he's lost it."

I feel her look at me.

I make an irritated grunt and rub my neck. "I don't think so, actually. I think that might be one-sided with Nomi, and I ~do ~think there is a slight chance for Raine or Pierce would not want to go that route."

"Maybe. Thetis seems to think Nomi is a fool." She sits up and stretches her arms. "She did say that Raine had two younger sisters."

"What?" I say, and look at her. "Sisters?"

"Yeah. Nomi was not talking directly to me about it, though, and the way she used their names in past tense leads me to believe they are no longer living," Sun Hai says, and shrugs. "Maybe there is something there?"

I stare at the floor, my thoughts firing like a machine gun. "Can you talk to Nomi? Like, one on one?"

"I can try, but she doesn't like her brother, and I'm sleeping with him, so . . . " she says, and laughs at my expression. "Sure am, and he's goooood," she purrs.

I laugh, watching her beam. "Well, if you want to keep it that way, pick her brain." I continue, "If it's about his sisters, then how would that affect Thetis? Did he have a part in their death, do you think?"

"I doubt it. Thetis is actually a good guy, despite being a little spoiled."

I bite my lip, not wanting to comment on that.

"Could explain the bad attitude," she offers, "but I will talk to Nomi, and how about you talk to the man himself, huh?"

Ask Raine?

That will go over well.

The door swings open, and I nearly scream. Sun Hai jumps up, and we both stare into orange flames.

"Raine!" I squeak.

I shiver, seeing a soaking wet Raine in tight black pants and a loose gray shirt that clings to his muscles like he just threw it on over his wet body.

~Yum~.

He eyes Sun Hai, and his gaze narrows at her. "Go," he says, and she rushes past him. His hair is slightly longer and wet, brushed back off his handsome face.

"You're talking to the woman Thetis is fucking?" He tilts his head at me and smiles. "You never cease to amaze me."

My heart is pounding like crazy.

Raine is way too big for this room as he walks in, eyeing me from head to toe. "Stand up," he orders. I frown and stand, and he sits in the only chair in the room, legs spread wide, eyes like fire. "Turn around."

I swallow and turn, and I hear him whistle. I fight a smile as I look back at him. "You like what you see?"

Of course he does. This suit makes me look naked.

His face is emotionless as he regards me, eyes glittering. "Bend over," he orders with that accent of his.

My whole body engulfs in flames, and I falter, heat pooling in my stomach.

"Do you remember that you are still my slave?"

I turn and cross my arms over my chest, trying to act normal, pulse hammering. "Are you going to kill Thetis?"

Have to stick to my guns, right? Maybe?

He laughs and takes a moment. "Almost did this morning," he murmurs as his gaze lands on my cheek. "I can hear your pulse. Relax."

"What are you, a vampire?" I ask, my pulse hammering harder.

"A what?" he asks with an amused smirk.

He smells good — like sexy-man and something fresh.

"Nevermind," I say, trying to relax, changing the subject. "Answer me this. What happened to your sisters?" I blurt out, and bite my lip.

Raine makes me act awkward, like I forgot how to act around a man.

His smile is gone, and I immediately miss it. That seemed to catch him off guard, and his orange gaze flickers, jaw flexing. "What happened to them?" he repeats, like it was an abomination to say in his presence.

I bite my lip. "I'm sorry, that came out thoughtless."

Raine looks down for a few moments then back to me.

"They both passed away of natural causes," he says, and studies me. "You are trying to find a source for my anger. You are quite easy to read."

I frown. "Maybe."

"I already told you there is no source, Camila," he says, and stands.

I can feel my anger start to boil. "I don't believe that," I get out, and tense as he walks up to me, backing me up against the bunk.

"If you want to know so much about me," he murmurs, and removes a hair out of my face, "then what do I get if I tell you some juicy tidbits of my life? Though I hate to spoil the mystery that has you so consumed."

"Anything," I blurt out, and redden as his eyebrow raise. "Well, not anything, but—"

"The place I grew up in was filled with nightmares and horrors. If you didn't sleep with one eye open, you got eaten by something. Poseidon kept resources from the people of Sose, and provided zero protection from sea monsters and Empire traffickers. We wanted independence because we were being mistreated, portrayed as low-life eels.

"It was then I found out that my mother's husband was a rival of Poseidon from childhood, and it's the famous rumor, the cause of our mistreatment."

"Your father?"

Raine tilts his head. "Yes, I did have one of those at one point. Then Poseidon took an interest in my mother, and the love story wrote itself," he says darkly. "It was a rags to riches story, truly touching, and after that, he has shown Sose mercy." Raine makes a face. "I think. Sounds good, though."

I pray Raine doesn't stop, so I slightly prompt him. "Your father? What happened to him?"

"Who knows, died somewhere," Raine says, and smiles down at me, but I can see the emptiness in his eerie gaze. "So, you see? I should be thankful. But, fun fact, I never knew why my father and Poseidon hated one another. It was a love triangle from way back. My father won—can you imagine the rage Poseidon felt? Someone from royal blood losing to a Sose?"

He gives me a pointed look. "I can."

I sense a deep, deep anger and a long generational battle. A part of me can't believe Raine opened up to me.

I feel Raine grab me around the waist, and he expels a breath.

"Do you have a better picture now?"

"When did you meet Thetis?"

Raine tilts his head. "And finally, the question of the hour. I did enjoy taking my anger out on him, making Posiedon love me like a son and not him. That, I think, was a great win."

"Why?"

Raine laughs and lowers his head to nip at my shoulder. "If you steal my power, I will kill Thetis the first chance I get," he murmurs, and the crush of his lips on mine is swift and desperate. His taste, his lips, the low groan in his throat, has me reeling.

The way his tongue works mine, I can't make myself stop. I want him, and I seem to be helpless.

And the fact is—he knows it.

I feel him smile against my lips.

"~Mmmm~, so responsive," he whispers against me as his hand lowers to my breast, grabbing it. We are kissing again, and my arms snake around his strong neck, deepening it.

His hands grab my ass, and he pulls me against his muscled body. The heat of him engulfs me, and I'm suddenly flat on my bunk with him looming over me, kissing down my neck.

Wasn't I supposed to stop this? Until he said he would not kill Thetis?

Whoops.

I get a glimpse of the predatory gleam in his fiery gaze.

Zero to sixty.

Our breaths are mixed and my eyes flutter. Our kissing is frantic as his hands caress everywhere, setting fire to my tingling body. Raine cups me between the legs, and I gasp, moan, pant, as my head arches back. His lips devour me, then trail down my neck as his hand and thumb work me through my wetsuit.

He blows on my neck, and the shiver racks my body.

"Raine," I pant, heat pooling in my girl parts like they are set on fire. I can feel my body perspire as I squirm and move with him, matching his intensity, his tempo.

I've lost my damn mind.

I can tell he's watching me now, whispering something that I can't quite make out as his hand gains tempo. I almost scream, wanting my clothes off. I'm overheating.

How can he make me feel this way through clothing?!

Of course he can.

"Raine," I grab onto this hand, trying to halt him. "C-clothes. OFF!"

I can see the dark light in his eye, and he smiles at me. It's incredibly sexy, hot — scorching. That did it, and when he sends a slight shock into my girl bits, I'm at my climax.

Colors blur together, and I grasp at his shoulders.

His mouth covers mine, drinking in my cries, his taste consuming me. Raine lifts his head and peers down at me.
"Camila, you can't withhold yourself from me, even if you try. I will prove you wrong every time." His teeth scrape down my neck, making me shiver.

"Hmm," I say, running my hands through his glorious hair as he lightly kisses my breast. "Maybe I will be armed next time. This is one slip — I mean what I say."

Ahem . . .

I mean, I'll try harder next time . . .

He lifts his head and stands, adjusting himself. "Can't wait," he whispers with a wink. "Stay away from Thetis and his men. You may come up when you are ready, my men will be waiting to escort you."

Then he is gone.

Well, I got some information out of him. Now to work on the real reason why the two men hate each other.

Quarantined with Raine and Thetis. Fun, fun!

"Steven!" I hiss. "Time to work."

CHAPTER 22

CAMILA

The night is ghostly on deck, the sub breaking the surface hours ago. The top deck of this submarine-ship hybrid is massive, with three levels.

I look up into the night sky and see two bright moons.

Full moons.

I close my eyes and shiver, remembering that the moon seductively warns you to be on guard and, at the same time, to be foolish.

It's a delicious contradiction.

I will never miss that warning again, though.

I tug the blanket around my shoulders tighter as my eyes scan the men on the upper deck on which I stand. The sea appears black, the choppy waves smash against the ship, rocking the massive rig. There is something eerily calming and terrifying about being out at sea in an alien world.

It's humbling.

I have not seen Raine since our hot little session. It was not supposed to happen until he gave me his word that he would not kill Thetis, but I'm proving to have no defense against him. I need to solve the mystery of Raine, and I'm running out of precious time.

I need a different strategy. He is making me vulnerable. That's when mistakes happen.

I have not seen Steven either in a couple of hours. He left saying he needs to scout with the other agents on board.

Raine has been on group scouts, trying to locate all of the Empire's battleships, to Thetis's disapproval. I think anything that Raine does, Theits tries to invalidate, fighting him at every turn. They both have different strategies. The two powerhouses are butting heads, and the tension is almost unbearable.

Sun Hai is terrified that Raine will try something soon—the two can barely be in the same room without a yelling match or a knife to one's throat.

I feel sick with nerves, not knowing how unstable Raine truly is. Will he try something and be successful? Will FGI put a large stamp on this mission as a failed operation, deporting us all from this enchanting world?

I sigh and feel the wind blowing my unbound hair. Pierce thought I needed to look natural, but still alluring, with my smoky eyes. My black suit is sleek, making me feel like a double agent—a woman with many mysteries.

Raine and I have quite a bit in common.

The sub has a faint glow to it, almost as if it really is just the spirit of what it once was. Half of the Nymph realm is illuminated, having the same power as a glowing jellyfish.

I see Raine's men mixed in with Thetis's men, seemingly working together despite their leaders.

Steven told me before he left that we had to break the surface, to pretend we are a ship instead of a Nymph submarine. The Gaya Empire will be scanning the ocean for any threats. We are posing as a ship instead of a sub, so I get why they chose this hybrid rig.

"Hey."

I turn to see Sun Hai, soaking wet in her wetsuit, the moon highlighting her body.

"Hi," I say, and frown, noting her wet appearance on this chilly night.

"Went scouting with Raine. We just got back," she says as the purplish skin on her neck slowly returns to her usual pale complexion.

"You went with Raine?" I ask, shocked. I'm sure he didn't like having Thetis's lover tag along.

"Well, we all have to work together. Someone has to keep an eye on Raine." She pauses and looks out over to the deck. "I can feel the tension on this ship starting to turn sour."

I take a minute to scan for Raine, but I do not see him on deck. I think I subconsciously do this every five minutes.

"So what did you guys do?"

"There are tons of battleships headed this way. It's not good. Raine is calling for more men as we speak. Smart move by him, he commands his men well," she says, wringing out her long black hair. "He surprised me."

"Raine?"

"Yes. It was clear he did not want me to tag along with his group, but he did make sure I was next to him the entire time." She glances at me. "I thought at first it was because he didn't trust me, but there were a couple of times he pulled me out of danger when I would have needed to use a lifeline." She pauses. "He could have let me get killed."

I think about that, not sure where she is going with this. "What are you saying? Raine is not the monster you thought?"

She laughs and looks down. "At first, I thought you were crazy for falling for a madman. But I can see the draw to him. He has this mysterious charisma."

I raise a brow, curious if she wants to jump on the Raine-train. "He likes Valkyries," I point out, feeling this intense possessiveness.

Back. Off.

"I'm aware." She looks at me and tilts her head. "This is a competition. After all, you should not think of Raine as yours just yet."

My eyes widen in confusion. "You want Raine?!"

I almost see red.

She shrugs. "I never said that. I have a good thing with Thetis, but you should know you are not the only Valkyrie on this ship that has noticed him."

I narrow my gaze on her. "Crystal?" I breathe. "Have you seen something?"

Rage.

"Her Valk name is Sonia, but yes. He is with her now because she has ties to the Queen of Zebia." Sun Hai turns to leave. "Have a good night."

"Why are you telling me about Crystal?" I ask, feeling jealous fury even though I try to ignore it.

Sun Hai looks back. "Well, you are not the only one seeing the hidden side to Raine. I am trying to prompt you to do something more than what you are, because if he kills Thetis, it's game over for everyone. I love it here, and I don't want your loverboy Raine to ruin it for me."

She leaves, and I wonder if Sun Hai is telling the truth about her not being interested in Raine. I saw her gaze when she spoke about him, and it was anything but indifference.

I close my eyes, taking a deep breath.
Raine will be the death of me, I'm sure. So many emotions to deal with.

My eyes shoot open when I hear a distant rumble, and the dark horizon flickers with orange light. I run to the far balcony rail to get a better look, seeing the vibrations in the water off in the distance.

"Dude," Steven suddenly says beside me, making me jump.

I look at him and frown. "Where have you been?"

"Scouting. I only stopped to eat a sandwich for a quick sec—like, it took barely any time." He looks at me with a guilty expression. "Swear."

"What did you find out?" I can feel my pulse pounding. "And what is happening? Are we under attack?" I gaze back towards the sea.

"Well, no, they cannot track us for the time being. Some technology Pierce was telling us about when I was eating my sandwich. But they are attacking in a way, sending out large drones to seek out Poseidon's army." Steven puts his hands on the rail. "The land Empires aren't stupid. They know what they are up against."

"What's Raine doing?" I ask, feeling a sense of panic.

"Not sure, but I did see Chelsey." He pauses with a frown. "No, wait, what's her name?"

"Crystal." I deadpan, and squeeze my eyes shut.

"Yeah. I hit on her, but I'm not sure if she was feeling it. Me and this wetsuit just aren't vibing." Steven looks down at himself with a scowl. "Kinda throwing off my game." He looks at me with a somber expression. "Be honest, does this suit make me look fat?"

We both stare at each other.

I open my mouth then shut it. "Uh . . . "

I hear a commotion and thank the Gods of Awkwardness that they saved me. My pulse jumps to life when I see Raine. I shiver and grab myself tighter. He renders me breathless every time I see him—such dark elegance and power.
He stands with his men on the mid-deck and stops right next to Thetis. My heart stops. I think everyone is silently holding their breath. Both men look

out into the dark sea at the flickering lights.

"First time Raine has not tried to slit Thetis's throat," Steven whispers. "I'm getting warm fuzzies," Steven says with round eyes.

Raine's body is rigid, his hard muscles tense. He crosses his arms over the billowy black shirt that still clings to his wet body, like he just came from the monstrous sea.

Thetis slightly looks in Raine's directions and says something. Raine takes a heavy breath and laughs cooly, responding.

"Aw. Look at that. They're actually talking strategies with one another. Thetis just asked for Raine's opinion," Steven whispers next to me.

I bite my lip as I watch Raine say something to his men, then turn towards Thetis, addressing him, hands on his hips. Raine's porcelain skin is luminous in the night, and his vivid gaze pins Thetis.

Thetis takes a moment to respond, and then I see Crystal walk up to both men, looking slightly timid. I don't blame her—Raine and Thetis are extremely intimidating men.

I'm instantly on edge, watching intently at Raine's expression as he walks up to her. He dwarfs her, looking down at her and saying something. His expression is of stone, unreadable.

Crystal is cute in her tight suit and blonde braided hair, and I wonder if Raine is attracted to her. I mean, she is an FGI agent. We are purposefully designed to be irresistible.

He must.
~Ugh~. I now understand the pain of competition.
"Raine just said your name," Steven says beside me, his eyes squinting in their direction.

I tense at that and see Raine's gaze immediately find me, then he glances back to Thetis, saying something. Does Raine always know where I'm at? It seems like he never has to look for me, he just knows.

"What are they saying?"

"Hmm, something about using you."

My eyes widen when Raine suddenly moves and makes his way towards me. All gazes land on me clear up here. I brace myself as I watch Raine swiftly make his way up toward me. He's now on the top deck, and his eyes hold me hostage. I swallow, my heart pounding through my chest as I watch him near. The wind blows his wet hair as he now stands before me.

"I need you."

I wish he were talking about something else. I look out to the men gazing up at us, including Crystal. I look back at him.

"For what?"

He reaches out and pulls the blanket from my shoulders, tossing it to Steven, covering his whole body. I ignore Steven's struggles to free himself as Raine inspects me from head to toe, tilting his head.

"We are going for a swim."

My eyes widen. "A swim?"

In the monstrous black waters?

Raine's gaze travels over my face and hair like he has not seen me in years, making me shiver. His eyes are so vivid in the night that I can see different hues of orange and slight hints of yellow.

"We need to disable a rod in the ocean. The empires are setting a trap, creating an electric force field with hundreds of rods. It will take a great amount of power to override one rod, but once we do, it will take down the entire force field. They will have a hell of a time trying to locate which one is out."

"You want me to take your power?"
I can see a smile pull at his lips. "Don't get too excited," he whispers in

that voice that has heat pooling in my stomach.

I take a breath. "Only mildly," I say, and roll my eyes playfully.

He makes a sound and closes his eyes for a moment.

"It's dangerous. You will stay close to me. I'm not even confident that we can override it." He expels a breath. "But we can't get close until we take it out. If we fail, it will put us in a vulnerable position."

"I will have no idea what to do," I say, feeling a wave of crippling fear.

Raine steps closer to me and grabs my face in his large hands, lowering his lips to mine. "Don't worry," he breathes, "nothing will happen to you." His mouth takes mine.

He could tell me anything right now and I would believe him.

Raine's lips are incredibly sinful.

I know he does not have to use his tongue for me to take his power, but mercy, he is kissing me, hard and demanding. I know we have an audience, but Raine does not seem to care what anyone thinks of him. Every sweep of his tongue makes my knees weak. The taste of him is addicting, making me want more and more. The way he slightly bites my lip and then sucks flatlines my rational thoughts.

See—this is why I am worthless.

Bring in more agents. I'm compromised.
He pulls back finally, "~Mmm,~ I needed that from you," he says against my lips. "Now take my power, Camila."
Raine's mouth locks to mine again, and all I can think is that I wish I could take a lot more than his power.

Possibly his heart.

***

I see the shocked stares as I stand on the ledge, ready to plummet into the dark, monstrous sea. My skin matches Raine's, and I feel so much power that it almost makes me dizzy and nauseous. I can see everything so clearly in the dark of the night.

When I take Raine's power, I feel such an intimate connection with him. I'm not sure if it's mutual, but if not, that does not change how I feel. Now, I guess, everyone knows that I have Nymph blood. I can see a lot of shocked expressions on the men's faces.

Raine stands behind me, one hand on my hip as he talks to his men. Every so often, I can feel his thumb press into my skin and gently caress me. Is it second nature for him to do this, or is he letting me know he is right here, calming me?

"Raine!" Thetis yells, walking up to us, taking off his shirt.

I tense. Raine's hand on me tightens.

"I'm coming with you. Your men need me," Thetis says, and exhales, locking eyes with Raine. "We need our best men down there. That rod is designed to be indestructible."

I can see Raine's jaw flex. "You will only get in my way," Raine hisses, and I can tell he is trying to hold back, his arm now circling my waist like I'm his lifeline. The only thing keeping him grounded.

"I'm coming, Raine. You need my help and you know it," Thetis fires back, and I can see the men around us placing their hands on their weapons, readying for a fight.

Raine laughs and closes his eyes, muscles flexing. "Fine. You want to come play, then do it, but stay the fuck out of my way."

Thetis glares at Raine and nods to his men. I let out a breath, not realizing I was holding it.

Raine turns towards me and lifts my chin to look at him. He is acting shockingly tender to me, and I see something in his troubled gaze.

"Are you ready?"

"Y-yes," I get out as the night wind hits me, blowing my hair around me.

"Liar." He smiles. I don't say anything as his thumb rubs my chin. "I will guide you. How much of my power do you have?" Raine asks, eyes searing me.

"Like twenty minutes," I say, and shiver in the cold wind.

"Can you take more?" he asks with a frown.

I shake my head. "Not unless I want to pass out, but I can take more underwater later."

He expels a breath and nods, tying something around his narrow waist. I try to ignore his large pecs and impossibly muscled torso. I give myself a shake and I look down and see he is now wrapping some sort of rope around my waist and hooking it to himself.

"I don't want you to get caught in a current."

I nod, feeling his hand tug on the rope at my waist, jerking me toward him. I look up and see a grin on his lips.

"What's funny?" I whisper.

"Do you know how to dive?" he asks, ignoring my question.

I feel my cheeks redden. "Yes," I say, looking at the long drop, like insane cliff diving. One of my talents is swimming, but it does not include expert diving from this height.

I feel my face pale. He makes a sound as he looks around.

"I'll take that as a no," he continues when I look up at him. "Just hold onto me, and we will go feet first. The water will not hurt you while you have my power, so do not be afraid."

I nod. Raine looks at his men and holds up his arm. "Let's get this done!

Watch out for drones." I start seeing Nymphs dive off the side of the ship and disappear into the thrashing dark waters.

Oh shit.
"You ready?"

I nod, my voice not working.

This FGI experience is like I joined the Navy SEALs.

I feel Raine pull me hard against him, and then we are airborne. I want to scream as I grip him hard, but it happens too fast as we hit the frigid waters.

Air bubbles all around me.

I'm weightless.

My mind blanks.

I open my eyes, and shockingly, I can see around me like it's crystal clear. The dark world is illuminated to my eyes as if the black ocean glows. I can feel vibrations, and I immediately know that they are solid objects all around me, like a map.

Raine is in front of me with his glowing eyes.
~"Can you hear me?~" Raine's voice whispers in my mind.
Wild.
Just like Steven.
~"Yes,~" I reply with my thoughts, hoping he hears.
~"You look like a goddess underwater,~" I hear him say in my mind.
~"Your eyes are like mine, but with a hint of violet.~"
Raine pulls me to him, and my arms wrap around his neck. His black hair floats around him, and I feel his hands grip my waist as they smooth up my ribcage.
~"Exhale your oxygen, but do not inhale. Your body will get what it needs from the water,~" I hear him say.
So strange. I still feel like I'm breathing normally.
~"We have a long swim, let me know if you need a rest. Or you can just hold onto me.~" His voice echoes through my thoughts.

I give him a thumbs up and he smiles, kissing my hand before we take off.

I see Nymphs swimming all around us, including Sun Hai. There are other subs with us, and I swear I see Nomi to my left, though I know she is not on our ship. It's so eerie and mind blowing to be swimming like this. It's peaceful, but also terrifying.

I can hear the water rushing by me as I create air bubbles with each stroke. Raine has to grab me a few times to avoid dark, lurking creatures with razor-sharp teeth. My heart pounds as our journey continues. I start to feel Raine's power slipping, and I tug on his powerful body.

He slows to look at me.

~"You need more?~" he asks. ~"We are here.~"

~"Yes,~" I say, and I can feel my panic escalating.

Drowning is one of my biggest fears.
~"Steven here. I'm watching your oxygen levels~——~you need to get more, dude."~

Raine's lips are on mine before I can think another word. I focus and suck in his energy, feeling my oxygen levels return to normal, calming me. I don't get a great pull like I usually do on dry land—underwater is much trickier. Maybe it's just being out of my comfort zone, submerged in the deep, scary sea.

~"Look at me,~" I hear Raine say. ~"If you need me to take you up immediately, you better tell me.~" His voice sounds intense in my head. -"Are you okay?~"

I nod, not wanting to scare him.

Thumbs up.

Nomi swims up to us, and I can see her eyeing me with her glowing blue eyes, then she looks to Raine. I wonder what she is talking about with him. The woman does not like me, and I can't blame her. I actually feel bad.

I tense.

I look to my left, then to my right, feeling slight currents in the water like something just swam right next to me. So damn creepy. I pray nothing touched my foot.

~"That was me, dude. OMG, I'm like this massive fish with tiny little shit-fins. I swear I hate this shit in the ocean. Some bastard Nymph bumped into me and I have been swimming sideways ever since.~"

I mentally laugh, trying to see him in the darkness.

~"I don't even know if I'm sideways anymore. I could be upside down for all the F I know.~"

I feel Raine jerk the rope at my hips, gaining my attention. He grabs me around the waist, his face right next to mine.

~"Tell me why you're laughing.~" His gaze sears mine.

He can hear me laugh? I stare at him like I don't know what he is talking about.
His gaze narrows. -"Let's hurry and do this.~"
I nod.

We swim for a little bit longer until we come up to a massive steel rod glowing in the dark ocean, with tons of Nymphs floating around it. I see Sun Hai with Thetis, inspecting it.

Raine waves his arm and the Nymphs respond. He pulls out a long, spear-like weapon and touches it to the metal post, the others following along. Raine pulls me in front of him, his arms coming around me, and he places my hands in his. I see Thetis hold up his fist to Raine and pull out his rod.

I feel Raine kiss my shoulder. His voice brushes my thoughts.

~"This will ground the electric current. When I give the word, I want you to put all of the energy you have into this with me. Do you understand? Are you okay?~"

299

~"Yes.~"

~"On FIVE. One . . . two . . . ~" I see him do something with his arm.~"Three . . . four . . . ~"

I focus and can feel the energy build up in my body.

~"Dude! I'm am not liking your oxygen levels!~"

~"FIVE!~"

I don't remember much.

Only white light . . . Raine's lips on mine . . . my body being jerked as if being violently pulled through the water . . .

~"This is Steven from mission COD-3-67. On behalf of Camila Mastos de Cruz, I'm authorized by Fairy Godmother Incorporated to use a lifeline on her behalf—~"

~"*Agent A32, Lifeline ACTIVATE!*~"

CHAPTER 23

CAMILA

"Camila?~"

~Beeep . . . beeep, beep . . . beep . . . beeep~—

I pry my lids open and see a bright light shining in my face. I swallow.

"Am I dead?" My voice is scratchy and dry. I need some water.

I hear a laugh. "Far from it."

That's weird.

I frown as I focus on three doctors leaning over me, while Pierce smirks at me. Why is he smiling at me like that?

My eyes focus on him, seeing the digital readings on his black-framed glasses. He's a strange man.

Wait . . . Why am I staring at Pierce?

"Pierce?" I say in confusion, my mind in fragments. "Why," I look around, "am I here?" I try to sit up and receive help from the doctors. "I used a lifeline?" I ask in awe, not remembering it. "Shit." I place a hand on my forehead.

"Well . . ." Pierce smiles at me and touches his glasses, changing the tiny digital readings to something else, slightly distracted. "You should have seen Steven. Acted out perfect protocol, gaining himself a white heart." He pauses. "A very high metal for an FGI shape-shifter agent."

"He had to use a lifeline on my behalf?"

"Correct."

My mind is whirring frantically, seeing flashes of myself underwater and Raine behind me.

"No," I breathe, remembering the bright flash. "What happened?"

Pierce takes a moment. "Well, you were in no shape to use that kind of power, with what little oxygen you had." Pierce gives me a pointed look. "We had to administer a shock to your heart to get you back. That was a close call, my dear." Pierce looks at the doctor next to him and laughs, patting him on the back. "First time I saw this guy sweat."

The doctor with half his face covered exhales next to Pierce, glances at me, and nods.

My eyes widen, my pulse jumping. "I almost died?"

Again?!
"I like to look at it in a positive light. You survived, not ~almost ~died. This actually makes me very hopeful, because I do love near-death experiences," Pierce says, and glances at the agents in black standing behind him.
"Zoya, please prepare for extraction."

I look at the woman in a sleek black business suit standing closest to Pierce. A stunning woman, with ice-blue eyes and hair that is pulled into a severe bun.
She nods and touches her earpiece, talking to someone. Really though, the woman looks like some Russian assassin from a ~007~ movie.
I look back at Pierce. "Did you just say that you like near-death experiences?"

Pierce winks at me. "You'll see for yourself. In my experience, the thought of losing someone will put things into perspective in a hurry. It does wonders for stoking burning embers into a roaring flame."

He continues, "Life can be too short, and being reminded of this is sometimes the missing ingredient."

"I see," I murmur, understanding the madness of this. Will it affect Raine as Pierce thinks?

"But you have one lifeline left," he warns. "Be smart, trust your instincts."

That's right.

Fear washes over me. "I only have one more?"

"One more, then on the fourth — extraction from the game. This is serious. The rules of these missions cannot be broken." Pierce takes off his glasses. "Are you ready to do this?"

I take a shaky breath. "Thank you, Pierce."

He tilts his head at me in question.

I almost feel my eyes cramp. "For pushing me outside my comfort zone. Being married to Brayja would have been a living nightmare," I say, feeling humbled, "and you knew that."

I still desire my riches and lavishness. But . . . it's not so blaring to me now. Other things have surprisingly squeezed their way into my soul, my inner desire shifting, flipping upside down.

It's confusing and mystifying.

Pierce smiles and reaches to pat my hand, squeezing it. "I take care of my girls," he continues, his blue stare seeing too much of me. "You will learn that we are family here. I will show you some tough love, when warranted. But none of my Darlings or Sweet Hearts have ever come out of this experience not being the best version of themselves."

I smile and nod. "I can see that."

"Steven here!"

I look past Pierce and see Zoya roll her eyes at Steven, touching the bridge of her nose.

Pierce glances back at Steven in his same black wetsuit, hair in a low, messy pony. "You finished your meal?"

Steven beams, closing his eyes like he is reliving it. "I didn't realize that the White Heart medal comes with a free meal. Soooo dope."

Pierce looks at me with an amused smirk. "We have the best buffet in all of the Universe here at FGI."

Steven nods, then looks panicked. "I might need a nap," he gets out, and grabs his stomach. A loud rumble is heard. "And tums." He swallows. "Legit ate like fifty hot wings in ten minutes."

"Pierce, we have extraction in 5 minutes," Zoya announces behind us.

He ignores Steven's crisis. "Camila, you will be revived by CPR. We will administer more oxygen in your body so you survive this," he continues at my gasp. "My team will have you monitored fully and will repeat the extraction if we have to. No lifeline will be at risk."

I open my mouth, then shut it, my heart pounding. I feel the blood leave my face.

"You'll be fine."

I think I nod.

"Extraction!"

Pierce's face distorts as my vision dots with black. ~"You'll be fiinnnnnneeeee~, ~trust meee ~. . . " is all I hear until I am fully out.

***

I can feel my body being violently pulled out of the water by strong arms before I black out yet again.

Flashes of Raine's face and glittering diamonds, all discombobulated.

Jewels and golden coins are falling to the ground, shattering. Tons of riches and lavish treasures flash through my mind's eye, almost to a point of madness.

The images won't stop, the flashing becoming more aggressive.

I scream, placing my hand on my ears and eyes.

Then the sparkling jewels vanish and in its place is a dark room, possibly a cold dungeon. I can feel and smell fear, terror. This place is not familiar to me, yet I seem to know it very well.

I want to leave. I can feel my heart pounding as I look around. Something is very wrong. The hairs on my neck stand on end.

I suddenly hear sobs, small sniffles making me tense.

My body is rigid as I listen.

My heart stops when I suddenly see two kids huddled in the corner, shivering, holding onto one another.

The older one is possibly in his teens, and in his arms is a frail little girl, who is the source of the small sobs. He strokes her hair as if trying to soothe her, even though I can sense his agony.

I place my hand on my mouth. My heart wrenches as I reach my hand out as if to gain their attention. My mouth trembles as I think of something to say. "E-excuse me? How did you get in here? I can help . . . " My voice trails off as an apparition of a man walks right through me as if I'm nothing but thin air.

I gasp in confusion, looking at my hands.

I must be dreaming . . .

My eyes fix on the man, and the girl's sobs grow louder, nuzzling her head into the boy's stomach. I can hear the boy hiss now, the man obscuring my view as he moves to the left.

~"Put up a fight this time, boy, and you'd wish you were never born~ . . . ~" came the low threat from a voice that sounds familiar.

His golden coat reminds me of the Valkyries, and the bright colored gems embedded into the sparkling fabric confirms this.

Guards pass through me, and the little child screams. The shrieks echo in my mind so loud that I yell in pain to make it stop.

It gets louder and louder.

The anguish—I can feel blood trickling out of my ears from the sound! Dear god, make it STOP!

"~CAMILA!" ~it shrieks like a phantom in the night.

I cry out again, but I make no sound as something flashes through my body making my muscles seize. Images scatter through my brain when finally my eyes open, a shock going through my frame yet again, and I scream in agony. My heart is beating wildly as I blink, trying to catch my breath.

~"Can you hear me?! Dude, we almost had to extract you again. The CPR did not work, so Raine freaked and shocked yo' ass! Shiiiit man. He got your heart beating again—you were like dead for a few minutes!~"

"Camila? CAMILA?!"

I hear his frantic voice as his hands cradle my face.

"I got her! I have a steady beat," I hear him yell to someone next to him. His handsome face comes into focus, the night sky angry and flickering behind him.

Raine looms over my body, dripping wet, eyes searching my face. The fire in his gaze is wild and intense as he examines my features.

"Raine . . . " I whisper.

His expression makes me shiver. So much emotion is there, like he is not hiding it for once. Poker face — gone.

He closes his eyes and whispers something. Water droplets fall from his pale skin, hair wild and soaking. Raine opens his eyes, and his blazing orange orbs hold something profound.

I shift, feeling the bitter wind as my senses come back to me.

"Raine," I whisper again, and look around.

In one sweeping movement, I am in his arms, and he is yelling things to the men around him, carrying me.

"Raine?" I ask, my mind still putting pieces together.

"Don't talk, just keep breathing," he pleads as if I could die at any moment. I feel Raine turn.

"Thetis! Get that sword of yours! NOW," he booms, his grip tightening on me.

My arms reach around Raine's neck, and I can feel the power in his body as he holds me. Though it does not escape me that he just called for Thetis. Why? I feel Raine turn, and his muscles are tense with each movement.

"I don't give a fuck. I want it off!"

"What off?" I ask into his neck, but he does not respond as we enter the ship and walk down long dark hallways. I can feel the tension in him, and I can tell he is not okay. I look around the black hallways with men following us and realize that this is not the way to my room.

"Thetis!" Raine yells again, and looks behind him.

I can sense he is flirting with a thin line of insanity. I can feel it in him. I don't know what he wants, but if I were Thetis, I'd listen.

~"Dude, I have no idea what Raine is doing. Just hang tight!~"

"Raine," I say, trying to gain his attention.

"Don't speak," he whispers through gritted teeth.
We enter a room, and it's a large bedchamber decorated with blacks and silvers. Sterile, but in that dark and gothic way. Raine sets me on the bed and turns to the men behind him.

"Is he coming?"

A Nymph nods right as Thetis walks in with a frown on his face, soaking wet as well.

"Not smart, Raine."

Something flashes over Raine's features. "I didn't ask for your approval," he hisses, eyes wild.

Thetis wipes a hand down his face and places his hands on his hips, muttering to himself. "The damn bracelet is enhanced."

Raine closes his eyes and cracks his neck, muscles flexing. "I don't give a fuck. I want it off."

Both men stare at each other, their gazes sizing each other up, tension escalating.

I look down at my bracelet with a frown. He wants it off? Realization dawns on me.

Raine wants to be connected to me again.

Maybe he blames himself for almost killing me, not that it was his fault.

No matter the reasoning, I feel a rush of heat at his possessiveness. Everyone in the room stares at me like I am a unicorn—the object of Raine's obsession. It's like this cold-hearted creature is actually showing signs of something other than hatred for someone.

Could it be love? Or just a brief fascination?

I notice how intense he looks as he stares at Thetis, as if he doesn't care what anyone thinks of him.

"Raine," Thetis grits out, water dripping from both men. "I need you at full power, and you being connected to her," he looks at me, his blue gaze piercing, "will put us all in danger."

"I want it off," Raine threatens again, like he didn't even hear Theitis's warning.

I feel my cheeks stain red.

"The Empires are coming for us, Raine. We didn't take out their force field. We are going to war!" Thetis yells so loudly that I flinch.

Raine smiles, and it's dark and sinister. "The bracelet comes off or I will take her with me, and you will have none of my help."

Thetis closes his eyes and flexes his fist. "How do you propose we get the damn thing off?"

A part of me is in shock at Raine's behavior, putting everyone at risk for me.

"Your sword," Raine whispers.

"That will cause a power surge," Thetis hisses. "We are a sitting target."

Raine takes a steadying breath and walks up to Thetis. We all tense. The men stand almost nose to nose. I can barely breathe. My pulse is pounding so hard, too much testosterone in this room.

"If anything happens to her," Raine barely whispers, my ears straining to hear, "I will blow this vessel up myself, understood? I want the bracelet off now."

Thetis's gaze widens slightly, seeing that Raine is completely serious.

My heart is pounding at what Raine just admitted.

Thetis takes a strained breath then nods, and I hear whispers around the room. I shiver as Raine, for the first time, glances at me, body rigid. The impact of his gaze has me breathless and confused.

I can't reflect on what I see there in the fiery depths of his eyes.

Raine walks over to me and kneels down in front of me, grabbing my wrist with the golden bracelet. I feel eyes on me as Raine regards me, his unnatural gaze tracing over my face. "You're still pale. How do you feel?" he asks softly.

I shiver and swallow, noting that his thumb is caressing my inner wrist. "F-fine," I think I say.

~Soaking wet, freezing, and confused by you. ~

He tilts his head at me and then glances to his left. "Give me something to protect her wrist from the blade," Raine orders.

Someone moves to fetch what he asks as I hear Thetis draw his sword.

"Raine," I whisper, trying to ignore the stares. "What are you doing? Why?"

He takes a moment to answer. "Protecting you," he whispers, not meeting my gaze, then he stands and makes room for Thetis.
~Protecting you~ . . .
Visions flash through my mind's eye as if those words were familiar and incredibly painful at the same time.

Raine walks around the bed and comes behind me, his strong arms circling me and steadying my wrist with the help of four other men. His heat engulfs me, and I shiver.

I feel his lips on my damp shoulder, and he nods to Thetis. "Do it fast."

Thetis nods and glances at me, his blue gaze holding concern. "Don't move."

Raine holds my wrist rock steady. I couldn't move if I tried. "Okay," I breathe.

I close my eyes.

His lips at my neck calm me from the sparks of light as Thetis brings his glowing sword down upon it. Hit after hit.

I flinch and gasp as the scorched golden bracelet finally goes flying off to the right. I'm breathing hard, wondering if I still have a wrist.

Sighs of relief sound around the room as Thetis stands, breathing hard. "Don't make me regret that," he hisses, and leaves. "I'll see you on deck."

The men leave.

Raine is still behind me and I'm scared to move. I feel his lips on my shoulder again as his hand rubs the skin at my wrist. I turn my head, wanting to know what is going on in his head.

"Raine . . . "

I expel a breath as I feel his energy all around me and through me. I shiver and suppress a moan, feeling my skin tingle. He makes a sound in the back of his throat and pulls me back to where I lay on the bed, his large body beside mine.

"Camila," he whispers, as his hand travels up my stomach, "don't be afraid."

"I'm not." My eyes flutter.

That's a lie.

"I will not lose you . . . "

"You won't," I whisper as his hand travels up to the valley between my breasts, my pulse beating hard. His gaze lowers, and I can see an inner torment there.

"You're so beautiful," he murmurs. "I want all of you." He looks larger than life laying next to me. Beautiful, powerful, stunning.

And somehow he wants me.

"Why do you want to kill Thetis?" I can't help the question. It just flies from my lips.

Raine closes his eyes and laughs, the sound chilling.

"Because he made me kill both of my sisters."

CHAPTER 24

CAMILA

"That's all you need to know," he whispers like he immediately regretted saying the damning words. I frown as I watch him, exhaling slowly, muttering something to himself.

My heart pounds as I watch Raine put his head in his hands, muscles flexing, his wet hair falling forward. Such a beautiful creature that's continuously tormented, and I'm finally getting glimpses of his pain. His bare torso almost radiates light as we sit in the darkroom, as if he could just be a figment of my imagination.

I can't deny the anguish I see in him, and with what he just said, my heart hurts. I swallow, knowing I must tread lightly here.

"Raine," I whisper, touching his arm, "Tell me . . . ~please~."

He laughs, eyes still closed, then finally he looks at me. I swallow, seeing something profound in his fiery gaze, confusing me.

"Not to change the subject, but feeling you is so addicting," he says, and tilts his head at me, studying me. The set of his jaw and the way he grabs the bedding, knuckles white, lets me know that Raine is teetering.

I have got to calm the rage that I see in his eerie gaze.

Now.

"I can feel you as well." I pause and inch closer, my pulse beating out of my chest. "I can see things as well," I slightly prompt, "when I'm connected to you."

He slightly grins. "Hmm," he says. "I hope for your sensibilities that you don't."

I look down, gathering my courage. "Was it you in a jail cell with a small little girl? I saw it—felt it." I squeeze my eyes closed, hoping I'm not pushing too much. "Long ago . . . "

The silence is terrifying.

I don't want to send Raine over the edge, but I also have to peel back his layers to start a healing process—if that's possible.

"Look at me," he whispers.

I look up at him and shiver at his dark grin. I wish I didn't find his wicked smirk so thrilling because I tread on dangerous waters here. I need to have my guard up, not to be entranced by his dark magnetism.

"You're scared," he says.

"No—I'm not," I say quickly, fighting the shiver that wants to wrack my body at his intense look. I feel like I'm sitting next to a wild animal, straining at its confines.

The energy coming off of him makes my body quake.

Raine blinks. "Liar."

I want to curse.

I don't say anything, then prompt, "Is it so hard to open up to me, Raine?"

"You won't like what you see," he murmurs. "And I can't have that."

It's tough to read him.

"You're deflecting. I know it was you in the cell." I swallow. "Was that your sister with you?" I grip the bedding as well, holding my breath.

He exhales.

Raine shifts and grabs me, making me gasp as he looms over me, his muscled arms braced on either side of me. "It doesn't matter, Camila." His voice is smooth, but laced with warning. He looks deadly. I feel like a twig with this godlike creature holding me hostage.

"You'll understand if I disagree," I get out, praying he does not hear my rapid pulse. He cannot put up his walls again. I have Raine with his walls on fire, cracks splitting right in front of me. I'm the warrior on the white horse, raising my sword as my army readies for a battle.

His gaze moves over my face. "I understand as well, but it does not change the fact that there is nothing you can do. I can see and feel that you desperately want to fix me," he whispers, and leans down to kiss my collarbone, lingering there. "I'm touched that you care enough to try."

"Bullshit. You're the liar now. You're not eternally damaged, Raine," I say through my teeth, hating that he wants to give up. "Stop giving up and let go."

Raine raises his head to stare at me, and I can tell he's surprised. "Careful."
"Or you'll get violent?" I tense.

He laughs at that and looks away for a second like he thinks I'm cute. "No, not with you. Never with you." He looks down, his gaze tracing over my body as he takes a shaky breath.

"It turns me on when I see the fire in your gaze." Raine glances up at me with that sexy look that drives my pulse into palpitations. "I might upset Thetis if I strip you naked and take you up against the wall. What do you think? I do love to upset him."

My pulse is pounding now, heat pooling in my lady regions. We have not

315

had sex yet, and I would be lying if I said I don't think about that every waking second. It makes me dizzy with desire. At this point, I will take him any way I can, and I'm not ashamed to admit that.

I'm being selfish.

I gasp when suddenly we both feel the sub shift violently to the left. Raine tenses then exhales, looking up towards the ceiling.

"We are outnumbered, I'm afraid. They know where we are because I gave our position away," he looks down to my wrist, "by removing your bracelet. Well, that and the fact that we didn't take out their force field."

I stare at him.

He tilts his head.

"Shhh. It was worth it." He smiles again. "I'm just relieved I didn't have to cut your wrist off."

My eyes widen.

He leans down to my ear. "I'm joking, Camila. You should know more than anyone that I would never hurt a hair on your head."

Before, I would call him a liar, but now . . .

Raine slowly lowers his large body onto mine as his lips claim me. The feel of Raine's lush mouth causes a moan to rise up and out of my throat as he deepens the kiss.

"Camila," he rasps as he swipes his tongue into my mouth over and over. "Take away the pain," he whispers into my lips as he lifts me, his hand at the back of my head as he devours my mouth deeper.

I barely have time to breathe in between each deep thrust of his tongue. ~Mmmmm. ~Raine kisses so fluidly, never missing a beat even through our rushed breathing.

In the back of my mind, I wildly wonder if he is a good dancer. I'd place all the gold in this world on it.

Raine lifts his head, and the look he gives me is all it takes. That wicked, primal flicker in his gaze has me on ~fire. ~

I can feel the beat of my heart echo in my head as I watch him lick his lips. How I got picked up and pressed against the far wall, I will never know. Or how Raine's lips suck against my neck and my legs wrap around his hips as they roll into me.

My hands leave his silky hair, and I unzip my wetsuit down the middle, desperately pulling it off. Raine makes a sound against my mouth as he helps.

Skin on skin.

My head falls back. My mind is in a tornado of pleasure, lust, and something profoundly deeper. I know he must feel it too, for he whispers into my neck in some language that sounds incredibly intimate as if he can't help it, lost in the moment.

I'm naked from the waist up, and I can tell from the light in Raine's gaze that it's driving him wild. His lips are everywhere, and I can feel the hard length of him as he grinds against me, reaching for the waist of his pants.

I reach down before he can, and I grab him through his wetsuit. I love the hiss that escapes his perfect lips, his arms flexing around me.

"I want it," I whisper into his neck, and bite his ear.

His hoarse moan almost has me undone, but I feel him lift me with one arm as he yanks the wetsuit and my underwear off me. He might have ripped it, but all I know is this is happening right ~now. ~

The violent tilts of the sub go unnoticed.

Raine needs me, or maybe I need him.

The ripped muscles of his torso and the titanium of his arms are a harsh contrast to my lush, golden curves.

Raine leans back, but keeps my legs wrapped around his trim waist to look at me, his chest rising and falling.

I'm breathing so hard I might hyperventilate as he lowers his black pants, freeing the hard length of him.

Swoon.

My face ignites with fire.

Our eyes collide, and I swear I see his pupils dilate.

"Breathe," I hear Raine say before his mouth crushes to mine. I don't say anything—I can't. I just moan as I feel the large heat of him at my entrance.
~This is it~.
I don't know what he is doing to my senses, but I'm burning up, delirious. The deep thrust impales me, and I scratch his back from the shock, holding on for dear life, panting.

Raine's hips start to pump into me with a rhythm that has me screaming his name, my legs gripping his waist. He takes his pain and aggression out on me, and all I can do is hold on for the ride.

He does this so effortlessly it's like he could do this in his sleep. I feel his lips on my neck as his hands grip my breasts, raising the tempo even further, driving me over the top.

He has ruined me for any man, so I'm putting all my chips in, praying that my cards are high enough.

His rhythm is so good that I blow up into an atomic bomb. My climax almost has me drawing blood on his shoulder, and I feel blissfully lightheaded, disconnected, my body is sizzling.
I feel his release next as he tenses all around me, claiming my mouth once again in a heated kiss. Such an intense connection that it's as if I'm eternally tied to him now.

Just the feel of the bare heat from his body is utter bliss.

The kiss on top of my head is broken up by the loud banging on the door. I hear Raine say something under his breath as he slowly puts me down, fixing himself, cleaning me with a nearby cloth.

Does he even realize that he acts so caring when he does not have his hardened wall up?

"Camila," he breathes, and kisses my lips lightly. "Get dressed. We have company—lots of it."

I watch as Raine fixes himself, almost in a trance, wishing I could have hours more with him. I look up and see him wink and me. "Don't look so sad. I'm far from done with you," he murmurs. "Far from it."

I shake my head, cheeks staining red. ~Focus~. I scramble to put on my wetsuit, relieved that it's not ripped. I work my clothes with shaking hands.

Raine looks back at me, making sure I'm dressed.

"Stay close to me, Camila."

I nod.

Raine gives me a look and a grin. "I want more from you, but we can talk later." He opens the door, and his men come in, guns strapped to them. Their eyes go past Raine to me then back to Raine.

"Raine, we are surrounded."

"Nomi and Thetis?"

"They are on deck, demanding we come get you," the man says, soaking wet like he just came from the water.

Raine cracks his neck and holds out his hand for me. "Maybe I will toss Thetis in the fucking water as bait."

The Nymph laughs, and I grab onto Raine's hand, never wanting to let go.
~"DUUUUUDE! Steven here, like . . . I didn't want to bug you guys, but Thetis is raging mad! Be ready for anything—both of these ninjas are loose cannons.~"

319

I curse, dread sinking into every bone in my body. Raine needs to be at a peaceful retreat to deal with his pain, not here. Not next to Thetis.

We arrive on the massive main deck, and I can see the sky already twisting above us, making me frown. Rain and wind hit me hard as Raine leaves me by the door, standing next to Steven and Sun Hai.

Raine's gaze, as it lands on Thetis, is murderous.

"Camila." Sun Hai walks up to me, wet hair blowing with the wind. "What the fuck is up with Raine? Is he creating this storm? A hurricane is building!"

I flinch at the crack of lightning, looking out onto the angry black waters. "I don't think so . . . He was with me."

She stares at me. "With you?"

I glance at her and give her a meaningful look.

"Homeboy made it to home base," Steven chimes in, and winks at Sun Hai. "A little dirty, dirty!"

"Steven," I hiss in annoyance.

"Sorry."

She huffs and glances at Raine, whose head is tilted up at the sky with his eyes closed. "Well, whatever happened, your man looks dangerous — unstable. We need him away from Thetis."

"Should I go to him?" I whisper, seeing Raine flex his muscles like he is trying to hold on to his sanity. All the men on deck look tense, weapons in hand. Tensions are high as if the wind and lightning mimic it.
"I'm getting a red alert," Sun Hai whispers, and glances back at Raine, breathing hard. "Pierce just told my agent to be wary."

My heart constricts. "Raine is breaking. The house of cards is falling, and he can't stop it. He needs to get out of here," I get out and make a move to go to him, but stop suddenly.

320

Steven grabs my arm and pulls me back as Thetis points at Raine.

The dreaded confrontation.

No.

"Raine!" Thetis throws his hands up in the wind and rain, his silver armor reflecting the streaks of lightning. Nomi runs up to Thetis as if she will get him to shut up, but he pushes her back. "Is this another trap? This hurricane?!"

Raine slowly opens his eyes to glare at Thetis, fists clenched. My heart is beating out of my chest as I watch.

"Come on, Raine! We are all sick of this. You are either for us or against us!" Thetis yells, taking a step towards Raine. "Or are you just fucking crazy like everyone thinks? Tell me!"

~Oh shit~.
I feel Steven squeeze my arm.

Raine tilts his head, jaw flexing like he is still trying to keep the beast hidden. The rain pours down his pale skin, black hair glistening as he tilts his head back the other way.

Nomi screams, "Thetis! Stop!" Tears trail down her face, eyes red.

Thetis scoffs at Nomi and points at her. "You, stop fucking pining after this lunatic! He doesn't love you, Nomi, and he never will. Never fucking ever will! Did that sink in?" he yells at her, then looks back at Raine, teeth bared.

"The Empires are closing in because of you. We are surrounded! All because," he pauses to look at me, "you have to be connected to this Valkyrie that has you begging on your damn knees like a bitch!"

"Thetis!" Sun Hai screams next to me. Thetis opens his mouth then shuts it, breathing hard. Eyes squeezing shut as he draws his sword.

Both men are losing it.

321

My heart is in my chest as I look at Raine, who is currently eyeing Thetis with hatred, chest rising and falling, two men holding him.

"Come at me, Raine. Let's get this over with!" he yells, and locks his eyes with Raine's fiery ones. "Why do you have to be connected to her? Why her?! Why is she the only one you care about? I have thought about this over and over." He pauses. "I mean, you almost killed your best friend, did kill your best friend's parents, and started a fucking war!"

Raine brings his hands to his head and yells, the sound painful. The storm picks up with force, making me frozen in fear. We are the eye of the storm, the hub of Raine's fury.

Thetis shugs and holds up his hands.

"I heard that you had two sisters. Your mother will not talk about them—why? She came at me when I tried to ask about them, almost slit my throat! Why? Or is she just as crazy as you?"

Raine lowers his hands, and the look on his face makes me gasp.

"Raine!" I yell, taking a step towards him. I can't have this mission be stamped MISSION INCOMPLETE: Game Over.

"Thetis, no!" Nomi looks mortified as she bares her teeth at Thetis, hitting him.

Thetis laughs coldly at her and grabs her wrist. "I don't know, Nomi! We all want to know what the hell drives Raine. I honestly want to know!" He looks back to Raine. "What? Is that why you like Daphine? Because she reminds you of the sisters you could not protect—"

Nomi shrieks.

Raine is on Thetis so fast no one can stop him, and the blade at his neck draws blood. Sun Hai has her spear pointed at Raine with ten other men. Thetis lays on his back, hands up, breathing hard.
"After all this time, you don't fucking know?! You're not worth the air

you breathe," Raine hisses at Thetis, the storm above gaining power, the wind howling eerily.

I can see the frown and question in Theits's gaze as I slowly walk up, body numb.

Raine presses the blade harder. "You were the only friend I had, someone who I called my brother." Raine says the damning words for everyone to hear.

I frown, trying to understand.

Thetis is still glowering. "What the fuck are you talking about?"

"I will kill you," Raine threatens, "and love every fucking second of it."

He raises the knife high, and Thetis raises his hands.

"Drop the knife!" Sun Hai screams.

"Wait!" Thetis swallows. "I have no idea what you are talking about. He's clearly out of his mind." He tries to look at Sun Hai.

"Of course you don't, you're too fucking stupid." Raine tilts his head with a dark grin. "Let's jog your memory. You betrayed me, left me for dead, with my two small sisters. You sorry piece of shit. Not surprising you don't remember."

Thetis goes to talk then stops, his brows furrowing more.

"Ahhhhhhh. You're starting to remember then? Bravo. Do you remember the screams? The pain we both went through together? I trusted you with our lives."

I see confusion in his gaze turn to pure horror. Raine bares his teeth, rain pouring down on them. "You fucking left us to their abuse, breaking your promise. You left and never looked back after I saved your life!"

"No," Thetis whispers. "No . . . "

"I had to watch." Raine pauses as if to gain control, eyes closing, hands shaking. "I h-had to watch Luci's life disappear right in front of me, too fucking weak to raise her damn head to kiss me goodbye.

"She was just a child! I had to end her life to end her suffering. She was only five!" Raine is breathing hard. "You promised her she would not die like that. Not like that—ANYTHING BUT THAT!"

We all flinch. Tears well up in my eyes—so much pain in his voice.

~Raine~ . . .
I feel so much agony, so much desperation.

"Impossible," Thetis whispers, mouth slightly trembling. "~Perseis?"~

Raine almost snarls. "That was my name long ago, but much has changed. After I survived, I took my middle name, unable to live with the pain that you fucking caused."

The only sound is the thrashing wind.

"You don't look like Perceis. I don't believe it," Thetis whispers, eyes wide with horror.

Raine closes his eyes and laughs. "Of course not. You were not fed the rock salt like all of the rest of us. You were royalty, secretly being abused under Brayja's father. "But for the rest of us, we were fed the drug so they could watch us slowly dwindle, and at the same time crave it. The Gaya dungeons were full of Sose Nymphs! Skinny and malnourished. They got off on that shit."

"My god," Thetis whispers, "it's you. Fuck."

"You betrayed me after I saved your life," Raine hisses, and closes his eyes, jaw clenching. "I screamed your name as you left us, and you ran into your dad's arms, and said nothing."

Thetis glances at Nomi. "You knew this?"

Raine silences Nomi with his hand. "Nomi saved my life. Of course, she knows!" Raine yells, and laughs, spinning his knife in his hand. "She is the only reason you were not dead ten years ago. My mother married your father to save my life!"

"My father knows?" Thetis whispers.

Raine takes a moment. "He knows who and where I came from, yes, and what my mother sacrificed. But not the coward you are." Raine tilts his head. "Actually, I think he does, thanks to me. He even told me I am the son he's never had."

Thetis closes his eyes, laying back on the ground, cursing. "I was young, Raine!" he yells. "Young and stupid, but mostly scared. I swear I came back for you, to look for you and your sisters, but you were gone!" He glances up at Raine. "Why didn't you say anything?"

Raine smiles. "Because I wanted to secretly destroy your life like you did mine," Raine murmurs, and glances up at Nomi. "Forgive me, Nomi, but I'm going to kill him."

"No!" I scream, but the knife in Thetis's side sinks deep.

My vision blurs

Sounds all around me.

This can't be the end.

It can't.

CHAPTER 25

CAMILA

I'm shaken, completely emotionally compromised. What deep scars and demons Raine must face every day when he looks at Thetis—like reopening a wound over and over again. I now understand the pain I have always seen in his gaze. The trauma replaying over and over.

But it's not the end.

At least not yet.

Raine is flirting with it as the hard punch to Thetis's face almost leaves him unconscious, despite the knife wound. And the second punch has Sun Hai drawing her sword.

But as I watch through numbness, it almost looks as if Thetis is letting it happen, not fighting back.

It's hard to see with the pouring rain, the storm howling in the air like a tortured phantom. Men grab Raine to hold him back, trying their best to restrain him.

Thetis hisses in pain as he grabs the protruding knife, Sun Hai by his side, helping him stop the bleeding. Men are screaming back and forth, trying to save Thetis's life.

Raine shakes off the men holding him back, soaking wet, cursing. He nearly glows in the dark of the night, heightening his dangerous appeal. He looks like some god of war, radiating fury with each flex of muscle.

I frown as my numb body makes my way to him, my heart still pounding against my chest.

"Raine," I breathe as he turns to look at me.

His eyes are wild. "I won't kill him," Raine whispers, "yet. For you."

I look back to the large group working around Thetis, wrapping bandages around Thetis's waist. Nomi stands and glances over the side of the sub.

"Raine!"

Raine's jaw clenches as he looks in her direction, lightning streaking across the angry sky. I suck in a breath as I follow their gazes and see what has their attention. I can see distant lights flashing in our direction. It still looks like we are surrounded.

Raine's fury suddenly morphs into a faint smile as he puts his hands on his hips, closing his eyes for a second.

Men are yelling orders to get ready for battle, despite the one happening on our ~own ~ship. Raine does not seem worried that, despite the storm he has created, we are still not in a good position.

I shiver, seeing the massive rigs barely visible through the rain and waves. Terrifying. I would have thought for sure these waves would have taken out the Empire's vessels.

~"Dude, you okay? I think I pissed myself. I seriously thought the mission was over. FGI headquarters is very tense. Empires are ridin' dirty in subs—they're going under for protection!~"

"Are we in trouble?" I whisper. "Where are you?" I look around the massive upper deck, squinting through the rain.

~"We might be, though I think Thetis will be fine. It takes a lot to take out a Nymph of his stature. I'm inside in this lounge area. I eat when I'm nervous.~"

Raine turns and looks at me, taking weapons from Nymphs. "Who are you talking to?"

My eyes widen, my heart jumping. "Myself."

Shit.

He tilts his head. "Liar." He looks at my wrist, then back up to me. "Come stand by me."

I nod and walk up to him.

He lowers himself, bringing his head to my eye level. "Do exactly as I say, understood?"

I stare at him, feeling my skin prickle at his blazing eyes. A slight grin pulls at his lips.

"We are not in trouble. Ask me next time and not," he pauses, "whoever it is you like to talk to."

"You can hear?"

He raises a brow. "Hear?" His gaze narrows, intrigue sparkling in his eyes.

My pulse is pounding again.

I'm a moron, was he trying to trap me?

"Er—me talk—to myself." I need a Snickers bar.

A Sose Nymph walks up to Raine. "We have a problem."

Raine gives me a look like we are not done with his conversation. I shiver, loving what his dark grin does to me.

I look around and see the Sose Nymphs holding up their weapons to Thetis's army, and vice versa, tensions high. This makes Raine laugh and clap his hands, eyeing everyone in that mocking way.

"You all just learned what a piece of shit coward Thetis is, and you still protect him." Raine shakes his head and straps more dangerous weapons to his bare torso.

I would not want to be on Raine's bad side.

Thetis stands with the help of one of his guards.

"Raine, I was young and stupid!" he gets out, pushing off the guard. "That day has haunted me my whole life."

Raine smiles, and it's frigid cold. "That must have been so hard for you."

Thetis looks away and chokes out a laugh. "I realize I should have died that day. It was what I deserved."

There is silence but for the waves beating against the massive sub.

"Well," Raine murmurs while he flips a knife in his hand, "fortunately for you, I survived to take the only thing away from you that you care about. Just like you took the only thing I cared about."

Thetis glares at Raine.

"Your father's respect."

I swallow, seeing the realization in Thetis's expression.

Raine, from what Steven has told me, is the apple of Poseidon's eye, and there are rumors that Raine could possibly sit on the throne instead of Thetis.

"You see," Raine continues, seemingly enjoying himself, revealing his executed revenge, "you did not tell your father that day for a reason. In fact, I don't think you ever planned to. You could have faced extreme backlash.

329

Brayja's father was one of Poseidon's closest confidants, too important for scandal. The alliance was strong and paved the way for success."

"You know nothing about that," Thetis hisses.

Raine tilts his head. "Oh? I watched you through the crack in the stone wall, the way Poseidon put his hands on your shoulders, praising you as you smiled like a betraying little bitch." Raine continues, "You left us, with a smile on your face, soaking in all the compliments."

All eyes are on Thetis. He exhales and clenches his jaw. "What you didn't see was the fear I felt. And what you didn't know is that I had a plan to come back and save you!"

"Lies," Raine hisses, twirling his knife.

"They are not!" Thetis looks at Nomi, pointing to her. "You remember Queen Hilda always sending for me when they stayed with us. Why do you think I have always hated the Gaya Empire? Especially Brayja!"

Thetis looks at Raine.

"The queen sent for me, using me, and if I didn't comply in secret, she would ruin the alliance. The night I planned to break you out she sent for me, the guards drugging me into submission."

I place a hand over my mouth and look at Raine, who is also frowning.

Thetis takes out a sword, ignoring the pain in his side. "By the time I was able to escape, you were already dead. Or so I thought. I should have told my father on the spot, instead of trying to do it my way. The abuse is not an excuse, just an explanation."

Raine turns his face away from Thetis and it feels like forever passes.

"You could be lying out your ass," he whispers. "I do not trust you."

"I could be," Thetis agrees. "But I care not anymore. All these years, I thought you were dead. But little did I know you came back for revenge. The guilt has hardened me, changed me even."

Steven is suddenly beside me, eating some sort of a sandwich, looking super high.

"Guys! You see, this is why communicating is sooooo important. Like," he continues at my horror, eyes heavy-lidded, "Rainy-boy over here thought you were this evil dude this whole time, and all along Theeetisss was just a poor scared little dude, forced to be that troll's plaything."

"Steven," I hiss in shock.

Steven points at Thetis. "Dude, I feel for you on that, that woman would give anyone the creeps. I mean, I don't even know how Brayjoo was conceived. Nom sayin'?"

"Who the fuck is this?!" Thetis yells, confusion and anger on his face.

"Steven," Steven happily provides.

I grab his arm and squeeze hard. "Shut up," I get out with rising hysteria.

"Why do I have to shut up?" Steven frowns at me, talking super loud even though he's whispering. "Look," he points to Raine and Thetis, laughing like a stoner, "you both are actually great guys! We can all go home happy now. It has all been a big misunderstanding!"

"I'm going to kill him," Raine says, facing us now, taking out a knife.

Thetis nods in agreement. "Throw him in the water as bait."

Steven's eyes widen as if now realizing his stupidity, and he looks from face to face, his chubby body wobbling backward. "Hey, heyyyyy, guys, I'm no threat to anyone, I swear. Er—except for maybe the food in, like, that break room on the second floor." He waves his hand. "I'm sure you know which one I'm talking about. Anyway, those salty cracker things are legit, did some damage to those. The ones with the white spots."

Thetis looks at me then to Steven. "The fucking whale bait?"

Steven frowns.

A Nymph laughs beside Thetis. "That's fish shit."

I scream as the ship jolts to the side violently, causing everyone to fall to the left.

Raine is immediately next to me with his arm around me, pulling me up as the ship rocks the other way, water gushing all around us.

"These bastards can't fight us in the water, the fucking morons!" Raine yells, and looks to Thetis. "I don't give a fuck about you or if you're lying. We all fight today and kill them all."

Raine nods to his men. "This shit is long overdue."

Thetis wraps some sort of armor around his midsection with the help of Nomi and Sun Hai. Thetis winces a bit, then nods when it's in place. "Surround them? Break down their defenses? Those golden vessels have tons of weak spots."

Raine takes a minute, eyes scanning the stormy night, then bends down and picks up Thetis's sword, making everyone tense. But he flips the blade around and hands it to Thetis with a nod.

"Let's get water in their subs and make them never see the light of day again. The fucking bastards will pay dearly for what they have done. I'm going to make it hurt, slow and painful."

Thetis looks at the blade then slowly takes it, a half-smile pulling at his mouth. He looks up at Raine and nods.

"You heard him!" he yells, turning towards his men. "Let's go fishing for gold!"

My mouth hangs open. I can see a surge of hope between all of the Nymphs, confused stares darting around as they get ready for battle.

"Dude," Steven whispers next to me, his breath smelling horrid. "Did they just become best friends?"

I shake my head. "I think Hell must have frozen over."

Raine turns towards me and points at Steven. "You—get lost." Then he grabs me by the waist, pulling me against his large body. "Now give me those sweet lips and let's try this again." He licks his lips like he can't wait, sending butterflies into my stomach.

My body tingles as his mouth hovers over my lips, the heat from his body making me shiver in this cold.
"What about Hell freezing over?"

I stare into his exotic eyes and fight a grin. "Just kiss me," I breathe into his smiling lips. The taste of him and the feel of his tongue makes my brain wander into a place of utter bliss.

And just maybe.

Quite possibly.

My story won't end with a knife in my stomach.
P.S. I don't believe in ~famous last words. ~

CHAPTER 26

CAMILA

I break the water's surface, gasping for air as an explosion of colors paints the black sky. My eyes burn, and my throat produces a scream of relief as my legs kick to stay above water.

Air.

I suck in a deep breath.

A glowing orb of fire followed by a loud siren from a distant submarine rings in the night air. The sound is frightening, monstrous.

I'm suddenly submerged.

Panic.

I go under the black waters again only to come up gasping for air and riding a wave, the seas making me choke for oxygen.

A distant part of my brain would never have thought I'd be in this situation—ever. A flash of lightning streaks across the sky, mixing with this madness. Raine and Thetis blew up half their subs, and now we are pulling back. My power from Raine has run out. I helped Raine, this time using his power correctly and safely with his help.

But after the explosion, we were separated underwater. It was like an underwater tornado.

I have no idea where our sub is, or which direction to swim in.

"Raine!" I scream as I forcefully tread water and ride each black wave, praying nothing pulls me under. "Stevennnnn!" I yell into the stormy night.

Terror and blinding fear are overrun by pure adrenaline and the will to survive.

I will not go down this way.

This mission's danger factor is off the charts. These are not silly Disney stories that FGI provides. Reality is stranger than fiction, and this is real. The danger is SO real.

~"I'm HERE! Dude, remember your lifeline. Sun Hai just used one—she was almost speared through the heart by a Valkyrie!~"

He continues,~"Where are you, man? I can't see shit down here! This is intense, maaan. Pierce says get to the sub now, on your left. No, your right! My left~—~your right!"~

I yell," HOW?"

I try to talk again, but I go under, and all I can hear is the rush of bubbles and my body being flipped in different directions. I violently kick and use my arms to right myself, but it's no use.

That's when real fear kicks in. I could be killed in a matter of seconds.

I'm literally about to use a lifeline, yet again.

Insanity.

But a strong arm grabs me around the waist and pulls me with great force. We break the surface, and I see Raine's body in front of mine as relief floods my body. "Camila!" he yells, his eyes searching mine, fear in them as his metallic, fire-colored arm holds me to him. "We are going back to the sub!"

His wet lips are on mine, and I realize he wants me to take his power for the trip back. I try to focus and desperately take what he offers, but it's not working.

I feel exhausted.

We go under for a split second and come back up. My lungs hurt, burning from the exertion and lack of rest after frantically treading water. I can make out a frown on his face, then Raine's lips are back on mine, desperately trying to give me his power.

I can't.

I feel faint.

Dizzy.

"Ahh! Camila!" I feel him start to swim, keeping my head above water, his strong arm securing me against him. "Relax against me. Let me do the work!"

I can barely make out his words, and just focus on staying conscious.

Stay awake.

Don't inhale water.

It amazes me how strong Raine is and what a powerful swimmer he is because we are moving pretty impressively. I don't care if I'm in the middle of an ocean with a war going on, I feel safe with him. I feel so strongly for him that my mind has been consumed with him since the first moment I set my eyes on his stunning fire ones.

He had me at first glance and never let go.

"Stay with me. Head up!"

I take a staggering breath. "I a-am good!" I yell back, gaining a little energy as he pulls me, my legs kicking.

"You better be," he gets out next to my ear, holding me harder against his broad chest. I feel him whip me around after some time, and I can see our massive sub right in front of us, giving me a sense of relief.

I made it.

I'm in front of him again, his body pressed to mine, keeping me above water. He looks at me, his head covered with droplets of pouring rain.

"You're safe."

"Raine!"

We both look and see Thetis on some sort of glowing ladder on the side of the massive rig, holding his hand out to us, rain hitting him hard. Then I see other Nymphs around the sub break the surface.

I'm hauled and pulled by Raine, but what makes me smile despite everything is the fact that he does not hand me over to Thetis.

"Wrap your legs around my waist," he says into my ear, then looks to Thetis, one arm gripping the ladder. "I got her!"

Thetis nods and we make it up into the sub, finally out of the dangerous waters. I literally thought I was going to use my last lifeline.

~"Dude, I'm safe! Holy shit that was crazy. I know you were, like, super worried about me!~" Steven echoes in my mind.

~"You have to learn to distance yourself from me emotionally. I'm an agent—a king. I know what I'm doing. I'll be nearby—AKA in the break room~——~no need to come looking."~
I smile.

Raine sets me down on the sleek deck, and I feel him lean down in all of his orange-mermaid glory. "You're smiling," he says in a sexy whisper, eyeing me curiously.

"Raine! Can I get a second? We might have a second wave," Thetis yells from our left as other Nymphs board. "Not out of the storm yet!"

Raine turns and nods, then looks back at me, a strange expression flickering over his face. "Taking power from me — it hurts you?"

I wipe my wet hair out of my face and step closer to him. My arms circle his narrow waist, making him raise a dark brow.
"No, it's not pain, I just think I need to do it more often to gain stamina."

Raine suddenly looks up and softly laughs, making a flight of butterflies take off in my stomach. He looks around then back to me, lowering down to make sure no one else can hear.

"After this is all over, I will enjoy improving your stamina."

The way his dark grin pulls at his perfect lips has my pulse beating hard.

My cheeks flush.

Are we talking about the same thing?

"Raine! Your presence would be appreciated!"

Raine never breaks his eye contact with me. "Thetis, you want me in a good mood or a bad one?" A smile pulls at his mouth again, and he waits for a response. His gaze lowers to my lips, then over my hair, like he's mystified.

I must look like a drowned rat.

~But mmm~, his eyes are so stunning this close — even in the dark, I can see hues of yellow and vibrant orange. His pale skin seems almost enchanted as it changes back to its normal shade.

I hear curses from Thetis. Raine looks down then back up to me.

"Thetis better fucking be glad ~my woman ~won't let me kill him," he says softly, and tilts his head. "And as much as I want to know why . . . I want her to know this more. That she is the only thing holding me together."

My heart is pounding now, my gaze searching his face.

He goes to say something else, but stops for a second, then, "I don't know where you're from or what your purpose is here. But every time you almost die, I feel such . . . "

He closes his eyes and looks away. "Something I have not felt in a long time."

I frown and feel my eyes sting.

He looks back at me. "I'm going to send you away to keep you safe for me."

"You're going to send me away?"

"I—" He pauses, and his hands go to my face to hold it. "Camila, I need to keep you safe. Your power is not ready yet for this. I was selfish to bring you along."

I swallow, knowing we have little time left here. My life has been so crazy on this adventure, I would not be surprised if we had but one week left. It feels like I have been here for years.

"I need you," I blurt. "I don't want to go." I hold his hand to my face.

Raine closes his eyes and leans down to whisper against my lips, "I need you more, trust me. But I need you alive. I want you gone before the second wave hits."

The crack of thunder is ignored.

I pull back and force a laugh, not caring that people are watching. "Raine, you're making me nervous."

"Why? Because I want to protect what's mine?" he says, and looks at me as if I would disagree, looking adorably insecure.

339

No woman in their right mind wouldn't call herself the luckiest lady being Raine's. He's a wet dream on a stick. He is my wounded hero. But he's also so much more than that . . .

"You want me to be yours?"

Raine rubs his thumb over my lower lip and makes a sound I can barely hear over the wind. "Maybe I should rephrase that this time, even though, know that I'm giving you false hope that you actually have a choice in the matter." He looks to his left then back to me with a boyish grin that I rarely see.

"Do you want me to be yours?"

My heart rate is through the roof, not sure what is taking place here. I glance to my left as if to drag out the suspense, trying not to show how full my heart feels just yet.

My eyes collide with Nomi's, and I falter.

It's not a nice look. But I don't have time to study it as Raine grabs my chin to look back at him. "Now remember you don't really have a choice. I'm taking you for myself, and I will indulge in being the evil villain if I have to. I am always up for a challenge."

I lick my lower lip and give him my best make-him-pant look. "Would it be bad if I would be into that?"

Raine stands to full height and grins, rubbing a hand down his face. He snaps his fingers and some of his men make their way to us. He is still smiling, making my skin tingle, and looks back at me with a wink.
"~Mmm~, sweet Camila . . . I already know what you're into, trust me."
My cheeks flush and my heart pounds.

He smiles more at my shocked expression, telling them to take me out of here ASAP. I hug myself and want to ask Steven what to do, but Raine will definitely hear me.
~"Dude, Raine is sending you away, man! We have a week left, which is not bad seeing how Raine is clearly already in love with you.~"

A week?

I thought it was a little longer than that actually, and a flash of nerves courses through me. But I also feel an overwhelming sense of excitement, for it seems that Raine's life long goal to kill Thetis has diminished—for now, at least.

That gives me hope.

A life with RAINE after this.

~Swoon City~.

How would that look? Still so many questions, but at least I know he seems to have my best interest at heart.

~"Hey, can we talk about that Nomi chick staring at you right now? My mystic talents are giving me warning sirens in my head. Though that could be just the big hit I just took.~"

I look up and see Steven looking down at us on the smaller second deck, chewing something with a frown, eyes wide. He looks really high, even through the rain.

I hug myself tighter as I glance to my far right and see Raine talking to the men that are going to take me out of here. Thetis joins them with a few of his guards, probably talking strategy.

Raine looks up and our eyes clash, and immediately heat pools in my stomach. Raine can do that with one look. A dark grin spreads over his lips like he knows and can feel what I am feeling.

He nods at Thetis, still grinning like he can't wipe it off his face. They might just think Raine is his crazy self, randomly smiling, but I know.

I love seeing him like this. In the mists of the war, he looks . . . happy.

Is that all from me? Maybe he just needed something to live for, something to overpower his deep scars and the need for revenge.

~"Dude, don't MOVE!~"

I freeze. My heart stops.

I hear Raine yell, "NOMI, NO!"

Quickly glancing to my left, I see Nomi with rage-filled eyes, gun pointed at me, hand shaking. She glances in Raine's direction then back to me.

"I-I thought you were just a Valkyrie fling! Something pretty and flashy." The sound of thunder makes me flinch. She looks past me. "One more step, Raine — Thetis — and I will do it!" Her voice breaks painfully.

My heart breaks, I can see so much pain in her gaze.

"Nomi," I hear Raine plead.

"Don't fucking use my name again!" she screams, tears streaming down her cheeks. "I loved you, Raine. I waited for you all these years!"

I hear Thetis curse. "Nomi, lower the fucking gun!"
"Fuck you, Thetis!" she spits. "You don't know shit! You don't know anything that I went through with Raine. You didn't even know it was him after all these years!"

"Nomi," Raine pleads, "come talk to me. Lower the gun," he urges. I can hear the desperation in his voice, the fear.

~"Dude, use your lifeline. I don't trust this bitch, never did. Get ready. This is what we call fatal attraction, man. She needs to smoke.~"

"Oh yeah, Raine." She sniffs, gun shaking. "You want me to talk to you? You knew how I felt about you, Raine! We were meant to be together. I thought you knew that. I have done everything for you!"

"Nomi, I can never repay you for what you did. You know I hold you in the highest regard. You have always been one of my few friends," Raine says gently, like he's trying to talk someone off a cliff. "Please come talk to me."

"Friend?!" She laughs and looks at me, red eyes full of hatred. "This Valkyrie bitch does it for you, does she? What is it about Valkyrie women that you love so much?!"

"Nomi," Raine warns, "lower the gun."

"No! I saw the way you looked at her, RAINE. I saw it!" She is crying now. "Fuck you, Raine. All I ever wanted was for you to look at me that way—you used me!"

"Nomi," Thetis hisses. "Sister . . . think about what you are doing. This can get worked out. We are in the middle of a war, about to be fucking ambushed! Can't this wait? I don't know why you have these delusions about Raine—" He pauses, and I see some guards nodding in his direction. "Stop this nonsense!"

She holds the gun up higher, making everyone tense. "You were right, Thetis. Raine will never love me." She looks past me to where I think Raine stands. "Remember when you kissed me? And you tou—"

"Nomi," Raine pleads, sounding closer, "I'm sorry if I misled you. I wasn't in a good place, and I thought you knew and understood that. I was incapable of giving you what you wanted. I can honestly say that I'm sorry . . . You know I mean that. You mean a lot to me, always will."

My heart constricts as I stand as still as possible, the rain coming down harder. I can see the pain in her eyes. I have a hard time finding fault in her obsession, and my heart hurts for her.

"I wanted to mean more to you." Her mouth trembles, tears gushing down. "I told you I would wait. You were everything to me!"

Painful silence, save for the crashing waves and the distant sirens.

"Nomi, I tried. You know that," Raine says gently.

She wipes her eyes with her other hand, and a curious expression crosses over her face. "Well, you're not thinking straight, Raine. I know you better than anyone. I know what you need."

She looks at me. "How long have you known her? Three months?!" She raises the gun higher again. "Don't fucking come closer, Raine. Why her? Why?! What does she have that I don't? I can wear gold jewelry and diamonds too. Is that it?"

"For fuck's sake, Nomi," Thetis yells. "Do this later!"

"Don't come closer. Get back, Raine!" she screams.

"Nomi — NO!" I hear Raine shriek.

I hear a loud pop.

Everything happens so fast that I barely register my vision going black and Steven's voice in my head.

~"This is Agent number B-0023 or something, on behalf of Fairy Godmother Inc. and blah blah~—~oh shit—LIFELINE ACTIVATE!"~

***

I come to screaming — visions of Raine tackling me. I jerk up as I feel hands on my body steadying me. White everywhere, and I quickly realize that I'm in the medical center of FGI. I'm out of breath as my vision rights itself.

"Shit!" I scream, trying to calm myself. "Was I shot?!" I sit up, heart pounding as I feel my body, breathing hard.

No blood.

The doctors part and in walks Pierce and that Russian woman, holding papers. Pierce takes off his glasses with a long sigh and smiles at me, though it's a little grim.

"Well, Steven is starting to prove his worth around here." Pierce winks at me, then glances at the woman next to him. "Zoya, extraction?"

"Ten minutes," she says in clipped tones, and looks at me. "You have officially used your last lifeline. On the fourth, you will be extracted from the game entirely." Her ice-blue gaze holds zero emotion, then she speaks into the radio on her shoulder.

"Dang, that is right." Pierce crosses his arms. "How far can we go back?" He glances at Zoya.

Zoya flips through some papers. "We have clearance for ten minutes. We can tilt Nomi's arm so that she misses."

Pierce nods and exhales. "That's good news." He looks at me with a severe expression. "We have clearance for the gunshot to miss you entirely. Seeing how you have zero lifelines left, it would not do to have Nomi hit a less vital area."

I swallow. "How far are you able to go back in time?"

Pierce hands the paper to Zoya, ignoring me. "Are we ready for extraction?"

"6 minutes out!"

A flash of nerves courses through me. Zero lifelines left.

I might be sick.

"Depends on the situation." He looks down then back up, his blue gaze intent. "You need to get the hell out of there. Understand that you have zero chances left. You use another lifeline, it's over."

I feel my eyes water, and I nod. This is heavy.
"Was I shot?"

He turns to grab a picture from Zoya, showing me the close-up image of a bullet mere millimeters from entering my body.

"Steven acted fast. One moment longer, you would have been in surgery."

"Where is Steven?"

"Eating."

I nod, feeling sick with fear. "I have to get out of there and wait it out till the end," I say, and wipe my eyes, not realizing I'm crying.

"Good plan. Lay low." He pats my knee.

I nod.

I can do this.

"Do not be a hero," he adds. "Other players will protect you. They will be informed that you are on your last lifeline."

I nod again as I hear them counting down.

I never felt real fear until right now. I am reminded that not all endings are happy, but I will fight like a damn wildcat to get it.

CHAPTER 27

CAMILA

I come to, sounds erupting around me.

"Grab her!"

Yelling and complete chaos. Men tackling Nomi.

I'm lifted and instantly realize that I'm in Raine's tight embrace. "Are you hit?" Raine yells, running with me through the rain, taking me into the main cabin and down hallways. "Medical staff!" he yells like I'm dying. "Are you hit? Are you hit?!"
Well, I would be, if not for FGI.

"No." I barely have time to respond as I'm laid on something soft. Raine frantically feels up my body for any signs of a bullet wound. "I'm not hit," I say again as his hands smooth up my ribcage, breathing hard, water dripping off of him. "She missed."

He closes his eyes, slowing his breaths. He turns his head and looks at the Nymphs beside him.

"Did they get Nomi?"

"Thetis has her."

Raine's eyes collide with mine. "Prepare Nomi to be transferred home—and Camila."

The Nymph nods and turns to leave, then pauses, looking back to Raine. "Camila?"

A hint of a smile pulls at Raine's lips, even though his whole body is tense, as he leans over me. "Daphine."

"Right. We have to hurry, Raine. We pissed off the Empires and they're coming straight for us," he says, then leaves in a hurry.

My heart is pounding as Raine meets my gaze. "Nomi . . ." I trail off.

Raine exhales, jaw flexing. "I should have seen that coming. I owe Nomi my life, and I would take a bullet for her if I had to." He looks the other way. "She could never accept the fact that I couldn't . . ." He pauses. "I couldn't get there with her, even though years ago I did try."

I bite my lip as I watch water droplets drip off his black hair. "I see. She saved your life, and in return, she wanted your heart."

He tilts his head at me. "Something like that," he murmurs. "She will be fine and realize she was acting rashly when she is back home. She has always been overly emotional, something I find nauseating about her."

Raine studies me as seconds pass.
"Raine, I'm scared," I blurt, feeling my panic boil to silent hysteria. "I c-can't die again, or it's over." I close my eyes. "I mean—I need to get to a safe place. I need to be safe. I can't be here."

Raine grabs my face, "I will get you out—"

The rig violently tilts to the left as tremors rack it.

"Fuck!" Raine's eyes are wide, grabbing onto me before I can fall off the bed. He looks up and listens, breathing hard, glancing back at me. "Stay in here."

I nod, now feeling what real terror is like for the first time here. I have zero lifelines, which means my luck has run out. I'm a sitting duck till extraction, and we are in the middle of an effing war.

I might be having my first panic attack.

I don't want this to be over.

"Focus." He leans down and breathes into my lips. "I can see and feel your anxiety, we will get through this . . . " He trails off and his gaze searches mine, and I realize I'm crying. "Camila . . . "

"I'm fine," I sniff, feeling my body shake, trying to look away, but he holds my chin in place.

"Liar," he quietly chides, eyes concerned, brow furrowed.

"Raine," I whisper as he wipes tears away from my cheeks with this thumb. "I-I love you," I say, knowing I spill my heart when I'm generally terrified. And right now, I don't care.

This incredible man needs to know.

"I love you," I say more firmly. I hope I'm not too emotional like he accused Nomi of being.

That does not matter to me right now.

I don't even care if he says it back.

I was head over heels for him from the first moment I locked eyes with him.

It's hard to read his expression as he lowers himself onto me, a slight smile spreading over his lips. My heart flutters at the deep stare he gives me.

"Well," he whispers, "now I won't feel so bad when I take you far away from here and lock you in my dark, ~dark ~lair."

I smile as his lips lower to mine, his strong arms lifting me and circling my trim waist. The feel of his mouth suctioning to mine almost makes me forget what danger I'm in. I readily taste the erotic sweep of his tongue, and I grind my body against him, wanting him so bad. I can feel my body heat instantly, my mind scattering.

Intoxicating.

I hear him groan low in my mouth, and it's primal, making my toes tingle in my boots. His hands grip me tighter as he deepens the kiss, smoothing up my rib cage to my breast. I wish we were anywhere but here.

"Camila," he breathes between his kisses, his eyes on fire, heavy-lidded and hot. "I'd tell you what I feel, but I don't want to terrify you quite yet. You're not chained to my bed, so there is the danger of you fleeing for your life."

He's smiling, and I can't get enough of it.

"Tell me," I urge, kissing his smiling, sexy lips.

I could eat him.

"After you tell me why you want Thetis alive," he says, eyes searching my face. "I can feel your response. I feel fear . . . Why?"

I swallow, closing my eyes.

"Camila," he urges.

I look at him. "I will tell you everything in five days, but just know I need him alive—to stay alive."

His eyes widen.
I don't know if I was supposed to say that, but I have to give him something.

"To stay alive? Why five days, Camila?"

I stare at him, not sure of what to say. "Trust me."
"Fuck, Camila. He has to stay alive for you to ~stay ~alive?! How's that

supposed to make me feel? Tell me how this makes sense," Raine says, his fire gaze piercing me, pinning me. He's getting riled up. "Though everything about you is a mystery, I guess it's all in the realm of possibilities."

He's not happy.

"Raine, it's complicated."

Very. Complicated.

"I bet it is," he murmurs, staring at me like he's trying to read my mind. He looks up as the ship vibrates with distant yelling. "Well, you're lucky I'm not in a position to make you tell me your secrets—"

The door opens, and men come in, out of breath. "RAINE!"

Raine jumps up like some ninja, body tense.

"They're here. They are about to board us! We need you now!" A guard says, eyes wide, loading a massive gun as blood drips down his forehead.

"Fuck, how many?" Raine asks in a low tone. "That was fast. They must have had a sleeper ship."

"That's what Thetis said. They got the drop on us," he confirms.

Raine reaches for me, pulling me up like I weigh nothing. He looks down at me. "New plan. Take my power, it will help you stay alive," Raine orders, not letting me have a word. The feel of his lips is urgent and desperate.

I quickly take his power, feeling his delicious energy like a drug, my body humming with his energy.

Raine pulls back and points to one of his men. "When the fight dies down, I want her fucking out of here. That's an order. I don't care who does it—just get it done."

They nod and look at me, then leave.

I hold my hands out, seeing the orange and maroon hue, shivering from the pleasure of it.

"Camila, look at me," he orders, voice authoritative.

I look into his pools of orange fire and shiver. "When I say go, you get the hell out of here and don't look back. You will be safe." He pulls me with him as we start to walk. "Do you understand?"

"Yes," I say, feeling sick. "What about you?"

Raine laughs harshly. "Don't worry about me. Stay back and out of the way until it's safe. You need to be on deck in case this sub goes down." He stops and pushes me against the wall hard, lips on mine, hands on my face in a breathtaking kiss. His tongue sweeps in my mouth like he wants to drink my soul, over and over again.

He rests his forehead on mine, seconds passing. "You have plenty of power?" he whispers, breathing hard.

I nod, feeling lightheaded.

Fear.

Panic.

He makes me walk in front of him, his hand grazing my ass as we turn a corner to exit. Raine jerks me back with an expression of horror. He opens the door into a war zone, a massive ship colliding with ours. Men everywhere.

Like one pirate ship trying to take over another.

Terrifying.

The loud siren of the Valkyrie ship sounds like a battle cry, causing my lungs to constrict. Steven is in front of us, looking pale, soaked by the rain.

Raine shoots me a look, but Thetis runs up to us, handing Raine his crown. Thetis also wears one, as do the other top-ranking Nymphs, looking like some mythological warriors.

"Raine! Now!"

Raine throws me to some of his men, tossing me into their hands. "Stay behind them!"

I gasp as I'm thrown to my right with Sun Hai and Nomi, guarded by his Sose guards holding up shields and gun/arrow hybrids.

Nomi and I lock eyes for a fleeting second, but Sun Hai has her sword out, covering me, blocking my view.

"Your last lifeline?"

"Yes," I say, getting drenched by the pouring rain. "I don't know how I'm going to pull this off."

"I got you," she says, looking only slightly terrified. "Let's be honest — if I were a Valkyrie warrior and saw Thetis and Raine coming at me, I'd shit myself and run the other way."

I glance at the men starting to fight the Empire's army, who are now boarding. The Nymphs look twice as scary, their size and amount of muscle make them dramatically larger than the short, brute-like Valkyries. Like Vikings that wear tons of gold.

I see Raine crack his neck right before he brutally beheads two Valkyrie men at once with his long, samurai-like sword.

Effortless.

A Valkyrie guard watches and backs up, swallowing.

I shiver, seeing how dangerous Raine actually is. He is so fluid, and the brutal way he wields his sword has a certain elegance. I find myself hypnotized, watching him, shamelessly fantasizing. It's thrilling to know that someone so dangerous can also be so pleasuring in the bedroom. It's like opposite ends of the spectrum.

A loud explosion sounds to my left, screams and yells as flames rise. The only way they can beat the Nymphs is with bombs. In one-to-one combat, they can't.

My ears are ringing.

Steven is beside me. "Dude! What the fu —"

"Steven!" I say, and he helps me up, smoke everywhere. "I need to get to a safe place!"

"Damn. This way!"

Steven leads me to the upper deck through the rain and smoke, coughing as we sprint. I look behind me and see Sun Hai following with her small Nymph agent.

A spray of bullets come from our left and bounce off Sun Hai's shield.

"Get down!" I hear Raine's voice, knowing he always has one eye on me.

We crawl on the top deck, huddling against the wall, shielded by Sun Hai. More ammo sprays, but hits way too high. I look at Sun Hai. "They are going to sink us!"

"It doesn't matter — Thetis says Raine's mother is coming. We just have to hold out for a bit longer. Kalypso will bring hellfire," she grits out.

We scream as another explosion hits the side of the ship.

Steven grits his teeth, his chubby body shaking. "This is shit. I dropped my pipe back there! Son of a bitch!"

I look at him. "Focus!"

"I'm trying! I'm stressed out, man!"

"Your weed won't matter if we get ejected from the mission," I hiss, wanting to shake him. I hear a lot of yelling about gun power.

"I have to see," I say, and crawl with everyone to the edge, peering over at the battle scene before my eyes.

Riane is yelling orders while wielding his sword. Nymphs are diving into the water to board and ambush the golden Valkyrie sub.

"We are winning!" Sun Hai says. "A lot of them are retreating."

I feel like I might throw up from all my nerves. I see Thetis fighting multiple men, knifing them through the chest.

Sun Hai stands and aims her weapon in Thetis's direction, killing a man running at him with a weapon. Sun Hai looks at me. "If Thetis dies, nothing matters."

"Pierce says to back off!" Sun Hai's agent yells. "Too dangerous!"

"Not yet," Sun Hai says.

A crash of thunder makes me tense, looking at Raine, wondering if he is causing the weather to pick up.

A brute of a Valkyrie nails Raine in the face with a metal weapon, causing him to fall to his knees. I hold my breath and grip the railing, my heart racing. Raine stands and spits out blood, dropping his sword, and turns towards the offender. He dodges his weapon and with a solid punch to the Valkyrie's face, Raine knocks him out cold.

~Damn.~

I see Thetis grin at Raine and toss him a weapon, then they start to work together back to back, almost seeming to have fun. One watching the other's back creates a force the Valkyries cannot compete with.

If I were not so scared shitless, I would think this is a big step for the two men. Seeing them work together and not try to kill one another makes my insides feel warm and fuzzy, despite everything.

"Homeboys are bringing the house down!" Steven cheers.

Raine slays another, and his gaze peers up at me, then his eyes widen. "Watch out!"

We all turn to see two Valkyrie men behind us, weapons raised.

All I see is a long sword coming down at me.

I scream right as an arrow pierces the man though the heart, the sword dropping to the wet floor. Raine is now beside me, grabbing my arm and jerking me up. "Stay back!"

More men are climbing up the side.

"Fuck!" Raine yells as he starts fending them off, gaining a slice on his arm, blood coating the ground.

I realize I'm on the ground in shock, unable to do anything in fear of using another lifeline. I feel Steven trying to help me up, yelling at me to get my ass back. I manage to stand, and I look out over the ledge, and my heart drops.

No way.
~Brayja~.
I blink through the pouring rain, thinking my eyes are playing tricks on me.

"Dude! Is that Brayjo?!"

Brayja.

His face looks beaten, swollen. Somehow he has escaped and is now with his people.

I hear Sun Hai scream. Brayja is raising his arrow-hybrid and aiming it straight at Thetis, rage filling his face. I hold out my hand. "RAINE!" I scream. I turn to look at Raine, who follows the line of my outstretched hand.

His eyes widen, and time seems to slow. I'm not sure how this happens—most likely something similar to when your life flashes before your eyes in a near-death situation. The look Raine gives me makes horror seep into every bone of my body. It's like I remember too many things in that one split second.

F.R.BLACK

Like me telling Raine that Thetis can't die or I do.

White-hot fear explodes through my senses as I see Raine react. He moves so fast that I'm just an innocent bystander. I feel like I'm underwater. Sounds are muted, my body is frozen, as I watch Raine jump over the ledge of the deck

.

"Thetis!" Sun Hai screams, causing him to look in her direction, confusion on his face. He is fending off another Valkyrie while trying to figure out why she is screaming through the rain and lightning.

She raises her weapon, but it slips out of her grasp. "Shit!" The rain makes it slippery with her frantic movements.

My hand reaches out as if I can stop Raine with pure brainpower.

Raine's speed as he races towards Thetis has my heart in my mouth, but seeing him push Thetis out of the way and take the arrow straight through the heart almost makes my vision go black.

It happens so fast my brain is rejecting it. I make a sound, not even sure if it was human.

Raine . . .

I hear and feel nothing.

Nothing matters anymore.

I see Thetis look at Raine as he collapses to the ground, and I can see the realization wash over his expression. Thetis finally turns towards Brayja with rage and fury painting his face, utterly horrified.

He charges Brayja, yelling in rage.

But that does not matter.

I feel my legs running, tears mixing with the pouring rain. Every part of my body tells me that he will be okay. It can't end like this.

357

It can't end like this.

How I dodge multiple Valkyrie warriors, I don't know, but I collapse next to Raine.

"Raine!!" I scream, seeing blood bubble in his mouth, the pouring rain washing away the massive amounts of blood spilling from his chest wound.

"Raine!" I shriek, as my shaking hands touch the arrow sticking out of his chest, praying I will wake up from this nightmare.

Sun Hai is next to me, but I don't see her.

Raine coughs, his heavy-lidded gaze finding mine. I look to Sun Hai, "Do something! Help me sit him up. We have to stop the bleeding!"

Sun Hai's agent is typing next to us. "Talking to Pierce—they are doing an x-ray!"

"So help me! Tell him to do something!" I cry, placing my hands over the wound, covering myself in Raine's blood. "Raine, stay with me!"

He sacrificed himself for Thetis—because of me . . .

This is my fault.

"Raine!" I say, tears gushing out of my eyes. "Can you hear me?" I lean down and kiss his pale lips. "Don't die, please. I need you. I need you . . . " I kiss him again, my brain misfiring. I feel his hand squeeze my leg, and my eyes shoot to his, my hand going to his face.

"Stay with me. You're not going to die," I whisper through my sobs. "I won't let you die!" I look at Sun Hai. "Can Pierce help?!"

I see tears in her eyes, and she shakes her head. ~No. ~

"Fuck that!" I scream. "You tell him to fucking do something. This is FGI—they can do anything!" I feel like I'm in a fog, seeing things around me that are not actually happening.

~This ~is not actually happening. It can't be.

I reject it.

Steven whispers next to me, "Pierce has his hands tied. It's against the rules to bring people back from death."

My eyes bulge. "Death?" I grab Raine's face. "Tell me what to do!" I scream at him, feeling hysterical. "You can't die. YOU CAN'T!"

His beautiful eyes flutter closed, but I feel his hand on my leg tighten. He lifts his hand and grabs my arm, pulling me to him with surprising strength. I lean in close to his face, my tears streaming like a waterfall of pain, blurring my vision.

"I love you," he whispers in my ear, then chokes.

"No! Raine, you will be fine. I know you will. Th-the wound is not that bad. We just have to pull it out!" I see spots in my eyes, my world collapsing.

A slight smile pulls at his lips. "Liar," he whispers, then his body goes eerily still.

I can't describe the pain erupting inside my chest.

I'm screaming, I realize. I feel someone pick me and take me in a hard embrace.

I'm punching whoever holds me, screaming my fury and cursing everything around me.

I push away from Thetis, feeling entirely out of my mind. I stumble to the left and grab Sun Hai, having made up my mind.

"You make sure Raine lives, do you understand?"

She wipes the tears from her face with a frown of confusion, more tears gushing out of her eyes.

"You keep him safe!"

They stare at me like I've lost my mind.

"You kill that fucking bastard Brayja. Have the men on alert, so this battle ends in victory!" I yell, and bend down, grabbing Raine's dagger that he dropped. I'm aware that all eyes are on me, and I can do only one thing to save Raine's life.

It was my fault. He should be alive right now, and I will make this right, even if it means that I'm no longer in the picture. I look up into the night sky and see that, since Raine has stopped breathing, the clouds have parted, and showing through is a blaring fucking full moon.

It seems my old friend is out again to say hello, ~long time no see . . . ~
I do a little nod to it, tears gushing down my cheeks.

I came into this game with a knife in my stomach, and it looks like I'm leaving it the same way. Thetis lunges at me, but it's too late.

The knife pierces deep into my stomach, fueled by my rage and agony, and I fall to the ground in a heap.

A lifeline can rewind history, thus saving Raine's life.

" . . . Lifeline . . . activate," I whisper, as tears stream down my face.

Goodbye, Raine.

CHAPTER 28

CAMILA

"This is bad."

"Well," Zoya pauses, "it's always hard when a sound player has to be ejected."

I curse.

I feel sick, having not eaten in two days. "When is Pierce coming?"

"Soon. He is still in meetings with our lawyers." Zoya sits down in front of me and places a rather delicious-looking club sandwich with some sort of fizzy drink. "Eat."

"How," I whisper.

She gives me a look, her piercing blue gaze pinning me. "I have been through this a few times, though it does not often happen in a love match. This is the worst-case scenario, and I usually try to prepare our shifter agents so this does not happen."

She shifts in her chair.

"But we all agree this has been a perilous mission, and I honestly didn't see another way. I would have done the same thing."

I feel my stomach clench, and I reach out to grab the sandwich because my stomach is eating itself even though I feel nauseous. "What are the odds?"

"I'm unsure, though Pierce is determined. He does fight for his girls, that I can say with confidence." Zoya grabs the other half of the sandwich. "Tabasco?"

I shrug and take a miserable bite with her. I didn't think someone like her ate this stuff.

"You know, Raine was my favorite. I knew there was more to him because our files did not flag him as a threat in the sense that Brayja was." She chews, putting drops of sauce on a bite. "I had a bet with Pierce that he was the one to watch."

My heart constricts.

Can't. Think. Of. Him.

"Is he alive?" I could not bring myself to ask earlier, too scared of the answer.

"Yes, you have succeeded in saving his life. Raine actually was the one to kill Brayja on a violent rampage." She swallows. "Because you . . . disappeared."

"How does that work?" I ask, relief flooding my senses.

"Well, you will always be a mystery in a sense. Though I think Sun Hai might tell him the truth. I have to check with Pierce on that. Until we receive the final verdict from the council, the reason for your disappearance will be unknown."

She puts down the half-eaten sandwich and wipes her hands. "I need you to know that I have enrolled you in counseling."

"Counseling," I whisper.

"Finish your sandwich," she says, not meeting my gaze. "I will check the whereabouts of Pierce and explore your options."

I swallow, feeling a rush of anxiety. "Will they let me go back?"

She pauses at the door "In my experience, it does not happen often."

I close my eyes.
"I'll be back."

I feel more tears stream down my face. The feeling of desperation is overwhelming. All I can think about is Raine. All I see is Raine when I close my eyes. His knee-buckling gaze and dark smile when he knows something you don't.

I wipe my face and push my plate away. He must be going out of his mind, knowing that I'm gone. He has to know because he was connected to me, so he must have felt the shock of the tie being broken.

I can't imagine his confusion.

The door opens and in walks Pierce and Zora, making me instantly tense. I stare, my eyes pleading with them to give me the good news.

"Camila," Zora begins, and glances at Pierce, hands folding in front of her white day dress. "Thank you for being so patient these past two days."

I nod, my heart in my throat.

Pierce leans down and grabs a piece of sandwich, assuming that I'm done. I'm too nervous to reflect on the fact that everyone is eating my food.

"I found a loophole I think will work, but your case is a tricky one. The fact that you took your own life and ~not~ someone or something from their world might give us leverage." He takes a bite and looks at Zora.

"Unless your sister really wants to make our lives miserable."

363

Zora exhales. "If we have a case, there is nothing she can do."

Pierce swallows. "You see, her sister hates FGI and wants to take over." He shrugs.

"Not happening, but she always makes us stick to the rules. She is rarely merciful unless we can prove her wrong, which is why we have the best FGI lawyers working on it."

I nod. My hands are sweaty and I feel disconnected. "Do you think I have a chance then?"

"Well . . . " Pierce pauses and swallows. "I do hope so because I feel that Raine needs you. You were the only one that could keep him in check."

The door opens, and in walks Steven, "Extraction is ready. Hey, toots." He looks at me then to the picked apart sandwich on the table. "Oh, sweet." He leans down and plucks up the rest, shoving it in his mouth, then points at me. "Were you done?" is his muffled question.

I make a face. "No, please give it back," I deadpan.

He chews. "You want it back?" Crumbs fall.

I close my eyes. "Sarcasm, Steven."

He still stares at me. "So . . . you don't want it back?"

"No." I look past him to Pierce's pained expression. "So what now?"

"Well, it will take a month for the hearing," he says, "then however long after that to finalize things. depending on the verdict."

I close my eyes. "A month?"

No . . .

That's too long.

Zora looks at Pierce. "Tell Zoya to ready her FGI package."

Pierce nods and glances at me. "Well, this might be difficult for you to hear."

I tense.

"Our time zones are different."

I swallow. "Meaning?"

"Dude," Steven pipes in. "Earth's time and the fifth dimension don't match up, ya know?"

Pierce frowns at Steven. "That almost sounded intelligent." Then he glances at me. "You will have to wait a year or two for the verdict, roughly."

I gasp.
Tunnel vision.

A year?!

"I can't stay here?"

"No, I'm afraid not." He leans on the wall.

"We give all of our players an FGI package for their participation. Plenty of money and other amenities for you in there," he says, and gives me a pitying look. "It will be difficult, but you can do it."

"What about Raine's world?"

"About the same, give or take a few months."

"What if he does not want me in a year?" I yell. "He could find someone else!"

Pierce takes a moment.

"Not many women can compete with my FGI agents. You are not just going to be replaced that easy — that's how love works. I'm willing to bet that

Raine will be on a quest to find you."

"You don't know that."

"I know a bit about this subject, actually. Raine is not an easy man to win over, and not just any woman will pique his interest as you did." Pierce smiles at me. "Trust me on this."

I close my eyes. "What the hell am I going to do for that long?"

"Find yourself."

"Perfect."

Pierce raises a brow. "I'm serious. This could be a very awakening time for you. Reflection is healthy for mental health."

Zora nods. "Prepare for extraction."

I feel like I am in a nightmare.

I can't!

I can't.

I can't . . .

***

A YEAR AND A HALF LATER . . .

MIAMI.

SOUTH BEACH.

The sun is beautiful today.

I take a breath and stretch.

Pierce said he would find me when he had an answer, and that was a year and a half ago. I'm losing faith that I will ever see him again. My hope dwindles every day.

Maybe they just punked me.

No.

I won't believe that.

I close my eyes and feel the dull pain that is ever-present. Late at night, I can still hear Raine's low laugh and the feel of his lips on mine, and it nearly drives me insane. If anything, my need for him has only heightened, especially when I'm hit on by men.

I laugh, wanting to tell them about Raine — the godlike creature that holds my heart forever. I dig my toes into the sand and adjust my black shades, loving the soothing feeling of the sun.

Once I craved diamonds and gold — lavish riches.

Now all I want is to be by the ocean. It's the only place where I feel like I'm close to Raine. My mind plays tricks on me, half expecting Raine to come running out of the water, his muscled torso the color of fire.

I don't cry anymore. I think I have permanently damaged that part of my body the first few months here. Now my tears won't come even though the pain is ever-present. I have no idea if the mission was even won. Did Thetis say yes to Sun Hai? Without a Darling or Sweet Heart necklace, I'm in the dark.

I'm willing to bet that Sun Hai had it in the bag, but it would help to know for sure. I'm living in a condo off the beach, a beautiful place that was bought for me by FGI. I have a savings account with a healthy amount of money that has assisted in my healing.

I will admit that FGI counseling has helped in giving me hope, though they have zero information about my case. Despite the fact that I keep pestering and threatening them.

I smile.

But get this.

Zoya did me a solid. I owe her, for she must have read my file. She gave the exact location of Lucas in the FGI packet I received, among other incriminating things.

I wonder if she did that in secret, because I can't imagine that being approved by the Fairy Godmother.

Or maybe it was.

So I sit here, staring at him as he eats lunch at an expensive coffee house with what looks to be an important person in cream slacks and a Hawaiian silk shirt.

Their laughter is carefree and relaxed.

That rat bastard.

Lucas is all cocky in his pink silk shirt with white slacks, relaxing with zero guilt about what he did to me. I stare at him, unable to believe that I was once attracted to him.

Anger seeps into every pore of my body. He's living life while thinking that I'm long dead.

Surprise, bitch. I'm back from the dead.

I smile as I sip my cocktail. I'm in a sexy black sundress just relaxing on a beach bed, my wide yellow sun hat shielding half of my face. It has taken me six months to track him down, but I did it, thanks to Zoya's information on his fake IDs and place of residence.

It's the only distraction I have from Raine, and maybe Zoya knew I needed that.
Nothing can distract a broken heart like a little revenge.

In all honesty, it was not that hard. He is sloppy now, getting too comfortable. Leaving a trail everywhere. I was more than happy to make an anonymous call to my friends in high places. I know a Russian man who would love to catch the thief who stole diamonds worth three hundred million dollars.
Oh ~Lucas~, what was the number one rule?
Never let your guard down.

It's time.

I stand up, setting my drink down on the table to my side, and make my way to the outdoor seating that faces the ocean. The slight breeze reveals my perfectly FGI-airbrushed legs, and it catches Lucas's attention immediately, stopping him mid-sentence. His mouth opens, and a slow smile spreads over his lips—wanting to hit on me, no doubt. I'm just a hot Latina, not the woman he stabbed in the stomach two years ago.

He did a kill shot, something that I should not have walked away from.

Lucas's luck has just run out.

I can see the rare black diamond on his finger as I get closer, something that will be a dead giveaway until they raid his home and find the remaining diamonds.

This is the moment I wanted for a long time.

I slowly take off my shades and grin at him, loving seeing the smile on his face slowly fade. His brown gaze now widens, almost to a point that would be painful. The man sitting across from him turns to look at me, wanting to see what caught his friend's attention.

I stop in front of them and tilt my head. "Lucas, wow. Fancy seeing you here."

He goes to say something, but nothing comes out.

"Damn," the other man says as he eyes my body. He laughs at Lucas's horror-stricken face. "Is this how you act around a gorgeous woman, Lucas?" He laughs more. "Forgive my friend." He is laughing harder now, getting red in the face.

"Oh, I have forgiven him," I say, and smile sweetly, but he can see the ice in my gaze. "But that doesn't mean karma has. She's a bad-ass bitch."

"Camila—how—er. You're here," he gets out, face pale despite his tan skin. He is breathing hard now, eyes still wide.

"Oh, Lucas. You look so adorable right now." It gives me so much joy to see him like this, on the other end of the barrel this time.

He blanches.

"You've gotten sloppy" I make a clicking sound with my blood-colored lips.

He frowns, a sheen of sweat on his forehead.

I put my hands on the short fence and lean closer to him, his friend now frowning at us in confusion.

"How fast can you run? I can't remember from when I was sitting in a pool of my own blood, but it looked like you could really move when warranted."

"Camila . . . " He whispers the plea, his eyes darting around now, slowly standing. "Fuck."

"Yes?"

"What h-have you done?" he barely gets out.

"Nice ring, it really fits you. Like the color of your heart." I laugh right as detectives round the corner, and I point at Lucas.

"Shit!" he screams, and tries to jump over the short fence to the beach, but his foot catches, making him crash to the ground awkwardly.

"I've done nothing wrong!" he yells as men jump on him, handcuffing him. "I know my rights! Fuck—Camila! She's the thief, not me!"

"We've had a search warrant for your Malibu flat for a while, which provided us with lots of stolen items that will put you away for a long time, buddy," the older detective says, and nods at me.

He's a nice guy. Been working with him for three months.

"I owe you coffee and donuts—and tacos!" I yell after him as Lucas screams for his lawyers. I glance at the guy who was sitting with Lucas and shrug. "He was a very bad man."

He barely nods, looking mystified.

I turn with a shit-eating grin on my face. "Yes," I whisper, feeling a wave of happiness. I start to walk towards the beach when something catches my eye, and I look to my left.

My heart stops.
~Pierce~.
My body is hot and cold.

I nearly scream, covering my mouth. He is clapping his hands as he walks up to me dressed in his beach finery.

"Bravo Camila!" he says, his blue gaze sparkling, "Now that was fun to watch! Did you see the look on his face?"

I still can't talk.

He's here.

Pierce is actually here.

I feel my eyes sting, my heart pounding. "Pierce . . . You have a verdict?" is all I can say, and I instantly feel sick with nerves.

He tilts his head at me. "How are you doing?"

"About to throw up," I whisper. "I thought I'd never see you again."

He smiles and reaches in his pocket, pulling out a necklace. I nearly pass out. Somewhere in my mind, I realize what this means.

"I can go back?" I guess I have tears left after all. I cover my mouth as tears fall down my face.

"You are finally granted a one-way ticket." Pierce smiles and laughs. "You have clearance, Camila. We almost lost it, but we all went to bat for you."

"Thank you," I say through my sobs. "Thank you."

I can't breathe.

My heart is going to explode.

"May I?" he asks, holding up the Sweet Heart necklace.

I nod.

Pierce stands behind me and clasps the most beautiful golden necklace around my neck. "It's stunning—perfect." The crystal is the color of sunlight, and it sparkles with each movement, entrancing me. It's attached to a shining golden chain that looks indestructible.

"You deserve this, Camila," Pierce says, and walks back around me.

"How's Raine?"

Pierce makes a face. "Not as well as you, I'm afraid, but he is still alive and thriving."

"What do you mean?"

"He is still searching for you. He never believed that you were gone. He took it pretty hard, as you can probably imagine," he says, and takes a breath with a smile. "I can picture the look on his face when he sees you."

I cover my mouth, feeling so much excitement and hope. "Does he know my situation?"

"No. Sun Hai and Thetis's lips were sealed until after the proceedings." Pierce looks out over the sea. "But he is smart. I'm assuming he knows you went back to where you came from, which will make the reveal not a major shock."

I nod, feeling my skin tingle in anticipation.

"When can we go?"

Pierce smiles and presses his ear. "Zoya, we are ready when you are. Tell Kevin in my design department to ready Camila's dress."

I close my eyes, never feeling so much relief and happiness before.

Raine, my love . . . I'm coming.

CHAPTER 29

CAMILA

I feel like I'm in a dream.

My body is humming with adrenaline. My fingers and toes tingle as I stand with my hands over my mouth, trying to calm my rapid pulse.

I had almost lost hope, and here we are.

"I knew this color was perfect."

I take a shaky breath, standing in the most stunning mermaid-style gown ever. It's the color of the tropical ocean on a clear day, and each sparkle reminds me of the sun's stunning reflection.

I turn to see Pierce with his hands in the pockets of his pristine gray suit. "You are one of the bravest agents we have had to date," he says, and winks at me. "You have completely transformed yourself. I can see in your gaze that you feel different than when we first met."

I smile, thinking of myself before this.

"Yes. After going through FGI bootcamp, it's impossible to emerge as the same person, and I'm so thankful for that . . . " I trail off and close my eyes, still unable to contain my excitement.

Raine. I see his beautiful face. His arresting gaze and dark grin.

I, Camila, will have my happily-ever-after.

Against all the odds.

"Raine needs you."

No. ~I~ need ~him~.

I look at Pierce right as the Fairy Godmother walks in with an adoring look on her face. "You look stunning, my dear," she whispers, and dabs her eyes with a white handkerchief. We pulled through. This was one of our toughest missions."

"Thank you," I say, and glance back to Pierce, feeling so much emotion. "Can you tell me anything about him? Like, how has he been? More detail?"

"Yes," Pierce says, and greets Zora with a side kiss. "Raine is currently on a voyage to find a mystic that may have the talent to contact the stars, in the hope of finding where you disappeared to."

Butterflies take flight in my stomach, and I can't wipe the smile from my face. "So, he must still love me . . . to still be searching for me."

Zora makes a sound and touches her chest with a chuckle. "That boy. When he wants something, he's not the type to drop it without a fight." She smiles at me. "You're one lucky girl."

Raine.

I can't stop saying his name in my head.
I shiver. "Is he okay? What about Nomi?"

"Well," Pierce puts on his glasses and takes out his virtual pad, "Nomi is fine. She resides at the palace with Thetis and Sun Hai. They are doing great, by the way — inseparable, actually." He looks up at me. "Thetis and Raine's relationship is surprisingly good. Thetis has gone to great lengths to help Raine find you, even though he knows his efforts are pointless."

I close my eyes, so thankful that Raine has begun to heal from his past. "That makes me so happy."

Pierce points at me. "They are mending their relationship like I had hoped for, and we have you to thank for that."

I glance at the Fairy Godmother and smile, holding back tears.

Zora smiles back. "I should rephrase what I said earlier: Raine is lucky to have you, my dear. You are perfect for each other. When Raine saw you, he never let go."

I take a shaky breath. The door opens and Steven walks in, wearing a fancy pinstripe suit that is two sizes too big.

"Steven!"

He smiles wide and runs up to me, hugging me tightly. "We are kings and queens—I knew we could do this."

I laugh. "Steven, your hands."

He moves them up. "Sorry."

I look at Pierce. "Can you hand me his gift, for being the best agent I could ask for?"

Pierce raises a brow. "You know you are just encouraging him, right?"

I laugh at Steven's shocked face.

"Y-you got me something?" he says, looking like he's won a Grammy and is about to give a speech. "I didn't get you anything, unless you want a hit," he says with wide eyes.

"Of course I got you something, Steven," I say, and grab the massive octopus bong I bought in Miami. It's purple and obnoxious. "I thought you would like this. It reminded me of those octopus monsters on Brayja's sub."

Steven's eyes are glassy, and he takes the bong, mouth trembling. "Duuuuude. I'll treasure this forever." He stares at it and puts his mouth on it as if to test it out, pretending to light it a couple times. He's crying now, hugging me again. "It's beautiful." He takes a staggering breath. "Can't wait to use it. Mystic mode will be soooo dope."

"Hands."

"Sorry." He sobs and moves his hands up. "I love you, man."

I laugh and hug him back. "I love you too, Steven. I will miss you."

Zora is smiling. "Are you ready, Camila?"

Steven snorts, like Zora is stupid. "Of course she is. She has not gotten laid in like two years, lady."

We all hit Steven on the head, Pierce rolling his eyes as we make our way to the pod.

I'm ready.

Here I come.

***

I'm breathing hard when I come to, and Pierce has to steady me so I don't fall. My long hair blows around my head. I feel the tropical breeze as my eyes adjust.

I cover my mouth. "I'm here!" I laugh and try to hold back tears.

"I'm really here," I whisper again.

I close my eyes, thanking the heavens.

It's bright and sunny, and I realize I can see the beach and the crashing waves.

"Now, you must tell Raine everything, but you already know that. The necklace will help, even though I doubt it will matter to him at this point," Pierce says, and I notice he's wearing a white Hawaiian shirt and slacks.

He lowers his Aviators. "Any questions?"

I glance at him. "Where is he?"

I can barely breathe, my nerves almost making me feel sick.

Pierce smiles and winks at me. "We sent him a very compelling message, though I didn't give away the surprise." He looks out to the water. "I do love surprises."

I stare at him. "So, he's here?"

I can't breathe.

My eyes search the beach for him.

"Soon." Pierce checks his watch. "In about five minutes, actually."

"Oh shit. I mean. Oh shit," I say, about to hyperventilate. "I'm nervous."

Pierce pulls me in for a hug, and I hug him back. "Good," he whispers. He pats me on the arm as he pulls back. "You look stunning, Camila. This is the first day of the rest of your life. I'm so happy for you."

I take a steady breath and nod, trying to keep it together.

"Relax," Pierce chuckles. "I will meet you later, but for now, I will give you your
      privacy. You deserve it."

I think I nod, and he leaves me standing by a tropical tree.

I'm alone.

Breathe.

I turn toward the water, watching the crashing waves, feeling like I will jump out of my skin. I'm wearing my nose ring and my many ear piercings, except in silver this time, not gold. I know Pierce made me look like a goddess, so I don't know why I'm about to throw up. My body shivers as my eyes search every part of the ocean for any signs of Raine.

I hold myself.

Deep breath in . . .

Exhaaaaaale.

Repeat.

I take another breath and freeze, my pulse jumping to life. I place a shaking hand over my mouth as I watch a figure run out of the ocean like some erotic movie that I can't turn away from.

Raine.

It's him.

Time slows.

His chiseled body, the color of fire and maroon, has my mouth instantly dry. Weapons are strapped to his powerful form as he emerges, his low-hanging black pants suctioned to his powerful thighs as he walks toward the beach.

I grip the tree next to me as my eyes take him in. I forgot how stunning he is. "Raine!" I whisper the cry as I feel my eyes cramp, my hand over my mouth.

Raine freezes.

As if he heard me.

He slowly turns in my direction, making me think he did hear me. He is breathing hard now—I can tell from the rapid rise and fall of his broad shoulders.

I feel tears stream down my cheeks as our gazes collide, and it's like the breath is knocked clean out of my lungs. I'm covering my mouth, crying, laughing . . . I'm not sure which one.

Raine drops the spear he's holding into the ocean, and even from this distance, I can see his burning gaze widen in shock. His mouth drops open as he takes a few steps in my direction, his skin turning back into his perfect ivory complexion. Raine stops on the beach, blinking as if to see if I'm some figment in his tormented memory. He is breathing hard, almost like he is frozen from utter disbelief.

My body is on fire.

My feet are moving of their own accord, and I realize I'm running at him, hiking up my sparkling skirts to get to him faster. As I near him, I can see on his face that he knows this is real, and he runs at me.

We collide.

Our eyes meet, and he grabs my face in his shaking hands. "Camila?" he says, the sound of his voice making my skin tingle. "You're here?"

"Yes," I laugh, tears falling fast. "I'm here for good now." I'm shaking. ~Raine~ . . .

My Raine.

"How?" he whispers, his orange gaze frantically tracing over my face, then lowering to my body, over my breasts in the dipping V neck. "How are you here?" he says louder, and I can see in his gaze that he is mystified.

"I'll tell you in a bit," I get out, and lock my arms around his neck. "Kiss me first."

He makes a sound, his hands grabbing me around the waist then smoothing over my ass as if he can't help himself. "Camila, I thought I'd never see you again," he whispers, lowering his mouth to mine, but not before I caught the glassiness of his gaze.

At the first touch of his lips, my body and mind are in bliss.

I want to get lost in him. I missed him to the point of madness.

"Camila," he moans in my mouth, then his lips devour mine, his hands pressing me to him. He grabs my face, walking me backward, then picks me up, my legs wrapping around his waist.
"How?" he whispers.

He is kissing me so well that my bare toes are curling, and he keeps repeating my name in those sexy moans that he does. Not being with a man for almost two years, then having a specimen like RAINE . . . I'm almost done.

Not kidding.

I don't realize that he has laid me on the soft beach, the full span of his arms on either side of me. "I almost forgot how beautiful you are. When I first saw you, I thought I had been struck by lightning," he murmurs as he stares down at me.
"You're not leaving me again?" Raine asks, his hands grabbing my thighs, my legs still wrapped around him.

"Never."

"How do I know this to be true?" I can see the fear in his gaze as he searches my face for any signs of doubt.

"I can prove it now," I say, loving the weight of him over me.

"Prove it," he says. "Now."

His intensity and his fear of me leaving makes my insides turn to mush. "Touch this." I grab the golden Sweet Heart necklace to show him as it catches the light beautifully.

Raine frowns as he reaches to grab it, water dripping onto me from his body. His heavy body collapses on me, but luckily I can still breathe. Minutes tick by as my nerves eat at me, my pulse hammering as I wait.

I wonder what Pierce shows him.

I close my eyes and pray.

Please . . .

I bite my lip as Raine suddenly lifts up, his fiery gaze wide and intense. He is breathing hard as his eyes trace over my face.

"Camila," he says again, as a slight smile pulls at his lips, and my skin tingles.

"Do you understand now?" I ask, my pulse pounding.

He suddenly leans back on his knees and laughs—I mean ~really ~laughs. The sound is magical.

Raine holds up his hands and lets them fall, getting up and pulling me with him. He picks me up and throws me over his shoulder, spinning me around, causing me to laugh out loud with him. He lowers me and the smile on his face could light up this world.

I love this man to the moon(s) and back.

Tears run down my face as he looks at me with so much love that my knees buckle, his hands steadying me.

"Yes," he laughs. "It makes sense now. Fairy Godmother Inc? Insanity," he continues. "That man Pierce said that you are mine now. I can do whatever I want with you."

He gives me a pointed look and slightly bites his lip like he is imagining something naughty, and I want to devour him. The sexual tension is almost too much.

I shiver. "I'm yours."

He can do whatever he wants.

For real.

Raine gives me a dark look that has my pulse thrashing. "You will like being mine, Camila." He continues, "I will prove it to you, over and over, every day and every ~night~."

It does not get any better than this.

I finally found my golden treasure.

Raine.

We hear cheers, and we both turn to see Steven, Zora, Pierce, Thetis, and Sun Hai.

I place a hand over my mouth as Raine picks me up again, spinning me around until his lips are on mine in a passionate kiss, stealing my breath away.

"I love you," he whispers to me, and takes me away for my ~happily ever after. ~

Zora glances at Pierce while dabbing her eyes. "Now ~that~ is a Happily Ever After." Then smiles at him, sniffing. "Race you back."

Pierce raises an eyebrow, hand in pockets. "Terms?"

"Speed boats."

"Amino?"

"Q7-1200."

Pierce laughs and tilts his head. "You're on, but you get Steven."

"You always like to cheat, you horrid man."

CHAPTER 30

CHRISTMAS PARTY!!!

I gasp and check my pulse.

Being beamed up does not feel good, but it also does not feel bad either. It's hard to describe the feeling that your internal organs might not all be in the same place. I look at Raine to see that he has his hands on his hips, a concerned look on his face. That must have felt weird to him.

I remember my first time, with a knife sticking out of my stomach. But damn. He's dressed in a very gothic black tux, red ruby cufflinks, and dark metal jewelry.

He looks delicious.
~My husband~.
~Yum~.
A slight shiver slides down my spine.

His pale skin with his stark black hair is stunning, not to mention his fiery gaze that ignites when he looks at me.
Raine grabs me around the waist, my golden gown glittering in the low lighting, jewels draped all over my body like some exotic queen.

As it turns out, Raine ~loves ~to spoil me with lavish riches and jewels. Who would have thought? We are truly made for each other. This past year has been like a fantasy for me.

Living in his underwater palace has been like an exotic dream. I actually ride sea creatures with saddles and harnesses, the dolphin-like animals being the ocean's horses. Thankfully I am able to sustain Raine's power for more than a couple hours now. The more I harness his essence, the more my tolerance builds. I feel like some enchanted mermaid, having to pinch myself every day.

I never thought I'd say this, but Thetis and Raine work together now, keeping the Sose Nymphs safe from Valkyrie cruelty. They are improving the ocean's slums and building new cities and shelters from the dangers of the deep sea. It's been scary at times, but Raine always makes sure I am safe.

But at night, when he comes to our underwater haven, dripping wet, I'm waiting. I already knew Raine had a thing for Valkyrie women, and now being with him, I know why.

His tastes are very similar to mine.

Let me tell you, this man's idea of lingerie is not lacy things and silks, but being draped only with glittering diamonds and priceless gems.
It drives him wild. His eyes burn with an unholy desire that actually intimidated me at first, in a very ~exciting ~way.
The man has an appetite, and just thinking about how he makes me feel gets my adrenaline spiking.

"Are you sure that was safe?"

I laugh, stopping my mind from wandering, feeling his hands smooth up my body.

"Probably not."

He raises a brow.

"Kidding. I'm sure we are fiiiine." I tug on his collar and pull him towards me, kissing him impatiently. I give him my tongue, then bite his lip playfully.

Can't help it.

He looks insanely sexy tonight with his dark appeal like some vampire king come to terrorize this place—or me.

Raine pulls back with a dark look. "Careful."

I give him an innocent look that always drives him wild.

"Or what?"

He makes a sound like I'm torturing him. "You know."

"Do I?" I say innocently. "Hmmm. I don't know what you're talking about," I say, and try not to laugh, loving that I know what makes him tick.

His hands grip me tighter. "You little liar." He smiles. "I will refresh your memory later on then. Or," he looks up to the massive coat room door, "maybe I'll just do it now."

"Excuse me," comes a male voice.

We turn to see some sort of gunslinger.

Very good-looking. Just an observation. But I'd imagine everyone here is that way.

"You are?" Raine says calmly, voice smooth and low. But I know Raine— it's a warning tone. Like a rattlesnake's rattle before the bite.

The cowboy raises his hands. "It's okay. I get it." He obviously senses the threat. "I was once in your shoes, a few years back. My wife was also on an FGI mission. Her name is Charlie." He waves his hand like he is getting sidetracked. "What I'm trying to tell you is, you need to hide." His very blue gaze pins us. "Like now."

"Why?" Raine grips my arm, pulling me behind him.

What is going on?

Surely no threat would be at FGI headquarters.

"Shit." He looks behind him, then back to us. "I'm not explaining this very well. You are in no danger." He pauses, getting frustrated. "Well, you are, just not what you think."

Two other men walk in, seemingly out of breath like they were running.

I tense. One man looks like Thor—no joke—and the other almost similar to Raine's gothic style, save for his tan skin and very pale gaze.

What the hell is happening?

All of the men look panicked. The one who looks like Thor approaches and pats the cowboy on the back. "Jules, I got this." He holds out his hand to Raine with a warm smile. "Apollo."

Raine takes a second, then his mouth slightly quirks, taking his hand. "I'm assuming you are all FGI targets?"

That makes the silver-eyed man laugh and say something under his breath, a hand wiping down his handsome face. "You could say that."

Apollo nods. "Correct. Listen, it's not safe." He pauses due to the throat-clearing to our left. A chubby man with an FGI name tag enters. "Excuse me. N-no weapons past this point." He looks terrified, eyes darting from man to man. "I mean it."

Then men ignore him.

"Hide in the coatroom."

Raine raises a brow at them. "From who?" He tilts his head.

All three say at the same time, "Our wives."

My eyes widen, and I can see the fear on the men's faces. Apollo takes a step forward. "We have been coming to these parties for a while now, and our wives became fast friends," he says in a low voice. "So they all talk to each other on this FGI chat room and watch FGI Entertainment Tonight. They have been following your story—religiously. They are waiting for you to arrive to meet you.

"Now, this meeting will consist of very excited females talking your head off, most likely to the point of madness. Thetis and Sun Hai were a little overwhelmed a couple of years ago. They mean well, truly. But for your first time here, it could be overwhelming."

I laugh and look at Raine. "I don't mind," I say with a smile.

Apollo gives Raine a look. "Coatroom, trust me."

Raine's fiery gaze pins me, then he gestures toward the coatroom. "I think I will take my chances in the coatroom." He nods to the men. "I appreciate the heads up."

The cowboy nods and looks relieved. "Give it ten minutes, then you will be in the clear." They all dart out like they are trained secret agents.

I laugh as Raine shuts us in the massive coatroom. "How bad could it be?"

Raine's gaze glitters down at me. "I'm not sure if I care," he says, and lowers his mouth to my neck. "I'm not sure if I like other men seeing you in this dress, either," he says. "This Pierce guy is brutal."

I smile as my hands snake around his neck, feeling his lips on me. He smells so good, something fresh like the sea with a hint of cologne. "That's what Pierce does best."

His hands grip me hard against him, not really hearing me as his mouth lowers to my collarbone, then to my cleavage.

My body ignites.

Suddenly we both freeze. I can hear lots of female voices, and they sound a little drunk, to be honest. Laughing and giggling with each other. We hear them searching for us, confused about why we are not in the beaming room.

"Red, this way!"

Shuffling noises.

More shhh-ing sounds, followed by laughter.

"I almost just twisted my ankle—look, my heel is stuck!"
Laughter.

"Holy crap, did you guys see how many people are here? Do you think we missed them?"

More giggles.

"Let's get another one of the Christmas treeeeee drinks!" They all agree, and their voices trail off with the sound of rapid heel clicks on the marble floors.

Raine smiles and kisses my forehead. "I'm glad they stopped us," he breathes.

I frown up at him. "That's surprising."
He laughs. "No, it's just that once I get started . . . We would never attend the party, if you ~know ~what I mean." He gives me a telling look.
I blush and laugh.
Raine and I have a record of not attending said ~parties ~because of this very reason.
"Fine, let's go."

I hear him chuckle behind me, and he grabs my ass with a deep sound in his throat that makes butterflies take flight in my stomach. "Don't be upset. I'll make it up to you later."

I laugh as we enter the massive hall of Christmas perfection.

His eyes widen as he takes in the loud music and the number of people. Santa's elves walk by with trays of drinks, and slutty toy makers are taking instant pictures and handing them to the guests.

This is spectacular.

I see large gumdrops and sparkling snowmen with massive trees, the bright colors flashing on and off.

"Camila!"

It's Pierce.

We both turn to see him walking up to us, checking his watch. "Camila! Raine! Welcome, I was worried you both had gotten lost!" He is wearing a sparkling black tux with a Santa hat on that is about to fall off.

"Pierce," I say, "this is amazing!"

"I know, right?" He shakes Raine's hand. "Come join the party. Steven is in the main room, hitting on a couple of girls from the accounting department." He gives me a look. "They would love to be saved from him." He points to Raine. "Thetis is here, arrived an hour ago."

Raine nods, still looking around the massive hall.

"So," Pierce puts his hands in his pockets, "you made it a year, and you both look great."

I smile, squeezing Raine's hand harder. "Thank you, couldn't be happier." Raine squeezes my hand back.

Pierce snaps for a drink from a passing waiter. "You must tune into FGI Entertainment Tonight to see the next top mission."

"I have heard about that." I look at Raine as he takes a drink, then hands me one. "So," I say, tasting the eggnog and whiskey drink, "what's the next mission? Are you allowed to say?"

Pierce leans in and looks around as if someone might overhear. "Let's just say that this will be a wild ride."

"How so?"

"This is a very futuristic world and mirrors ours very closely in an odd sense. Think of the Big Band, swing dance era, paired with Gatsby extravagance."

My eyes widen. "Oh wow," I say, intrigued.

"Our main target is a dark genius, the Puppet Master. The man in the shadows, almost like a legend that's more of a myth. But he is real, and we are going to take him down—or, bring him to his knees with one of our agents." Pierce chuckles, sipping his drink.

Raine makes a sound and shakes his head. "Poor man, he won't have a chance in hell," Raine murmurs. He winks at me, making my body tingle.

"Like the Great Gatsby? This man?"

Pierce makes a face. "Yes, in a sense. This man is exceptionally brilliant, developing perfect female and male androids for purchase by the wealthy. Mostly as maids and the 'help' in a sense. This world is made up of them, to create this perfect 40s-ish utopia. Dion Lieto Le Rose is this crazy mastermind target. They say he's half machine himself."

"What? Really? How strange."

"I'm not sure if that's true, it could be a myth—we are still looking into it."

"So why is he bad?"

Pierce waves at a slutty Mrs. Claus and winks, then sips his drink again. "Well, he's under the watch of the FBI. They say he's guilty of very criminal activity. Like, trying to take over the world with chips and robot stuff. Dangerous man. The FBI is trying to take him out but have nothing on him yet. Dion has his tracks covered pretty well."

"Yeah, that sounds like a movie I might have seen before."

He chuckles and waves at another person. "This world is all about singing and dancing, and being perfect in every way."

I laugh. "Like a 50s musical?"

"Kinda." Pierce smiles and exhales looking at his watch again. "The girls are about to be picked. It's a very exciting time for us. I get to do a whole new fashion line of amazing dresses and accessories. Very exciting."

"I bet. I can't wait to see what happens," I look at Raine, "because it really does turn out to be a happily ever after in the end." I grin at Pierce. "Even if you do have to ~almost~ die a few times to get it."

"I'll cheers to that," Pierce says.

We cheers, and make our way into the winter wonderland of FGI.

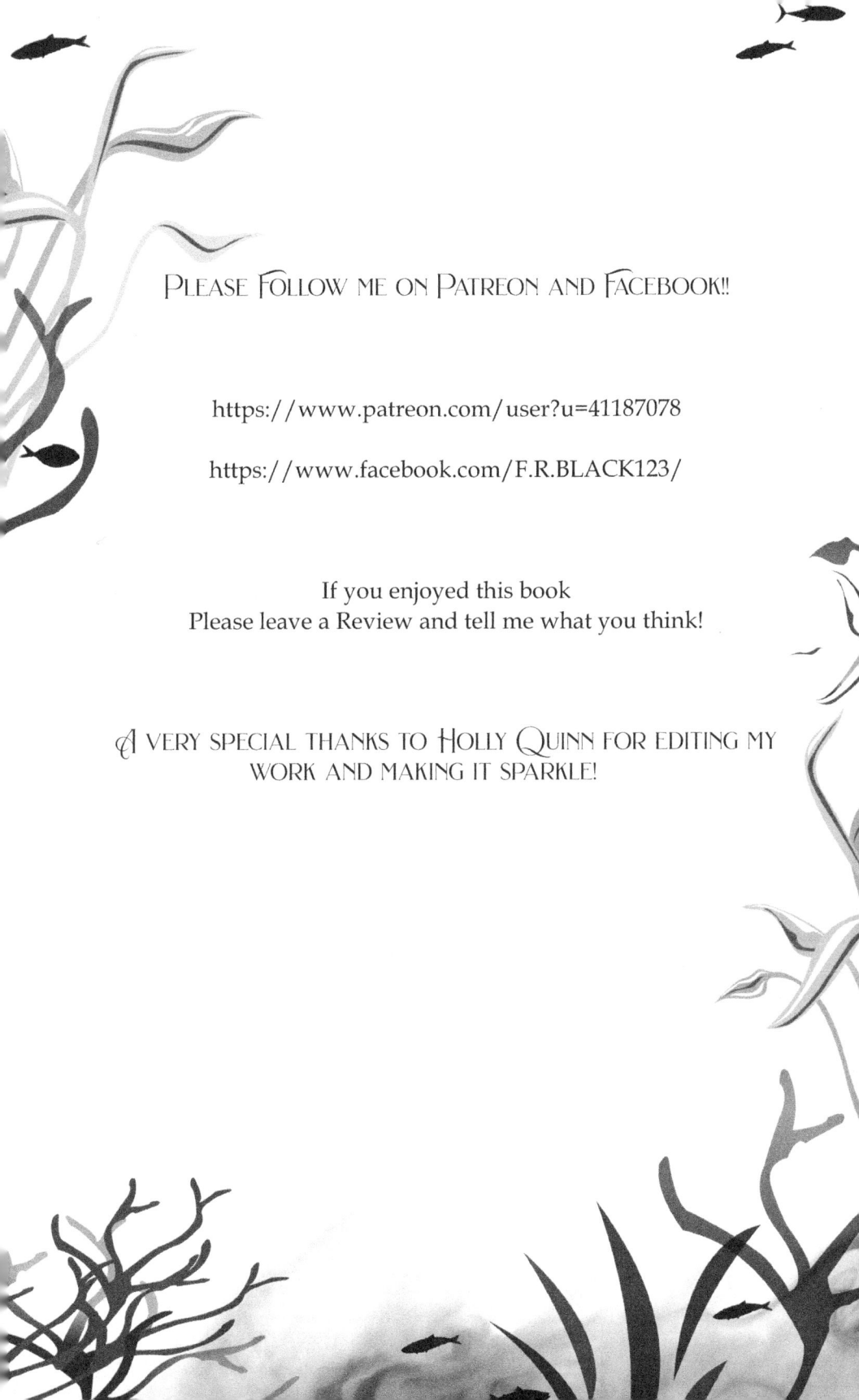

PLEASE FOLLOW ME ON PATREON AND FACEBOOK!!

https://www.patreon.com/user?u=41187078

https://www.facebook.com/F.R.BLACK123/

If you enjoyed this book
Please leave a Review and tell me what you think!

A VERY SPECIAL THANKS TO HOLLY QUINN FOR EDITING MY
WORK AND MAKING IT SPARKLE!

Made in the USA
Las Vegas, NV
30 April 2024

89332063R00223